Justice For Emily

Derek McDonald

Published by Derek McDonald, 2023.

This is a work of fiction. Similarities to real people, places, or events are entirely coincidental.

JUSTICE FOR EMILY

First edition. November 13, 2023.

Copyright © 2023 Derek McDonald.

ISBN: 979-8223452201

Written by Derek McDonald.

Justice For Emily

By Derek McDonald

Chapter 1

September

SEVERAL TIMES HARRY stops, ponders and fights against the easy option. He has travelled a long way, rehearsing word for word but still those nagging negative thoughts surround him. *How will it end? Will it end up in violence? Perhaps embarrassment? Maybe shame?* He is approaching a house and the lights are on. There is still time to turn around and walk away but he feels this is a "now or never" moment. He stops once more, looks around the quiet cul-de-sac. A total of only seven houses exist, most of them in darkness. He observes a line of conifers at the end. Probably over two metres high and stretching the width of the street. He also realises the sound of the busy main road behind them is somewhat muted. Hardly any lights shine through. He notes this because he has parked his black Audi in that road just behind the conifers about five minutes earlier and had to walk around to get to where he now stands - outside 6 Cherry Walk. It all looks so familiar as he has been there several times before. He takes yet another deep intake of breath as he fumbles with a large black wooden gate. He is in. He then gently turns and closes the gate quietly. Still his good manners are at the forefront of his pleasant personality but this is no time for politeness and certainly charisma will not be needed. Unexpectedly a bright security floodlight momentarily blinds him. Once more he stops and considers walking away. He is now only about two feet away from the doorway. Suddenly his thoughts actually turn to the family living there - wife and children? They will surely be devastated by the revelations Harry is about to bestow upon them? It will surely mean the breakdown of the marriage and possibly the whole family? Now Harry has another thought to deal with and wonders how well his conscience may fair should he be the one responsible for such painful news? He realises this is not the right moment and quickly returns to the black wooden gate.

On his long drive home to Becclesfield, he once again practices his breathing exercises. He needs to somehow get his adrenalin and heart rate down. He knows it is particularly bad for him when he is driving. It will take over an hour until he reaches his home and much will go through his mind not least the appointment in the morning with his therapist, Jacob and he knows he has to somehow get through this first.

It is approaching eleven o'clock on a Tuesday morning and Harry is always punctual when it comes to his sessions. He has carefully chosen his slightly baggy cream trousers and a blue checked, short sleeved, cotton, buttoned down shirt, which is also a little loosely fitted. He likes to feel comfortable when laying down. The lift doors open with a sound of a bell noise. He slowly walks out and turns left. He is walking very slowly. Probably not even a conscious or deliberate decision but a walk of dread. Approaching half way down a darkened corridor he approaches the second door on the right hand side. He stops, stands still and takes his usual deep breath for courage more than anything else. He is not particularly looking forward to these sessions but he really does not have much choice in the matter. A court order for a road rage incident three months ago means it is this or a heavy fine with perhaps a prison stretch. He knows the two months off from driving was the right course of action but now he has to participate in some form of therapy. He gently knocks on the door and takes two steps backwards. It appears he is showing some form of apprehension to what may lay behind the door and hopes there is no one in.

'Come in.' A familiar voice calls out from inside the room.

He slowly enters the room, again taking one long deep breath as he feels something disagreeable is about to occur.

'Ah, good morning. It's great to see you, Harry. How's your week been?' This is always the same reception Jacob has given Harry over the last five weeks.

'Okay, I guess,' he says, appearing a little hesitant as he always is on these occasions. He smells the paint of the freshly painted room. It is darkened blue on all the walls but to Harry, it may as well be a prison cell. He looks at Jacob as if he is an opponent of sorts. He makes eye contact with him. Sizing him up in some strange way.

'Please sit or lay down. Whatever you prefer.' Jacob points over towards the left hand corner of the room. 'Sorry, for the paint smell but it has improved the room?'

He completely ignores the attention made to the interior design of the room and wanders over to the left hand corner where there is an inviting looking cream coloured couch. He lays down. 'Thanks Jacob. I'll lay down as usual.' He tries to relax immediately but is unable to do so and so consciously does some breathing exercises. He knows Jacob will be somewhat impressed. He is.

'Oh good. I see you are using the techniques, Harry. Now please relax as there is only you and I here.' He takes up his usual position sitting upright in a dark leather chair. The middle aged therapist is wearing casual clothing as usual. He finds this approach puts his clients at ease more than a suit and tie would. On this occasion he has a pair of light blue trousers and a white cotton buttoned down shirt. His short black hair is exactly as it always is on these occasions, well groomed. His sleeves are rolled up. They always are. Perhaps it is done to show off his gold coloured watch on his right wrist? Or perhaps he needs to see his watch to ensure the timing of the session does not run over schedule? Either way, it is always on display.

At this point Harry frequently takes a look around the room. It is part of his ongoing therapy. This is done to put him in the present time and clear his thoughts a little by focusing on the here and now, not the past or the future. He notes, as he always does, the room's design. The old oak desk, the modern chair behind it. He then spies the laptop, open as usual. To his right are the kitchen items: sink, kettle, crockery, fridge and a large mirror. At the rear of this area there are three large windows but bizarrely they never appear to let much light in. This looks planned to Harry as being some form of aid to help with the ambience of the room. Also, there always is a quiet but conspicuous sound of water running. This is the thing that always puzzles Harry for no matter how hard he looks he can never see any speakers. All around the room are qualification certificates on the walls along with a number of paintings of tranquil settings. Lovely golden sands, sea and blue skies. They all have blue skies. The other thing Harry always wonders about is the large brown leather seat in the middle of the room. It never appears to have been moved at any time. Even the cleaners look like they clean around it. It is Jacob's chair. It has a swivel so he can gently move around, so if a client gets up and walks over to the window, he can still observe from a three hundred and sixty degree angle anywhere in the room.

Jacob sits down on the large leather chair in the middle of the room, crosses his legs and looks really comfy. 'Are you relaxed, Harry?' he says.

'Fine thank you. All ready to go?' There is an element of sarcasm in his voice but it is more to do with his nerves. He is at that point again. *What's he going to dig up now? What shall I tell him?* A great deal of thoughts are flowing through his head.

'Now just relax, Harry. Last week you told me about your anger management issues. Have you tried out the relaxation and anxiety techniques we have been practicing over the last few weeks?'

There is the usual wavering from Harry as he analysis every single question before answering. He always feels one mistake and it can be more weeks of therapy added to his sentence. 'A lot better.

Although there was this one incident last week.' Harry stops as he realises he may be saying too much all ready.

'Please continue. What incident was that?' Jacob shows genuine interest.

'It's the usual,' he says, 'no one out there seems to know how to act at those mini roundabouts. It's so simple. Just give way to the right. I did initially get upset but I used the breathing techniques instead of my voice or gesticulations and you know what?' he pauses to gauge the look upon Jacob's face and it is looking favourable, 'it really works. I use it every time I feel a little strained. I feel so much better now,' he pauses once more realising he could be over selling the point.

He smiles in an approving manner. 'That's good. So no other issues going on. Remember it is really important and this is your chance to speak up.'

Harry hesitates. It appears there have been many issues and not just recent ones but he looks determined not to reveal his inner most thoughts. 'Nothing really,' he pretends.

He is forced to acknowledge his answer but deep down is a little troubled. 'Nothing really? That means there is something going on. What is it, Harry? You cannot ever recover fully if you are not truthful. Remember what we spoke about at our very first session?'

He is once again cautious. Still trying to hold something back. This is the one thing he is desperate to avoid but it is also the one thing that still keeps him pounding up and down on his bedroom floor in the early hours of each morning, every night for the past year or so. He understands he needs help and Jacob is a good listener but can he overcome the depressing thoughts swimming around in his head? Where could he possibly start? The major problem he is now having is - Jacob. What would he do with the information and how much longer will it mean attending therapy once the secret is out in the open. Not to mention the other consequences. The other thing is, he has only known Jacob for five weeks, well five hours really but the patient confidentially laws do slightly add a plus to all of the negatives and perhaps he will really feel better for lifting the burden off his shoulders by talking to him about it?

Chapter 2

HARRY IS STILL being probed by Jacob. He knows once he gets the scent on something he is never going to let go. Just like a bloodhound on a trail and Harry now feels he is the hunted. Jacob fires another question. 'If you have something serious on your mind you really need to let go of it, Harry. If you do not, all the techniques and the counselling in the world will be unable to help you in anyway. You have to talk about it. You will feel better for it and we can then move forward but I can tell it is holding you back.'

He imagines he is in a boxing ring and Jacob being his opponent, has him pinned up against the ropes raining blows down upon him. Perhaps it is his youth returning to his aid. His days of learning the boxing game and more importantly the training of how to avoid the blows. This is the philosophy he is now adapting. He needs the bell or even his trainer to throw the towel in. He has neither. He looks around the room. There must be an out? He cannot just get up and walk out that will most certainly add several weeks to these sessions. He remembers back to the one defeat he had in those boxing days many years ago and it is a familiar feeling; unmanageable sweat appearing on his forehead, a feeling of total despondency and strangely - dizziness. He is floundering but then he spots the kettle and recalls he has the right for a break at any point when things appear to be getting tough.

Jacob has been tolerantly waiting for him to react. One thing he does have is plenty of patience but not much time. Just one hour sessions is all they have been allocated each week, so it is vitally important the time is used wisely. He eventually and ever so selflessly says, 'Harry, are you ready?'

Harry times his response to perfection. 'Can we have a little rest please? I Feel like some refreshment.' He tries not to grin but inside he feels he has made it to the end of the round. Time is precious and he has wasted plenty of it.

Jacob smiles but really tries his best not to show his displeasure. He stands, walks over to the small kitchen area and fills a kettle.

Harry knows what's coming next. 'No sugar please, Jacob.'

'Oh yes, I remember. No sugar.' He attempts to pretend he knows his patients' preferences when it comes to refreshments but really the one thing on his mind at this time is to get Harry to open up and make the breakthrough he so desperately wants.

Harry looks closely at one of the paintings and really wishes he was there. He can actually visualise himself lying on the beautiful golden sand, staring up at the blue sky and soaking up the sun. How he could do with not being at this session now. He knows the second part is about to begin and he can no longer delay the inevitable - more sparring.

Jacob at this moment has sat himself behind his oak desk and peering into his laptop. Harry hates this part. He knows all the notes from their sessions have been kept religiously and perhaps he may find some clue as to what really lies at the heart of his real problems. He goes through his routine of breathing exercises once more. This occasionally clears his head a little of some thoughts and doubts.

He returns back to the brown leather chair in the middle of the room. Harry smells his own fear as he knows this is all about to begin again but will he still be able to hold out?

'Fully rejuvenated, Harry?' He asks.

Harry nods his head in agreement, even though he is never prepared. Never comfortable sitting or laying in these therapy sessions but he knows he has to go through with it all.

Jacob crosses his legs and calmly says, 'Try to relax now. I noticed you doing your breathing exercises, that's really good. You were telling me about the real challenges before our break. Please go on.'

Harry conspicuously flinches. He knows his opponent never gives up and will prolong his attack. He ponders whether to actually give in himself and start telling him the truth. It would be a weight off his mind and perhaps it lies at the root of his anger management issues? He sits up a little. 'You are right, there has been something disturbing me. It has been on my mind now for the best part... I mean the worse part of the last six years.'

Jacob is trying to conceal his real elation of what finally looks like a major advance. He knows one wrong word or even movement could prevent him from revealing his thoughts. So he just nods in a perceptive way.

Harry pauses, questions himself once more but overcomes the demons in his head and says, 'you have been so patient with me Jacob and you are right, as usual, so here we go. It is something that started during my school days...' He pauses once more to see the look upon his face. He knows childhood trauma is always of great interest to most therapists but as it is the truth anyway, he continues. 'Leo Parker was a boy I knew from school. He was a bit of lad. You know with the girls? Anyway, we both had strong feelings for the same girl, Emily Banks. She was a lovely looking girl. She had long black hair all the way down her back and the most beautiful pair of hazel eyes...' he pauses to gauge the look upon his face once more but Jacob is as usual unmoved. Harry often thought of him as having all the attributes of a great poker player, he could never fully read his thoughts or body language. He would have the same look upon his face whether he was holding a full house or just a pair of twos.

Jacob sees the deliberate pause and so encourages him to continue with a smile and a nod of recognition in order to coax him further.

He continues. 'Emily came running to me one day. I think it was a Monday?... Yes, it had to be a Monday because it happened over the weekend.' He deliberately pauses once more. This time he was beginning to tease him a little by dragging it out. He knows there is probably about ten minutes left of this session and he still has not revealed his real secrets. He slows it all down and is now playing for time. Just like a footballer dancing around a corner flag in the dying moments of a game.

Jacob is also fully aware of the time as well. 'Please continue, Harry.'

'Clearly I asked her what was wrong and she told me Leo had got her drunk. She could not remember a single thing. She was you know? - worried if he had taken advantage of her.' He pauses as he tries to remember the events in chronological order and kills a little more time in the process. 'So, a week later she approached me again. She told me Leo could not possibly be my friend as he had been insulting me all evening on that dreaded night. I guess he was just trying to score points with her and when that failed he got her drunk? He was obviously promoting himself to get into her favours and put himself ahead of me!'

He stops writing his notes and sympathetically smiles and nods to him in order to encourage him along once more.

After yet another deliberate long pause he continues. 'The thing is it actually backfired on Leo because it brought Emily and I closer together. Really closer together - you know what I mean?' he grins.

He nods again to show his understanding of the situation and says, 'please continue, Harry.'

Harry starts to wrestle with his shirt for some reason. He has become uncomfortable but he knows there are just minutes left and decides not to say anymore. He has calculated that how things stand at the moment the secret is still hidden away in the back of his mind and Jacob has not got any information that Harry did not wish him to have.

He quickly changes the subject. 'Did I tell you about Emily's father? He was a lovely man. He gave me a job. He ran the big saw mills in Ferry Lane. You know - behind the station?'

Jacob uncrosses his legs and leans forward as he knows time is running out and says, 'yes I know the one. That was the one that burned down some years ago now.'

He smiles and looks a little impressed how Jacob knows about the local history and community. 'Do you live around here then, Jacob?' He asks a personal question for once.

For the first time Jacob becomes a little uncomfortable and wishes to avoid the question. He decides this to be a good time to finish the session. 'Oh it looks like we have run over a little, Harry. Have a good week and don't forget keep up the exercises and the medication. If at any point things get a little tough you should ring your GP in the first instance but if anything gets too much, I'm sure it won't, you should head straight to A & E.'

He sneakily sighs a relief and gets up to stretch his legs. 'Thank you very much, Jacob. Really appreciate your understanding and help. I feel these sessions have helped me a great deal. I feel a different person now. See you next week unless you feel I'm okay to...'

He gets up from his chair and wanders over to his desk. 'Yes, eleven o'clock next week please. We are making really good progress, Harry. So I look forward to seeing you then. Goodbye.'

Harry walks out through the open door much quicker than the way he had actually entered the room. He feels he has dodged a bullet. Although, it is the first time he mentioned some of his trials and tribulations in one of the sessions. He is already beginning to dread the next session, which is a week away. Another week of staying up each night, drinking decaf coffee and another week where he may once again feel the need to visit 6 Cherry Walk. How much longer can he keep avoiding the real reasons for his current state of mind?

Chapter 3

HARRY ARRIVES BACK home in Becclesfield. He lives on the second floor of a small block of apartments in Waverley Road. To the side elevation are some playing fields. There are swings, roundabouts and a see-saw. He looks at this area every single time he enters his building. He uses it as some type of nervous tension relieving therapy and he often drifts back to his happy childhood days. They were happy times and he was a dissimilar person back then. He recalls taking the short cut through the park to the beach, where there are still half a dozen concrete barges used during World War Two moored up and rotting away with every passing season. Thoughts wander to the tremendous days spent on the golden sandy beaches with his adoring parents, neighbouring the rock pools to the right of the beach. As he enters the building a mature neighbour from the ground floor apartment on the left hand side opens his door. He is a little frail. Early eighties? He is wearing a grey cardigan, which matches his grey thinning hair and is wearing a pair of brown trousers. He always opens the door to greet Harry with a friendly smile.

'Hello, Harry,' he says, 'have you been anywhere nice today?' He smiles agreeably towards him in an affectionate way.

He smiles back. He knows the man is nosey and always asks him the same question. He puts it down to being a little lonely since his wife died last year. 'Hello, Fred, nowhere exciting. In fact, quite the opposite. How are you? Do you need anything from the shops tomorrow?'

Fred looks a little cunning. 'Oh thank you Harry. If you wouldn't mind getting me some milk and bread? I would be ever so grateful.'

He nods. 'No worries, Fred. I'll knock tomorrow with them. Have a nice day.'

Fred looks ever so unassuming. 'Thank you, son, where would I be without you? The others don't even visit anymore. Not since Elsie - you know?'

Harry looks genuinely saddened and reassures him by saying, 'Please don't worry. I'll pop in tomorrow for a game of chess as well.'

He smiles in gratitude and looks forward to their games of chess but more to their lengthy conversations on how to put the world to rights. He turns and closes his front door. Harry climbs the twenty or so concrete steps to his landing. His apartment is the last on the right. He stops and peers over the balcony every single time he approaches his front door. He appears to be looking for someone? He has for nearly a year had a sensation deep inside, a gut feeling, he is being followed but has not actually seen anyone loitering around his apartment. He opens the front door, takes one last look and enters his apartment. He cannot wait to get into bed. He feels fatigued as he always does after these sessions. It is just as well he is still unemployed as this allows him to come and go as he pleases. He has been in this state for nearly a year but is reasonably well off having received an inheritance three years ago from the sale of his late parents home in Tranby.

Meanwhile, Jacob does not have this extravagance. He knows he will have to get his notes made up tonight and ensure the files are ready for his six weekly review with his boss about the status of some of his patients. He is under pressure at these meetings as his boss always tries to persuade him to discharge some of the patients. There is a long waiting list and the practice is under constant demands. The stress levels within the local community appear to have tripled since the epidemic of COVID, which is at long last under control with vaccinations nationwide.

Wednesday morning and Jacob has everything in hand. He arrives at his office. Picks up some files and makes his way to the third floor via the stairwell. He knocks on a door on the third floor.

'Come!' Mohammed shouts out.

Jacob always finds this a little off putting and somewhat daunting. He enters the room. It is in stark contrast to his office downstairs. It has a contemporary feel to it. Even the kettle is new. There is a metal framed glass desk with a pale blue chair, which Mohammed is at this time sitting on. There are a number of windows, which allow a good amount of light into the room but it still looks a little drab.

'Ah morning, Jacob. How are you on this lovely gracious morning?'

'Great thank you, Mohammed.' He nods in agreement.

'Now we have got the niceties over with we can move on to the work in hand,' he says in his usual abrupt manner. He slowly rises from his chair, walks towards his bookcase and pulls out a large red box file. 'Not all of these I hope?'

Jacob smiles. 'No just the ones with the yellow highlighting. We would be here to Sunday if we had to discuss every one of them today.'

'Yes, I thought that would be the case and have read up on them this morning. Just three?' He says as he opens up one of the files. 'Which one do you want to discuss first, Jacob?'

He is not really worried which one goes first but he is keen to keep Harry's one until last. 'What about Amelia Roberts?'

Mohammed opens her file. He ponders over it for a little while. 'She appears to have made some good progress. Her paranoia has now abated and her obsession with her twin sister is now under control. What about discharging her?'

Jacob knew he would have to give at least one of them up today. He nods in agreement. 'Yes. She could be monitored with phone calls and perhaps her GP can check on her - say every three months for the first year?'

'Agreed. Next.' He leans back in his chair and affords himself a full stretch of both arms. His jet black hair is shinning as the sun breaks through the large windows behind him and enters the room with a sudden flush. He is as always smartly dressed in his grey suit, white shirt and grey silk tie. He still has all of his hair, which he is proud about because soon he will be retiring after forty years of service.

'Millie Sanderson. Have you got her file?' Jacob says.

He fumbles through the main file and pulls it out. He studies it for five minutes. 'Definitely not. She needs more help.'

'I agree. She still has the obsessions mentioned in the file and remains a little potentially dangerous. I am still awaiting further reports.' Jacob pushes her file to the bottom of his pile. Now he only has Harry left.

'I read through his file this morning. Very complex. Court order as well I see. I feel there is a lot more going on here, am I right?' Mohammed looks over the top of his black spectacles. He always does this when he feels he could be one hundred percent correct in his analysis and he is.

Jacob is pleased. He is getting closer by the session of a major breakthrough with Harry. 'Yes. Another one who needs further help.' He deliberately left it brief. He did not want his boss to start going over it all.

'Is he cooperating though? That is the important factor here.' Mohammed takes his spectacles off and rubs his brow with his left hand as if to signify a sudden rise in room temperature.

'Yes he does at times but I feel he is sometimes trying to play the system. He just wants to get this all over as soon as possible but there are some complex issues going on and I need to get to the bottom of those. I am making good progress but the issues appear to be with his past. Like so many of our patients.' Jacob says in a self-assured manner.

Mohammed puts on his spectacles, stands and places the red file back on the bookcase. 'That wasn't too painful but we need to see if we can hurry up on some of these cases a little. Funding is tight and the waiting lists have now grown to three months minimum. I would take some on but I have this centre and the two other ones to organise each day. How are you coping now Sarah has left?'

Jacob smiles as he rises to his feet. 'We are all busy down there but we pull together. We are a team. Oh, I have an eleven o'clock to attend to. Will you kindly excuse me please?'

'We can't keep them waiting can we? Keep up the good work and it's good to see you are in such good spirits.' Mohammed smiles as Jacob turns and walks out onto the corridor, down the stairs and back into his office.

Chapter 4

A NOTE HAS been posted through Harry's letterbox and it is telling him Leo Parker, the man he has been trying to trace, will be in a pub in Tranby this evening. It is anonymous but somehow this does not matter to him as he feels this is the moment he has been waiting for and cannot resist the urge to check it out. He is a great believer in "what comes around, goes around". It is Friday afternoon and he is readying himself. He grins at himself in the mirror and looks quite pleased with how he looks. He brushes his fair hair and takes one last look before leaving his apartment. He sets off in his car to head the forty miles to Tranby. He knows he will not drink and drive, so has pre-booked a room at The Lodge, a five minute walk to the town centre. For some reason, maybe paranoia or even spite? he has booked it under the name of Leo Parker. He has also expressed he will pay cash upon arrival, it is as though he does not wish anyone to know he has visited Tranby.

He arrives one mile outside the town centre and finds a free parking spot in a quiet street. He does not wish for anyone to notice his car. He picks up a small holdall bag from the passenger seat and locks the car up. He is walking fast. He looks like a man on a mission. He has something on his mind and probably thinks the answers are close by. He stops to look at The Lodge, the place where he will be staying overnight. It has a big blue triangle sign and a row of exterior lights shining down from a large canopy. He looks at the large glass automatic doors and takes a last long breath. Having never in all of his years of living close by, has he actually ever entered the building. He finally makes it to the reception area where upon entering through the automatic glass sliding doors, there is a smartly dressed young lady smiling as if she has known him forever.

'Good Afternoon. How may I help you?' she says, sounding like a well rehearsed scripted line from some play.

'I've booked a room,' Harry feels he is stating the obvious but knows he has to communicate in this way in order to get booked in. 'Leo Parker,' he just remembers in time not to give his real name. 'Paying with cash. I know it is a little old fashioned but I don't want my bank to know everything I do.' He grins.

She smiles but she would smile at anything. It is her job to smile and be polite no matter what. 'Oh yes, Mr Parker. I have found you.'

He hands over the cash and does not need a receipt. He is given the key and a short instruction of how to get out of the building if there should be a fire or any other kind of life threatening emergency. He takes the key and ponders the thought of such a tragic fire but quickly manages to get it out of his mind using his breathing techniques. He hastily finds his room, mid way down a darkened corridor. He affords himself a little smirk and with a hint of sarcasm he thinks about the fire once more and how anyone will be able to see their way along the corridor at night in any event, that is even without the added hindrance of smoke. He uses the card to get into the room. Places it into an odd looking socket and abruptly the room comes alive with lights. It has been a long journey for him so he is quick to get his shoes off and lay on a large cosy white looking bed. Everything is white: the pillow cases, the sheets and even the duvet. He wonders how they manage to keep everything looking so clean and fresh. He has in the region of two hours to kill and drifts off to sleep.

He awakens in a state of panic. Thinking he has overslept he quickly grabs his phone to see the time and even though he thinks he's been asleep for hours it turns out to be just forty minutes. Still tensed and a little anxious his thoughts are running wild. Unexpectedly he has some mixed feelings; he feels both stimulation and a little trepidation in equal measures. His anxiety levels have risen dramatically. He uses his "in the moment" techniques and looks around the room. He sees a large widescreen tv on the wall in front of him. To his left are three large windows with curtains. There are tea and coffee making facilities to his right, and he is fully aware there is a shower and toilet behind the closed white door, slightly to the left. The room has a large painting above his head. It shows a beach and a blue sky. *Always a blue sky.* He gets up and heads to the shower room. Has a refreshing shower and gets dressed in some clean clothes he has brought along with him. He goes to the long mirror by the door and says aloud, *'got to look smart for Leo. I can't wait to see the look on your face. You took everything from me and now it's payback time!'* He looks one last time to make sure he looks his best and he leaves the room without the need to speak to himself once more.

He exits the building and starts his five minute walk to the town centre. As he gets nearer he notices there is an increase in young people milling around. They all look smart, happy and above all optimistic. It is Friday night and the area is getting busy. He approaches the town centre. There are a great deal of shops but all closed for the day, some closed forever. He looks down the High Street and reminisces over how the shopping centre looked many years ago when he grew up in the area. He recalls; Woolworths sited next door to the Midland Bank. Two units up and there was Wilko. Debenhams was opposite and next door to C&A. The market square looks so different and in such a short space of time as well. Another big change in the area, it has been made totally pedestrian safe - no motor vehicles of any kind allowed to drive in this area. He has a flashback to the days when he had to dance in between cars and vans to cross the road. There must have been a market there during the day as he spots two street cleansing operatives clearing rubbish off the pavements. As he wanders along the market square he sees The Swan directly in the middle. He stops to take it all in. It looks as though it has always been there. It has a large frontage, very wide. Black beams with white paintwork all along the front. The roof looks like it has just been redone with old looking tiles. There are lots of people on foot and Harry hears the first hint of music coming through the open and hospitable entrance.

He enters the pub knowing he will in all probability have to wait to get served for some time judging on the number of people already in the pub. He takes a quick look in the region of the bar without looking too obvious. It was just a quick glance, he will look in more detail once he is served and finds a quiet place to observe from. After around ten minutes a pretty looking bar person approaches him. 'What can I get you?' she politely asks. She has a lovely, warm and friendly smile.

He takes a moment to observe her. He thinks he has seen her before somewhere. He is struggling to find words, any words and his face is one of disbelief. Finally he regains his composure. 'Two pints of lager please.' He feels that is not enough time to spend talking and so thinks up something quickly. 'Do you accept cash?' He smiles to show it is meant to be taken humorously.

She laughs loudly. 'If you've got it, we'll take it!' She walks off to get his beers. He watches her in an admiring fashion. He once again tries to think if they have ever met before somewhere as she looks really familiar to him. Even the silky white top and pale blue jeans seem familiar. He is thinking of asking but thinks better of it as he knows that is the oldest pick up line in the book. He has one more look around the pub but this time it is done with real intention and not one of his "in the moment" exercises. He is looking for Leo. It is the sole reason why he has travelled to Tranby. His thoughts are fully focused on finding him and his demeanour has changed for the worse. He does not really want to bring attention to himself so he stops scanning the bar area.

Out of the blue his thoughts become sporadic but then he hears the calming voice talk to him. 'Here you are. Two pints of lager. That will be fourteen pounds please.' She smiles and then says, 'oh but as you are paying cash - that will be fourteen pounds please!' she laughs aloud once again.

He is truly stunned at the price. He has not been in a bar for some time now but still he cannot help but react. 'Fourteen pounds? That's almost a pound per inch!'

She laughs. He quickly realises she thinks it was intended as a joke and so he laughs. Then unexpectedly he has become convinced just where he knows her from. He takes a quick look at her and notices she has everything Emily Banks once had; long black hair, hazel eyes and a slim waist but it is too hard to believe. He feels it cannot be her though or could it? The similarities are remarkable. He looks her directly in the eyes and says, 'there's plenty more where that came from.' He realises it sounded a little lame but could not think of anything else to come back with.

She promptly responds, 'I bet there is and I wish I had the time to hear them.' Her manner has slightly transformed as she rushes off to serve another customer along the bar area.

Just as he is gathering his thoughts and his two pints of expensive lager, she returns to the area with another glass in her hand. Probably realising she had been a little sharp with him, she says, 'I hope you both have a lovely evening, enjoy.'

He is taken aback a little but smiles and nods. Then he thinks why she said "you both" when he is on his own? He realises he has two pints in his hands. He chuckles to himself as he has bought two because of the crowded bar area and did not wish to waste any time up at the bar. He wanders past a large group of girls standing in a circle guarding their handbags in front of them. They suddenly scream aloud. *What's that all about - it isn't for me, is it?* Then he realises by their wiggling and arm waving in the air, their favourite song has just started playing. He chuckles to himself and begins appreciating the nice atmosphere. He takes up a strategic position by the front entrance. He knows he can see everybody coming and going from this advantage spot. He settles by the door. He vigilantly surveys the entire pub but there are so many people and the disco lights are rolling about in his region. They have been strategically placed to shine out of the front doors. It is so the people outside on the street can see them and it may bring more punters inside. This is making it even harder for him to see people's faces, even those now coming and going through the main entrance. So he focuses on the bar area. He has reasoned with himself that the majority of the individuals inside the pub will at some point go to the bar to buy drinks.

He drinks the two pints in a record forty minutes. He is not sure whether it is because he feels a little edgy or whether he just wanted to connect in banter with the pretty bar person. So he makes his way to the bar area to where she is serving hoping to get her again. She looks as though she intentionally rushes up to him, leaving one or two customers looking a little bemused as to why he is being served before they are.

'Hello. Two pints of lager or have you seen something else you fancy?' She attempts to tease him and it works.

He hesitates and knows full well that timing is of the utmost importance. He is thinking on his feet and quickly replies, 'I do feel a little lonely over there on my own.' Then he feels the urgency to explain further. 'I only bought two pints because of the crowd in here tonight. I wouldn't want you to think I'm an alcoholic or something?'

She smiles once more. 'Oh you're on your own. That's a shame. On a Friday night as well. If I wasn't working so hard tonight, I'd come over and keep you company. What can I get you?'

'That is a crying shame. I'd love to tell you my interesting life story. I am working on it at the moment. When it's finished it'll probably be about twenty pages long unless I get to know you better of course. That would really be worth writing about.' He smiles and gazes into her eyes, which was a little hard considering the flickering of disco lights flashing all around the place.

'Really? You have plenty of chat here tonight. So I'm pretty sure you could write a lot more than twenty pages. I bet you've had a lot of happy experiences with your looks?' She did not mean to pay him such a nice compliment this early on, she fears she may have let her guard down far too prematurely.

He looks extremely smug at this point and says, 'that is so nice of you to say but if we are talking about looks - then you only need to look into the mirror... you're stunning! I think I had better have those two pints of lager as some of your regulars are giving us evils. Besides, I have dipped into my savings account so can probably stay for the rest of the evening now at these prices.' He has chosen similar repartee that earned him a favourable reaction before and it works once more.

She laughs but suddenly realises she has been chatting to him for a little while longer than anticipated. She grins and then goes off to the pump.

Harry is unable to take his eyes off her. He thinks she is witty and friendly with an uncanny resemblance to Emily Banks. She not only looks like her from face on but even from the back and sides. Even her mannerisms appear indistinguishable in every way. The only dissimilarity he can find is concerning age but then Emily was just 17 years of age when he last saw her six years ago. He takes a few moments and reminisces about the happy times he spent with Emily but always cuts it off towards the last days they saw each other.

She comes back with the beer. 'There you are.' She stares him in the eyes. 'You should stay around this evening. You never know who you could meet on a Friday night?'

He is a little flushed but knows there is some sort of connection going on. He feels a shiver go down his spine as he senses he has seen that gaze before. He says, 'what's your name?' Suddenly he realises he may be over stepping the mark and tries his best to clarify. 'Oh. I want to leave some feedback about your wonderful service. I'm going to give you five stars.'

She is delighted he asked. She leans over towards him and whispers gently in his ear, 'my name is Millie but don't tell anyone else but surely I'm worth more than five stars?' She teases him once more.

'Well it only goes up to five but if there were some sub sections I'd give you five stars for personality and five stars for beauty.' He has gone all in and there is no turning back. She will either like it or hate it.

Fortunately for him she giggles. 'You've made me feel embarrassed now.' She takes his money and wanders off to the till in the middle of the bar area. She grabs a pen next to the till and writes a note.

She comes back and hands him change of the twenty pounds note he had given her to pay for the drinks. 'Here you are. Now don't go losing any of it will you?' She smiles and then rushes to the next customer apologising for the short delay in service.

He just stuffs the change into his pocket and then wanders back to his surveillance position by the main entrance. After around thirty minutes, he decides to visit the restroom. He thinks it a good time to have a tally up. He does not want to use his cards anywhere in this town for some reason but needs to know how much money he has left for the rest of the evening. As he fumbles through his pockets a piece of paper falls out and drops to the ground. He does not recognise it, so he bends down and picks it up. There is some writing on it. He reads it; "*Would you like to meet up after work? Meet me at the burger stall around midnight. If not, don't worry have a nice time. Millie*". He is elated. He really likes the look of Millie and has to actually calm himself down. He is thinking far too quickly to be in control of his emotions. So decides to go back to the entrance and leaves his drink on the table untouched. It has gone eleven o'clock and he wants to be as sober as possible for the rendezvous. Suddenly the one thing which has been niggling away at him for the best part of six years has all but vanished; for the time being, anyway. He tries to avoid eye contact with her but catches her gazing over in his direction a couple of times. So he waves, nods and smiles all in one action.

It is now approaching twelve o'clock so Harry visits the restroom one last time, only this time he is refreshing himself up. He leaves the pub and goes in search of the burger van in the market square. He finds it and takes up a position a few yards along. He can smell the cooked meat and onions but knows that having one is the last thing he should do before meeting Millie no matter how tempting it is. He looks at the front entrance, only this time he is not looking for anyone other than Millie. It is a different kind of expectation than he had experienced all evening when looking at the entrance, this time the tension is a little exciting. For a moment his mind turns back to Emily Banks and the good times they shared but as always he has managed not to remember the ending.

Chapter 5

THE TIME IS after twelve o'clock and still no sign of Millie. Suddenly his mind wanders into thoughts of negativity. Serious doubts enter his head. He starts to wonder if it has all been some kind of sick joke or has someone conspired with her. To make matters worse, he has started thinking about Emily Banks. He thinks of leaving at this point but some positive thinking came into play at a crucial moment. He quickly makes a list in his head of the positives and the negatives. He then discounted the ones on a percentage of reasoning. He had quickly killed off the thoughts of there being a conspiracy involved or the trouble she has gone to for some practical joke to what is after all a stranger to her, besides, he could not see anyone in the square videoing anything on their phones. Suddenly he feels a gentle tap on his shoulder. He turns and sees a smiling Millie standing in front of him. He once again has an overwhelming feeling of joy.

'Hope I didn't frighten you creeping up like that. If you think that is scary you should see me in the mornings.' She laughs again, it appears to be a wonderful, blissful and contented laugh.

Harry sort of hugs her but a little awkwardly as once again he does not wish to overstep the mark. 'You look amazing, Millie and I would....' He was going to say "love to go for a walk down by the canal".'

Millie senses he is a little insecure at this point so breaks the ice once more by interrupting him and says, 'I know. You would love to buy me a burger but no onions for me please.'

Harry is reassured and also pleased he gets to eat one of those tempting burgers he has smelt cooking for the past twenty minutes or so. 'Oh lovely. Just what I was thinking. No onions, just tomato ketchup. Would you like ketchup on yours?'

'A burger without ketchup would be a sacrilege. It would be like having a full English breakfast without beans.' She giggles and wraps her arm around his waist showing her appreciation. They head towards the burger van and get their burgers. They then wander off towards the canal. They appear comfortable together considering the little amount of time they have known each other

They slowly walk away from the market square feeling fully revitalised after eating their burgers. Millie has the first question of the night. 'So what is your name? You know mine.'

He smiles. 'Of course, sorry I forgot to mention that.' Suddenly he wonders whether to give his real name or that of Leo Parker - the name he has used to book into The Lodge. He does not wish to take the chance. 'My name is Harry - Harry Sutton and I live in Becclesfield.'

Millie stops in her tracks. 'Becclesfield! You are kidding me? That's where I live.'

Suddenly he is unsure of himself. He does not know whether to be happy or cautious. He plumps for the former. 'That's truly amazing! Why are you working so far from home?'

'I stay at my sister's, Chloe's, home at weekends and her husband, Colin is the manager of The Swan. So I just help out sometimes. Mostly Friday nights funnily enough. I know it sounds like nepotism but you know?' She shrugs her shoulders.

'Sounds to me Colin is getting the better deal out of it. A beautiful, polite hard working barmaid... err sorry I meant to say bar person.'

She laughs again. 'I know what you mean, Harry. Oh I sound like that Frank Bruno guy from the eighties who my dad used to like.' They both burst out laughing.

'I know what you mean, Millie!' He says quickly. Once again they laugh together.

She looks at ease but for some reason, a little awkward. They hug and within a moment they kiss for the first time. It is not a lingering kiss but just one of appreciation. He feels a strange but welcoming presence. It is like Emily is by his side and helping him to overcome his anxieties. It is heartening and encouraging because he has not had any meaningful relationships for many years.

'Hope you didn't smell the burger on my breath.' She appears a little embarrassed but tries to make light of it. 'At least we didn't have the onions!'

He laughs. 'It's the same for me, Millie but glad we didn't have the onions as well!' He leans forward for another kiss, this time it is more passionate and longer lasting than the first kiss. After a while they start off to the canal and find a bench. They sit and gaze out over the water.

He is first to speak. 'It's lovely how the lights reflect in the ripples of the water and how gentile it all looks.'

She looks impressed with his lovely description. 'Yes it is amazing at this time of night as well. No one around acting silly, except for us!' She giggles once more. He has an appreciative smile upon his face. They kiss again. It appears comfortable and natural. In such a short time they have discovered so much common ground and basically like similar things in life. They live just minutes in the car from each other in Becclesfield as well. She is first to break the long silence as caressing and kissing had provisionally prevented conversation. 'I have to confess something to you Harry.'

He has a look of dejection and shock at the same time. The appearance generally displayed by an individual when news of a death in the family has just been relayed to them.

'I thought you looked familiar when you walked into the bar. You know, like we had met before somewhere and now you have said Becclesfield then it could be possible we have at some point in time crossed paths without realising it?' she says as she looks more closely at his face. 'I'm a strong believer in fate. You know? Like things are meant to happen for a reason. You know what I mean, Harry? Ha, I've done it again, sorry but you do understand?' It appears quite important to her that he does.

He cannot help but laugh. She is naturally funny, he seems to like that. After he regains his composure he says, 'this is going to sound corny but I had the same feelings about you. Honestly, I didn't want to say that in the bar as it would have sounded creepy and you probably get that sort of thing a lot.' He is now sitting upright looking sincere. He likes the idea about things are meant to happen. He can see her face looking a little serious though, he had not noticed that much up until now. So he tries to change the subject a little. 'Wish I had brought my paintbrushes and easel. It would make such a great painting.'

Her face changes and looks a little more familiar. 'Wow! I knew you were an artist, Harry. I could tell by the way you talk, act and the sensitivity you show about everything you say.'

He smiles with pure contentment. 'I'd love to paint you. Those beautiful hazel eyes and apart from the obvious beauty on the outside I can tell you are whole. I mean beautiful in and out.' She kind of melts and just pulls him closer for another kiss.

Suddenly he has another major issue brewing up inside his head. He wonders how to go about solving it. He has a room just minutes away, all paid for and just sitting there. He holds off for a little longer. 'So Millie, someone like you must surely have a partner, boyfriend - husband?' He holds his breath momentarily as he anxiously awaits her response.

She deliberately hesitates, knowing he is looking stressed out. 'Well, there is Tom. I can never give up on him. I would be totally lost. He is such great company and he makes me feel safe, in a funny way.'

He bows his head in disappointment and frustration. He thought at last he has met someone caring, beautiful and funny. However, he thought deep down it was far too good to be true. Once again he becomes plagued with negativity.

She rubs her right hand gently through his short fair hair. 'Don't be too downbeat about it. I've only been living with him for two years.'

'Two years! That's a lifetime. Really Millie, I thought better of you.' His thoughts of going back to his room have taken a serious fatal blow. The last thing he needs is to get mixed up in a relationship where there is an interested third party.

She feels he has waited long enough. 'Oh Tom. Oh sorry, I mean Harry.' She pauses and can no longer hold it all back from him. 'Tom is my cat. Well he's my sister's cat really.' She laughs aloud. 'Got you!'

He is delighted but still not fully recovered from the shock of it all. 'You certainly know how to play practical jokes, Millie. Anyway, I had better be going as I have an early start tomorrow.'

She looks disappointed. 'Oh okay Harry.' She looks closer at his face and can see a flicker of a grin.

'Got you! One - one.' He laughs aloud and they kiss once more.

'I suppose there is no point in asking you about your love interests at the moment, you'll probably come out with something like - football, like most guys do these days?' She smiles and sits back on the bench expecting the worse.

He does not wait to respond. He is not going to waste any further precious time on practical jokes. He says, 'no one and guess what? I don't even like sports.' He snuggles up to her and they kiss again. He feels it is a déjà vu moment. She is running her right hand inside his shirt and gently caressing his chest but the last time this happened it was Emily doing it. He tries to break the thought and concentrate on the here and now. They stop kissing and embrace each other. Suddenly he fiddles around in his pocket and pulls out the door key to his room.

She is distracted and wonders what he is doing. 'Everything okay?' she asks.

'Oh yes. I had a strange sudden feeling that I had lost the key to my room.' He thinks this is probably the best way of getting the news to her about his room without frightening her off or being too forward but he feels they are approaching that moment. The moment when two people look into each other's eyes with that serious look upon their faces and suddenly there is no more words necessary. Well, Harry is certainly at that point but is Millie?

She goes all quiet and looks across the canal. 'So you have a room? Is this your move on me? You get me back, undress me and we end up in bed together making passionate love all night?'

He is genuinely embarrassed he stutters. 'No... I, I...'

She rises to her feet. 'Really, Harry? Really!' She picks up her bag and starts to walk away. She turns to face him once more. 'I cannot believe you are like that. We've only just met. Shame on you, Harry. Is this how you treat your girls on the first night? It doesn't show much respect - does it?'

He is devastated. He is obviously once again dejected, disappointed but above all he feels extremely foolish. Being a stickler for perfect timing, he realises he got it terribly wrong this time.

Suddenly she turns and says, 'well, are you coming then Harry?'

He nearly falls over getting up from the bench so quickly. She giggles and is enjoying teasing him and he appears to fall for it every time. Yet still he is reluctant to walk towards her. 'Okay?' he says, not knowing how to handle this situation.

She says, 'are you coming then?' Suddenly she bursts into a song, 'hurry up Harry, come on. We're going down the pub!' She laughs as he rushes over to her. 'Your face. I wish I had taken a pic of you Harry. It was so funny.'

He grins as he recognises the lyrics are from a song from the eighties. He affectionately kisses her on her left cheek. He likes her banter, he finds her so amusing but above all very sexy. Now he has yet another new worry cropping up in his head as it has been a long time since he has been intimate with anyone and that last person was Emily Banks. He still sees flashes of Emily within Millie at times and now worries - will he live up to her expectations?

Chapter 6

THEY MAKE IT through the back door of The Lodge. There is no one around to witness their entrance. They enter the darkened corridor and find their way to his room. They are both giggling, a little like school children who have just sneaked the last piece of candy into their mouths after cleaning their teeth. They enter the room. He fumbles with the card slot near the door. He manages to get the electricity turned on. At this point he is now behind her and he takes a sly look at her curvy figure. He is excited but a little afraid. He really wants everything to be perfect. For once she looks a little coy and is probably experiencing similar emotions of insecurity. Her mind appears to be elsewhere.

'Make yourself comfortable,' he says, looking at the only place in the room where this would be possible - the bed.

She has gone a little quiet. Perhaps she is thinking how little she really knows about him but she needs this to work. She moves towards him and says, 'I would like to take a selfie of us both.'

He is happy at such thought of his picture being inside her phone and wants a copy for himself. Besides, this will be a good excuse to exchange phone numbers. She takes the picture. A nice cosy photo of them both huddled together looking very happy. They exchange mobile phone numbers as she sits on the bed looking a little anxious for some reason. To make matters worse Harry then says, 'Okay. We've had the camera, lights and now it's time for the action!' Still she shows little enthusiasm. If anything it appears she is looking hesitant and is attempting to slow things down.

However, he is getting more aroused by the second but as he always thinks, everything is about the timing but can he get it right this time? He slides onto the bed next to her, close enough to embrace once more. Words now appear to be a thing of the past.

She has started to react more favourably towards Harry but it still appears she has something on her mind. They begin caressing each other. They are kissing passionately whilst attempting to remove their clothing at the same time. She is first to be totally naked, whilst Harry still has his Calvin Klein undershorts and his black socks on - typically English.

She slides easily underneath him, there is so much tenderness but she is still holding back for some reason. There is an abrupt lack of self-confidence beginning to surface in her. She actually appears very anxious and vulnerable. She whispers a little breathlessly. 'Have you got something?' Perhaps this is the issue she has been worrying over?

At first, he does not understand the question but suddenly the penny drops. 'Oh you mean a condom? No - I wasn't expecting to be in this... this position.' He laughs at his comment but is also looking extremely pensive as he realises this is serious. Very serious. Yet another error from his part. Being an ex cub, he has failed one of the very first things he was taught; "always be prepared", now he has to overcome this huge lapse in organisational skills.

She gently pushes him aside and sits up in bed. 'Oh Harry, I can't believe it. Go and get one. Get three.' She sort of smiles but secretly she appears relieved. Her anxiety levels drop. Harry is desperately disappointed but mostly with himself. He feels he may have blown it and may find it hard to recover the mood.

He asks, 'where am I going to get those at this time in the morning?'

'There's a twenty four hour garage on the outskirts of town.' She pulls the duvet over her body as suddenly she has become embarrassed about being naked. He also rushes to pull his under shorts back on but he still cannot hide his excitement. She looks at him standing in front of her and says, 'apart from having a cold shower first, you had better get some wine while you are there. I think we'll need a drink?'

He browses his phone to find a number for the local cab office. All the time cursing himself for really ruining the moment. He mutters under his breath; *'Just a little piece of forward planning - prevents a long time of family planning'*. He looks miserable and is probably thinking whether or not he has ruined the moment with Millie for good?

He overcomes all the hurdles thrown at him; getting the cab, finding the garage and the embarrassment of asking a young girl behind a small glass window for three packets of condoms. He also buys two bottles of wine and a half bottle of vodka. He feels it will be of some assistance when he gets back - if she is still there that is? He pays the cab driver and quickly races back to the room. He stands outside as breathless as he was when they were passionately lying naked in the bed earlier. He takes a deep breath. Does one or two breathing exercises and brings most of his anxiety levels down. He can see a light shining under the door gap - a good sign? He looks for the card and realises it is inside. It is still in the socket otherwise the lights would not be on. It also means if she has done a bunk he will be locked out for the night or at least until he can find a receptionist awake. He knocks gently on the door and patiently awaits to see what will happen next. A few moments, which to him seems an age, passes by. He knocks a little louder. He cannot shout out to her as it is now around two in the morning and he will wake others up. Still no response from inside the room. This time he bangs as loud as he feels will be acceptable to the sleepy neighbours in rooms along the corridor. He thinks he can hear a little rustling going on inside the room; this brings on an air of excitement as he realises for the very first time, she has waited for him. The door opens slowly he pushes it open and sees Millie is still naked but rushing to get back into bed before he sees her. The sight of her pretty little body sends erotic ripples through his entire body. He cannot wait to re-engage the passion and intimacy with her but wonders whether some wine will be needed first, in order to regain the mood for he has what can only be described as "stage fright" and it could not have happened at a more inopportune moment.

She is first to speak. 'Did you have a successful trip?' She sits up dropping the duvet a little lower down exposing her left breast. She is back to her teasing antics once more. Still, he does not mind one bit.

'Guess what I got?' he says, as he fumbles through his carrier bag.

She looks intrigued and interested. 'I hope it's not a book for each of us to read through the night.' She tries to keep a straight face.

He pulls out two bottles of Rose. 'I hope you like wine. Unfortunately, I don't have glasses but we can use these cups.'

She looks genuinely happy. 'Great! Could do with a stiff drink!'

He is busy opening and pouring the wine. 'Nice and cold, she got it out of the fridge.'

She looks at him as if to ask a question but just nods towards him, encouraging him to continue talking. He continues to pour the wine. He picks up the cups and takes them over to the bedside shelf. Still she looks at him, as if there is still something missing.

He realises exactly what she is looking a little concerned over and so tries to keep it going a little longer, not just for a joke but he is hoping the wine will help settle his nerves. He timidly removes his top as she sips her wine and sneaks a glimpse of his muscular chest once more. She says, 'do you work out? It looks like you take great care of your body.'

He smiles in appreciation and some of his early nerves have slowly disappeared. He looks her in the eyes and says, 'Only twice a week. I'm not one of those fanatics who go nearly every day. Thanks for the compliment though but you obviously know how beautiful your body is. Did I tell you that before?'

She takes another sip. She thinks the wine is going down well. Too well. 'I think you did mention something about being whole - I think you mentioned in and out!'

He laughs. The wine is definitely going down well and his inhibitions are shrinking by the sip.

'Okay, I surrender!' she says, 'did you get the condoms or a book?' She puts her empty cup down. He spots it is empty and gets up out of bed still wearing his shorts and black socks.

'Oh you're empty, Millie. Let me top you up again.' He moves over to the small table in the corner. Pours the remains of the first bottle into the two empty cups and places them back onto the bedside shelf again.

'Come on, Harry. Answer me.' She has become a little impatient.

'Hurry up, Harry, Come on!' he sings in a rough tone, one he generally reserves for the empty bathroom in his apartment at home. 'It's a really great book. It's by that new author everyone is raving about? You know the one who wrote that bestseller; The Story of World War Two?'

She turns over as if to show she's had enough of his teasing. She can certainly dish it out but is not very good at receiving it back. Suddenly he thinks he is messing up the timing again. 'Yes, I got them. Three packets, like you said.'

She turns back to face him again with a grin upon her. 'Three packets? Are you expecting company?' They both burst out laughing. 'You do know there's three in each pack?'

He says, 'Well the lady at the garage did say she was free later - only kidding!' They both laugh loudly.

Millie is looking a little serious. Perhaps having doubts about the situation she now finds herself in? Maybe, just a bout of nerves again but she is definitely playing for time and it becomes obvious she has something troubling her. She says, 'let's have another drink. I'll pour it for us.' She gets out of bed with a sheet wrapped around her naked body. She has become bashful. A little afraid, perhaps? She pours two more cups of wine and encourages Harry to drink with her. 'Let's celebrate The Swan,' she says as they clatter cups together. 'Drink up, Harry. We'll have a right old party tonight.'

He turns to her and says, 'if I did not know better, I would have thought you are trying to get your wicked way with me. You do not have to get me drunk for that, sweetie.' He moves closer.

She giggles and sips her wine. She is first to finish and slides out of bed to get two more cups. 'Here you are Harry. Make this the last one and she slowly drops the sheet to reveal her naked body to him.

He gulps his wine down in one go and places the empty cup on the bedside table. Then he leans over towards her and they kiss but it is not as passionate as their previous encounter. He looks quite drunk but Millie appears to be in control of her emotions. She is taking it very slow considering the position they find themselves in. She whispers, 'take it easy, Harry. The night is young.'

He finds himself feeling extremely tired all of a sudden and is struggling to stay awake. He thinks about the medication he took earlier and the effects of drinking alcohol. Then his mind turns to something a little more humorous; *we only need the fire alarm to go off now and that will make the night complete!*

Chapter 7

HARRY STIRS SLOWLY and attempts to focus. At first there is insecurity. The environment appears unfamiliar. There is nothing making sense. His throat is dry and his head is aching. He has not felt this ill for a very long time. Not since the last time he saw Emily Banks. He realises for the first time he is alone. Then two empty wine bottles on the floor come into view. They are quickly followed by an empty half bottle of vodka. Then he winces a little from a deep pain on the left side of his neck. It feels as though he has been bitten by an insect or something? He feels a little dizzy and there is a sharp pain coming from his lower abdomen area. Still he wonders what an earth he is doing in this strange room and what the hell happened overnight? He can smell perfume on a pillow case and it smells familiar. Suddenly a minor breakthrough with his memory occurs. He remembers Millie but where is she?

The longer he thinks the more depressed he is becoming. The fact she is no longer in the room is a real big negative. He scans the room for further clues and finds one by his side of the bed; an empty condom wrapper. He now thinks at least they had sex but he cannot remember any of it. Why did she leave without waking him? This does not look good for any ideas he has of having some kind of future with her. Feeling really low, his thoughts wander back to how he met Emily Banks and the last time he saw her. He is preparing for the worse possible scenario. He calls her name out and gets no response. He gets up and prays Millie is not in the shower room. For if she is, it will be bad, very bad as there is only a stillness within the entire room. Still he struggles with his thoughts and still no sounds coming from the room. The door handle has what looks like a blood stain showing over the top of the brass. There are further splashes over the walls but they seem like someone has tried to wipe them off. They are lighter in colour than the one on the door handle. He does not wish to open the door but he cannot just leave the room. He knows he has to look in. With trembling hands he pushes open the door slowly and refuses to walk in. Once again he shouts her name aloud. Once again there is no answer. He must somehow pluck up the courage to look inside. He peers through the open crack of the door and sees a pile of white towels on the floor. They look to be covering something. He physically bites his thumb in fear but urges himself to go in. He has to go in. He has to know. He approaches the towels and slowly lifts one off and discovers they were lying on top of a stool. He sighs a huge relief, she is not in there. Perhaps everything went well and the stains on the wall could even be rose wine splashes. They were in bed together, drinking wine, laughing and so possibly the remainder of the night was not so tragic after all?

He begins to put his belongings in the bag, hoping, no praying his memory will return and everything works out for the best but negativity now surrounds him again. He remembers making that promise to himself several years ago - the promise most people have made at some point in their lives when they have a huge hangover and have embarrassed themselves at some point. The promise, which is generally quickly broken; "I'm never going to drink again!"

He is ready to leave and something on the mirror by the front door entrance catches his attention. He walks over towards it and can see it is writing. It looks red. *Surely it's not blood?* He reads the message scrawled in big letters:

HI TIGER - CALL ME - MILLIE XXX

He is still intrigued as to what substance it has been written with. At this point he notices a large red and bluish mark on the left side of his neck. The area he found to be so sore when he first awoke. Now he can see it. He gets closer and puts on a vanity light. He can see what appear to be tooth marks. He is ashen faced and can barely focus his eyes. He nervously touches the substance on the mirror with his thumb. It looks like blood. His imagination kicks in and suddenly fear overcomes him. He tries to reassure himself that he has not been bitten and attacked by a vampire. He raises his thumb to his nose to smell. Then he discovers the substance to be lipstick and the bruising on his neck to be none other than a love bite - hickie. Relief fills his body and this is quickly followed by actual excitement as reality takes over. It must have been a successful night after all? There is a change in mood - a change in everything. He feels ecstatic and the hangover has now become insignificant. Throwing his bag back on the floor, he runs down to the reception area. She is there again. The lady from the day before, smiling happily towards him, only this time he is also genuinely smiling back.

'Good morning, Sir. Have you come to check out?' She says.

He smiles towards her and says, 'no, quite the opposite actually. I'd like to pay for another night please.'

'Will you be paying in cash again?' she remembers him from yesterday.

'Yes please,' he quickly answers but almost immediately he knows he has little cash left from the night before. 'No. Sorry to mess you around I will pay by card.' He fumbles in his pocket for his card and then recalls he has given a false name on the original booking. So he is unable to use a card with his real name on it. 'No second thoughts - make it cash. I'll have to go to the market place and get some cash out.'

She nods in agreement. 'We take cards if you want to use it but otherwise that's fine. I can keep your room open for you. Will you be long?'

'Not long and thank you for your kind help. I'll give you five stars when I do my feedback.'

She really is genuinely pleased. 'Thank you, that's so kind of you, sir.'

He rushes to the market place, returns to The Lodge and hands over the cash to the receptionist. He is now back in his room unpacking once more. After this he takes another look at the mirror. Stands back and admires it. He then takes a picture, no one has ever called him "tiger" before, he kind of takes it as a compliment in some way. Whilst still standing there, he recalls it is time for him to take his anti depressant tablets. He has to take two a day as prescribed by his GP. It then dawns upon him about the possible side effects. So he grabs the enclosed leaflet that came with the drugs. Looks at the side effects section and it clearly warns against consuming alcohol whilst taking this medication. He reads on and discovers alcohol and these tables can cause intense energy bursts and temporary loss of memory, followed by extreme drowsiness. There is also something about migraine attacks. These are just some of a long list of possible side effects. Despite all of this he pops two tablets into his mouth quickly not allowing any time for him to have a quick change of heart and not take them at all. He actually now thinks this medication mixed with alcohol had worked the night before even if he cannot remember anything.

It's gone eleven and so he plucks up the courage to ring Millie on the number she provided. The phone rings at the other end four times before she answers it. 'Hi.' She says.

'Morning Millie it's, Harry.' There's a nervous silence. He wonders if she is going to speak with him.

'Oh hello, Harry. How is your head this morning? More to the point, how is your stomach?' She is nervous. They've only had one date. Well, a few hours really. She is in deep thought. This call is crucial to her. She is desperate to keep this relationship going on the right path for as long as she can. There appears to be much riding on it all.

He responds quickly as he gets a *so far so good* vibe. 'Not too bad.' He is actually shaking at the knees at this point. He even contemplates doing some breathing exercises but thinks better of it as it may not sound too good at the other end.

She giggles. 'I am a little surprised to hear that after you fell on top of the table and landed on your belly. Not a pretty site being naked at the time.' She laughs. Still there appears to be something holding her back. Some nerves, perhaps? She begins to feel anxious as there are awkward silences in their conversation and she is doing all the talking. She needs a sign from him. Some clue as to how he feels about her after spending the night together.

He is a little stuck for words. She continues to lead the conversation. 'Mind you, before you did all that - wow! You were so strong. Did you take something? You had so much energy and so gentle.' She portrays herself as being extremely vulnerable. Perhaps she should not have said too many compliments in one sentence but she desperately wants this relationship to progress forward.

An elated look upon his face unexpectedly appears and he says, 'oh, it was a lovely night. Sorry about the table incident. I'm not normally into table hugging naked!'

She laughs. 'So you usually just do it with your clothes on? And there was me thinking you wouldn't love me in the morning.' She says, as she teases him once more.

He is still tense and searching for words to say. 'I'd love it if we could meet up today. I've decided to stay another day and booked the room again.'

'Wow! You don't mess about do you. So you want to get your money's worth from the garage purchase of last night?' she purposely laughs but still there appears to be something more on her mind. Her thoughts are wandering. She looks very serious but obviously, Harry cannot see this. 'Shall I come over to the room and we can send out for a takeaway, when we're ready to eat?'

'Fantastic! I can't wait to see you, Millie. Bye sweetie.'

She is so desperate to see him again. She says, 'I'll come over about four and bring the wine and some glasses. I'm pretty sure you would prefer them rather than those old cups?'

They both agree to the time. Harry has another chance but he has already taken his daily medication. He worries about mixing it with the alcohol and feels he does not want another night like the last - or does he?

Chapter 8

October

ALTHOUGH HE HAS little memory of the nights of passion with Millie, they appear to be getting really closer in their relationship. He returns home to a quiet looking Becclesfield after a very happy weekend and now he has something more to look forward to in his life. It is a nice sunny quiet Sunday afternoon as he drives past the memorial church in the middle of the High Street; it has a large clock on all four sides of the tower and each of the individual clocks have a different time. He knows this church very well. It is where his parents are buried in the rear of the grounds. He looks to the left and remembers his first job in the old derelict building that used to be the library. In fact, he knows every inch of the shopping centre, he has walked it a thousand times. He turns sharp left along the coastal road and glimpses the open sea where the top of an old wreck is still managing to survive the turbulent tides and holds desperately onto the seabed. He then turns right just before The Crown, which brings him into a one way road, turning right once more into Waverley Road where he lives.

As he walks through the main entrance towards the communal stairs, his neighbour, Fred is standing as if he had been awaiting his arrival for some time. 'Afternoon Harry. Did you have a good weekend?' he winks to him as if he knows something good has happened. 'You didn't say you was going away, son. I would've kept an eye on your place for you.'

'Afternoon Fred,' he says, looking at him affectionately, thinking he probably wants a little more than just a quick greeting. 'Yes something popped up.' He laughs aloud.

Fred smiles and is genuinely happy for him. 'What's her name?' He remarks rather candidly.

Harry grins and has a little admiration of Fred's sharp wit. 'Well, you are very wise, Fred. Her name is Millie.'

'That's my most favouritist name, Rodney.' He laughs as he knows Harry likes to watch the Fools and Horses tv show.

Harry laughs and says, 'have you got everything you need, Fred?'

'As you are asking, son. I am a little short of milk. Other than that I'm great thanks. Just wanted to make sure you was okay.' He smiles and winks at him once more.

'I'll bring you a litre when I next go out.'

'That's very kind of you, thanks. I'll pay you for it when I see you next.' Fred turns and gently closes his front door.

Harry continues up the stairs onto the landing, he pauses and looks over the balcony. This is something he does as a matter of fact. He is looking for something or someone? He will not enter his apartment if he feels there is something suspicious going on down below. On this occasion he feels free to enter his apartment. He shakes his shoes off and stretches out on a small blue corduroy sofa in the living room. He grabs his mobile phone to make sure he has got Millie's phone number and not done another stupid thing, like accidentally deleting it somehow. He looks all around his living room as appearing to complete a ritual of some kind. Perhaps it is comforting in some way? He promptly drifts off to sleep for several hours.

For Jacob it is the start of another busy week. He is sitting patiently behind his desk. It is Monday morning and he is awaiting his first appointment of the week. It has been hastily re-arranged due to a cancellation. She is late and he expects this as she has been late for most of her sessions. He rustles once more through his notes even though he knows this case inside out. It is his most complex and challenging. It's not very often these types of cases get passed to him but amongst other issues she has obsessive and identity challenges.

It's heading towards ten past ten. There is a sudden but gentle tap on his door. 'Please come in,' he calls out.

In walks a young beautiful woman aged in her late twenties. 'I'm ever so sorry for being late. It's those buses. I should've got a taxi or even walked, it would've been much quicker.' She nervously smiles in his direction hoping she has said enough to get excused.

She has. Jacob smiles back. 'Please feel free to either sit or lay down, which ever you prefer?'

She lays down and gives her short skirt a gentle but slow tug downwards. 'I should really wear something more appropriate for these sessions.' She likes to try and tease, perhaps put Jacob off but it hasn't happened as far as she can tell yet in over twelve sessions but she enjoys trying.

He walks over and sits in his large leather chair as always, situated in the middle of the room. 'How has your week been? You look quite content in yourself.'

A big smile appears on her face as she recalls some of the events over the past few days or so. 'Much better thank you.' She is holding back because even though she cannot read Jacobs thoughts or see much of any reaction, she knows he will be disapproving of the real truth and she needs his support.

He can tell there is more to come and so pushes home the point. 'So what has led to this sudden change in yourself?'

'I have just had a better weekend than the norm. The weather is fine and still no sign of the horrible winter approaching... yet.'

'So no feelings about Paul or Alex anymore?' He knows if anything will open her up this will.

Somehow she resists her emotions and on this day they are not overreacting by the mention of her former lovers names. 'I have overcome those misplaced feelings I had for them both. They no longer flash up in my thoughts. I am in a much better place now. They are both a pair of losers. They'll never amount to much - just a pair of users.'

He believes this part but shows no emotion upon his face. 'You feel you have moved on then?'

'Ooh, I have so moved on.' Her face has not changed from looking happy and content. 'Life, at long last has suddenly brought some joy. I was beginning to give up a little, I don't mind saying but when you least expect it... something turns up.'

He takes a long look at her and even her body language is giving off a better vibe. 'That's really good, if a little sudden as only last week you were tearful at the mention of their names. That's really good - Millie.'

She smiles back at him in appreciation of this recognition and encouragement. The one thing she feels she has is - Jacob's support.

He still wishes to get to the bottom of this quick turnaround. Most of his patients are not able to manage this well so soon under her circumstances. 'Did you go out anywhere special this week?' She blushes a little. He knows. He knew from the moment she walked into the room.

She just nods her head and then deliberately crosses her legs allowing her skirt to rise higher in the hope it will distract him somehow. There is a short pause. 'Just some drinks with friends - you know?' She says.

He then gives her a mini lecture on drinking whilst on medication to which she pretends to be surprised but really takes no notice of it whatsoever. 'Millie, you have made good progress over the weeks but you may remember what we said during the early sessions? So long as you can express the real feeling you are having, we can progress further but if you are going to hold back then we just go backwards.'

She sits up and says, 'I may as well tell the truth - after all that's what I'm here for. I met someone over the weekend. So nice and I received a bouquet of flowers everyday this week. I really think this could be the one!'

'That is nice, Millie but please be a little careful of jumping into a serious relationship so quickly. You remember why you are here and I know you are doing so well at the moment. If it is making you happy then that must be a good thing but please give yourself time to adjust to this new relationship. A few days together is not really ideal to have such strong feelings. I mean you know very little about him or her. It takes time to fully trust somebody.' He looks intently into her eyes. 'Please just be careful to protect your emotions - ok? Time is up for this week. See you again next week. Hope your new relationship continues on its happy path.'

She gets up, wriggles her skirt downwards a little and smiles as if to thank him for such good advice. She then leaves the office.

He immediately gets to work on updating her file. There appears to have been some kind of improvement but he knows this to be really a critical time for her and things can so quickly come tumbling back down from such great highs. The important thing now is to monitor her closely and with some luck he may be able to move on to some of the other issues she really needs help with. He has a really good day and was able to fully discharge two more of his patients. He knows that will please Mohammed a great deal and perhaps take a little pressure off the growing waiting list.

Harry is lying asleep on his couch and is still recovering from his adventurous weekend with Millie. Suddenly he is awakened by the sounds of The Great Escape ringtone from his mobile phone. He picks up immediately as he sees the beautiful face of Millie flashing on the screen. 'Hi, Millie. How are you?'

'Oh, Harry. The flowers are so lovely. Thank you ever so much. It's such a nice thing to receive, especially on a moody Monday morning.'

There is a short pause but then he says, 'flowers?...'

After a few more moments Millie says, 'I was just thinking who on earth would've sent them to me for a moment there.'

Got you!'

'You are getting better at this game. Thanks so much.'

'What have you been up to today?'

Millie hesitates but then says, 'not much really. As I told you over the weekend, I have been working from home since the epidemic.'

He has no idea and cannot remember but pretends. 'Oh yes. Have you been busy with it all today?'

'For a moment I thought you had forgotten. You are still buying that house aren't you? Only you haven't sent over the deposit you promised to do this morning.'

There is a long silence as Harry tries to work out just how to get out of yet another corner. 'Well... I still have a few questions.'

'Thought you would. Just as well I'm not really an estate agent otherwise I could have fleeced you, Harry. I do deliveries. I'm a midwife. Knew you wouldn't remember.' She laughs to show she is not offended in any way.

After a few moments he says, 'knew you was a midwife - just thought I'd play along with you for a while.'

'Whatever? Now more to the serious points in hand. When are you taking me out again?'

'I was going to suggest coming over here on Friday night for a Chinese takeaway or something else?'

'Something else? You mean there is something else on the menu. What have you a "House Special" in mind?'

'I meant any takeaway you prefer but there is always a "House Special". It is of course reserved for "special" guests. Are you going to be one of those?'

'Only you could think of something like that. You had better think I'm Special, Harry. After the nights we've just spent together. Anyway, it sounds like a plan. I'll bring the wine. Do you have two glasses as I know you live alone?' She laughs again.

'I am pretty sure I have more than two but I will check. I'll have to get the cleaner in early this week though.'

She knows he really does not have a cleaner but goes along with it.

He hangs up and tries once more to recall the events of the two nights they spent together and can only recall her naked body and a cup of wine.

Chapter 9

IT IS NOW Tuesday morning and approaching eleven. He knows the next person to walk through his door will be Harry Sutton. He is actually really looking forward to seeing him as there was nearly a major step forward last week. Jacob will be keen to get to work with him from the off.

Harry knocks on his door. He has arrived a little early. He actually looks forward to this session for some reason. In fact, he has looked forward to each day since Saturday.

'Come on in,' he calls out.

Harry walks in with a good look about himself. Always smartly dressed for the occasion, there is something different and Jacob can tell immediately. He smiles in a warm welcoming manner. 'Good morning, Harry. Please make yourself comfortable.'

He is already laying on the couch as Jacob takes up his usual seated place in the middle of the room. 'Now last week you mentioned a Leo from school and the problems with Emily Banks. I think that is where we left off?' he crosses his legs as usual.

He is a little put out how he has gone straight to that area. 'Don't you want to know how my week's been first then?'

'I can tell you have had a good week but you are right we should talk about that first. Please go ahead Harry.'

'Well I went away for the weekend and guess what?' He pauses but little reaction is forthcoming. 'I hardly even thought about Leo, 6 Cherry Walk or even Emily come to think of it. I spent the whole weekend with a beautiful young lady.'

'Have you known her long?' he asks.

'All weekend,' He grins. 'We know each other a lot more now though!' He is quick to resort to his usual suggestive way of answering.

'Oh I see. So you were intimate?'

He is hardly analysing the questions this week. 'Yes and she lives local to me - happy days!' He tries to recall the intimate moments but his mind is a blur.

'Are you going to meet up again then?'

'Definitely. She's coming over to mine on Friday night. We're having a Chinese takeaway and probably lots of wine.' He feels he has just let his guard down.

'Have you been taking your medication? You do know you are not allowed to drink alcohol whilst taking your pills?' He knows he probably has not been taking it but had to ask.

He is disappointed with himself. He has also relaxed soon and fallen for a sucker punch but fortunately it is early in the bout - he still has time to recover though. 'Of course, Jacob. She'll be on the wine and I'll have the non alcoholic one. I wouldn't be that silly to drink at the same time as taking my meds - it gives you some nasty side effects you know?'

'I'm pleased you know about those. It can be dangerous as your medication is quite strong but you are living proof it is working.' Jacob shows him some encouraging support.

He is happy with those remarks. He has recovered from the early blow well but he's not out of the woods yet.

Jacob fumbles through his notes once more. 'So tell me about Leo?'

He is not too defensive. 'There is not a problem about him anymore.'

'Why was there a problem? What caused you to think about him and Emily Banks so much in the past then?'

The mention of Leo did little to move him but the mention of Emily really brought it all back. 'I told you about Emily and what that scumbag did?'

'Yes. He got her drunk and may have had intercourse with her but you said it brought you and Emily "closer". You then worked for her father at the sawmills in Ferry Lane. The one that burned down several years back now. Can we take it from there please, Harry?'

He wants to resist. Once again vivid memories of that era comes to mind but after a lengthy pause he decides to open up. 'Well, after the fire her dad went bankrupt. Emily moved away and we never spoke or saw each other again.'

He cannot help but look puzzled and so asks, 'what happened to Leo?'

This is now obviously getting extremely uncomfortable for Harry as he fidgets and eventually sits up. 'Leo - always the lucky one. Always come out on top. Always got the girls. I think we should have nicknamed him -"always" more suitable than "dick head", I suppose?' He allows himself a private little chuckle.

Although a little humorous, Jacob basically ignores and continues with his line of questioning. 'You say lucky. How?'

He looks a little subdued as he recalls some of the events. 'Got in the school football team even though he had two left feet. Got that apprenticeship at "Blue line Garage". He knew I had applied for it. Also got Emily.'

'Got Emily? What after all he did?' He really appears not to understand this answer from Harry.

He knew another mistake had been made but this time there would be no coming back. So he thought he may as well continue on. 'I meant that he got her that night. You know when she was drunk?' He looks full of anger.

Jacob then asks, 'how is that lucky? If he won over her affections in a natural way - that could be deemed lucky?'

He gets fed up with all the questions and calls for a break. They have not spent time on the subject he really wished to discuss further - Millie.

They finish their short break and this time it is Harry who prompts the first question. 'You haven't asked much about my marvellous weekend. I thought it may have been better to speak about the positives in my life not all those negative times from the past?'

He is quick to respond. 'Yes, I am really happy for you but we need to deal with those past events as they have had a real impact on the present and could affect you in the future. You have had Leo and Emily on your mind for so long now it has really affected you in a negative way.'

He stares out of the window in apparent disgust and a little contemptuously . 'If we must,' he reluctantly says.

'Good. That's really positive of you. Now you were saying Leo had been lucky and he got Emily. Did they start seeing each other after that incident? That appears a little strange given the events of that evening?'

He feels he needs to find something, anything to get him off the scent because Jacob is closing in on him. 'Yes. She was a very forgiving person. They started dating after... well, after we broke up. I saw the two of them in Tranby walking over some wasteland.'

'So he was going out with her after the fire at the sawmills? Did you have any thoughts of revenge, aggression or anything of that nature towards Leo? I mean you and Emily were "close". You knew and probably spoke with Emily about what Leo may or may not have done?'

'He did do it! Emily was heartbroken. She regularly sobbed on my shoulder. I was going to get him but...' he deliberately pauses and takes some deep intakes of breath. He is getting over anxious and afraid of disclosing his real problems whilst in this state.

'Take your time, Harry. You are doing really well. It helps to talk about it.' he says, knowing it does not really appear to be helping Harry at this precise moment in time.

Once again he looks at the time and there are just minutes left. He has said enough for one session, so plays for time again knowing he has all but made it through this one. 'Her father was such a nice guy. It was a shame what happened to him.'

'Okay, Harry thank you for today. You may not realise it but we are making real progress. Look forward to seeing you next week... oh and good luck with your new relationship.' He smiles as warmly as he did when Harry first entered the office.

'Thank you, see you next week.' He leaves but is concerned now. Can he continue withholding the secret?

Chapter 10

HARRY FEELS DEVASTATED and extremely anxious after this last session. He heads to The Crown. He not only feels like he needs a drink there has been a sudden urge inside making him want one but he fails to really understand why. It is so strong he has not even given a thought to two things; the fact he has taken his pills and how only two days ago he said to himself he would not drink again.

He pushes open the door to The Crown. It sounds a bit creaky as it slowly opens but it has been there a long time. He once again questions himself as to why he should even be wanting a drink and especially as he is alone. He shrugs it off and marches directly to the bar. He is in such a state, one pint will not last long and so gets two pints of lager. He finds a nice quiet spot in an alcove area. He sits and carefully places his beer on the table in front of him. The first pint is gone so quickly, it is as if he has just crawled through a sweltering desert on his hands and knees gasping for a drink in order to survive. He actually feels a bit better. More relaxed and less stressed but suddenly his thoughts have once again turned to Leo. He attempts to shake these thoughts off by concentrating on the five senses method Jacob had taught him right at the beginning of his treatment. He looks at the fruit machine in the corner with it's annoying flashing lights. He smells pizza cooking from behind the bar area. He listens and hears some mumbled voices in the background. He tastes remnants of lager still in his mouth and he touches the smooth finish of the wooden table in front of himself. It has worked yet again. These distractions have cleared his thoughts, at least for the moment.

He rushes back to the bar and buys another two pints of lager. He gets back to his seat without spilling a single drop. He carefully places them on the table. He is busying himself by minding his own business. Thoughts of the weekend are now fresh in his mind and he is slowly loosening up. When all of a sudden a tall man with short black hair breezes past him and stands up at the bar area. He is wearing a black leather jacket with large writing on the back. It says, "Route 66". He has seen that jacket before. It has something to do with Emily Banks and so he takes a second look. He thinks the guy looks familiar, more than thinks that, he is convinced he knows who it is. He gets out of his seat. He is trembling uncontrollably. Having waited almost six years, this opportunity is not going to pass him by. He suddenly realises where he has seen that jacket before and is convinced it belonged to Leo Parker. So he taps the guy on the shoulder. He turns and looks at Harry. He has a puzzling vacant sort of look. Harry realises he has made an embarrassing mistake.

'I'm so sorry you look like someone I knew,' he says.

'You don't mean there is another poor bugger running around who looks like me do you, mate? Poor sod.' He replies with a smile, which crinkled his nose a little.

Harry laughs as he appreciates his sense of humour. 'Yes, so sorry about that, I should've gone to Specsavers!'

Now it is time for the stranger to laugh. 'Nice one, mate. Here let me buy you a pint - it may help improve your eyesight?'

He is slightly taken aback with the generosity and kindness of the stranger. He forgets he has a full pint on the table. 'Oh thank you. I'll take a chance with a pint of lager please.'

The man orders the drinks. 'By the way, my name is, Alex.' He puts his hand out.

'I'm Harry. Nice to meet you.' They shake hands. 'I've got a seat over there if you fancy sitting down?' He points to the left side of the pub.

Alex nods in agreement. 'Sounds good to me. I've been on me feet all day.'

'So are you local?' Harry asks.

'I am now. Moved down here about five years ago. Used to live in London before that.' He notices Harry's other drinks on the table. 'Are you with friends? Only I see there are a few pint glasses knocking around, mate?'

'Oh, no. I just got two in to save interrupting my thoughts too often.'

'I've heard some excuses before but never that one. Don't mind if I use that when my boss comes to get me out of the pub at lunchtimes, do you?' He laughs. 'So are you from around these parts?'

'Most of my life. Went to the local schools but there's not much work here now. Not since the saw mills in Ferry Lane closed down. Old man Banks was the largest employer then.'

'Yeah, I was lucky to get a break. My mate Paul got me a job not far from here. Still have to use the motor though. Are you working here?'

Harry pauses for a moment and not really sure how much he can reveal about himself to who is after all just a stranger. 'No. I'm taking a little break from it all. Feel sometimes, anyone who can that is, should take some time to appreciate the better things in life.'

Alex nods in total agreement. 'Yeah, I know what you mean, mate.'

Harry takes a rather large gulp of his beer and then asks, 'what about your friend - does he live around here?'

Alex is a little taken aback and answers a little nervously. 'Not any more. He moved out when she divorced him. He's gone back to London but only recently. It took an age to sell their house, what with Covid, Brexit and now the cost of living crisis. They're just not selling at the moment.'

'Bloody Covid! Who would have thought it?'

'Yeah. That's when he met her.'

'Oh his wife?' Harry looks a little puzzled.

'No. "The Witch", as we used to call her. If I tell you about it you'll have to promise to keep it to yourself, mate.'

'Definitely, mate,' Harry realises he has started using Alex repetitive common word "mate", probably in attempt to put him more at ease as he describes more about Paul and The Witch.

'You know The Angel pub. It used to be over the road. Like so many now is has turned into a restaurant.'

Harry nods in agreement.

'Well we were in there, me and Paul. Having a great laugh. It would've been one of those nights you could look back on at some boring time in the future and roll up about.'

Harry is not certain but he surmises "roll up" probably means laugh but he certainly is not going to interrupt him unnecessarily.

'I noticed this bird looking over at us. She was a little cracker, mate. Long dark hair, short skirt really lovely friendly looking face. Not just one of those bird's you think you've met before but one you are praying you have met before.' Alex pauses to take a gulp of his beer. 'She only comes over to us both. Right forward gal. She starts rabbitting on about some party that is gonna happen later that night. Of course, we're all ears. It develops in a way it becomes obvious she has Paul in her sights and so I do the right thing - walk away and give 'em space.'

'Very noble Alex, if I may say so. What happens then?' He is getting right into the story and can't wait to find out what goes on next. He has even stopped drinking - momentarily that is.

'Well, Paul being such a nice guy,' he winks, 'gets into a cab and makes sure she gets home safely. So much worried about her wellbeing he stays over. I get a text to say if his wife asks at any later point, he was drunk and stayed over at mine. What could I do, mate? He's a close friend and even though I was friends with his wife, Maxine, I had no choice?'

'Wow! You are a really good mate, mate,' he realises how silly that sounded and then accidentally repeats another of his common grammar uses; 'You know what I mean?'

It all goes over Alex's head he is far too busy recalling the events, he continues, 'Paul thought it was just sex for the one night. He hadn't figured for the trouble coming his way after. She went crazy, mate. You know real crazy. She kept ringing him. Hunted him down to where he worked and when she found out he was married - well that was it.'

Harry looks genuinely shocked. 'You mean he didn't tell her he was married? Wow!'

'I think she really knew deep down but wanted to have a bit of fun but when she gets serious and he doesn't - same old story. Anyway, he asks me to take some heat off him and proposes I go instead of him. He arranges to meet up with her and so I go along. I pretended he got delayed at work and I get her a lot to drink. By the time ten o'clock comes around she is giggling and hugging me. We kissed and as they say, "the rest is history". Then it started. She left Paul alone and came after me when we broke up.'

'Oh, what the stalking thing?' Harry looks to be listening very intensively.

'More than that, mate. Only this time she couldn't blame it on me being married as I was still single.'

'You're well rid of her by the sounds of it.' He says rather sympathetically.

'What do you mean? She's my wife!' he replies ever so sharply.

He is stunned. The last thing he wanted to do was go and insult Alex in this way. 'Bloody hell. Sorry mate. I - only meant....'

Alex laughs loudly. 'Really got you there, mate. Who in their right mind would want to marry her? I have a restriction order against her. Especially after what she did to Paul's new car.' He pauses and takes a big gulp of beer. It looks like he needs it as he continues to reflect back to that tragic day. 'He had a brand new BMW convertible parked proudly on this driveway. Two weeks old. He wakes up one morning and someone - no guesses who - has painted "Paul is a dick head" down both sides of his shiny black car.'

'Bloody hell. I suppose he reported it to the police then?'

'Not at first. He hid it from his wife for two days but when she received some anonymous photos on her phone. You know the ones you wouldn't want your mother to see. That my friend was that. She put in for a divorce and he went to the police. She was taken to court, paid a large fine for damages and agreed to therapy. She was also issued with a restraining order.'

'Wow! What a horror story. Glad I never bumped into her. Have you seen her around here lately?' Harry looks genuinely shocked and quite wary.

'No. I think she moved in with her sister somewhere. Probably taken her dopey cat with her. I swear she loved that more than any person she ever met.' Alex has an empty glass in his hand.

Harry feels it is time for him to go. 'Thanks for the friendliness but I have an appointment. Perhaps we can meet up next week. Exchange mobile numbers and text over the time and place?' He leaves the pub.

Chapter 11

ANOTHER WEEK HAS passed and being Tuesday morning, eleven o'clock, means it is yet another session between Jacob and Harry. They have already taken up their normal positions. Jacob has welcomed him as usual and Harry is laying on the couch not looking at all comfortable. He knows Jacob is on the verge of extracting part of the secret out of him. He shuffles and wriggles until he is ready for the next onslaught.

Jacob, as usual is first to start the session. He says, 'you said last week, Leo and Emily had started a relationship after their drunken night together but how did he go about winning over her affections?'

He knew this was coming; the frontal assault but he sees a golden opportunity to verbally abuse Leo at the same time. 'He was a nasty piece of work, I can tell you. I would not have trusted him with my mother - I saw the change in him over the passing years.'

'Okay, putting that aside. How did he actually go about it?'

'He waited until she was vulnerable. That's how he always does it. Sets a trap and slowing draws them in - just like a spider. On this occasion, he was there to comfort her after her father's factory caught on fire. He knew her parents would be ever so grateful for him being there at their worst moment. So it was easy.' He is satisfied with his response.

'What happened next with them both? Did they stay together?'

This is the question he has been avoiding for the past six years - ever since the fire. 'I don't think so but he's lucky as I have always said. I've been to his house several times but haven't seen Emily since that fateful day when the factory went up in smoke. It was as though she left Becclesfield in a hurry... come to think of it, perhaps she started the fire for some reason and then ran away.

Always thought how those two occurrences could have been linked in some way? Then there was that man I saw her with that day, over the wasteland in Tranby whilst I was attending to my allotment next door. He looked a little familiar but even to this day I've not been able to place him. Perhaps he was her accomplice?'

'So the man you saw her with was not Leo then?'

'Strange, I always see him when I go back to that day in my head but this leather jacket is the real thing that makes me think it was him. He was wearing it and I only saw them in a distance. Although, I suppose he could've had it stolen by someone else before that day and the stranger could've been wearing it. He may've even lured her there, pretending to be Leo?' Harry looks quite bewildered.

'So you have been to his house? Does that mean you are on friendly terms with Leo now?' He looks a little surprised by this new revelation.

He quickly recovers and says, 'no we'll never be on friendly terms. I mean I have been past his house a few times. Never gone in. Not seen him in six years. Thinking back now, I think they probably eloped. Yes, that's what they did - eloped. That's what I am getting so confused about. They both disappeared at the same time. It must've been Leo over the wasteland that day if they went off together, right?'

'Why did they elope? I thought he practically had her parent's blessings?'

Harry begins to fumble with his shirt - a clear sign of nerves kicking in. He knows this next answer has to be good or part of his secret may come out. 'I think it's down to that fire. Emily's father lost everything that day, as he had no insurance for arson. Leo did the honourable thing for once, knowing her father could not now pay for an extravagant wedding, he took her away from it all. Then the old man fell ill and died shortly after from a stroke. Thankfully he had life insurance though - no good to him of course.'

Jacob uncrosses his legs, a sure sign of an imminent breakthrough in his mind. 'Leo sounds to have mended his ways a little?'

'Never!' he shouts in an aggressive manner. 'He is a slime ball! Always has been and always will be. He will never mend his ways. I hope he is dead!' He calms down a little and sits up now expecting the worse.

Jacob leans forward. 'Okay, Harry, please calm yourself. Do your deep breathes?'

He scratches his head and replies, 'Perhaps they didn't elope? Someone told me Parker was sent down for the arson attack and did 5 years in prison. He would be out now though. Knowing him, he would return to this area, even if just to show he is not fearful of any repercussions. I'm pretty sure there would be many awaiting in line to exact some form of revenge upon him, if they knew where he was. Still no one can tell us what happened to Emily or where she is?'

Jacob's eyes light up with a flicker of emotion. 'So you are not sure what happened to either of them and not sure whether Leo started the fire or not. So why such distaste towards Leo then?'

'I'm confused. I don't trust him but I could've been wrong about some of my memories of him. I really don't know what to think. I know one thing though - he is the only reason why Emily and I are not living happy lives together.'

Jacob feels they both need a little rest and calls a refreshment break. He sits behind his desk and looks into his laptop. Harry peers over at him and grunts a little under his breath but not loud enough to be heard. He knows Jacob is looking at his notes again.

The second half begins with both looking quite relaxed. Jacob asks, 'you met a young lady last week - how is that coming along?' He decides to concentrate on the present and a little on the future.

He is pleased to answer on a subject he really likes to talk about - Millie. 'Fantastic! Millie is such a fun loving and gentle person - just what the doctor ordered!' He laughs a little at the irony of his comments.

Jacob refrains from showing any emotion as usual, he just continues with his thoughts. 'So she looks like she could be your calming influence?'

'She is! Do you know I hadn't thought about her in that way before but you're right. She's so loving. Take her cat, Tom she absolutely idolises him. She took me this weekend to meet her sister. They have a pub in Tranby and boy did we get into one on Saturday night.'

Jacob has a sudden stern look upon his face and says, 'have you been taking your medication?'

He knows what the problem is and so answers immediately. 'Yes of course but obviously not on Saturday as I knew I was going out for a drink. I have sent her a bouquet of flowers everyday this week, that's how much I like her. She is one in a million. That sounds like it could make a good title of a song or a movie but in her case it is true.'

He nods in approval. 'So when are you seeing Millie again?' he says as he feels a strong feeling of déjà vu.

'I'm meeting her in the town centre tomorrow. She has a ten o'clock appointment with the opticians first. We are then going into The Crown for a bite of lunch - of course I won't be drinking - I nearly forgot to tell you I made a new friend in The Crown this week as well. Alex is such an easy guy to talk with - he reminds me of you.' He is pleased he remembers to put the proviso on the drinking part and to pay Jacob a long overdue compliment.

Jacob feels a little humble. He is not used to getting many compliments in his line of work. 'That's really good but please be careful with alcohol whilst on your strong medication and I look forward to seeing you next week.'

Harry leaves with a little bit of a skip in his step. He is happy but still a little confused as to why he practically stood up for Leo Parker in front of Jacob. He puts it down to the medication as it sometimes causes confusion when not taken properly. He has gotten quite a bit off his chest in the last session and is in a much better place. He has not visited 6 Cherry Walk for several weeks and he rarely thinks about it but it is likely to be short-lived because he has not revealed the final part of the secret thus far - that is probably because he may not know it - yet?

Chapter 12

JACOB HAS ARRANGED an immediate meeting with his boss. He is patiently waiting in his office. Mohammed has had to rush over from one of the other centres he manages as he realises the importance of the meeting.

He walks in and jokes, 'don't get up.' He has a wry smile upon his face. Jacob just looks up and nods. 'So what's going on? Have you suddenly become a matchmaker?'

Jacob is a little annoyed with the flippant attitude he is appearing to take. 'I think it is a bit more serious than that.' He dares to reply.

'Yes but nothing we haven't in this industry come up against before. I have read through these files and we will need to monitor them both very closely. Maybe bring them in on an extra day here and there?' He gently rubs his black moustache as he begins to mull things over a little more.

Jacob is quick to point out. 'They'll know there is something wrong if we do that. They are both very clever. It would also appear neither of them wants the other to know they are having therapy as well but the main issues in Mr. Sutton's case are things from his past. He frequently talks about persons he used to know and one of the is the missing Banks girl. She was the 17 year old daughter of the owner of the Banks sawmills in Ferry Lane. It burned down about six years ago. I think I will take a closer look at how that all happened. He also has a number of contradicting conspiracy theories including either Leo Parker or Emily Banks, and maybe even both, actually set fire to the factory. If memory serves me, the police did charge someone locally with the arson attack.'

Mohammed caresses his black moustache again and says, 'I am more concerned with the relationship with Ms. Sanderson and Mr. Sutton. If this goes the wrong way it could become a bit dangerous given their current state of emotions. Well they haven't committed a crime together and we don't know as to any plans to do so. It is obviously what may happen if they break up their relationship - it could then be argued it would be in the public interests to reveal their issues to the law courts or police but we would have to tell them both we are doing that.'

He agrees by nodding his head. 'Of course if we did that this would have a catastrophic impact on their current treatment programmes. Perhaps even push one of them or both of them over the edge?'

Mohammed gets up off his chair, turns and looks out of the window behind him. 'What a small world this really is. Keep a close eye on this situation for now - and Jacob... tread very carefully. Keep me informed of any progress, one way or the other. Thanks for coming up.'

He gets up and leaves the room, heads downstairs back to his office to contemplate his next moves on this fast developing situation. He scourers through his laptop files. Going over and over each of their cases. He knows whilst they are happy in their relationship everything will be great but should they break up - well it could be extremely dangerous for either of them or others closely linked to them.

He gets out the almanac, it is really referred to as the "bible" in his industry. He looks at "public interests" and breaking confidentiality laws. He has spent his lunch hour reading but has not come up with any solutions other than the one Mohammed suggested - keep monitoring the subjects. The only trouble he has with that is it is only one hour per week and a lot can happen in a day, never mind a week. The one thing he appears unable to solve at the moment is whether the new friend Alex is the same person who had an affair with Millie before or whether it is just pure coincidence. After all, there are many people called Alex but if it turns out to be the same Alex, then what is he up to?

Harry and Mille are having a drink in The Crown. They may get around to having something to eat but it is unlikely. They are in great spirits, already had four drinks and onto their fifth. He suddenly remembers to ask a question. 'How did the opticians go today?'

She looks somewhat baffled at first and then sighs, 'oh yes. It's such a pain. You spend all that time having your eyes tested, sitting in a chair outside, going back in, sitting outside again and what for?'

'A new pair of trainers!' He laughs loudly.

She laughs having realised the strangeness of her question. 'Of course. Why didn't I go to specsavers?'

Harry laughs. 'I used that one last week - now where was I?' He is unable to recall and so moves on. 'Shall I get a bottle and two glasses?'

'Rose - great!'

'I'm Harry not Rose.' He jokes.

He leaves his seat and makes his way to the bar area. Orders the drinks and goes back empty handed. He is feeling great. He has not taken any of his medication for five days now and feels he has turned the corner with his stress and anger management behaviour.

'You haven't done a "Jack and the Beanstalk" on me, have you Harry?"

He is a little puzzled he has not heard that one before.

She sees he is still looking bemused. 'You know his mum sends him out to sell the cow and instead of coming back with the money he buys the beans. You know the beans for the beanstalk! God do I have to explain all of my jokes?' She laughs again.

He laughs as the penny finally drops. 'I see. No, the waitress said she'll bring it over. It's all about the presentation you know?'

She has a serious look suddenly come upon her face and says, 'Harry, I have to ask you. Who is Emily? You kept saying her name the other night whilst we were... and in your sleep you kept mentioning a guy called Leo Perkins?'

He has an instant blush and rush of anxiety but it is not out of embarrassment. He pretends to struggle with his memory of such a people and then says, 'I hope you are not going to hold anything I say whilst under the influence, against me? I probably meant to say your name - it's so similar, Millie.'

She is quick to respond. 'No, of course not but you wouldn't like it if I was to say someone else's name to you whilst we were - you know - being passionate?'

This time he is embarrassed. 'Oh, I didn't know I had done something like that. I don't know anyone called Emily or Leo but I know I have nearly called you it sometimes by mistake. Especially when we first met for instance. It is very similar, you have to agree?'

'I hope you remember our passionate moments as I do, Harry? Only it sounds a little vague all of this.'

'Wow! Who could forget being with you Millie? Such beauty and tenderness. A truly remarkable soul and such great kindness.' He has really tried to put himself back in her good books.

She says in typical Millie fashion. 'Oh, thank you so much, Barry - Oh, I see how easy it can be.'

He is not sure whether she is being serious or sarcastic but for the sake of an agreeable outcome he chooses the former.

Right on cue, a blonde slender waitress approaches their table with a tray containing one bottle of rose and two glasses. They look really pleased and both thank her at the same time. It is enough to save him from any further grilling on the subject.

'Shall I be mother?' He pours the wine into each glass. 'How's Tom today?' He has changed the subject superbly. He knows the mention of Tom always melts her heart.

She is pleased he asked. 'He's like all blokes - bloody spoilt!'

He is not certain whether to grin or take a little offence to being labelled as "spoilt" but knows she did not mean to infer anything. So he chooses to laugh. 'You love him really. Just like me?' He is fishing for the answer he is longing to hear even though they had not been together long.

She smiles, hugs him and they steal a quick kiss before anyone in the pub can see them but she either chose not to reply or did not realise it was a serious question. With snowfall getting heavier, Millie turns to him and randomly says, 'I don't know how they do it? Apparently every single snowflake is unique. So they must've someone standing outside with some form of instrument. Imagine doing a job like that, you'd be an abominable snowman by the time your shift was over.' She giggles.

He laughs and knows she is just joking but just in case tries to clear matters up for her. 'I think you'll find they would use computers of some sort. It would be millions of flakes to take into consideration.'

'I've just won my bet with my sister. I told her I could get you to talk about the snowflakes.'

'Oh I'm pleased to be of some assistance. Will I be getting half then?'

They drink their wine and stroll back to Harry's apartment, which is just a five minute walk away. Although both being quite inebriated it takes more like ten minutes to reach the apartment. As for Tom, well he has a caring neighbour looking after him.

It is Sunday lunchtime and Harry has made his way to The Crown to meet with Alex. It had been arranged by text messaging earlier in the week. Harry arrives first but no sign of Alex. So he just orders a pint of lager and tries to find a spare seat but it is difficult as the smell of Sunday roast dinners being cooked and consumed fills the air. There are many people sitting down and so he stands by a pillar in the middle of the pub. It has shelving all around it and he rests his pint on it. Even the stalls are being used. He cannot see the entrance from where he is standing but he is sure Alex will be able to see him if he looks hard enough. There is a small party of people in close proximity to him and they appear to be in full celebration. Perhaps a birthday or anniversary? They are quite noisy. So Harry keeps a watch on all the tables in his view and notices an elderly couple begin to finish off. They stand as though they are leaving. He rushes over but is beaten by two young guys. They have extremely smug looks upon their faces as if they had just finished a race in gold medal position. He is annoyed. His temper is frayed. He can feel aggression building up. He also feels they have belittled him. He gives them a look. The kind of look, which tells the receiver "you have over stepped the line!" He carries on walking towards them. His temper is getting out of control. He is going to teach them a lesson in good manners. Suddenly, a thought enters his head and tells him to calm down. He uses the breathing in the moment techniques - urgently! He is now within two feet of them. He grins at both of them so they can see him and he has worked out, which is the weaker by the looks upon their faces. He has learned these things from his old boxing days. "No fear!" echoes through his mind - the words of his late trainers voice said on a daily basis for many years. Still he is thinking about the techniques and starts to use the emergency one. The one Jacob showed him from week one of his sessions. It is just enough for him to carry on walking past them but he cannot resist a devilish grin at them again. They look away and somehow this is enough for Harry. It is like a victory without there being a prize or the need for a punch to be thrown. It is enough for him to calm down.

He walks towards the door oblivious at this stage he has left his pint way back on the shelf. He needs the fresh air from outside to cool down. He gets out of the pub and begins his deep breathing and senses techniques. It works but he does not wish to walk past the losers again, so he remains standing outside. Still no Alex and it is getting on for over forty minutes past the agreed rendezvous time.

He gives it another ten minutes and decides to call it a day. His mind then turns suddenly to 6 Cherry Walk. It is as if any slight disappointment or disruption triggers these thoughts. This time he wants his revenge and knowing Millie is at her sister's for the weekend in the same area, he decides to plan a journey there. His main objective is to get this sorted out once and for all. He also thinks once he has done this he can meet Millie at some point; *A win, win situation whatever happens?* He is determined not to get drunk this time as he still is unable to remember any of their nights of passion. He rushes back to his apartment picks up some belongings and sets off on the forty mile journey. Whilst driving he appears to be having some desperate thoughts. He shouts aloud to himself; 'I knew you'd go for her. Leave Millie alone - she's mine!' He begins to speed down a country lane. There is a cyclist ahead of him approaching a bend. He narrowly misses him but swerves a little out of control and ends up in a ditch. Fortunately, only his pride is hurt but that is enough. He clambers out off the car and the cyclists races towards him.

'Are you alright? You were in a bloody hurry. You could've killed me and yourself!' The cyclists shouts.

Harry has the red mist come all over him. He is blaming the cyclist and grabs him around the neck. Punches him to the ground. He then rips off his little camera from his helmet. 'Prove it now you dick head! If you say anything to anyone I'll come back for you and finish you off for good. You won't even be able to sit in a saddle again, mate!'

The cyclist is nursing his bloodied nose and knows he is no match for him in a fight and says nothing. He just shakily gets up and pushes his bike a little up the road. When he feels he is in a safe enough distance he shouts back. 'You're a bloody maniac! Don't worry, you'll get yours!'

He thinks about chasing after him but he needs to get his car back onto the road. Fortunately, he is able to reverse back up a small ridge but there is damage to the under carriage. He knows there will be a hefty repair bill to pay. He is getting worked up again. He punches the steering wheel in anger. He shouts aloud, 'I'll get you Leo! This is your bloody fault!'

He manages to get his car back home but his problems have not just resurfaced but appear to have escalated. He has gone from being able to control his anger to appearing to actually write a plan of action down on paper and it will no doubt only be a matter of time until he enacts upon it.

Chapter 13

HARRY IS WALKING in the local park. It is Monday, 14th October. He often goes for walks when he is particularly stressed and needs time to think, to work out the future, and manage in the present. He is ashamed of himself for the actions he took on Sunday. He is also concerned whether the cyclist has his registration number and whether he will report him, for if he does, his current probation period will be revoked for sure. He already has a court order to attend therapy until discharged, which is taking longer than he thought it would. Again he appears to be struggling with his thoughts. He looks a tortured soul. He is back to venting his anger towards Leo and really now he wants his revenge upon him.

He is about half way around the park when his mobile phone rings. He looks at it and it is Alex. He answers it in a cheery voice. 'Hi Alex. How are you?'

Alex replies immediately. 'Ever so sorry for not making it on Sunday but had a problem with Paul.'

'Oh, I hope he is okay,' he says as he shuffles along a green wrought iron park bench.

'Not really, mate. He took too many pills. He's in a right state after what "The Witch" has done to him. I spent all weekend at his bedside. It is touch and go. She really needs sorting, mate.'

Harry is sympathetic. 'Is there anything I can do?'

'That's really nice of you but there's really nothing anyone other than a doctor can do for him now. He's still in the intensive care unit. I swear if anything happens to him I will get her good and proper.'

Harry relates to the venting of anger. He has been feeling nothing else for the past twenty four hours himself. 'It's a shame as he only has you left now. I don't mean only just you. She probably hasn't even got a conscience - I wouldn't mind betting. People like her never do.'

Alex sounds pleased with his supporting remarks. They arrange to meet in The Crown within the hour. Harry rushes around the narrow footpath in the park towards the exit area and heads home. He has a shower and changes clothing in record time as he is really looking forward to a drink. He needs one after the events of the past twenty four hours and so does Alex by the sounds of things.

They are both comfortably seated in the pub and there are two pint glasses of beer on the table in front of them. It has returned to being fairly quiet and there are many vacant tables available. They have chosen one in an alcove for extra privacy.

Alex looks Harry directly in the eyes with a serious look upon his face and says, 'he's the best friend you could ever wish for. I am so grateful you could meet me at such short notice. Boy, did I need this.' He grabs his beer and takes almost half a pint in one go.

'Wow, Alex! You really did need that!' he tries to imitate him but unsuccessfully manages to drink as much in one go. Alex does not even notice.

'So you've been up against it this week as well? What's been going on with you, mate - not gal troubles?'

Harry slightly hesitates. He knows he has to protect himself a little about his sessions and of course the poor cyclist he punched in the face. So he pretends, 'bird troubles, mate.' he tries to speak in a tone of language he knows will be appreciated and better understood by Alex.

'Bloody hell not you as well. There must be something in the air around here?' Alex sips a little beer. The pub is starting to get more busier as the lunchtime crowd begin to arrive for their Monday specials.

'You know how it is. One minute she loves me and the next minute - it's no good me telling you - mate.' Harry is trying to raise his own profile by pretending to be a man of the world, even though he feels uncomfortable acting this way as it is completely out of his character.

He sort of grins a little. 'Have you known her long, mate?'

He is not sure whether to tell the truth as it may have sounded a little premature to mention the "L" word after what has just been a matter of weeks. 'It seems like a lifetime on occasions.' They both laugh loudly.

Alex goes up to the bar and comes back with two more pints and a couple of shots. 'This'll liven you up, mate. We'll soon get rid of our bloody Monday Blues. I am certainly going to be very careful when I meet another bird in the future but at least I'm a lot more experienced now.' He grabs his shot and says, 'Come on Harry my, son, after three. One, two - three!'

After hitting the table three times they down the shot. Harry watches him to see how it is done because he has never had one before and by the look upon his face that becomes obvious. 'Wow! That was rather interesting,' he says as he quickly recovers his composure.

Alex is quick to keep on where they had last left off. 'So is she local? You know the gal you're seeing at the moment?'

He is a little hesitant to discuss his love life as he has not had much opportunity to talk or in his case, brag about it much to anyone so far. There is yet another reason why he does not wish to dwell on it too much and that is because he is still unable to remember one single moment of it all. 'Yeah, she's here in Becclesfield most of the week but helps out at her sister's pub at weekends in Tranby.'

'Here in Becclesfield. That's nice and convenient. Whereabouts?' Alex is showing some real enthusiasm for a friend he has not know that long.

'Oh, Minster Way. The last building on the left or the first on the right if you're coming from the other way.' They both laugh about the obvious.

Alex has yet another large gulp of lager and has to wipe his mouth with the back of his right hand to stop it dribbling down his chin. He grins and then asks, 'so she shoots off at weekends. What time does she have to leave then? It takes a good hour to get there, doesn't it?'

He nods in agreement. 'She's a creature of habit. She leaves at dead on six every Friday night and leaves at the same time on Sunday evening to drive back.'

'That is being really disciplined. I couldn't do that. I suppose she takes the Denbar Lane route? That's certainly the quickest but it's miles of country lanes and in the dark it gets a bit tricky.' He looks at Harry quite intensively.

He immediately answers, 'oh, she's not worried about the dark and is a great driver - not like me.' He pauses as a flash memory of the cyclist incident comes to mind. Recovering he continues, 'she always uses that route. Both ways. I've been with her and she handles everything great.'

'Everything?' Alex jokes.

'Oh, I see what you mean. Certainly no problems in that area. We - let's just say, we get along really well.' He takes the empty glasses to the bar and comes back with two pints and two shots, making sure he avoids the subject of intimacy as he still is unable to recall any.

'Top man, Harry!' Alex shouts as they are presented nicely on the table. 'Dunno which one to go for first.' He need not to have worried as Harry was already thumping his shot on the table three times and down in one. 'Blimey, mate. You're ahead of the game now.' Alex does the same with his shot.

They remain in the pub for around three hours, say their goodbyes and leave both looking rather inebriated. It would be several hours of deep sleep for Harry, which is greatly appreciated these days but will it have helped him to overcome the recent spates of aggression he was having or will it make matters worse? He will not have to wait long to find out, for in the morning he has another session with Jacob and things are beginning to be revealed more with each passing week.

He arrives back at his apartment and is lying on the bed when we receives a call from the medical centre advising him of Jacob Lyall's short term illness. The sessions will be cancelled for at least three weeks. Harry feels reprieved and is keeping his fingers crossed the illness lasts a lot longer, although he does not wish Jacob any personal harm but it feels like a sudden unexpected holiday.

Chapter 14

November

IT IS TUESDAY, 5th November but the only fireworks Harry is thinking about are the ones concerning the recent rows he is having with Millie. It has been three weeks since his last session due to Jacob's bout of flu. Harry sits on the chair as he thinks this will unsettle Jacob because he has always laid on the couch. He is trying everything in his power to hold onto his thoughts, which have haunted him for nearly six years. He is fully aware how desperate Jacob is in trying to unravel this information from him and so needs to bring his 'A' game today.

'Morning, Harry. I see you are sitting this week. You always lay on the couch. Is there any specific reason you have chosen to remain seated this week?'

'You don't need to analyse everything, Jacob. I just fancied a change. I know you probably want to talk about my current relationship and the nearly four weeks I've had since we last met. So let's not just dwell on the past. My mate, Alex tells me, we can't do anything to change it - so why bother worrying over something you have no control over? - You know? He's bloody right as well. Anyway, are you feeling much better? It's not catching is it?'

'Thank you for asking, Harry. It was just a bout of flu but it lasted quite a while and because of my patients, I had to make sure it has completely gone before I came back to work. Now you mentioned your friend Alex. Have you seen him again this week?'

'Of course. He's my mate.' He smiles looking very proud he has a friend to talk about.

'He lives local then?' he asks.

'Not too local but near enough to meet up for some drinks - and no I haven't been drinking whilst on my medication.' He grins as though he has just gotten away with something special.

He has no option but to take his word for it but knows deep down he is lying. 'Good. So the first time you met Alex was a couple of weeks ago in the pub?'

He nods as if looking a little bored. Then he gets up and lays on the couch. It is yet another disrupting tactic he has deployed.

Jacob has not been affected by this sudden change in seating arrangements one iota and continues with his questions. 'What about Millie? How are things going with her?'

He looks a little uncomfortable to answer as he recalls having an argument on the phone last night and it was a huge one. 'She's a woman. You know how they can be sometimes? One minute up and the next down.'

Jacob does at last show some emotion and it is one of a little shock. 'It's not like you to be like this? Why the sudden change about women? You are normally respectful about them and their needs.' He looks really concerned now. He is convinced his new friend Alex is having a very negative effect upon him and it has been over such a short amount of time.

'Well, she wouldn't let me come and see her the other night. I think she's probably going to end things with me. Sounds to me she's got someone else, otherwise why wouldn't she want to see me? Don't quite know what I did wrong but that's how it is - if you must know?'

'It is only I can see a change in you today, Harry. You are not yourself. Do you wish to continue your relationship with Millie?' He is awaiting with abated breath as he is fearful of just what Harry's answer to this question is going to be.

He thinks about the question very carefully and after a long pause says, 'I don't feel for her in the same way as I did. I don't trust her. She is not acting in the way I want her to. Did I tell you she lives near 6 Cherry Walk?'

Jacob is quick to remark. 'I thought you said she lived in Becclesfield? Tranby is over 40 miles away from here.'

'Ah I'm glad you are paying attention, Jacob. This is what she does when things get tough, she moves in with her sister in Tranby. You remember? The Swan pub. That's where I met her.'

'Is this just temporary?'

'Temporary, permanent - who bloody cares. The further away the better as far as I'm concerned. Even though Alex has never met her before he says she is selfish and I'm better off without her in my life. So far he's been right.'

'Okay but you mentioned you did not like the way she is acting. What did you mean by that? What way do you wish for her to act?' He looks a little annoyed.

'I expect her to be more loyal to me and if I want to see her then she should be happy for me to come over at short notice. It leads me to think she's probably got someone else over there at her apartment staying.' He looks at one of the paintings on the wall and goes off into a short daydream. 'Anyhow my mate Alex tells me to treat them mean to keep them keen.' He has a sinister look appear upon his face.

'That sounds a little controlling , Harry. If she is unavailable for some reason then you need to respect her wishes and do you listen to everything this Alex tells you? Is he in a relationship?'

'He is worldly. I enjoy our conversations and so far he has been spot on in everything he has said to me.'

Jacob decides to move away from Alex and says, 'you mentioned 6 Cherry Walk again - who lives there?' This was a long overdue question.

Harry is no longer even concerned about analysing his answers before answering and just comes straight out with it. 'That is where I last saw Emily. Back then it was just a large wasteland with a huge lake. I used to love playing over there as a child. Even did some fishing in the lake with my father - when he was talking to me that is.'

'That sounds a lovely memory, Harry. I suspect they have built on that land now and is that where 6 Cherry Walk now stands?'

'Yes. In fact, the lake would most probably be right at the end of the back garden to number 6. Strange that day though, I can see it clearly as daylight. I was wandering around the allotments next door when I saw Emily and a guy. He looked familiar but I could not place where I've seen him before. Anyway, she must've met up with Leo at some point. I knew she would end up with him. As I watched her walk away from me for the last time, it felt like a light inside of me went out. Something I still cannot work out though, is why he was wearing Leo's leather black jacket with "Route 66" written in large letters on the back? The only thing that has kept me going all of these years is that I feel I was meant to see her one last time even though we didn't speak. That was the very last time I saw her alive.' He has said it now and cannot take any of it back. He has a sudden fear build up deep inside and is showing it by physically trembling. He has revealed part of the secret he has been harbouring for over six years now.

'You just said "alive". Is she dead then?'

He knew it was coming but how to answer it was still causing him concerns. 'Well, no one has seen or heard from her in over 6 years. I think even the most optimistic of us would have reached the same conclusion, don't you?' He has managed to get himself out of a tricky moment but is no longer up to any further questioning so he says, 'don't want to discuss this load of crap any more. Move on. It's upsetting me and I thought you were here to make me feel better not...'

Jacob smoothes things down by calling a short break and gives both of them a chance to reset their emotions. They quickly return to their respective seats. Jacob respects his wishes and does not push any further on that side of things and so asks, 'how are you going to tell her it is over?'

'I'll probably just text her or email. Don't fancy telling her face to face. My mate Alex says I shouldn't see her again if I'm not committed as it is only like keeping a sick pet alive when the kind thing would be to put it out of its misery.' He grins rather wickedly.

Jacob is actually finding it extremely difficult to show no emotion but even stronger emotions are building inside on how he is going to help Millie. Things got so bad before when breaking off a relationship and of all people she has had to contend with now she has Harry. This is potentially dangerous and may even be too traumatic for either of them. After much obvious thought, he says, 'so how would you feel if Millie gets someone else after you break up with her?'

He looks angered and it was immediate. 'No one will want her after I've finished with her!'

'What do you mean? Please clarify.' He is immediately concerned for Millie's welfare.

He realises he has used the wrong choice of words and tries to correct his error. 'I meant once people know she went out with me and Leo, no one will want to know her.'

'Oh, you didn't mention Leo went out with her first?' He looks genuinely confused by these new revelations.

'Really? must've crossed my mind. That's what caused the row. I've been looking for him and all the time she not only knew him but probably been bedding him all along. It's a conspiracy, mate.'

Jacob is horrified deep inside but being the professional shows no or little emotion. 'I'm shocked to hear this - Harry. How did you discover - Leo has been emotionally involved with her?'

'I was heading through the country lanes on my way to see her last Sunday. I bumped into this cyclist and he stopped me to ask directions. I told him I was on my way to see Millie Sanderson in Tranby. He said he knew of her. He then said about her being currently involved with Leo Parker. Well, I could hardly believe my ears. Bloody Leo - up to his old tricks. It doesn't take a rocket scientist to work out I've been scammed. All that nonsense in the pub when we first met. I thought she was a bit easy. All a con. It would appear everything in my bloody life revolves around Tranby and it's **all about Leo**.' He actually punches the couch in anger.

Jacob is quick to diffuse the situation. 'Take a deep breath, Harry. Remember your exercises. Have you been taking your medication?'

He just nods even though he is lying.

They stop for a refreshment break. Jacob peers into his laptop. He is extremely concerned. Harry has gone backwards. Even worse than when he first turned up all of those weeks ago. Millie is in danger, he feels. Harry is in danger also. He looks carefully at every note he has about Alex. He thinks since Harry has met him his personality and demeanour has changed for the worse. The one thing he has personally been dreading is this relationship to falter. He ponders just how Millie will take it. He thinks Harry is lying about meeting a cyclist and discovering some sort of romance going on with the elusive Leo. That, he thought, would not be probable but how should he now proceed with him? He only has twenty minutes left to calm him down and get some positivity back.

'So this Leo Parker, where is he now?'

Harry snaps; 'Hell I hope! I don't know anyone who has seen him. Although someone put a note through my door the other week telling me he was in... you guessed it - Tranby.'

'Did he have any family living around here?'

'He did but they died. It was awful for him losing both parents in that way.' He looks somewhat morose.

'How did they die, Harry?' He is looking extremely interesting to hear the answer and leans a little forward on his chair.

'Lucky Leo was out at the time but when he got home the street was full of smoke and flashing blue lights. There were a number of firemen trying to put his house out of fire but when they got inside both had died of smoke inhalation. You see what I mean? Lucky Leo even managed not to die.'

Jacob for once is unable to conceal his horror at Harry's description of events. 'I would not call it lucky to lose your parents and probably all belongings to a house fire. How did it start?'

He has gone all silent and once again has decided to call a halt to this line of questioning as he feels it serves of no real importance in making him feel better. There is a break coming up and so indicates he is ready for it now.

They get ready for the second half of the session. Harry is sitting once more. Yet another change of tactic. Jacob crosses his legs and begins. 'Now Harry, you know how important it is to keep up with your medication? All of the progress you have made will mean nothing if you suddenly stop taking it. You do want to get out of this programme and I am here to help you but I need your full cooperation. So - have you been taking your medication?'

He has listened carefully and something came over him. It was probably the calmness of Jacobs voice and his positivity. He knows he has to tell the truth. He does want to get out of the programme. 'You're right, Jacob. I've not been taking them. I ran out weeks ago and been too busy to get around to the chemist.' He tries to justify the reason with a feeble excuse but it was all he could think of at that moment.

'Oh, Harry. You must take the medication. Coming straight off like that will make you delusional and maybe even extremely paranoid. They are just two major effects. Promise me you will go and pick up your repeat prescription when you leave here today. Promise?'

He half nods in approval. He knows deep down he has no choice really. He just wants to get out of the office and will say anything he can to achieve this. The session draws to its conclusion and whilst in the lift he receives a text from Alex, it reads;

HI HARRY, HOW'S IT GOING MATE? FANCY A JAR OR TWO THIS FRIDAY LUNCHTIME ONLY I HAVE TO FLY OUT TO MY FAMILYS HOLIDAY HOME ON SATURDAY FOR A COUPLE OF WEEKS. CHEERS - ALEX.

Harry agrees and sends his acceptance back to him. The state he is in with his stress levels and anxiety leads him to think he needs a drink. Besides, he thinks Alex has been around a bit and wants to pick his brains about what to do with Millie but first he has to avoid her for three more days yet.

It is Wednesday, 6th November, ten o'clock in the morning and Jacob is preparing for his next important patient. This is one he has been really getting himself ready for. He needs to find out more about this mysterious Alex and her relationship with Harry. She is late yet again.

She finally shows up. She looks rather dressed down for her. The short skirt has been replaced by a pair of navy trousers. There is little sign of make - up and she has flats on - no high heels. He knew this may happen and has been prepared. 'Good morning, Millie. How have you been since we last met? I am sorry but the flu got the better of me. I am fully recovered now'

She looks him deeply in the eyes and then hangs her head a little. She says, 'I've had better. My cat has just gone missing. Two days now. He never leaves the apartment much, so it's unusual for him. I have put notes outside on lampposts. I hope he is alright?' Tears are welling up and she is visibly shaken.

He leaves his seat and returns with a box of tissues. 'There you are. I am sure he will turn up. Our one goes off for days on end but he always returns. Perhaps, it may have been all of those fireworks. They seem to last for weeks these days. I know, Tammy hates them.'

'You're right. I forgot about that - I didn't know you had a cat. Oh, how lovely.'

He smiles but needs to press more. 'How are things with ... Harry?' He pretends to struggle a little in remembering his name.

She wriggles a little uncomfortably and says, 'he didn't like the fact I went down to my sister's for the weekend without him. I've been doing that for months now and I can't take him with me every weekend - it wouldn't be fair on her and Colin. They do have a business to run. Then the other night, he just rings out of the blue and insists to come straight over. I told him I had just washed my hair and it was not at all convenient. He then practically accuses me of having another guy in the room with me. He was rambling on. I think he'd been down the pub again - I hope it's not drugs?'

He sympathetically nods in agreement. 'So he expressed these opinions in an aggressive manner, did he?'

'Yes. He seems to have something else on his mind at the moment. Whatever it is, it is not helping our relationship - perhaps he should come to see you - that would help?' She giggles.

He remains calm as usual and continues. 'What about the other guy - oh yes, Alex?'

She looks a little puzzled. 'I thought we had passed that point. I haven't seen him or thought about him for weeks - until now that is.'

He would not have brought this up usually but he had to find out if he is dangerous in anyway. 'Did he at anytime threaten you?'

'You could say that. When I was having my troubles with his friend Paul, he tried to put the frighteners on me. One night he rang me and asked how I was feeling being in the apartment on my own. Did I have CCTV? Was there any Neighbourhood Watch in the area? Then he told me a young girl had been assaulted only that week. It wasn't for my benefit and he sounded kind of weird. Then another time, in the early hours, I saw a car parked up opposite. It was there all night and the person sitting inside didn't get out of the car at any point. I am pretty sure it was him but he always denied it.'

'So how did you two get together after this?' He looks quite puzzled how this could have happened given their obvious distaste to one another right at the beginning.

'Strange, I keep asking myself that. He was a shoulder to cry on when Paul finished things with me. I thought we would last a lot longer than we did. Then one night we met up when Paul failed to show up. We were drinking heavily and one thing led to another. After that he kept calling me and we met each other a lot.'

'Were you intimate?' He feels he has to ask.

'Yes.' She blushes ever so slightly.

'How long did this relationship last?' he takes a quick glimpse at his watch and sees time is running out.

Millie looks a little awkward but knows she must answer the question. 'It lasted about two months. I thought we were in a good place then he just disappeared for about a week. When he resurfaced, he sent me a text telling me he'd had enough.'

'That must have been a shock and hurt you, especially as you did not expect that and the way in which he did it?'

She starts to sob. It takes a few minutes for her to regain her composure. 'He was just like his other mate - the loser. That's how I ended up here. It's so obvious they were in it together and I felt such a fool being played like that. I'm getting too old to be messed about in this way. Now look at me: once again on my knees and another lover hiding away somewhere. This is what they do when they want out. They're all bloody cowards. Call themselves men - huh!' She is back to sobbing once more.

He writes some extra notes on his pad before continuing. 'So what are you going to do about your current relationship?'

She ponders and says, 'I know where he lives. The car he drives and I'll convince him that I am worth it.'

'You are not going to fall backwards now are you? You have come so far now it would be a shame to ruin things. Besides, I am sure you wish to get out of this programme one day. So you have to know sometimes these relationships end and just accept it - try to move on.' Jacob has tried his best to soothe some of the obvious pain.

She realises she needs to keep calm and say something positive. 'Oh yes. I only meant that I'll probably go over to his and see if his car is outside, then knock. I just think these things are better done face to face. So many guys these days just have what they want and then break up by text message - the useless cowards.'

He nods his approval to this explanation and the session draws to a conclusion for yet another week but he is concerned as he ponders the thoughts of which one of them will strike first - Harry or Millie?

Chapter 15

Wednesday, 6th November

MILLIE ARRIVES HOME and there is still no sign of her cat Tom. She goes out looking for him once more. Tom has been known to wander over to the park opposite on some occasions and so she searches over there. Whist she is approaching one of the old cricket pavilions she notices a strange looking man in a dark tracksuit with what appears to be a dark hat. Suddenly he ducks behind some trees in the left hand corner. She immediately becomes distressed as she recalls the man parked up outside of her apartment the other night as well. She stops and turns back but continues to look over her shoulder. An elderly man walking his dog comes towards her on the pathway and nods to her. She talks to him and says, 'good afternoon. You haven't seen a black and white cat running around here at all, please.'

He says, 'oh you mean Tom?'

Her eyes light up. 'You've seen him then?'

'Oh no. Sorry - but I read the poster on the park gates. I have been looking and Toby normally picks up their scent. I'll phone you if I see him.'

She thanks him and walks on, taking one long last look over her shoulder but the weird acting man appears to have disappeared. She walks out of the park gates and crosses the road. All of a sudden there is the sound of a car speeding up and she looks in horror as a black car heads straight towards her. She just manages to get to the pavement in time. She is not sure but it looked like the man in black she had just seen over the park? She is trembling and shaken up. Somehow she regains her composure and dusts herself down. A resident has seen what has happened and rushes out to offer help but she refuses it. She wanders home but keeps her eyes out for the car along the way. She will not go to the police because of the dealings she has had in the past with them. She calls Chloe. She needs someone to talk with. 'Chloe, I am being followed by some maniac.' There's a pause at the other end.

'What do you mean - a maniac?' Chloe responds quickly.

'First he was in the park and then he tried to run me over. The other night he parked outside my house all night and Tom's gone missing.'

'Tom's missing? What do you mean missing? How long has he been out for now?'

'Getting on for over a week now.' Millie begins to sob.

'He's done that before, Millie, he'll just come waltzing back in when it suits him. Try not to worry about Tom but these other incidents are worrying, have you notified the police yet? Did you get the guys reg number?'

'No. I was far too shaken up. It was a black Golf or Polo car and looks like the same one which was parked outside my apartment the other night.'

'You know you have to be careful of him? If it was him in the black car, you could be in danger. You'd better come here and we'll work on something together.' Her voice is sounding nervous and shaky.

'Thank you sis I'll do that - but wait, what if Tom comes back, I won't be here for him? No I had better wait until he comes back but thanks anyway.'

'Okay but keep me informed. If things get any worse I'll come and stay with you instead. Remember how dangerous he can be.' Chloe is doing a good job of calming her down and help her clear her mind of so many negative thoughts.

Millie is pleased to have such support. They say their goodbyes. She decides to drive around to Harry's apartment and take a closer look at his car to see if it jogs anything in her memory about the incident outside the park.

She pulls up outside and notices his black Audi parked up outside with some damage to the side. Her thoughts begin to wander again as she has not been made aware of any accidents he has had recently. She looks around to see if anyone is following her as she has a strong sense there is. She panics and rings the number Jacob has given her to call in an emergency. She spends some time speaking with a kind and considerate voice on the other end but there is little the person can do for her other than make an urgent appointment with Jacob on Friday morning.

She heads for her home in a rush. She has remembered about Tom and hopes he is waiting for her outside but he is not. She goes inside and notices one of her windows wide open. She does not remember leaving it open, especially that wide. She puts it down to the windy conditions outside and closes it. She knows the sensible thing is to go to the police but without anything concrete, there are serious doubts in her mind that she will be taken seriously. She opens the fridge door and takes a bottle of rose wine out. Pours a large glass and tries to calm down. She switches on the tv and puts the local news station on. She knows that is a bit of wishful thinking on her part but there may be something about her cat, Tom? She has several glasses of wine and falls off to sleep.

She awakens in the dark and is a little fearful but soon she realises where she is. She feels safe. All the windows and doors are locked. She looks at her art deco chrome figurine clock on the wooden mantle shelf. It is two thirty in the morning. So she wanders into her bedroom and starts to undress for bed. She has not drawn the curtains. Something inside tells her to look out of the window, she does. To her horror there is a black car parked opposite with one occupant inside. She grabs her mobile phone and dials the emergency services number. The occupant, looks male, has seen her pick up her phone and the car drives off at speed. She cancels the call but feels afraid, very afraid. It is too early in the morning to call anyone but she does have a friendly neighbour on the ground floor. She decides it is even too early to wake her up. So she goes to bed leaving many lights on all over the apartment. She knows she will be unable to sleep but lays on the bed. She will now be counting the hours down until she sees Jacob on Friday morning. This is the first time she is actually thankful she has Jacob. She is growing more concerned with Harry. Her desperate thoughts match the worried look upon her face. She is all alone and there is someone, at the very least, stalking her.

Having spent an uncomfortable night wrestling with her duvet and pillows, she is sitting up on her brown leather settee in the living room sipping a cup of strong coffee, brewed from the day before. Having checked the calendar she keeps up on the wall in the kitchen, she notices the new session booked in for Friday morning. Just one day to go. She has looked out of her window and checked the door but still Tom is nowhere to be seen. Then her phone rings and she answers. It is the receptionist from the medical centre he has managed to get an earlier appointment for her with Jacob and it is in just over one hours time. She gets up and races into the shower. She needs one and feels much more refreshed. This is the best she has felt for over twenty four hours. Although, tired and fatigued, she still manages to choose some trendy clothes. She has her self esteem to think about as she recalls how badly dressed she was at the previous session. She is ready to leave within fifty minutes for her short drive to the centre.

She arrives at Jacob's office early, for the very first time and has to sit outside in a small waiting area but at least she is alone with her thoughts.

The time has come for her to enter the room. She smiles towards him and it is reciprocated. 'Now Millie, please make yourself comfortable. Feel free to sit or lay down, whatever you prefer. It is nice to see you again.' He takes his seat in the middle of the room. He crosses his legs, which is always a sign of relaxation and the session is about to begin.

'So, Millie - in your own time please begin with why you needed an urgent appointment. What brought that on?'

She is looking really anxious and afraid it may not come out right. She takes a deep breath first. 'I told you my cat is missing. He's still not showed up. The man in the black car has been parked outside my apartment again only last night but before that I went for a walk over the park and he tried to run me over - I think it was Harry.' She looks pleased she has managed to get so much in.

He tries to catch up with his notes as she waits patiently for some sort of response. He says, 'perhaps the car outside of your home is just pure coincidence. There could be many reasons as to why the guy was sitting in the car alone. You have done the right thing coming in so quickly. You cannot afford to be alone and dwell on these things too much. Have you notified the police about the car that drove straight at you. That sounds like something which needs reporting to me?'

'They already think I'm crazy woman. How is it going to look if I run around there telling them things that I can't prove?' She is looking extremely frustrated with herself. Perhaps even helpless, certainly defenceless.

'You should tell them about the road incident part. Was there any witnesses? If someone saw it and they support your allegation then they have a duty to investigate it.'

Millie pauses for thought and then says, 'you're right. There was someone who spoke with me after. She must've seen it. I'll go around there afterwards. Thanks, Jacob.' Suddenly she appears to be more her old self. Comfortable and relaxed.

He is pleased with this early turnaround in her demeanour but worries about why Harry has gone all radio silent. 'Have you had another argument with Harry?' He has already really gathered that but wants to hear it from Millie herself.

'We have had a number of big rows lately. They have all been down to his selfishness. As I told you before, he wanted to come down my sister's pub at the weekend but it wasn't fair to keep burdening her with our company when they have that pub to run and then the other night, he rang out of the blue and insisted on coming straight over. I told him it was inconvenient. Then I got a few random text messages, which didn't even sound like they had come from him. They came from his phone and then nothing for days now. Chloe has always told me not to be treated like a doormat. Anyway, the last time he spoke with me on the phone, his voice changed by the second. It was as though I was talking to a complete stranger. It sent shivers down my spine to be honest. He sounded sinister and aggressive. Then he accuses me of having some guy with me in the room. He said he's coming over and I told him not to. Then, I suppose it was him parked up outside my apartment all night. Probably hoping to catch me with this illusive lover - I should be so lucky. I think he is obsessed with me but not in a nice way.'

He fumbles through his notebook once more but still he is concerned. 'Have you actually seen him since we last met?'

She hesitates and looks awkward. 'No.'

He feels she is lying and asks, 'so no waiting outside his home then?'

She has to tell the truth. 'Well, I did visit the area and look at his car. I just wanted to know if I could pick up on something from the other day - you know the one that tried to run me over?'

'And did you? Was it the same car do you think?' He looks at her very intensely. He needs to know. She needs to know and really the police need to know.

She looks up to the ceiling and her eyes are filling up with tears. This shows her true vulnerability. 'It is hard to say. It certainly looks like it.'

'You must inform the police immediately, Millie. If he has tried once, he will no doubt try again. This is a criminal offence and needs to be reported. Did you get the number plate?

"No, unfortunately I didn't get it but I'm still worried about Tom.'

He sighs and then says, 'you have done everything you can to find him. Perhaps he'll come back when he is ready. They do wander off a lot.'

She is looking more morose as she ponders Tom's welfare. 'I know you are right but it is difficult for me. I am all alone at night and it can be very daunting when things like these are going on. I just wish I knew what is going on in his mind?'

'As I said earlier. If you feel you need some company then perhaps your sister, Chloe is the one to turn to? You mentioned a friend from school during our earlier sessions - what about her?'

'Yes, she may be able to go out some time. I'll give Sam a call when I get home and I will ring Chloe. Just hearing their voices will make me feel better - I am sure.' She looks much happier than when the session started and Jacob is pleased as he has done a good job in turning things around for her.

'Now how do you feel at this precise moment?' He stares intently towards her.

She is struggling a little with her thoughts but responds, 'I feel a lot better having spoken with you today. At least I know you have my back and I will go to the police, if I can get the witness to back up my story. It is beginning to get real scary. What if it is Harry waiting outside my apartment at night and driving his car at me? He knows my every movement. He even knows where I go at weekends.'

'I think you must go to the police. If you do not then I have a duty of care to inform them if your safety is at risk. It would be better for you to report it because you will not have to reveal any of your confidential case notes but if I report it they may request to see everything.' He is trying his very best to give her the right advice.

She starts to sob again. 'Why do I keep picking these types of guy? You're right I will go straight to the police. Promise me you will not go to them as I will be devastated if anyone should get their hands on my file?'

He feels this has to be acceptable and does not wish to stress her anymore. He nods in agreement and smiles. He reminds her what she has to do in a crisis again and ends the session.

Chapter 16

Friday, 8th November

IT IS FRIDAY morning of the 8th November and although feeling better after the session from the day before, she still has plenty going through her mind. Still Tom is missing but she has a decision to make about him now and it is made. She has decided she needs to go off to her sister's for the weekend as usual. This way she will be safe and Eileen from the apartment below will naturally keep an eye out if Tom should turn up while she is away. One of her worries sorted. Now what about Harry? She drives around to his apartment at lunchtime. She rings the bell on the door below. It is Fred's apartment. He comes to the door; pyjamas, slippers and navy blue woollen gown. She says, 'I'm ever so sorry to trouble you but do you know Harry from upstairs? Only I have arranged to meet with him and unable to get him on the phone.'

He is pleased. He feels he can be of use to her. 'Oh that's right. I've seen you waiting outside for him. You've just missed him. He's gone over The Crown for a couple of jars, my love.'

She smiles. 'Thank you ever so much.' She turns and walks away.

'If you see him, tell him I still have Check. He'll know what you mean. Have a lovely day, dear.' He then closes the door behind him. This reminder is unlikely to even be remembered by the time she gets to the pub and certainly has little chance of being delivered as she races around to The Crown.

Harry is seated in The Crown drinking a pint of lager and has at long last switched on his mobile. He sees there are numerous voicemails and text messages from Millie. He is a little wary of reading them before he meets Alex at The Crown. He does not wish to get stressed, so he switches it to airplane mode.

He drinks his first pint and goes back to the bar. He orders two pints of lager as per usual and returns to a quiet seat in an alcove to the left hand side of the bar. *It's fish day - Friday -* the odour makes its way out of the double doors from the kitchen every time they open. His peaceful drink is suddenly disturbed as an angry Millie approaches his table. 'What the bloody hell is going on, Harry?' She says rather loudly. A number of people stare over in their direction but she wants that. She feels a lot safer being in a public place with plenty of witnesses.

Harry is shocked and taken aback. 'Oh, Millie. Did you get my text this morning?' He is looking more uncomfortable by the second.

'Yes, at long last. I thought something had happened to you and why have you decided to end it with me? What the hell did I do wrong?' She is getting worked up and is visibly upset.

'It's not you, it's me,' he realises immediately this is the last thing he should have said. 'I mean, I am not worthy of your affections.' That sounded just as bad.

She looks perplexed as she still refuses to sit. 'There must be something else going on? Have you met someone else? I'd rather know.' She begins to shake a little and it looks like her temper is beginning to boil over.

'Huh, me? What about Leo then?' he looks rather smug he has at last been able to say it.

'Who the hell is Leo? I don't know any Leo. I haven't seen anyone other than you. Just because I went to Chloe's for the weekend without you.'

'You're too much aggro. I'm meeting my mate in here for a quiet drink. So if you don't mind buggering off. We are through, Millie!' He tries to take a gulp of beer but just at that point she picks up the other pint glass and pours it all over his head.

'That's for not being man enough to end it face to face. Bloody text message. Nothing but a coward and a loser. Hope you find someone else who will put up with your...' She has shouted so loud, even the people in the conservatory extension are staring through the windows to see what is going on.

He immediately loses his temper and shouts, 'you bitch! Think you can get away with doing that? I'll come for you when you're sleeping. You won't even know until it's too late, bitch!'

'Oh, I'm so scared. What you going to do, run me over?' She turns and walks out of the pub.

Harry rushes to the toilet to try and clean himself up. He still thinks he got off quite lightly considering the temper she was showing. He goes back to his seat where a bar person is cleaning the table and seating area with a cloth. 'Okay, Sir?' he politely asks even though he has practically heard and seen everything that has just gone on.

He nods back to him and smiles a little. He wipes his hair and forehead. 'I think I need to replace that pint that was err... spilled.' He goes up to the bar and notices Alex standing at the other end of the bar. He signals to him and Alex walks over to him.

'Bloody hell, mate. Was that the bird?' Alex looks quite concerned.

Harry tries to look a little cool and just grins. 'Can't live with them and you can't live without them. Pint, Alex?'

He nods. 'She looks a right handful. Not even worried about what other people think. You're better off without her.'

He agrees once more as he pays for two beers. They move further along the pub to the next alcove. 'Bloody ringing wet. I did what you said and text her but she didn't take it at all well.'

'It's not easy but you did well, mate. Shame about wasting so much beer though!' They laugh.

Alex is quick to get some more drinks. He comes back with two pints and one shot. 'Think you need these. This will help you overcome any doubts you have and remember they're like buses: they'll be another one but not sure when and when they do arrive, you see two at the same time. Drink up! there's more where that came from, mate. I had a little win on the horses so the drinks are on me today! I couldn't wait so sunk my shot up at the bar.'

Harry looks well pleased and finishes his lager and shot. 'Thanks, Alex, that's very nice of you. Same again?' He laughs loudly. He hasn't even realised some of the customers are still talking about the row he just had.

Alex stands up. 'I told you, I'm getting them today.' He goes to the bar. Once again he comes back with two beers and one shot. 'I dunno what's wrong with me today. I am downing those shots like there's no tomorrow. The barman is giving me a look as well.'

Harry is too busy downing his shot to even realise what Alex said but is really appreciating the free drinks. He goes off to the toilet and when he returns there are two pints of beer and another shot waiting for him on the table.

'Here you go, mate. Get that down yer neck. Just forget about her and have a good time.' Alex says as he slowly takes a sip from his pint.

'Wow! At this rate I'll be... how do you say, Alex - Brahms and List?'

'You're getting the hang of it now. I'm just off for a gypsy lee.' Alex stand up and heads off to the toilet.

Harry is pleased to have such a kind and considerate friend, especially at this current moment in time but he is still considering how to get back at Millie for embarrassing him in the way she did at the pub and for hitching up with Leo? The mood is a happy one and lasts for another three hours. Alex helps Harry out of the pub and walks him home to his apartment. Harry is drunk, very drunk but Alex appears quite sober considering he is holding him up and is basically supporting him up the stairs. He gets the front door open and places him on his bed. Alex leaves and heads out.

It is now Saturday 9th of November, early afternoon and Harry is stirring again. He cannot remember what or where he has been for the past day or so. It is worrying him. He has a number of abusive voicemails on his landline from Millie together with some nasty insults about his manhood amongst other things. He had expected some backlash but this is really overkill. He does not have much of a hangover, which surprises him but he has a thumping headache as if someone had hit him over the head with a heavy object. He is uncomfortable, anxious and concerned over the threats he has received from Millie on Friday afternoon on his answering phone. He cannot remember what type of conversations they had on Friday but guesses they must have been threatening and abusive, judging by her sharp responses. He is unable to locate his mobile phone but is not too bothered as it will most likely contain more abuse from Millie. Under the circumstances he decides to go away for at least a few days while these hostilities are occurring. He knows where to go, a place where there are no need for mobile phones or any other form of communication. He gets his camping things together and decides to knock at Fred's on the way out.

Fred opens his door. He is in. He's always in. 'Hello, son, how are you?'

'Hi, Fred. I'm as well as can be expected. Have you still got Check?' he asks.

Fred winks at him. 'Yes. Are you coming in to finish last week's game?'

'I'm sorry but I've got to get away. Best not to tell you in case she comes back around calling. Got women troubles. You know? She may come looking for me again. Can you tell her I've gone away and will be untraceable. Not taking any phone with me. Can't find it at the moment anyway. You were right about those things, they're nothing but trouble. Even when you don't use them, people can find where you are.' He grins a little. 'I'll bring you something back.'

'Okay, Harry. Thanks. I'm running a little short - if you get what I mean? Still, I don't need to worry about having to share it with anyone, do I?' He winks again as though it is some sort of code only they know.

Harry laughs a little and winks back. 'I know exactly what you mean. Perhaps you should take a little more water with it?'

'What water it down? Never! Have a great trip and I hope you find the peace you are looking for. You certainly won't find it around here, son.' Fred smiles and closes the door.

Harry leaves the building in a hurry as if he is running away. He is running away and cannot wait to get to his next destination, wherever that is?

Chapter 17

Sunday, 10th November

JACOB IS AT home in his fully detached cottage, two miles outside Becclesfield in a quiet village known as Priory Park. Having only recently moved to the area with his wife Ayaka, a beautiful Japanese lecturer in History. They appear to have settled in quite well in that short space of time. They have been married for over ten years but have no children. He is reading a Sunday sports page of his favourite paper whilst she is busy piling the week's laundry into a small washing machine in a utility room at the back of the cottage. She sees a note fall out of Jacob's trousers pocket. It says; "MUST FIND MORE OUT ABOUT ALEX THIS WEEK". She takes it out into the rear lawn area at the back of their large gardens. He can sense someone is behind him and turns to face her. He smiles.

'You have left a note in your trousers again. What will happen if I wash them one of these days?' She smiles ever so graciously. She always does when she is happy.

'Oh, thank you, Ayaka. I can see why your name means colourful flowers in Asia now. So sweet of you to take care of me in this way.' He smiles back with affection. Ayaka bends down for a short kiss and then heads back to the kitchen. He reads the note and floods of memories begin to haunt him as he recalls the traumatic week with some of his patients but in particular Harry and Millie. He knows he must try not to bring his work home with him at weekends, as he has in the past. This can cause some unnecessary strain upon their relationship. He has so many times advised his patients to calm down and relax, yet here he is doing quite the opposite. He has a genuine fear for both of them but is now a little transfixed on Alex. He does not like the way he has suddenly become a huge influence on Harry. There has been a decline in both Harry's and Millie's well beings and it all happened when Alex arrived on the scene. He must find out more about him and what his motives are? So he gets up and goes back into the house. Ayaka is now preparing some lunch and a little wine. Jacob is a little hesitant how to break the news to her that he has got to go out. He does and she is, as always, ever so understanding.

He gets into his black Golf and drives to Becclesfield. He is going to visit Harry. Maybe, a little unprofessional but things look a little more desperate to him now. He pulls up outside and goes to the main entry system. He rings the bell a number of times. There is no response but he notices an elderly man peeping out of the curtains on the ground floor apartment and so buzzes his number. The main entry door opens and in he walks to find the man (Fred), dressed in his pyjamas, slippers and nightgown even though it is past midday.

'What can I do for you? Are you from the Housing Association?' Fred says looking both interested and a little mystified.

'No, not from anywhere like that and thank you for answering the door for me. I am sorry to disturb you but I am looking for Harry Sutton.' Jacob is smiling as if to tell him he is friend not foe but Fred is not too sure himself.

'Harry? Now let me see.' He gives himself time to think more and then says, 'are you a friend of his then?'

'I am ...' for once he is unable to think on his feet of how to describe himself. He knows not to say therapist or doctor and so says, 'yes we are good friends. Thought I would look him up as I was nearby. I am not going to get the opportunity to do so after today.'

Fred is still suspicious and thinks of something to ask that may help him make up his mind whether or not to tell him any information. 'How long has Harry lived in Becclesfield?'

He answers immediately. 'Most of his life. Worked at the Banks' Sawmills in Ferry lane in his early twenties.'

'That's right. He's always telling me about that and how it burned down. I remember exactly where I was when that happened. It's one of those Kennedy moments.'

He interrupts as he can see there could be a little rambling on to follow. 'Oh, yes, I suppose it is. So is he coming back today?' He is actually showing a little restlessness and loosens his beige woollen tie a little.

'I had to be careful. You know, what with strangers just turning up out of the blue like this but you look quite respectable... he's gone off somewhere. He wouldn't tell me where though - so no point in torturing me for the answers - Ha. Reckon if anything like his other ventures are to go upon, probably two weeks or more and definitely somewhere secluded - if you get my meaning?'

'Oh, okay. Thanks ...' He is disappointed but there is nothing more he can do but to thank him and depart.

Fred then proudly interrupts him. 'Fred is the name and always on top of my game!'

'Fantastic! I like the introduction. Well it was a pleasure meeting with you, Fred. No doubt Harry will be in touch soon then. Thank you very much for your time.' He smiles once more to show he is friend and definitely not foe.

'Time - one thing I've got plenty off, son.' he sort of says a little sullenly. 'When you live on your own, the time just drags by.'

Jacob feels a little sympathy but fails to conjure up anything magic to say, which would make him feel any better and so simply smiles. He turns to walk away when Fred suddenly says, 'oh, if you do hear from him first, can you tell him I still have Check?'

At first he nods but then his inquisitive mind will not just let him leave without finding out a little more. 'Who or what is check?'

Fred grins. 'He hasn't told you about Check? That's the cat he's been kindly looking after for a female friend, if you get what I mean?' He winks and then says, 'she's away on her holidays. Isn't that a nice thing for Harry to do. It shows you what a kind and caring gentleman he really is. Just tell him he's ok, please.'

Jacob looks shocked. 'Yes, I'll tell him. What colour is Check?'

Fred laughs loudly this time and it takes a little time for him to stop. He thinks it is hilarious and then he says, 'don't you know? It's obvious. Black and white of course. That's why he's called 'Check' after the chess board.' He gauges the look upon Jacob's face but it is pretty emotionless. So he nods, smiles and then turns, gently closing the door.

Jacob rushes back to his car thinking about Millie and how upset she was when her cat went missing. He had wondered who would strike first in their relationship and it would appear to have been Harry. He knows he has to go to the office and look over his notes. He cannot recall whether Millie said it was a black and white cat. One thing he does know for sure is the cat's name was certainly not Check.

He has spent best part of two hours thumbing through written notes and browsing his laptop but no reference has been made to the colours of Millie's cat. He realises Millie could now be in serious danger and he should take the short drive to her home in Minster Way. Once again he worries whether it could be deemed inappropriate and if she sees him again outside her apartment it may frighten her even more but it is something he has to do. It is the only way he can put his mind at rest - seeing Millie is well and okay. He would never forgive himself if she comes to any harm whilst having the opportunity to prevent it from happening. This would naturally have a catastrophic effect upon him personally.

He parks up and chooses to observe from across the street. He sees a figure at the window looking out and then appear in another room. He decides to call her mobile but she does not answer. Still he stares up at her window but cannot be sure it is her. He knows he cannot go knocking on her door. Suddenly he notices a woman with long blonde hair coming out of the entrance and she is heading straight towards his car. She taps on the window quite abruptly. 'What are you doing?' She says sternly.

He is taken aback. A little fearful as the woman looks aggressive but she does look a little familiar. Perhaps an ex patient? 'I am just waiting for someone to turn up.' He is still not quite sure why he had the need to answer her question in the first place but if it gets her out of his way then so be it.

'You're the one! I can tell. I've seen perverts like you before. Why are you stalking my sister? What's your name?' She is looking extremely menacing.

He is really nervous and tries his professional calming influence tactics on her. 'I mean you no harm. You have me mixed up with someone else. Take a nice long deep breath in and out.'

It works a little but is just temporary. She has something in her hand and points it at him. He does not know what to do and starts his engine to drive off.

'Don't worry nonce. I've just taken your picture and got your reg. The police will catch up with you!'

He speeds off realising it is probably for the best. He thinks in all probability it is Chloe but was it Chloe in the apartment he saw or was it Millie?

Chapter 18

JACOB ARRIVES HOME feeling rather concerned and a little upset by the recent events in Minster Way. Chloe has his registration number and if she goes to the police, like she is threatening to do, he will surely get himself entangled in these state of affairs but now he has a secret. He has real anxiety and stress. He finds himself actually sitting on the other side of the fence - even though he knows how to treat himself, this is unlikely to work under these circumstances. He has resigned himself to the dreaded knock on the door and the bent up fear that most suspects get moments before that happens. Still he worries about Millie and what Harry may be up to, running off like that. He decides in keeping things in his life as normal as possible and for as long as possible. So he heads into his large dining room. 'I'm home, Ayaka. Sorry it took a little longer than usual.'

She is pleased to see him and rushes towards him for the usual welcoming; a long hug and appreciative kiss. 'I can warm up your dinner for you, Jacob. Please be seated and relax yourself. Your patients' are so lucky to have you as their confidant.'

He kind of bows his head and smiles awkwardly. 'Thank you my sweet flower. It means a lot coming from you, blessed one.'

She giggles a little but really likes the affection he always shows towards her.

Just over two hours of sitting watching tv there is a knock on the front door of their home. Jacob answers the door to find two uniformed police officers standing in front of him. 'Hello, sir. We are sorry to trouble you on a Sunday evening like this but just need to ask you a few questions.'

Jacob is in shock and nods his head in full agreement.

'Is that you're black Golf on the driveway, sir?' The taller one says.

'Yes it is, officer.' he answers a little hesitantly.

'May we ask what you were doing in Minster Way earlier today?' The shorter officer is writing in his notebook word for word of what is being articulated.

Jacob is finding it hard to answer. He knows really that he should not have been there but that is not all he is concerned about. 'Yes. I went to check on one of my patients.'

'Oh, you're a doctor then?' His eyebrows are raised at the thought.

'A therapist.' He has to correct him.

The officer looks a little puzzled and asks, 'so how many patients do you have on your books?'

Jacob laughs a little. 'About thirty at the moment and growing by the week.'

'So do you go around all of their homes to check on them?' The officer looks content with his line of questioning but for Jacob it is a realisation process. He now knows how it feels to be cross examined in a way he has to do to his patients on a daily basis and he feels uncomfortable.

He pauses for a short time and knows if he does not answer soon they will become suspicious of him. 'I am unable to say too much; you know, patient confidentiality and all that.' He has avoided answering a tricky question and relied upon a technicality to get him off the hook.

'I see. Perhaps it may be more suitable for you to come down to the station at some point and help with our inquiries?' He looks a little frustrated with Jacobs apparent refusal to cooperate fully.

'I really do not know what else I can tell you. Am I being accused of something?' He asks a little abruptly.

The officer realises he may have pushed him a little too hard to begin with and has not given him any information at this point about why they are really at his front door. 'Oh no, sir. Nothing like that. We are just trying to piece together some of the events over the past thirty six hours or so. I forgot to ask you, what is the name of your patient in Minster Way?'

Once again he has hesitated and it is not looking good for him in front of the two police officers. He regains composure and says, 'Millie Sanderson.' He felt he should answer that question but had a little reservation over whether he should have or not.

'When was the last time you actually saw her; either professionally or socially?' The officer continues to keep a stern look upon his face.

'I've never seen her socially - that would be unethical to say the least but professionally, I saw her Thursday morning at The Merryfield Medical Centre, Warwick Road.'

'So why did you feel the need to visit her at home?' He looks a little confused.

Jacob suddenly feels isolated and a little fearful. 'I thought she may be in danger and that is all I can say at this point. I will need to speak with my boss and see how we can help you further but what has happened to her?'

The officer looks pleased with his sudden shift in cooperation. 'She hasn't been seen since Friday 8th November evening.'

'She goes to her sister's in Tranby some weekends, if that helps?'

'Thank you, sir. We already know about that. Her sister has informed us she did not turn up there and she also hasn't heard from her since Friday morning. Has she contacted you since then, sir?'

'No. That is a shock!' He is looking rather edgy and the more he tries to conceal it, the worse it feels.

'You say she may be in danger? Can you please tell us more about that?' The officer's voice has mellowed somewhat as he really needs some answers to take back to the station.

'I am sorry, I unable to do so until I speak with my boss in the morning but I promise we will help wherever we can. We want her to be found safe and sound. I will make this a matter of utmost urgency and talk with my boss first thing in the morning.'

'Ok thank you very much, sir. We will pass this information to the detectives being assigned to the case and they may wish to talk with you but it will be of great help if you can consider releasing the files given the current circumstances. Thank you for your time, sir.'

'So long as all the protocols are in place, then it should be no problem, officer.' He smiles and quickly closes the door.

Ayaka has been patiently waiting just inside the living room and could hear every word that was said. 'Everything alright, Jacob? That poor girl gone missing. It is a shame. Do you know her well?'

'Yes. She has been a patient of mine for some time now but obviously I am unable to speak with you about it due to the confidentiality rules. I will need to speak with Mohammed first thing tomorrow morning. We need to see about releasing our files. Would you like a nice cup of tea?' He walks into the kitchen area and puts the kettle on, trying to bring some normality back to their lives.

Jacob arrives into work an hour earlier than normal and is studying all the notes he has on Millie Sanderson. He knows there are no notes about his "home visits" as he did not want anything suspicious to come back on him about being involved with a patient, this would be so unprofessional even if it gathered any small amount of credibility could cause an internal investigation. Now the police have him being outside her home that is going to make thinks very uncomfortable for him to explain. He wonders whether to "doctor" the notes to show he has been outside her home on official business but knows if that is discovered as being entered after the event it will look very suspicious indeed. He decides to leave the notes as they are but needs to give his boss the heads up about it all and see what he makes of it. It is the only real option he has. He really needs Mohammed's support now. He goes off to their nine thirty meeting in his office on the third floor.

He knocks on the door. 'Come on in, Jacob'

He walks in and says, 'good morning, Mohammed. How are you?'

'Fine thank you. So what is all the urgency about?' he asks.

'Millie Sanderson has gone missing. Since the 8th. I have been questioned by the police?'

'How did they get to you so quickly? The notes are all up to date, I take it?' He looks over the top of his plastic spectacles to engage Jacob in the eyes.

He nods in agreement but is a little hesitant. 'Well, the notes are up to date - except there is something else I need to explain. I had more reason to be fearful for her safety after meeting with Harry Sutton last week. He basically called off their relationship and was sounding really strange and aggressive. He made a couple of remarks, which led me to believe he was going to do something. It was late on Wednesday night when I left the office and did not wish to trouble you with any of this at that point. Ms Sanderson informed me on Thursday at an emergency appointment she had made with me the day before, she was concerned about Harry's behaviour as he had been getting more aggressive and they had rows. There is another person involved, Alex. He appears to be a bad influence on Harry.' He pauses to recollect some more thoughts.

He continues. 'Sunday morning I had a little time spare so I thought I would check to see if Harry was okay. I could get no answer but a neighbour told me he had gone away for a few days or so. I got talking with him more and he said he was looking after a cat for Harry who in turn had told him he was doing the same for a female friend who was on holiday. It appears it may be the cat that went missing from Millie's home about two weeks ago. I then went to check on Millie - only from the outside but then, I think it was her sister, came out from the building and challenged me for being parked outside. She informed the police about my presence and at the same time reported Ms Sanderson missing. The police asked why I was outside the apartment and I told them I was concerned but I would talk with you about the case notes being released.' It has sounded like a well rehearse speech and it had been well rehearsed as there was much lying on this.

Mohammed takes a deep breath and tries to take it all in. 'So you went around a patient's house in your own time using your own initiative?'

'Yes.'

"The police now want all the notes but this part is not included - in other words it is unofficial and worse of all - unauthorised? This looks bad, Jacob. I have to ask - is there any more to this? It happens in our profession on the odd occasion where a patient gets infatuated with their therapist or the other way around.'

'No. Nothing like that at all. Well, certainly not on my part and I would know if she was like that about me - she isn't. I acted on impulse in the best interests of the patient concerned.' He tries to convince himself as much as he is trying to persuade his boss that his intentions were honourable if a little unethical.

'Yes but you know you cannot go around doing things like that. You should have reported it to the police - these are the things they get paid to do. This is a right mess, Jacob. I'm struggling to see how you can get out of this. There's nothing I can do but go over our previous notes. You never indicated you was concerned this much and we both agreed to monitor the situation for a little while longer. That's what you should have done.'

He replies immediately, 'yes I know we agreed to monitor and we were monitoring the situation but it developed a lot faster than

I had anticipated. I could not go to the police with the lack of information or real intent needed to break the Confidentiality Agreement. So I did what I could do and see if they are both safe. It appears they are not.'

'I'll have to take advice on this, Jacob. I will do my best with HR and perhaps we need to just check with legal about the steps needed to take before the files can be handed over. Is there anything I should know? Now is the chance to tell me Jacob. You haven't crossed the line?'

'No, of course not. She is a patient. I am upset with myself that I could not have prevented whatever it is that may have happened to her?'

Chapter 19

Monday, 11th November

A MAN IN his mid fifties, dressed in a black suit, white shirt and navy blue tie enters the Incident Room at Becclesfield Police Station. As he walks towards a big old oak desk at the centre of the room, he tenderly touches his balding head. He gently caresses the last few remaining precious hairs he has left before addressing all the other officers in the room. He is in command of this investigation; Detective Chief Superintendent Beau Cole. In the room are many detectives, police officers and support staff. They are all gathering in connection with the disappearance of Millie Sanderson, who has not been seen for four days. Up on a large white glossy board behind Cole are arrows and question marks. "Millie Sanderson" is written in large blue capitals at the top of the board together with a recent photograph. They are working on establishing a timeline of events occurring in the weeks up to Millie's disappearance and searching for clues from the 8th November to present.

DCS Cole opens up the meeting. He introduces himself even though everyone in the room are fully aware of who he is - the boss. He then goes on to say, 'DCI Davies will lead this investigation from today forth. We all know DI Simpson and Jenkins, and of course DC Wilkins. We also would like to welcome aboard, T/I Thompson a trainee officer who has just transferred over from Tranby Central.' He pauses and awaits the usual sounds of dissatisfaction at the mention of Tranby Central. 'Settle down. I know but we are all trying to achieve the same goals here. We need to clear this one up asap, as we don't want another Emily Banks on our hands. So I'll leave you all to get on with things and let DCI Davies take over.' He smiles a little awkwardly and leaves the room as if he had not really wished to enter it in the first place.

DCI Davies walks behind the desk and points to the board behind him and says, 'you see all these blank spaces? I want them filled up within five days. I want suspects names, clues and evidence. You have by now read all the case notes, if you haven't then you should not even be sitting in this room.' He pauses to gauge the reaction and it appears everyone is up to speed. He continues, 'Simpson, I want you to question the therapist guy, Mr ... what's his name?' Most of the team know it is his deliberate way of finding out if everyone is really actually up to speed.

T/I Thompson calls out, 'Jacob Lyall, sir.' He looks rather smug and pleased with himself. It is the young man's first day at this station and as a trainee he is ultra keen to learn.

Davies replies, 'well done young man. Glad to see someone has studied his case notes.' He grins as this was just a ruse to wind up some of the more experienced officers and it worked.

DI Jenkins whispers to Simpson, 'we'll have to keep our eyes on Thompson. Only been here five minutes and already trying to score points with the governor.'

Simpson whispers a reply, 'don't worry about the shrimp, we'll make sure he gets the usual treatment. Just like we had to go through when we started out. Just hope he likes making tea?' They both snigger a little but without bringing any attention to themselves.

Davies addresses the team once more; 'Jenkins, you get the pub. The Crown. See what you can find out from staff and customers who would have been in there on the morning of the 8th. Oh and take T/I Thompson with you.'

Jenkins groans aloud and pleads, 'why do I get to do the babysitting? Surely Wilky is better suited to look after him?'

'I want him to have the best training. You do remember all of us have at some point in time had to go through extensive training to gain our experience. So look after him out there.' Davies pauses to recollect his thoughts and then says, 'Wilky, you get the background, neighbourhood, workplaces and check with forensics for any DNA clues on the vehicle, they should be through by now. We need this board filled up so let's not hang around. Any questions? No, good.'

Jenkins turns to Wilky and says, 'bet Thompson's bloody useless. Tranby sent him over probably to hinder the case?'

Wilky replies, 'yeah he looks well wet behind the ears. Still everyone deserves a chance just like you... you've had loads of them.' They both laugh and quickly finish speaking as Thompson wanders over towards them probably unsure of where he should stand or even act in front of these vastly experienced detectives. He is a little in awe of them but his will power and gritted determination is not going to allow anything or anyone stand in his way of achieving his main ambition of becoming a fully fledged detective.

Jenkins and Thompson head off to The Crown in order to question staff and perhaps ask some customers if they were in the pub on Friday, 8th of November. They have found a bar person who remembers seeing someone fitting Millie's description. His name is Raymond Barker and he has worked there for the past four years. He says, 'yes, I remember her well. She didn't have a drink,' he pauses to laugh, 'he had it for her. There was a right row going on at the table over there.' He points to an alcove area. 'It was really aggressive. Everyone in the pub must have heard it. So she gets right upset and pours his pint of beer right over his head.'

Jenkins asks, 'were there any threats made by either of them that you can clearly say you heard?'

'Oh yes. Everyone within three metres would have heard him say;"Bitch - I am going to get you when you are sleeping. She shouted back to him; "You are not going to run me over then?" That's how I remember it but you see the guy on the table over there.' He points to a middle aged man reading his newspaper alone and sipping his beer. 'He was here. He always is. Ask him, I bet he can back up my story, officers.'

They both look over. Jenkins says, 'stay here son. I'll handle this.' He then approaches the man, flashes his badge and introduces himself. He relaxes the man as this sudden interruption appears quite a shock but once they speak for a little while it is confirmed; a person answering the description of Millie Sanderson was in the pub and a row did take place between a man and woman in the alcove area as Raymond had described. The two officers leave the pub and return to the station.

DI Simpson dressed in a brown suit, white shirt and brown tie, decides to make an impromptu visit to Jacob Lyall at his home in Priory Park. He knocks on the door and it is opened quite quickly by Jacob's wife, Ayaka. She smiles gracefully.

'Oh good evening. I would like to speak with Jacob Lyall, please.' He flashes his badge at her and she looks rather worried. He tries to put her at ease. 'It's nothing to worry about. Just a few more questions about Millie Sanderson, a patient of his.'

'Oh that poor girl. Still not turned up? I hope no harm has come to her. Please come on in. He is in the lounge reading.' She leads him through the large hallway into the first door on the right. The tv is on but hardly any sound can be heard. Jacob rises to his feet. He appears to know just who the person is and exactly why he has turned up at his cottage. He puts down the book he is reading; World War Two - In Rhythm.

'Good evening, sir. I am DI Simpson. I am sorry to call unannounced but the investigation is moving very quickly and we really need any help you may be able to give us.' He slowly sits down upon a large red leather chair.

'Still no sign of her?' Jacob asks looking extremely concerned.

'I am afraid not, Mr. Lyall.'

'Please call me Jacob, detective. I am in a better position to speak about things today as I know the files are being released tomorrow morning, I think? So please fire away and I will do my best. We all wish to find her as soon as possible and to turn up safely.' He crosses his legs as though he is about to undertake another therapy session in his office at work.

'Thank you kindly, sir. How was Ms. Sanderson when you last saw her?' Simpson is fully aware questioning a professional person like Jacob needs to be handled politely and intelligently, if only not to offend.

'She was quite upset. We arranged an emergency session as she had serious thoughts about being followed. She also had an incident where a car looked as though it drove straight at her.' He could say more but feels little is probably best at this point and in order for the detective to keep up with his note writing, which appeared to be on the slow side of things.

'You say a car drove straight at her? Did she report it to the police?'

'I told her she should and she actually said she was going to if she could find the witness in the street to come forward. I guess things progressed so much so that she did not have the time to do it? Then on top of all of this, she was in a relationship with someone and it had begun to deteriorate quite fast.' As he was explaining all of this to the detective, he suddenly realises, he should probably have reported this before but hindsight is a wonderful thing.

Simpson shuffles a little in the chair for comfort and says, 'deteriorate? what in a violent or obsessive nature?'

It is at this moment he figures the police have no idea who she was in a relationship with and most importantly of all, the person was receiving counselling from him as well. 'Oh, I think you need to know the person Millie was in a relationship with is also coming to me for sessions of therapy with his anger management, amongst other issues. His name is Harry Sutton. It is by a court order.'

Simpson is shocked by this news. 'Did they meet at your office?'

'Strangely, no,' he says, 'a chance meeting in Tranby. Her sister runs a pub there and Millie went to work behind the bar - I think it is called The Swan?'

'That is a coincidence? Where does Harry Sutton come from?'

'He lives here in Becclesfield.' Jacob is quite relaxed at this present moment in time. The questions being raised are not personal to him - yet.

'So, I have to ask, Jacob, you felt she was in danger and went around to visit her, did you visit Harry's place as well?' Simpson has at last touched on the sensitive subject of why Jacob should, in his own time on a Sunday, go to such lengths.

He is annoyed and knows exactly what the detective is trying to insinuate and says, 'I went to Harry's home first actually and he is away at the moment. I then went to see if Millie was okay and she was not there neither. So I waited outside in my car. One thing you should know is Millie's cat has been missing for weeks now and a guy called "Fred", Harry's neighbour is looking after a cat for Harry. I have not been able to find out if it is the same cat - could just be yet another coincidence? But if it is the same cat then that points to Sutton acting menacingly and intention to cause her harm?'

'Thanks very much, that sounds interesting. We will follow that up. One last question please, if I may?' he pauses for a response.

'Please go ahead detective.'

'You obviously appear to have had genuine concerns about her safety, why didn't you come to us with them?' He stares directly into Jacob's eyes.

'It is a very thin line. We have to assess the real danger and the negative affect it will have upon a patient if we are wrong in our assumptions and act too soon. We were monitoring the situation very closely and to be perfectly honest, this sort of thing where two patients are seeing each other is certainly not the norm. So retrospectively, I wish I had gone more with my gut feelings rather than using the long drawn out processes but if I was wrong it could put our patients back to square one, and of course then the weeks of building up trust is destroyed. Not to mention the devastating emotional upheaval it will no doubt create upon the patient. Perhaps, in Millie's case, this may actually become irreparable.'

Detective Simpson is satisfied with the information he now has. He thanks both Jacob and Ayaka for their time then leaves the property.

Chapter 20

DC WILKINS HAS started to follow up on Chloe Richards statement about the disappearance of Millie. There were so many references made by Chloe Richards as to his aggressive outbursts directed at Millie, this needs to be done as a matter of urgency. He chooses to pay Harry Sutton of Waverley Road a visit. He rings the main door entry system to his apartment but there is no answer. A face at a ground floor window appears from behind some netted curtains. Suddenly the buzzer to the door entry systems sounds signalling it has unlocked. Wilkins walks in and is greeted by an elderly gentleman standing dressed in a blue nightgown and red striped pyjamas.

'Thanks for letting me in. Is Harry Sutton around today, do you know?' He is smiling in a friendly manner and trying to hide the fact he is a detective.

'He's away at present. No idea where and no idea when he'll be back. I already told his other mate who came knocking a few days back the same thing. He is very popular all of a sudden. By the way, my name is Fred.'

'Hi Fred. I should have realised he wasn't in. His car's not parked up in its usual spot.' He tries to encourage some information about the vehicle.

'The love of his life that Audi. Although he has recently found a new love of his life - a human and not a piece of metal.' Fred laughs to himself.

'Is it still that blue one or has he changed the colour of it now?' Another attempt to extract further details.

'No. It's black. Don't remember him having a blue one but he's only been here a year or so. If you catch up with him will you tell him I've still got that lady's cat.'

'Cat? What's that all about?' He is genuinely puzzled but feels it could be worth pursuing a little.

'Yeah, he's been looking after it for his lady friend while she's away. Thought she would've been back by now, though. Thought he'd be back by now.' He smiles.

'Is he still seeing... Oh, I'm terrible with names, Stan.' He deliberately tries to get Fred onside. He needs him to say the name of the woman Harry is currently seeing.

Fred replies immediately. 'It's Fred not Stan. He hasn't told me her name but she is a cracker. Long black hair and pretty. About the same ages. They'll make a lovely couple. It's about time he got hitched. Don't see why he should be happy all of his life!' He laughs once more.

That was just as good as giving him the name. A description from a witness, a neighbour as well. He smiles in appreciation and thanks him. Fred turns and then closes the door behind him whilst DC Wilkins gets into his car and writes some brief notes about the conversation he has just had with Fred.

It's Thursday morning and time for a team briefing back at the station. It appears from the activity on the blackboard the investigation is progressing quickly. There still has been no sign of Millie Sanderson with all the surrounding fields and buildings in Denbar Lane having now been thoroughly searched and a number of media requests for help have so far not yielded much. House to house enquiries in the immediate area of Denbar Lane are still underway. DCI Davies is standing in his usual position behind the oak desk in front of the blackboard. 'As you can see, we are making progress. So let's have your updates. Jenkins, you go first.'

Jenkins rises to his feet. 'I, err, I mean "we" visited The Crown. We have statements from staff and a customer confirming her presence at the pub during the lunchtime session. There was a row and it appears Ms. Sanderson threw a pint of beer over some guy's head. The guy was heard to threaten her by saying,' he looks at his notes and says, 'I quote; "Bitch - I am going to get you when you are sleeping." She then shouted back to him; "You are not going to run me over then?" This wasn't backed up totally by another witness but he did say the guy made a threat of sorts to the woman. The bar staff have a difference of opinion on his name; one thought it Larry, another thought it Barry but it is possible not to be either of them. He is described as late 20's, fair hair, medium build and local dialect. However that sounds? There was another man described as 30ish, taller, slim and a cockney. They moved to another seating area and had several drinks. They were well gone by the time they left the pub, apparently.'

'Good work, Jenkins! - Simpson, did you talk with Lyall yet?' Davies asks.

He gets to his feet and says, 'certainly did, sir. I can reveal we have a suspect, Harry Sutton. He is the current interest in Ms. Sanderson's life. That's not all, guv. He is undertaking therapy with the same therapist, Mr. Jacob Lyall, although they didn't meet that way. They met in Tranby. Get this. Ms. Sanderson had a cat she absolutely adores and it went missing. Harry Sutton has all of a sudden got a neighbour looking after a cat. Their relationship has deteriorated recently and it would appear he has shot off somewhere, almost at the same time as Ms. Sanderson. I'm thinking he could be an animal lover? He has premeditated the kidnap and made sure the cat would be taken care of when the appropriate time came? Added to this Ms. Sanderson told her therapist that she had been stalked by a guy in a black car; possibly Golf or Polo and then a black car tried to mow her down in the street. Sutton has a black Audi not a million miles away from a Golf or Polo...

Jenkins quickly interrupts. 'I know what one I would rather have out the three.' It appears to have been appreciated by most in the room judging by the sniggering.

Both Davies and Simpson give Jenkins a stern look. Simpson continues with his assessment. 'She has not reported any of this to the police but I guess when we get her case files tomorrow, all will no doubt be revealed.'

'Good, Simpson - Thank you for your tuppence worth, Jenkins. Forensics on the car - anyone?' Davies asks looking quite pleased with the progress so far.

Wilkins rises to his feet. 'Forensics say there are two sets of DNA found in the car. Obviously one is that of the potential victim and the other is of an unknown person. The sister's statement mentions a Mr. Harry Sutton as being recently in a relationship with Ms. Sanderson and so I paid him a visit yesterday but he is currently away. He left on the 9th November and hasn't been seen since. He drives a black Audi, I got the reg from DVLA. The details are up on the board, sir. I have uniforms checking neighbouring CCTV in and around the area of Denbar Lane on 8th November to see if we can place him anywhere near the scene at the time of her disappearance. I have checked the database and Harry Sutton is clean apart from a road rage incident about six months ago.'

'Great work! We'll have to get Harry Sutton's case notes as well. Definitely need to bring Mr. Lyall in to help us some more with our investigation. We need to find out just who the cockney guy in the pub is and what his intentions are. Overall, a very good start. Crack on and we'll all meet up on Monday morning at 10 sharp. We'll also have the case files by then.'

The meeting ended with some of the detectives exchanging notes. A major search for Harry Sutton is now being organised by

Davies with forces up and down the country being given a copy his photograph taken from Millie's phone. The registration of his black Audi car, HARR3, has been despatched nationwide. They appear confident it will just be a matter of time until they meet up with their current main person of interest.

Chapter 21

JACOB AND AYAKA are sitting in front of their tv awaiting the local news bulletin. Jacob has been informed there will be something on tonight about the Millie Sanderson disappearance. They are huddled together on their red leather sofa. They both look extremely concerned about what the news is going to relay. Suddenly, the main news switches to the local area broadcast and the presenter is sitting on a cream coloured couch in a small studio. She says, 'good evening. Tonight we are bringing you an important update in the Millie Sanderson missing case. We can go live to our reporter at the scene, Alisha Nicholson.'

In an instant the picture on the tv switches revealing a slim woman with long black hair in her early thirties. She is holding a small microphone in her left hand. She says, 'I am here in Denbar Lane where on the 8th November, Millie Sanderson's vehicle was found abandoned. Police have been searching the fields and surrounding area for the missing 29 year old. They have in the past hour released this photo.'

A photo of Harry Sutton and Millie Sanderson showing them hugging each other is revealed. It is the selfie Millie took when they were staying at The Lodge in Tranby.

The picture on the tv reverts back to the reporter once more and she says,' police are looking for a Harry Sutton, 28 years of age from Becclesfield. He was last seen in the area on Saturday, 9th November driving a black Audi car registration number HARR3. He is described as being five feet ten inches tall, short fair coloured hair and is of medium build. If you have any information please contact Becclesfield 77559. Your call will be treated strictly confidentially. This is Alisha Nicholson reporting from Denbar Lane, Becclesfield.'

Jacob turns off the tv using a remote control and Ayaka can see he looks mortified. She hugs him and brushes his hair with her hand. 'You could not have done anything to prevent this. You are a really good therapist, Jacob.'

He raises his head from her shoulder and looks her in the eyes and says, 'I do not know where I would be without you? You are so sweet and loving. That was definitely the best thing I ever did, marrying you.' He knows all the love and words of wisdom will be of no use, for deep inside he has real torment. He feels accountable. Over and over in his mind, he retraces the signs, the red flags that kept cropping up and feels he had been far too passive with Mohammed. More action should have been forthcoming and she (Millie) really needed support and this was not as helpful as it perhaps should have been. For Jacob, there are going to be further sleepless nights, more feelings of guilt and thoughts of whether he is up to the job anymore are beginning to already gather. Being a therapist, he has been trained how to help people with certain techniques but he is now realising for the first time, perhaps for him, they may not work as well as he had always thought they would. He is now undergoing the sort of thoughts, emotions and anxieties that some of his patients have but who can he turn to?

There has been a break in the Millie Sanderson case. A woman in her thirties has come forward and is voluntarily giving a statement to DI Jenkins. She goes by the name of Evita but it is certainly not her real name. She walks into interview room 7d at Becclesfield Police Station. She has a mini skirt on and it is so short it reveals she is wearing black stockings and suspenders. She is wearing a low cut red silky top, long drop dress earrings and her lipstick is a darkened red colour. She has long black hair and hazel eyes. DI Jenkins is joined by Constable Wicks, a young woman aged around twenty two years of age and she is just out of the Hendon academy.

Jenkins greets her and thanks her for coming in. She smiles and looks him up and down then says, 'you look a sweet person, honey.' She sits down on a wooden chair the other side to the police officers who are also now seated.

Jenkins says, 'thank you. Now you wish to make a statement about Harry Sutton I understand?'

She looks a little confused but understands why. 'Yes, honey. Only he didn't want me to call him Harry.'

'What did he want you to call him?' Jenkins is already getting interested.

She crosses her legs revealing even more of her thighs to him or maybe even to Wicks, she had been eyeing from the start? 'He wanted me to call him Leo and I had to play the part of a girl called Emily.'

'Are you sure it was not Millie?' Jenkins immediately asks.

'No, definitely Emily. I should know.'

'Okay, Evita. Can you start from the beginning. How you came to meet and where you went, what you did...' He gets a little flustered at this point and hesitates.

She picks up on this. 'You want all the sordid details, Hun?' She grins.

He just nods in agreement.

She begins by saying, 'he called the "hotline" and wanted someone in their late twenties, long black hair and hazel eyes.' She pauses to see if there is any questioning of her appearance as she is actually thirty four years of age. She smiles and takes their silence as a form of a compliment. 'Anyway, he says I'll pick you up...'

Jenkins interrupts. 'Where?'

'Give me a chance, Hun. He said he would pick me up in Chancery Street. The one near Tranby railway station.' She pauses as Jenkins and Wicks both encourage her along more. 'He turns up in a black Audi. I remember thinking to take a mental note of the registration - it's something us girls learn early on in the trade. If they come on a bit strong then the reg is passed along to all the other girls - you know for safety? The reg was easy to remember it was one of those personalised plates - HARR3 - yes, that is what is was.'

'Okay, so you get into his car. What did he say?' Jenkins feels this is an important question and is looking a little wary in case of the wrong answer.

'He says, "my name is Leo and please do not say anything to me yet. I want you to be Emily and do everything I say. I will pay you extra". We'll we can all do with extra cash, Hun but I didn't care much for the seriousness of it all but a job is a job.'

'Okay, Evita. So you have - agreed terms. Where did he take you in the car?' Jenkins is looking rather pleased with himself. He is getting some very detailed and useful information.

She uncrosses her legs and appears a little defensive. 'Strange. He drove over to a small cul-de-sac in Tranby. He must be one of those thrill seekers. You know the ones that risk being caught out in the open? Who am I to question his motives?'

'You say a small cul-de-sac, do you recall the name?'

'Yes. It's such a lovely name. Shame he took us down there. It is called Cherry Walk.' She asks to stop for a cigarette break outside. Constable Wicks accompanies her. They leave the room and walk outside the police station. Evita turns to her and says, 'I think you're in the wrong game, sugar. You could earn a lot more with your pretty face and that uniform would go down a bunch.' She laughs.

Wicks knows she has to keep on her good side and so laughs with her. 'I don't think they will let me take the uniform with me if I left?'

Evita lights up a cigarette and blows the smoke in a sexy looking manner. She is trying to excite Constable Wicks but it is not working at this point. She finishes her cigarette and they return to the interview room where DI Jenkins is sitting patiently waiting for them and says, 'so you mentioned, Cherry Walk, what happened once he parked up?'

She crosses her legs once more. This time she is trying to tease Jenkins and it is working a little. 'We'll he pulled up in the corner near some conifers. He waited ten minutes after turning off the engine and lights. He then started whispering sweet nothings in my ear. None of it made sense but you have to play along, don't you?'

Jenkins eyes light up. 'What sort of words was he whispering to you?'

'The usual; "You look and smell great. I wish I had not gone and ruined everything". Then he said something a bit eerie.'

'Go on, Evita.' He is all ears.

'He said; "If only you had not said no. We could be together now. This is the closest we have been since - " Then he stopped talking and started the action. He was getting rougher as we embraced. He ripped my knickers and I told him that would be extra, Hun but he did not even calm down. He just kept saying; "You are mine, Emily. All mine, Emily. Hope you can feel this from where you are?" He then slapped my buttocks hard and then it was all over.'

Jenkins tries not to show any emotion but he is excited about the information but it is not Millie's name he was saying. 'Are you one hundred percent sure he was saying Emily and not, perhaps, Millie?

'I'll never forget it. Weirdo. Definitely had some issues with a girl called Emily. Just glad I'm not her if that is the way he treats her.' She fiddles with her large red leather handbag. Looks at the time on her mobile and says, 'we'll that's it, Hun. Any more time and you will have to start paying me.' She stands up and looks both of them up and down. 'You two would go well together. Let me know if you need any company at any time?' She signs the statement with her real signature.

Both Jenkins and Wicks blush uncontrollably. Constable Wicks escorts her out of the building and thanks her for her help. Evita pecks her on the cheek and says, 'I mean it, sugar. If you ever need any company. I'll make a reduction if you wear your uniform.' She grins and walks away. Constable Wicks tries not to imagine things too much but the thought has been planted in her head.

Jenkins has walked up to Davies office and placed a copy of the statement upon his desk. He is disappointed Davies was not there to greet him and discuss the statement together.

Chapter 22

JACOB LYALL HAS been asked to attend Becclesfield Police station following some information relating to the CCTV footages in Minster Way. He is only too pleased to attend on a voluntary basis. He arrives a little early, 1750 hours and is shown to a small room on the second floor. There are just three chairs and an old scratched looking wooden desk. It looks as though various persons over the years have been using it to pass the time of day by etching their initials upon it whilst waiting to be interviewed. There is a big round clock on the wall above the door and it has a loud ticking action sound. The door lets little light in as it has a small enforced glass oblong shape frame. The whole room, including the door, could do with a paint as it appears not to have been done for at least ten years or more. Jacob sits on the single chair, assuming the other two chairs opposite are for the police officers. There is a type of cassette recorder and small microphone in the middle of the table. It is a very bleak and off-putting room and it probably just adds to Jacob's sudden feeling of agitation. The detectives are either running late or are deliberately keeping him waiting in order to unsettle him from the start of the interview.

At last a ray of light shines into the room as the door opens and in walks DI Simpson and Constable Wicks. Simpson apologises for the hold-up but fails to give the reason for the fifteen minute delay. The following is the written transcript of the interview that took place:

Jacob Lyall transcript d/d 16th November @ 1815 hrs

5111000366 case number 0207 660 6027 DI Simpson and Constable Wicks

P We have evidence that places your car outside Ms. Sanderson's home in Minster Way on two separate occasions; one of them, Thursday, 7th November shows you sitting in your car all night. The other occasion was on Sunday, 10th November. Can you confirm it was you sitting in your car?

JL That is correct. I did stay overnight on one occasion and the other time was the Sunday when her sister Chloe approached me.

P You failed to tell me that when I visited you at your home on Sunday evening. Why is that?

JL I did not think it was relevant and still do not think any of this questioning is.

P There is a young lady gone missing and we need to find out where she is. I'm sure you agree, the sooner we do this the better?

JL Of course but our time will be better spent doing just that. We need to find Harry. He holds the key to all of this.

P We are doing our best. I'm sure we'll catch up with him soon. It will only be a matter of time. So, if you wouldn't mind answering the questions, sir?

JL Yes. Please let us continue.

P So is it normal to sit outside a patient's home all night?

JL I was concerned and it proved right.

P How many other patient's homes have you sat outside all night before?

JL None but she was extremely vulnerable and may have been in danger.

P Why was she more special than any of the others?

JL She was not more special but it is a unique experience to have two patients like this to treat at the same time.

P So you said you thought she was in danger?

JL Yes

P If that was the case, you are duty bound to inform us. You may have been able to prevent this all from happening?

JL Well, I spoke with my line manager and we were monitoring very closely.

P So he agreed you should stay outside all night then?

JL Well, no.

P Why did you do it then?

JL I was more concerned than -

P Your boss?

JL Well, I know the cases more than he does, of course and there were some significant developments, which I had not had the opportunity to tell him about.

P Ok. So all this information will be logged somewhere; laptop, diary or logbook?

JL The case files are all up to date and secure.

P What about your movements concerning the two visits to her apartment?

JL I have never been inside her apartment.

P No but you have been seen on two occasions "observing" in your car outside the apartment. Where would these be kept?

JL I did not log them.

P Why not?

JL I had not got around to it.

P But you said all the case files were up to date and secure. So you didn't want anyone to know you was outside her apartment, in your own time and because she may be in danger, which you failed to report to the police? None of this important information logged anywhere? You can see how it looks, Mr Lyall?

JL I have not done anything. I would not harm her or anyone.

P Where was you on the evening and night on Friday, 8th November?

JL I was on a course in London.

P Can anyone vouch for you during those hours, sir?

JL I would imagine the Caledonian hotel in Baker Street will have up to date records.

P What time did you book into this hotel?

JL Around 10pm.

P Why so late?

JL Had a flat tyre in the country lanes. Took me ages to change the spare wheel. Not used to doing that sort of thing and in the dark.

P What country lanes? Can you kindly be more specific?

JL You know. Tenby Lane but before you ask, no I did not see Millie Sanderson or anyone else I knew. It was dark and dangerous.

P So you were in Tenby Lane? From what time?

JL From about 6.30pm till about 8pm, I guess?

P Did anyone see you?

JL I suspect some probably saw a man struggling in the dark to change a spare wheel but no one stopped to speak to me and I doubt if anyone will come forward to verify such a unexciting occurrence.

P Did you have Harry Sutton's mobile phone in your car or on your person?

JL Of course not! Why would I have his phone? I have not even seen him for some time now.

P Why did you not get a train from Becclesfield?

JL I drove to Tranby. I parked at the station and caught the direct train to London. It appeared to be the best route but as it turned out, it was not.

P Do you have any idea where Harry Sutton has gone?

JL Do you not think if I knew, I would tell you? There is nothing obvious in his case files. The only places he mentions are Becclesfield and Tranby. He has just met up with a character named Alex. These details will all be in the case files. Have you not read through them yet?

P Unfortunately, there has been a little delay in getting them. Something to do with the process, I would imagine. It usually is.

JL Shame. We could all do without this regrettable delay. Time is of the essence. I am sure you do not need me to say that?

P Thank you. I have one last question and I think I need not really ask but would you be happy to give us your DNA?

JL See no reason why not? Please go ahead. Anything to help find that poor girl.

P Okay, thank you, sir. We will arrange the test. Interview over 1855 hrs.

Jacob leaves the police station. He is somewhat bewildered by this experience. Not sure if there is an accusation being made about him and uncertain as to whether he should really now get some legal advice. His thoughts turn away from himself as he imagines the fate of poor Millie and regrets profusely not informing the police about her possible peril but the biggest regret he has is probably the decision he made to park up outside her home on that Thursday night. Even more concerning is; what will his wife, Ayaka make of this? Will she understand he was just being concerned about one of his patients? Will she forgive him for lying to her over where he really was that night?

Chapter 23

IT IS SIX o'clock in the morning. Jenkins has just arrived at Becclesfield Police Station. As he wanders along the corridor he can hear voices coming from the incident room. He walks in and discovers many of the team are seated. 'Blimey, what's going on? Must be something big to get us all in like this? We were all due in at ten anyway. Something must've happened?'

Wilkins is first to respond. 'Reckon they've found her body. It's the only time I ever get a call in the middle of the night - dead bodies.'

Simpson adds, 'definitely big. At least it is nice to hear it before seeing it on the news or social media.'

'Saw the gaffa pull up in the car park. You never see him much before lunchtime normally.' Jenkins says rather sarcastically as he raises his eyebrows and sniggers a little. 'Blimey even Thompson's here. Better than that lot at Tranby Central - hey? Bet they don't all stick together and commit like we do?'

Thompson has already learned not to get drawn into the politics of the two local police services and so just nods in agreement - more in a diplomatic way than anything else.

At this moment both DSU Cole and DCI Davies enter the room together. They appear in high spirits. Cole stands in front of the desk and says, 'at around 02.35 this morning, Harry Sutton was picked up and arrested. This followed on from a call received about a man acting suspiciously in a parked car in Cherry Walk, Tranby. The clock is therefore already ticking and we need to build a case over the next day or two with the evidence we already have and hopefully, the new evidence you will no doubt be collecting over the coming hours. We will need you to commit yourselves fully for the next seven days at least. Overtime has been authorised. Well done for your efforts to date and keep up the good work. I will hand over to DCI Davies. Thank you all.' He taps Davies on the left shoulder in an approving manner and a he leaves the room there are cheers of happiness and a little clapping.

Jenkins cannot resist a little swipe and says to Wilkins, 'I suppose the next time we'll see him will be when the case has been solved and he'll be standing in front of the cameras taking the credit.'

Wilkins replies, 'not if it goes tits up, he won't.' They both grin at each other.

Davies takes centre spot in the room. He has abandoned the front desk area and wants to be right amongst his team. He says, 'right we need to get things moving; so Jenkins I need you to visit that Merryfield Centre first thing when it opens and insist on having the session notes on Sutton and Sanderson. We need them this morning. Simpson arrange for Mr. Lyall to attend this evening on a voluntary basis. Oh and Thompson, I want you to go to London and check Lyall's alibi at the hotel where he allegedly says he stayed on the night of the 8th.' He pauses and takes a look at the board to see what other facts or evidence needs verifying. He turns back around and says, 'Wilky, chase up any CCTV footage in the Denbar Lane and Minster Way areas. Let's see if we can find Sutton's black Audi in the vicinity at the important times. Unfortunately, we still have no leads on Sutton's buddy, Alex. So Constable Wicks, can you question the staff and regulars in The Crown and go to see the residents of Cherry Walk. See if you can find what Sutton was doing there in the middle of the night. Great job so far. Let's get cracking, we really need this sewn up asap.' Davies appears to be in a hurry and leaves the room abruptly. He does not stand around discussing theories with his team like he normally does.

DCI Davies is back in his room, when there is a knock on the door. 'Come on in.' It sounds as though he was expecting this person by the friendliness in the tone of his voice. The door opens and a tall man, aged around 26 years of age with thick brown hair, parted in the middle and dressed in casual clothes is soon seated opposite.

'Ah Tony, it's great to see you again.' He smiles appreciatively towards him.

'Thank you, governor. It's been a few weeks since we last spoke.' Tony is sitting quite rigid in the chair.

'How are you getting on at The Swan? Have you any news yet?' Davies is more relaxed and looking quite hopeful.

'I managed to get in okay. I work behind the bar. The first few days appeared to be exactly what I would have expected. All the staff were upset. They were all hugging Chloe and Colin. Some of the regulars were also visibly saddened to hear the news of Millie's disappearance. I kept an eye on the description you gave me of the Alex guy and a strange thing happened just as I was leaving on Saturday night. It may be him, he entered the pub around eleven o'clock and Chloe ushered him around the back of the pub. The area usually reserved for staff only. She actually looked shocked to see him and certainly wasn't expecting him. He has a London accent and I tried to listen outside the door but the only thing I heard was muffled voices. So I walked in to the room pretending to get my coat and they stopped talking immediately. I looked for a little while and then made my excuses and left. It seemed weird but I think it is definitely the guy. So I waited outside the pub and he came out around one in the morning. Chloe drove him off but being on foot, I could not follow them.' He pauses to recollect further thoughts and can see an admiring look from Davies.

'Did you get anything else?'

'No, I'm afraid not but I did hear him say to Chloe something about all meeting up on the 23rd November. If it is at the pub, then I will be there that night and can report back further. The other thing I feel is odd; there seems to be too much normality going on. Chloe and Colin are laughing with the punters. They are acting as if nothing has happened. If it were my sister gone missing, guv - we'll I don't know what I would do? I certainly wouldn't be drinking and socialising until she is found safe.' Tony has finished his current state of affairs from his undercover work at The Swan.

Davies is delighted at the progress made in such a short time. 'That's great work, Tony. Carry on in there. No one suspects you do they?'

'No one. Besides, it's one of the safer ones I've been on, guv.' Tony stands and smiles. Davies gets up as well. He is showing his respect and gratitude.

Davies says in a whisper as he approaches the door. 'We'll have someone in the pub and a car around the corner. So keep it simple and wait for back up, should he show up.' Tony nods in approval.

Davies calls Constable Wicks to his office. It takes her five minutes to get herself ready and arrive. Davies says, 'thanks for coming in. The guys downstairs are pretty impressed with you. They say you can keep a straight face when things are getting a bit tough - is that true?'

'Yes, sir. It's very nice to hear I have made a little mark on the team already. Thank you for telling me that.' She is smiling and proudly sitting upright in her seat.

Davies steps over to the door and makes sure no one is within earshot. 'What I am about to tell you is top secret. Only I know about it and it is important you don't tell anyone. Are you happy with this?'

She looks a little flushed but it is to do with the level of trust her boss is placing upon her. 'I am deeply honoured, sir. The secret is safe with me - I promise.'

'Okay then. I do not want you to go to The Crown but go to The Swan instead. You'll be in plain clothes and no need to question anyone. I need you to go on Saturday, 23rd November. Mingle in with the customers but keep a close eye on Chloe and Colin Richards. Also, my informant tells me the man known as Alex is going to be there at some point. We desperately need to track him down. If you think he is in the pub, you must urgently call for back up. Do not try to arrest this man alone as we do not know his capabilities yet. I will have a car parked up around the corner with two uniformed officers. They are totally dedicated to this operation, even if there is a mugging going on right next to them they are not to be diverted under any circumstances.

Now when you go back to the incident room, they'll probably be questions from some of the team as to what I wanted - just tell them it was a short brief on questioning the staff and customers at The Crown. You must report to me anything you feel is important. Here is my personal mobile phone number, I will be awaiting your call - even if it is nothing, just ring at the close of play. Ok?' Davies raises his eyebrows in a reassuring gesture.

She is happy. So much responsibility given to her so soon but the Academy gave her a five star rating and her qualifications are unquestionable. She says, 'thank you again, sir. I will do my best to see what is going on and report straight back to you on the mobile number you have given me.' She gets up and leaves the room with a skip in her step but she knows to calm herself down before going back into the incident room. So she changes her facial expression to a more solemn look before entering the room.

Wilkins rushes into the incident room. He has a couple of memory sticks in his hands. He rushes over to Simpson who is typing on his laptop. 'Hey governor!' he shouts, 'do you know what I've got in my hands?'

Simpson continues typing but says, 'without looking - I shudder to think.'

'I have CCTV images that places Sutton going into Denbar Lane at 1805 hours and guess who is two cars in front of him?'

Simpson quickly turns around as he knows the importance of such evidence. 'What! You have him following Sanderson?'

'Yep and neither of them came out. He must've gone out through Long Lane. Clever bastard knows there are no cameras down there but he slipped up big time going in Denbar Lane. Can't wait to see the gaffers face when I show him this.' Wilkins turns to walk away but Simpson is not ready for him to leave. His competitiveness has kicked in and he wants to be the one to take it to Davies.

He stands and says, 'Wilky, I have a meeting arranged with him in five minutes. Can you finish off my notes for me and I'll take it with me. Don't worry - I'll tell him you got it.'

Wilkins looks bitterly disappointed, all of his mornings work and excellent results are not going to be directly appreciated by Davies. He knows how career minded Simpson is but as he is superior in rank, has no choice but to agree to the request. He sits down and looks at the laptop whilst Simpson rushes to see his boss.

Simpson is seated in DCI Davies's office and is awaiting his arrival. He looks around the room; he sees a picture of Davies with a commendation medal upon his chest, there are pictures of his family sitting proudly upon a large oak desk, the desk is full of paperwork but it appears orderly and not scattered around. He looks to the windows on the left side with a little envy as his open plan office has just a little window and certainly does not overlook the playing fields as the ones in this office do. There is carpet on the floor - this must have been personally arranged by Davies himself.

He respects the cleanliness of the entire room and even the filing cabinets look dust free, which is a rarity in this station and in many more across the land. His thoughts are interrupted as the door swings open - it is Davies returning from a short lunch break.

'Hi, Simpson. Hope you haven't been waiting too long? What have you got for me?' He sits down behind the old oak desk.

Simpson cannot wait to tell him the news. He says rather excitedly, 'I sent Wilkins to Denbar Lane this morning as you requested, sir and he has these footages from the day in question. I did say to him to keep persevering as I had a hunch one of those houses close by would have a CCTV camera installed and it has paid off, governor. Apparently they show Sutton following Sanderson into the country lanes at around 1805.'

Davies rises to his feet and has a smile to match his excitement. 'Well, don't just sit there let's stick them in and see what we have. If this turns out to be true - then it must be game, set and match?'

They view the images on the laptop and it confirms Harry Sutton's car is just two cars behind Millie Sanderson's car as they entered Denbar Lane. This does not quite prove the case but the anticipation of what is on their respective session notes and perhaps any DNA found by forensics being carried out on the suspect's car may add substance to an ever growing amount of evidence, which could lead to charges being made within a matter of hours.

The tv is switched on in Jacob's home as he readies himself for another day at the office. The newsreader announces there has been a breakthrough in the Millie Sanderson missing persons case. She passes the link to her reporter on the spot.

The camera then goes live.

'This is Alisha Nicholson reporting live outside Becclesfield Police Station where a 28 year old man is being questioned by police in connection with the Millie Sanderson disappearance. You may recall the 29 year old has not been seen since her car was found abandoned in Denbar Lane on 8th November. Police then issued photos of a person of interest they wished to interview; 28 year old Harry Sutton. It has not been confirmed whether the man they are currently holding is Harry Sutton but they intend to call a press conference at some point soon. Stay tuned for further updates. This is Alisha Nicholson in Becclesfield back to you in the studio, Roberta.'

Jacob switches the tv off and ponders for a short while. Once again regretting not having acted a lot sooner as far as notifying the police is concerned. He blames himself and is now hoping more than ever she is found safe.

Chapter 24

AT SOME POINT in the afternoon, Davies receives information from forensics' relating to Harry Sutton's car. He calls back Simpson, who is still working in the incident room. They meet in the canteen. A dull affair. It has just a couple of self service paying machines for hot drinks and snacks. There are numerous small metal framed tables and seats, similar to those in primary schools but a bit bigger. Davies cannot wait to tell the news to Simpson. 'I have just had the results back on Sutton's car. There are a number of blood spots found in the boot. They are being tested as we speak. It could well be that of Millie Sanderson. So I need you to stay around - just in case we charge him tonight.' He smiles with an air of satisfaction.

Simpson looks elated and says, 'that is fantastic news, governor! Obviously not so for the Sanderson's if it turns out to mean what we think it does but at least we may be able to find her - wherever that may be?'

'Yes it's great news for the team! All the evidence is stacking up now and pretty soon we'll have the full story. Except, he may not give up the location of her whereabouts that easily.' Davies stands and says his goodbyes.

Jenkins has spotted the two of them talking in the canteen and pretends to bump into Davies in the corridor by chance. 'Oh guv, I have been going through the case files. They are very interesting. He mentions Emily Banks and Leo Parker quite a lot. He says he has lived in this area all of his life but we can only trace him being here for just about a year. Perhaps his DNA will show us more? Get this - he has been to Cherry Walk on a number of occasions. It is like he is obsessed with it and Leo Parker. Strangely he hardly mentions

Millie Sanderson but keeps going back to Emily Banks. I looked that case up, guv' He pauses to see the look on Davies face turning much more cheerful. 'Leo Parker was the number one suspect in the missing Banks case but no evidence or body was found. He did however, get put away for burning down her father's factory in Ferry Lane. He got seven years and was released after five for good behaviour. I can find no mention of Harry Sutton around this area at that particular time.'

'Come up to my office and well get our heads together. Are the notes from the sessions on the computer?'

'Yes, sir.' Jenkins is pleased to be taken up to his office. He knows Simpson has been with Davies both in the office and in the canteen but more urgent to Jenkins is cracking this case, no matter who scores the brownie points along the way - so long as it is not Simpson, that is.

They are both seated in the office. Davies looks at Jenkins and says, 'how long you been on the force, Jenkins?'

'Just over 15 years, sir.' He replies as his mind wanders off trying to think where this is leading.

'I have been impressed with your work and of course, Simpson's. I think there could be a promotion coming up here in the spring. Would you be interested in going for it?' Davies smiles. He knows how competitive they both are and would do practically anything to get the post.

He tries not to overreact and smiles. 'Of course, sir. It is what we all are trying to achieve in our careers.'

Davies nods in approval. 'Let's get back to the case. What do you think about it so far?'

He crosses his legs and says, 'well, sir. Something doesn't seem right with it all.'

'Please go on.'

Suddenly Jenkins feels this could actually be a pivotal moment in his career and treats it like an interview for a job. 'Harry Sutton does not appear to be real. He is either using someone else's identity or he's lived on the moon for most of his life. It doesn't sit well with me. I have Thompson looking into it at the moment. I'm confident we will find out his true identity soon, sir.'

'Good. What else do you think?'

'All the witnesses from The Crown are saying Sutton was legless when he left with the Alex guy. How on earth could he have carried out such a kidnap? How could he have driven to Denbar Lane, got Millie and disposed of her so quickly? It doesn't add up, sir. This other guy - Alex is really puzzling me as well. Where did he shoot off to? What are his motives? Where the bloody hell does he live? There is much still to do, sir but I know we will get there. Everyone in the team is as committed - well all committed to bringing this to a conclusion. One last thing, sir. I have been reading up on the Emily Banks notes and there are obvious similarities. Wilkins has been looking into Leo Parker's movements when released from prison and he went to Europe three days after being freed. There is no sign of him having re-entered the Uk since, sir. So the chances of this being linked to him are pretty remote unless he bunked back into the country somehow.'

'Fascinating. There's plenty of logic but very little evidence. Keep working those theories and let me know if you need further resources. Good work, Jenkins.' Davies picks up the landline and rings forensics whilst Jenkins stands and then walks out of the office. He feels good about himself. There were plenty of selling points put across to the governor and they may just count when the time for promotion comes around in the spring but he could do with being able to back up one of those theories.

Davies has called Jenkins back to the room immediately. He rushes back at speed. He does not have time to sit. Davies says, 'we've got him! DNA found in the boot is that of Millie Sanderson. It's just been confirmed by forensics. I'd like you to sit in with me. He is being brought up for questioning.'

Jenkins looks as though he is the most important person on the planet and cannot help thinking just how Simpson is going to feel when he finds out he has been favoured over him. 'Great, sir!'

'Now, Jenkins, what I am about to tell you is confidential at this moment in time. You were right, Harry Sutton has only existed for over a year and the DNA swabs have revealed they are one - he is Leo Parker. He changed his name when he got out of prison. Now we know from his therapy case files, he has distanced himself from his former identity, so much so, he believes Parker to be a completely different person. A person he really dislikes. We can use this when we go downstairs. So whatever happens, we must not let him know we have discovered his true identity. This is crucial and that is why I haven't told the rest of the team just yet. I doubt if we will be able to charge him today as we are not ready but let's see what he has to say.'

'I fully understand, sir. Great tactics, if I may say so.' Jenkins looks pleased to have been taken into confidence by his boss. They leave the room having drawn up a number of questions they need to ask Sutton.

They all meet up in the interview room 7b. The following transcript was taken from the questioning;

Harry Sutton - representative Mr. Ian Barnwell (Stewartson and co)

Transcript d/d 19th November @ 1325 hrs

5111000377 case number 0207 660 6030 DCI Davies and DI Jenkins

P You agreed prior to the interview that it is okay to call you Harry. Is that still the case?

HS Yes. That's my name.

P Are you comfortable? Do you need anything?

HS Please go ahead. I have nothing to hide.

P You own a black Audi car registration HARR3 - is that correct?

HS Yes that is right.

P You were seen in this vehicle in Cherry Walk in the early hours of Monday 18th November. What were you doing there?

HS Taking a trip down memory lane. I remember some years ago before the houses were built, it was just wasteland back in those days.

P Can you remember when that would have been?

HS Well, those houses were built about five years ago, so it would have been before then of course and I was only a child when I used to play over there. So probably about twenty years as a guess?

P How long have you lived in Becclesfield, Harry?

HS Most of my adult life. I moved there from Tranby when I was about ten years old.

P Where did you live prior to your current address in Waverley Road?

HS Oh, I forgot. I was travelling for about five years.

P Where did you travel?

HS Here and there. Anywhere that took my fancy. I was having a "free as a bird" moment back then.

P Whereabouts in Becclesfield did you live prior to travelling?

IB What is the point of these mundane questions? My client is here to help you with your enquiries in to the missing woman.

P Yes we do wish to get into that part soon but we need to get some background information. If you will prefer we can come back to that later. So who lives at 6 Cherry Walk, Tranby?

HS Surely you know more than I. Have you checked the voting register or knocked on their door?

P You keep visiting the street - why?

HS I have memories. Happy memories. I told you it used to be a wasteland and as a kid I played there with my friends. I know every inch of that plot of land, especially the lake.

P Tell me where is Leo Parker?

HS I think he is dead. I know he went to prison.

P What makes you think he is dead?

HS Well he is dead to me. I hope I never see the likes of him again. What he did -.

P What did he do, Harry?

HS Set fire to the Banks warehouse in Ferry Lane and then run off with my girl - Emily Banks.

P Where is Leo Parker?

HS Already told you, either dead or with Emily as far as I can tell.

P What makes you think that?

HS They both vanished at the same time. After the fire.

P I must agree with you, Harry - this Parker guy sounds a nasty piece of work. Would be great if you could recall where it was when you last saw him?

HS He went to prison for arson. I have not seen him for many years.

P Do you think he is capable of kidnap or dare I say - murder?

HS He was capable of arson - so who knows?

P How is it you know so much about the fire, Parker and Emily Banks? You were travelling at the time, you said?

IB I must ask if you intend to ask my client any questions on the missing girl, Millie Sanderson?

P Yes. We'll move onto Ms. Sanderson. How did you meet her?

HS I met her in Tranby. She was working in The Swan and we just hit it off.

P What was your reason of travelling to Tranby?

HS I had an invitation to a celebration do there that night. I must have got the wrong dates mixed up.

P Who was the invitation from?

HS Just someone from the school days. No one to worry over. Anyway, we went back to my room at The Lodge. They will be able to confirm this. I also got a taxi in the early hours to get some... wine from a 24 hour place.

P Your neighbour - a Fred Watkins says he is looking after Check for you. Who is Check?

HS Probably means the chess games we usually play.

P What happened to Millie Sanderson's cat Tom?

HS He probably had enough of her nagging?

P So the cat Fred is looking after for you wouldn't happen to be Tom?

HS Not answering as have no idea what you are going on about. What has a cat got to do with me being locked up here for the past two days?

P Okay, moving on. What were your movements on the 8th November?

HS Remember it well. That was the day that stalker poured a pint over my head in The Crown. I had already sent her a text message telling her we were through. Why did she have to come to the pub and embarrass me in front of my mate?

P Stalker? Who is the stalker?

HS Millie Sanderson that's who.

P What is the name of your mate who was in the pub at the time?

HS My mate Alex.

P What is his full name?

HS Do not know. Only know him as Alex.

P Where is he from?

HS London - I think?

P How did you two become friends?

HS I met him in The Crown one day and we started meeting up for drinks on a regular basis.

P Thank you, Harry. Are you okay to answer a few more questions?

HS Anything, so long as I can get out of here.

P What was you doing on the 8th November around 1800 hours?

HS I was sleeping off a heavy drinking session from the lunchtime.

P Did you drive your car at this time?

HS Of course not. I could not even stand never mind drive.

P Did you loan your car to anyone or give someone your keys that day?

HS No one but me is allowed to drive my baby - so no.

P Have you got Alex's phone number please?

HS It is on my mobile phone but I lost that in the pub on that day.

P So you didn't lose it in Denbar Lane on the 8th?

HS I haven't been near Denbar Lane since - since I last went to Tranby.

P Has Millie Sanderson ever been inside your black Audi at all, Harry?

HS No. We have always been too drunk to drive anywhere.

P So you are certain she has never been inside your car HARR3?

HS I have been advised not to answer that or any further questions.

P We have evidence showing Millie Sanderson has been in your car. Your car was captured on CCTV following Ms. Sanderson's car into Denbar Lane at 1805 hours on Friday, 8th November and your mobile phone was pinged at the same time. So you certainly had your mobile with you inside your black Audi. This is your chance to get it all off your chest Harry. Tell us what you did with Millie Sanderson?

HS This is stupid. I never left the apartment. I was drunk. I lost my phone and my car was parked up outside - well, certainly it was there when I awoke around Saturday afternoon. You must be mistaken. Can I go now? I have answered all your questions and you do not have anything on me, otherwise you would have charged me by now.

IB You say you have evidence. What sort of evidence to show Ms. Sanderson was in my client's car?

P We have her DNA. Let's just say that for now. So Harry Sutton you will be detained pending further enquiries - interview ceased at 1408 hrs.

Davies and Jenkins go back upstairs for a brief over the interview with Harry Sutton. Davies says, 'well what do you make of it all now?'

'Now we know for definite who he really is; the main questions appear to be about Emily Banks and the similarities with the Millie Sanderson missing persons case. I still believe he was unable to drive and accomplish a kidnap from the information received from the staff at The Crown. Then he would have to dispose or hide the body somewhere. The DNA in his car? Perhaps, he doesn't remember her being in the car?' He has satisfied himself of not leaving anything out.

'Of course, you wouldn't have known this but the DNA found in his car was blood stains in the boot. I think further questioning of staff at The Crown and see if they have any CCTV in or around that pub. Remember, we are investigating Harry Sutton.'

'I'm straight on it, sir. I'll get Thompson to check the shopping centre for any footage from the day.' Jenkins leaves and heads to the incident room to pick up Thompson on his way out.

Chapter 25

CONSTABLE WICKS HAS been called up to see DCI Davies. She is seated and waiting inside his office. He has just gone to sign the overtime slips for the past week and it is high. He races back to his office. Sits down and welcomes Wicks with a friendly nod and smile.

'Now, Wicks, what do you have for me?' he asks.

She gets out her notebook and it looks quite full. 'Cherry Walk was a wasteland six years ago. There was a large lake, probably would be right at the back gardens of 4,5, and 6. I spoke with a Mr. Walsh who lives at number 6. He moved in when the houses were first built. He tells me that a person, who fits the description of Harry Sutton, has been pestering him a little. He says he has been in his grounds on at least three occasions. He had CCTV and security lighting fitted. He called me in and showed me the footage he had saved. It shows Sutton approaching the front door, as if he is going to knock on the door but he never does. Another time, he was seen at the end of the garden on his knees as though praying. He has reported it to us and there are a number of entries on record but obviously we had no idea of the identification of the trespasser. It goes without saying, we never managed to apprehend him.' She pauses as she can see he is in deep thought.

'Okay, can you link up with Jenkins and swap notes. He is looking into an old case; he should be made aware of this. It is the Emily Banks disappearance around the same time as they started to build on that land by the sounds of it and you may as well know now, Harry Sutton's former identity is Leo Parker. He was number one suspect in the abduction of Ms. Banks. See if you can be of assistance, please.' Davies picks up the phone, this is a sign for Wicks to leave and get on with things. She ups and leaves the office, making her way to see Jenkins. She is not sure what sort of reception she will get from him as he is known for being a "lone wolf" and may not cooperate fully.

The investigation is picking up pace at it approaches the end of the second week but still the detectives have been unable to locate, Alex Shaw, the man who has befriended Harry Sutton in The Crown pub. There has been some media coverage running the latest developments and like so many local people, Jacob Lyall has been watching with more than a public interest. He is at home with the tv switched on awaiting the breakfast local news and suddenly it flashes up on the screen;

"We go over to our reporter from Becclesfield for the latest update on the missing, Millie Sanderson case."

The screen switches to outside Becclesfield Police station and there is a young reporter holding a microphone in her left hand.

"I am here live reporting from Becclesfield where police still question a 28 year old suspect, Harry Sutton. They continue to search an address in Waverley Road in connection with the disappearance of 29 year old, Millie Sanderson. Police have just a further five hours to question him otherwise they will have to apply to the courts for an extension. They still wish to question Alex Shaw who is about six feet tall in his early thirties. He has short black hair and has a London accent. If you have any information please call the hotline below. Your calls will be handled in the strictest of confidence. I will be back as soon as this investigation has any further information. This is Alisha Nicholson reporting from Becclesfield".

Jacob turns off the tv. Gets his tie on and takes a long look at himself in the mirror. He still blames himself for Millie's current plight, whatever that is? He now regrets so many actions he could have taken prior to her vanishing but some may argue, he has done more than most by sitting in his car overnight outside her home to ensure her safety?

He gets in his car and heads off to work. He is not looking forward to it for it is Wednesday and normally he would be looking forward to treating Millie. He also knows he may be living on borrowed time as far as his career is concerned. Mohammed has set the process of an internal investigation into operation to see if he has acted unprofessional, unethical or has done anything else that could turn up leading to a disciplinary hearing.

Jenkins has discovered he now has to share all of his information with the unproven Wicks and is not happy. He has no intention of showing her anything other than the routine files.

'Wicks, the witness statements. Can you go through them word for word and see if there are any clues we may have missed?' Just as an afterthought he says, 'please.'

She is clever. She knows a dead end when she sees one but how to handle it is another thing. She agrees to do just what her superior has requested even though she knows it is a waste of valuable time and resources. These statements have been read by everyone in the team already, including her but she goes and sits down at a desk, opens up a laptop then downloads the statements.

Jenkins leaves the room rather quickly. He is adamant Sutton could not have pulled off the kidnapping in his drunken state and so he decides to go back to where there may still be some evidence - Waverley Road. He knows Wilkins questioned one of the neighbours and has decided to back that up for his own peace of mind - nothing to do with being competitive or being personal in any way with DI Simpson. He arrives at Sutton's block of apartments and buzzes the apartment on the ground floor, number 1. He knows just who lives there. An elderly gentleman buzzes him in and is standing outside in the landing area just in front of his dark oak front door. He is dressed in blue checked pyjamas and grey slippers.

Jenkins says, 'hello, Mr Watkins?' he flashes his badge. 'I'm DI Jenkins.'

'Please call me Fred. Fred's the name and always ahead of the game.' He smiles as he adjusts the cord on his pyjama bottoms.

'They told me you are a character. May I please come in?' He says as he carefully puts his badge away.

'I suppose you wanna talk about 'Harry?' He invites him inside and they walk through to a lounge area. Fred is cheerful and happy. He is so glad of some company. 'Please be seated. I'll just put Check out.' He lifts a black and white cat from a two seat light grey fabric settee that appears to be a hundred years old. It is threadbare on both arms and the cushions are dented in a way to suggest they have also been there all the time, but it has great sentimental value to Fred. It is where he spent hours sitting with his late wife.

Jenkins sits and scans the room. It is quite dark considering it is around eleven - thirty in the morning. He notices a large portrait of a woman in her mid fifties hanging above the mantel piece. Below that there is an old gas fire. He turns his head to see a set of patio doors that are not letting much light in because there are two heavy looking velvet red curtains covering most of the area. The only real source of light is coming in from a large window to the right of the patio doors. Just in front of this window is a large dining table. Placed carefully in the centre is a chess board with chess pieces looking as though some game is in progress. To the right of this area is a medium sized tv and on top of the tv is a picture of a couple in wedding attire. He is not sure if it is Fred when he was younger or it may be one of his family. His thoughts are interrupted as Fred re-enters the room and sits on the settee.

Jenkins makes an early attempt of relaxing Fred. 'That's a lovely portrait.'

'Yes. It's me late wife, Elsie.' he appears tearful.

'Oh, I'm sorry to hear that, Fred.' He is quick to reply.

'It's been a long while now. I do still miss her you know?'

'Of course.'

'It's been very lonely around here since she's been gone. The family very rarely visit these days but they do have their own lives to lead. That's why I was so grateful when Harry came into me life. He moved in about a year ago now. He always came down to play chess; we were in the middle of a game when he... he stopped coming. He used to buy me stuff like; milk, eggs, bread, sugar, beer and whisky. He couldn't have done this kidnap stuff. He's too nice a bloke. Would you like a cup of tea, detective?' he asks as he rises to his feet in anticipation.

'Thanks, Fred. Don't mind if I do. Just one sugar please.' Jenkins is content with the way things are going and feels there is much more information to come.

'You know he did well to get over his last girlfriend. She was a piece of work. His latest girlfriend is a much better person. I can see them two getting married one day. I mean he is getting on a bit now.' Fred is speaking from the nearby kitchen room whilst he is brewing a pot of tea. He soon returns to the living room with a tray; a pot of tea, two cups and saucers, spoons, sugar, milk and a tin with biscuits inside. He places them on the table in front of where Jenkins is seated. Fred sits on the settee.

'Thanks. You said he had a bad relationship. Who was that with?' He has not waited too long to restart the questioning. He now sees Fred as a reliable witness but he still needs to find out what he actually really knows.

Fred puts his cup carefully down on a saucer and says, 'yeah, that right. Her name was Emily. She broke his heart. He looks pretty cut up every time he mentions her name and yet it was over five years ago. Shows you what a nasty cow she was.'

'What about his current girlfriend? Do you know her name?'

'No but I can tell she is much better for him than the other one. Harry says she has so many of Emily's good points and none of her nasty ones.'

'You would say he is serious with the new girlfriend?'

'He was at first head over heels. I could tell. Something must've happened recently? Perhaps one of those bad patches we all have to go through?' Fred passes the biscuits over and Jenkins takes one.

'Thanks, very nice, Fred. Have you ever seen his new girlfriend?'

'Yeah, she called here on that Friday. She's a stunner, detective. I may be old but I'm not dead yet.' They both laugh. 'I would say she's around thirty, got long black hair and the most wonderful hazel eyes.'

'I know what you are saying, Fred. You mentioned "that Friday", which Friday was that please, Fred?'

'The day that horrible cockney bloke brought Harry back from the pub. I'm guessing he never met up with her that day judging by how drunk he was. I offered to help him take Harry up the stairs but he basically told me to mind my own business.' Fred is deep in thought as he tries to recall those moments.

'Don't like the sounds of him. what'd he look like?' He is busy scribbling down his notes and knows he could be onto something new in the investigation.

'Six footer with short black hair. Tattoo of a dagger with a snake around it on his left arm. Looks like ex military to me.'

'So what happened next?'

'I'm a bit ashamed to tell you anymore.' Fred blushes uncontrollably.

'You don't have to worry about anything, Fred but if you want to help Harry you need to tell me everything. I am with you, I don't think he kidnapped her either.' Jenkins is very convincing.

'Ok but remember I live here alone and he could come get me at any time he wishes. I'm far too old to defend me self as I used to be able, son.'

'Let's put things another way - did Harry drive off in his car at any time in that afternoon or early evening?'

'Drive! You must be joking. If he tried to walk down the staircase he would have fell to his death. That's how drunk he was?'

'What about the cockney guy, was he drunk as well?'

'I hope not as he raced off in Harry's car. I know it wasn't Harry because the bloke had to adjust the driver's seat and mirrors. He's a lot bigger than Harry you see? Then he headed off towards the town centre. I know I should've reported this to the police but I was scared of him. He looks pretty evil.' Fred bows his head in despair.

'Please don't get down about this. Sure it would've helped us in our inquiries but I doubt if it would've stopped the kidnap and we'll be no further up the road than we are now, really. Also, our detective who visited you a week ago or so should have been able to get this information. Did he ask you any questions about Friday, 8th?'

Fred looks genuinely concerned and a little confused. 'I honestly dunno. I only remember that incident because of how intimidating that bloke was and the car speeding off. I must admit, I was shocked to see it parked back up again in the exact same spot as it was the night before - perhaps he stayed over? I always look out the patio doors first thing in the morning just in case Check is waiting outside.'

'Okay, Fred. You have been great. Would you like to give us a written statement? I can get this lovely young lady, Constable Wicks to drive you there - tomorrow if you wish?' Jenkins is very pleased and excited at making a real breakthrough. He now has a reliable witness and another bonus is it was one of DI Simpson's team that had already questioned this witness a while ago but did not extract this information.

Chapter 26

JENKINS NEXT STOP is Tranby. There is something nagging him. A gut feeling something vital lies there and he wants to be first to find it. He is going over things in his head; Cherry Walk, The Swan, The Lodge, Chloe and Colin Richards? Something is not right. The other thoughts disturbing him are the way Millie vanished and the drunken state Sutton was in. He now has a witness putting Alex Shaw to the top of his list but he wishes to know what the Richards' involvement is in all of this.

Simpson is sitting once again inside DCI Davies office. He has some hastily written notes in his hand and cannot wait to share his latest discovery. Davies saunters in and nods before sitting in his chair opposite Simpson. 'What have you got for me, Simpson?' he says as he fondles a silver Parker fountain pen; it was a gift from his colleagues for reaching the milestone of twenty years service earlier in the year.

'Sir, I have just found out that Millie Sanderson was married but is now separated from her - let's say, estranged husband. Not only that, sir, it was quite a turbulent and violent relationship according to the neighbours either side of their house they shared in Willow Street. Her husband at the time was a Julian Sanderson. A squad car went to his last known address in London but he has not been there for over three years now. So we are now trying to piece together his profile and his whereabouts.' He is pleased with himself and smiling.

'What! The sister failed to tell us any of that. I wonder why? I cannot but help to think she has deliberately withheld that information but why? Who was supposed to be checking Sanderson's background? - they need a rocket up their arse for missing this important piece of information. What about "The Missing Persons Unit" didn't they have this information? Look into this Simpson. I want to know why this information has only just landed on my bloody desk.' Davies is red with anger and sweating at the temples.

'I think it was Jenkins or one of his team, sir. Unfortunate mistake - should we bring her and the husband in for further questioning? They certainly need to explain all of this. They may even know the whereabouts of Julian Sanderson?'

Davies appears to be shocked by this sudden change of events but is quick to respond. 'No, that is the last thing I want to happen. I have an undercover operation going on at The Swan on Saturday night and if my information is correct then we will have the Richards' in custody by Sunday morning along with Alex Shaw.'

'Saturday night? Who is doing the undercover work, sir?'

Davies believes he has to now tell him. 'Keep this to yourself but I have got Constable Wicks going into the pub in plain clothes. Tony Stevens has already got himself on the inside as a bar person and a squad car will be waiting around the corner to assist in any arrests that may take place. So you see, I want that place left completely alone until Saturday night.'

He smiles but is a little put out he was not either made aware or given a part of the action. He says, 'she will probably blend in quite well at her age.' He shuffles around in his seat as he is not really comfortable with such an inexperienced officer being given such a good chance so early on in her career.

Davies knows he would not be happy finding out he had no say in the matter but tries to comfort him by getting a half bottle of scotch out of his drawer and two glasses. 'You've not got to do any driving over the next few hours have you?'

He smiles. All is both forgotten and forgiven as he accepts his glass. 'Lovely aroma, sir.'

Davies nods in agreement and then says, 'so where's Jenkins today? I haven't seen him all day.'

'He's gone to the pub, sir.'

'What? Gone to the pub while we have all this going on?'

Simpson then says, 'I see what you mean. No, he's gone to Tranby.'

They suddenly then both realise and say together. 'The Swan!'

Davies is quick to say, 'get Jenkins back immediately. Make sure he does not go anywhere near The Swan. I don't want his size elevens stumping all over our operation and Simpson, can you get all the team gathered for a four o'clock?'

Simpson nods, ups and leaves. He races down to the incident room. 'Thompson! I need you now.'

He goes towards Simpson's desk. 'Yes, sir?'

'I've got a job for you.'

Thompson is unsure whether to be pleased or a little reserved until he knows what it is because he has only been given mundane jobs since his arrival from Tranby Central.

'I need you to ring Jenkins and tell him under no circumstances to go to The Swan. Tell him and the rest of the team to be here four o'clock sharp.' He then taps in his password on his laptop and just before Thompson sets off on his tasks he says, 'oh Thompson - thanks.'

He is pleased with the sudden politeness. He has received very little since his transfer but was kind of expecting it given the competitive relationship with the two stations.

An important meeting is taking place in DSU Cole's office and Brad Willis (CPS) together with DCI Davies, are seated. Cole is a little delayed but arrives ten minutes later. They are discussing the case and the possibilities of carrying out excavation work to the rear of 6 Cherry Walk, Tranby. Top of the agenda though are the potential charges of Harry Sutton - formerly known as Leo Parker.

Willis is first to speak. 'So this search of Cherry Walk. What makes you think Millie Sanderson has been buried there?'

Davies answers, as he is expected to do most of the prosecuting presentation. 'We don't think she is there. We are still searching for her but we have evidence to support the theory that Emily Banks is most likely buried in that vicinity. We have discovered as per our notes you have that our Harry Sutton used to be known as Leo Parker. He was the one guilty of burning down Emily Banks father's sawmills and did five years in prison for that. He has been caught on CCTV visiting 6 Cherry Walk on a number of occasions and when we picked him up he was outside that address in the early hours. There is the statement from "Evita" who had dealings with him and part of his sexual fantasy was for her to be called Emily and he was to be called Leo. It got rough and some of the conversation leads us also to believe this address is of vital importance to him.

Here's the catch 22. We have evidence to suggest he is involved in the kidnap of Millie Sanderson but we have not been able to locate two other persons of interest so far. Alex Shaw a so called friend of Sutton's and a Julian Sanderson, the ex. We have reason to believe this marriage was an abusive affair and so it is vital we find him as well. Sutton's car was used to follow Ms. Sanderson into Tenby Lane and blood matching her DNA has been found in the boot. Sutton's mobile phone was detected at the same time as the crime took place in the exact spot in Tenby Lane. He disappeared the next day but returned to Cherry Walk a few days later when he was picked up. There's a lot more.' He stops to take a breather and to see if he has said enough to get the nod from Willis.

'I don't have a problem with the intention to charge Sutton with suspicion of kidnap. That will at least keep him on remand so you can get your full case together. It looks like it is him by the evidence and if as you say he was involved with the Emily Banks girl back then, this may be worth a crack. You will need to convince a judge first and I see it only 50-50 at the moment whether you will get it. Remember, we are going to dig up someone's back garden and totally disrupt the neighbourhood for about ten days. It's hard to call. Do you have any other evidence relating to Cherry Walk?' Willis is showing restraint and caution. He has seen so many of these investigation requests turned down in the past for lack of evidence.

Davies pulls out some additional paperwork from a small brief case. He hands both Cole and Willis a copy each. 'Please read the highlighted areas taken from Sutton's therapy sessions. You will see he is obsessed with 6 Cherry Walk. He distances himself from Leo Parker. It is as if they are two different people. He mentions Emily Banks, Cherry Walk and Parker as if all three are linked. I'm pretty sure that is where we will find Emily and as a result it may lead us to finding Millie Sanderson.'

Cole looks over admiringly towards Davies. He knows the case has been confusing at times. He says, 'I have to agree. The evidence does point to something significant being at 6 Cherry Walk. What do you think, Brad?'

'Having read this piece of evidence. I think there is not a judge in the country that will not support your application. My advice is to go straight ahead and lets' nail the bastard.' Willis has given his full support.

Willis rises to his feet and shakes hands with Cole and then Davies. He leaves the office. Davies has not finished discussing the evidence and says, 'there is one thing. I have an operation going down on Saturday night at The Swan. I think one Alex Shaw will be there meeting with the Richards'. So I don't want to start the dig until Saturday early afternoon because if the press get a hold of anything they will throw a spanner in the works and it could ruin the operation.'

Cole nods in agreement and says, 'that sounds rather sensible but so long as we have all the paperwork in place we can go as you prefer but we will of course have to give the occupants of number 6 Cherry Walk a little notice to get out of the property for a couple of weeks.'

'Of course. I'll send Wilkins around there as soon as the ok is given.'

Davies smiles then leaves the room to take a team brief.

He walks into the incident room. All of the team are gathered. He nods and then takes a quick glimpse at the board behind him. There has been a lot more activity since yesterday. He appears content with how the team are working the case. He says, 'well done to you all. Great effort so far. I know it is still disappointing that we haven't got there yet in terms of finding Ms Sanderson but I'm here to tell you of some significant developments in the Emily Banks case. We have all the necessary paperwork to carry out a thorough search of properties in Cherry Walk, Tranby. We will no doubt be using the heavy machinery and it will all commence on Saturday afternoon. Now it goes without saying we do not want the media to get hold of any of this information, especially as on Saturday night we have an operation going on in Tranby, which we hope, if my information is correct, to arrest Alex Shaw. We will definitely be questioning the Richards' on Sunday morning, whatever happens. The latest person of interest is Mr. Julian Sanderson. He is the ex and we haven't been able to locate him at his last known address in east London.' He stops and checks his notes to make sure he has explained everything correctly. He has so far. Then he continues. 'The CPS has given us the green light to go ahead and charge Harry Sutton on suspicion of kidnap. We will be doing that this evening. So, Simpson, stay behind as you will be accompanying me and handle everything.'

Simpson smiles at Davies, turns and grins at Jenkins but it is short lived as Davies then says, 'well done, Jenkins on reworking the Tranby clues. Sorry we had to pull you out. Did you discover anything new?'

Now it is Jenkins turn to look rather smug. He replies, 'indeed, sir. I found out that our Mr. Sutton did stay at The Lodge but booked in as one Leo Parker, paying cash.'

'That's interesting. Wonder what his motives were for doing that? Perhaps he had intentions of committing a crime in Tranby that evening? Great stuff, Jenkins. Now I want Wilkins and Thompson to spend all their time trying to locate Julian Sanderson, we desperately need to question him. He is at the top of our list along with Alex Shaw, so get straight on it guys, the clock is ticking. Any questions team?'

Thompson reacts first by saying, 'why didn't the Richards' tell us about this Julian Sanderson. He would've surely been top of our list right at the beginning of the investigation, sir?'

'Good question, Thompson and hopefully we'll have the answers on Sunday when we bring them in for further questioning. Any other questions? No, good. Wicks can you see me please and Jenkins can you stay behind as well please?' Davies sits down and signals the end of the team brief.

Wicks approaches him and says, 'yes, sir?'

'Saturday night,' he says, 'just observation and reporting back. We don't need any hero stuff. I will be parked opposite with Jenkins and there will be a squad car just around the corner. If you positively identify Shaw then go outside the pub and start brushing your hair. Obviously make sure you are in a well lit up area so we can see you.' He smiles and then sends her off to get Jenkins. He walks over to where Davies is seated.

'You doing anything on Saturday night, Jenkins? No, good. I need you to come with me on a surveillance job of The Swan pub.

If my tipoff is correct then we will be making some arrests. Wicks will be inside in plain clothes of course and she will signal to us if he turns up.'

Jenkins looks pleased with being chosen to accompany him. 'Yes, sir. What time? Good move using Wicks, she'll blend in perfectly, sir.'

'Be here at nine and well get a driver and car booked.' Davies gets up and goes back to his office, taking Simpson with him.

Simpson is first to speak. 'Has the charge sheet been prepared, sir?'

'It's all in hand. Now, I want you to handle the charging process. I'll be with you. I just want to watch his face turn colours as we lay the charge upon him. His legal representative is due within the next half an hour. So let's go over everything and make sure we get it right.' Davies produces his file on Sutton. 'Here's some light reading to get you in the mood. I'm off to the canteen. I'll bring you a cuppa back. No sugar, if I remember right?'

'Yes. I mean no sugar. Thanks.' Simpson is happy even though he has a lot more reading to do but he is going to charge Sutton and feels it is an honour to do so.

The time has arrived and so has Sutton's legal representative, Ian Barnwell. They are all waiting in interview room 7b. Also present is pc Barker. Davies and Simpson walk in and Sutton looks up at them from his seated position. He says, 'about time. I hope you have come to release me after all of this wasted time. You could have caught the real suspect by now.' His legal representative, Barnwell whispers an air of caution and tells him not to say anything else.

The detectives say nothing at this point as Simpson hands over the charge sheet detailing the alleged crime. Sutton and Barnwell read it thoroughly. Simpson then charges Sutton with Suspicion of kidnap and informs him that he will appear before magistrates in the morning in Tranby Magistrates Court. He is taken back to the cells.

Davies takes Simpson back to his office to discuss the case further. He takes out his old half bottle of scotch and two glasses. 'Think we have earned a wee dram, don't you?'

He looks very pleased and nods in agreement. 'Thank you, sir. I don't mind if I do.'

'Great piece of work, Simpson. We have him exactly where we want him - banged up. Now let's hope we get a break soon on either the Banks' case or Sanderson.'

'Yes, sir and did you see his face towards the end. It looked like he was ready to go ten rounds with Tyson Fury!'

'I've seen that look a hundred times. First they look all smug, then sudden shock as reality kicks in and then the bent up anger at being caught out. This can happen in some cases in a matter of moments. Just like him. The thing is we need Shaw and Sanderson. Either way. Eliminate or prosecute. I just hope the weekend brings in some important results one way or another. Anyway, I have things to do tonight even if you don't.' Davies gets up with a smile on his face. It has been a good day and Sutton is safely locked up. He knows if no other evidence is found soon this investigation will probably be seen as a failure by the bigwigs of the force.

Part Two

Chapter 27

SEVEN YEARS EARLIER and five weeks before the fire at Banks Sawmills, a twenty two year old, Leo Parker has made it to the main entrance with at least ten minutes to spare but even he cannot disguise the sweat upon his forehead. He has much riding on the next half an hour or so. He takes another step forward and goes through every word he has been rehearsing in his head for the past two hours. Failure is not worth contemplating. He takes a long look at the frontage of this familiar building. He has seen it from the road, from the railway lines and the rear from the golf course that backs onto it. He also knows this business is the most successful in Becclesfield and employs more of the local community people than most in the area. He already knows a couple of people who work there from his school days although he would not class them as friends. He has brought with him some documentation, which he is hoping will be enough to win over the interviewer. He enters through the large double doors. There is a sign directing visitors to the first floor. He slowly climbs the stairs and then sees a large sign above a hatch window - "Reception". Everything inside the building looks exactly as he had imagined it to be, except the offices are located on the first floor and not the ground floor.

'Hello, please come on in.' A voice comes from the other side of the hatch. Then a large yellow door buzzes and clicks. He pushes it open. *This is it. No turning back.*

'Good morning,' a beautiful smiling young lady is standing to greet him. Her eyes are drawn to his physical athletic body shape and good looks.

'Good morning.' He keeps it brief. Nerves are still getting the better of him although he quite likes the look of the woman standing in front of him. She looks so pretty and has a pleasant manner about her.

'You must be Leo Parker?' She says, as she puts her hand out and shakes his. She smiles and then deliberately gazes into his eyes to let him know she is friendly.

'Yes, that's correct. I've come for an interview.' *First question correct, tick.* He amuses himself.

'Please be seated. I see you are local. That's good. We like to employ people from the local community and I see you have been working locally at JD'S Fencing?' She sits down and takes a good look at him. Her body language is giving off a very friendly and calming aurora. She wants him to be comfortable and relaxed.

He is not sure what the receptionist is doing asking him these sort of questions and is caught a little out by it. 'Yes. I have a forklift licence.' He has said that part already. He had not rehearsed that to come out so soon. He was hoping to use that towards the end in what he thought may be important at a time when he may be under pressure to impress the interviewer.

'That will be really useful here.' She passes him a form to fill in. He takes this moment to look at her. He has only been glancing every now and then up to this moment in time. He really wants this job more than ever now. She is standing looking down at the factory floor through a large window. Her lovely long black hair is glowing as the light flashes in through a skylight in the ceiling. She has a slender figure. Black ski pants and white silky top. She turns back to face him. He notices for the first time her lovely hazel eyes and diamond shaped earrings dangling either side of her pretty little face. She is young. He is wondering about eighteen, which would be three years younger than him.

'Have you finished filling in the form, Leo? The work downstairs can be heavy at times but I can see you have the right tools for the job.' She grins cheekily.

He fails to notice the personal compliment but just smiles back at her. He takes her comments as a positive sign though. 'I'm good with lifting things and have plenty of stamina.' Still he wonders when his actual interview will begin.

She nods in agreement. 'I've just asked Bob to come and join us. He'll be your foreman. He can be a bit of a moaner at times but so long as you're not late and turn up in a healthy physical condition, like now, you'll be just fine. By the way my names, Emily.'

Once again he has failed to recognise the deliberate compliment she has bestowed upon him. 'I'm Leo... of course you already know that.' They both laugh. He then says, 'so how long have you worked here?' He has reverted back to his normal self. Much more relaxed and confident.

'I don't work full time. I just help out when they need me. Julie's on her hols right now. So I am covering for her. I am awaiting a place in university to come up.' She leans over her desk to pick up a stapler, even though she has no real need for one. She is deliberately attempting to draw his attention to her curvy figure and it certainly works.

He notes how perfect her body outline is and feels he would like to paint her but he has to focus on the here and now. 'That sounds like a lot of fun and hard work. What are you going to study?'

'Economics. My father says it will do me good as I cannot hold onto money that long - I just spend it.'

'That's what it's for and father's are not always right.' He says with a one hundred percent conviction and knowing full well just how well these comments will go down with Emily.

She laughs in appreciation of meeting someone with the same attitude to money and secretly applauds his naivety relating to her strict father's principles.

He still wishes the conversation to carry on as he feels some connection with her. 'I should have gone to uni' but ...' They are interrupted as the door buzzer sounds. She actually looks more disappointed than he does.

'Perhaps, we can continue this conversation some other time. Wish you all the best of luck in your new job.' She stands as the door buzzes and in walks a man in navy blue overalls with a badge on his left shoulder strap showing the word - "Supervisor" upon it.

He sizes Leo up and down as if he was taking measurements for his coffin and then says, 'hi. Is this him?' He asks a bit abruptly. Still eyeing him up and down but Leo is used to having this done to him, both when he was in the army and when he was about to start a boxing match in a ring. It does not hold any intimidations whatsoever.

She stares over to Leo as if to say, "see what I mean". 'Yes, this is Leo Parker he'll be starting with us on Monday. His references all check out fine and he is another local guy.'

Bob looks a little put out that he has not had a say in matters but is used to being overlooked when some of the decision making occurs in this room. 'Okay, laddie follow me.' They walk off to the shop floor. She watches him as he goes off into the yard at the back of the factory. She appears to be expressing a little more than a business interest in him.

'So you done this type of work before, laddie?' He probes.

'Well, I've worked with wood before.' He is puzzled why such a question should arrive. All his work experience is down on his application form and has been approved by the office. He senses that the foreman wishes to give him a hard time but it will not deter Leo's determination to get started at this new place of work. He takes a long look at the 5'10" slim built middle aged man and sees a frustrated person. Someone who really wants to be somebody others look up to.

'I did at school. I mean what work experience have you got now?' He is hoping for Leo to slip up in some way so he can then go back to the office and gloat a little.

'I worked at JD'S Fencing for two years until the receivers got their hands on the place.' Leo is still keeping one eye on the office windows on the first floor and he can see Emily moving around.

'Good man, Joe. Shame about his business going under like that. He used to work here when he was about your age you know?' He softens considerably. He really likes Joe and feels genuinely upset at the news of his business failing.

'We got along really well. The girl in the office, she has a lot of responsibility for a receptionist, doesn't she?' Leo is trying to find more out about her and he does.

'Keep your eyes off her if you value them. She's the governor's daughter and she ain't for the likes of any of us down here. That's what you should think. She is up there in that office and you're down here. Banks' is not a person you want to cross, trust me.' He leads him to the side of the factory where there are two fork lift trucks parked up being charged up for the next shift. 'This will be your first job when you get in on Monday morning, plug these in and then go work on the sander with Stefan. He's a good worker you'll do well to copy his attitude, laddie.'

Leo has had this style of regimental orders from his time in the army and so does well not to show any emotion. 'I've got that. It seems quite straight forward.'

Bateman looks at him in a sly way. 'I hope so, laddie or it will be curtains for you if the forklift trucks don't start up first thing Monday morning. Anyway, Stefan will be here when you arrive, he always gets in early. We like that here.'

'You can't beat exceptional punctuality, I always say.' He is purposely saying the things he knows Bateman wants to hear.

Leo will spend twenty minutes being shown around and being told the rules - the rules of his foreman that is - Robert Bateman but the one rule he will find the hardest not to break does not originate from Bateman.

Chapter 28

LEO HAS BEEN working at the Banks Sawmills for over two weeks now but in all that time he has not seen Emily again. Julie has returned from her holidays and is now working alone in the office. He really wishes to meet up with Emily but cannot figure out a way. Then a piece of luck comes his way as Terry Banks calls him up to the office to speak with him. At first, he is rather fearful as he did make a mistake or two on his first day. He walks up the stairs to the first floor and finds the door with "Terry Banks" written on a brass coloured sign. He knocks gently on the door.

'Come in,' a husky sounding voice calls out from inside the room.

He walks in with a fixed smile readying himself for whatever may be coming his way. 'Morning, Mr. Banks.' He takes a quick glance at him as this is the first time he has seen him. His first reaction is one of caution. He notices the broken nose, the small scar above his right eyebrow and there is a piece of skin missing from his right earlobe. They appear to be old injuries of some nature.

'Morning young man. I understand you ruined a pallet of wood last week.' He looks serious and a little stern.

'Yes. I am so sorry. I'll try and make up for it.' He is looking quite fearful now. The last thing he wished to do is upset the boss so early on in his new career and he looks like a person you would not wish to get on their wrong side.

'Do you know what I did on my first day, young man?' He laughs loudly. 'I crashed the forklift into the sanding machine. Lucky for me though, the boss was my dad. You don't have that comfort do you?' Still he plays with him.

'No, I guess not Mr. Banks.' he bows his head awaiting the worse. It looks bad in terms of getting through his four week probationary period.

'Don't worry. I haven't called you in for that. I am looking for someone like you. Someone who may wish to make a bit more money at the weekends or even some evenings.' He stands up and looks out of the office window down to the factory floor. 'I can see a lot of things going on from up here. Anyway, you have come to my attention and my daughter, Emily interviewed you, so you must be okay. Now I'm looking for someone to cut my lawns, dig out the weeds and general maintenance work. Is that something you may be interested in young... Leo?'

He immediately realises he will see Emily more often and answers. 'Definitely. I'll take it. When can I start - this weekend?'

'Slow down. I haven't even told you how much you'll get yet. She did tell me you were keen. Okay, I'll take you out of the yard some days as well. Any extra work you do for me in your own time I'll pay you cash in hand. No need for anyone to know is there? If you get my meaning?' He stands and opens the door. 'See you at mine on Saturday morning. Ten o'clock. I'll get Simon to introduce you to big Bertha.' He smiles as he opens the door and suddenly appears to be more approachable.

'Thank you, Mr. Banks. I'll be there.' He stands up and tries to leave the office.

'You had better take a note of my address. "TIMBER VALE" 4, Front Lane, Becclesfield. Have you got that. Thanks and carry on with the good work. I think you could go far if you keep your nose clean and follow instructions, young man.' He is now smiling in a friendly manner.

Leo has left the room and Terry then picks up the phone, dials a number and waits a short while for someone to answer at the other end. 'It's me. I've got a job for you.' He has a sinister look upon his face. 'I gave you all the details last week. It's a green light. Get back to me. I need this as soon as. Thanks bye.' He turns off the phone and places it back into a secret compartment he has built into his desk. He then grabs his jacket and heads out of the factory.

Leo has been counting the days down to Saturday and it has finally come around. He looks the smartest gardener in town. He has a pale blue Ralph Lauren Polo shirt on with a pair of Calvin Klein jeans. He is hoping Emily will be there but he has not figured out how he is going to approach her. He wonders if any of the family members are going to be in attendance and who on earth is Big Bertha?

He drives up to a pair of large black gates. He still cannot quite clearly see the house on the horizon. The gates open. They have seen him on the CCTV outside the property. He drives down a long winding road past a lake on the left hand side. Then he sees the magnificent house. He drives past a large fountain in the middle of the frontage to the property. He parks next to a Mercedes Sports convertible brand new car. He parks his old Ford Fiesta the other side to it. He is now having serious thoughts of whether this was a good idea or not. He recalls Bateman's words of warning and how he described her as basically being out of his league. He gets out of the car and Emily comes out of the big oak wooden front doors to the home.

'Hello, Leo. How are you?' She looks really happy to see him and has worked on her appearance all morning. She is looking immaculate.

He is a little taken aback. He looks at how beautiful she looks in her chequered white and black shorts with a red top, which looks to him as though it had been shrunk on its first wash. 'Good morning, Emily. I have not seen you around lately.' He tries to act all nonchalant as he does not wish to be seen as being overly keen.

'Yes. Julie is back from her hols. I am in next week for three days though. It's the monthly salaries to be calculated and paid out.' She pauses and bends over to pick up a bottle of suntan lotion she deliberately dropped on the floor. She takes her time picking it up as she gauges the look upon his face. She is trying to tease him a little and it has worked well. She continues. 'There's no one around here at the moment. My sister is staying in Oxford this weekend with her boyfriend.' She pauses and sticks some fingers in her mouth as if to signal the sound of him makes her want to vomit. 'My parents have gone to Tranby Golf Club for a day of...'

'Golf?' he interrupts.

She laughs. 'There's no flies on you is there, Leo? Come on around the back. I've got sun loungers and drinks. I think you are going to love it around there. Here follow me.' She actually grabs his right hand and leads him down the side of the house towards the rear area.

'Are you sure. I'm supposed to be meeting... Big Bertha and Simon.'

She laughs once more. 'You've already met Simon. That's the Rottweiler you passed as you pulled into the yard and as for... Big Bertha - He names everything around here. That's after his driver.'

'He has a big female driver then?'

She laughs out loud again. 'Oh you are so funny, Leo. No, Big Bertha is his driving club for golf. He is referring to the large lawn petrol mower. He calls that Big Bertha. Anyway, don't fret, it will only take you three hours or so to mow the lawns. Come let's get round the pool area?'

'You've got a pool as well? What a Lovely place. Whose car is the Merc?' He is somewhat overwhelmed by everything but his mind is really focusing on Emily as she walks in front of him to the rear of the buildings. He cannot take his eyes from her petite figure and the way she gently wiggles her bottom.

'Oh the Merc. That's a present.'

'Present? Who from?'

'Daddy bought it for me. He is trying to encourage me to pass my driving test. I have taken two already this year and failed. He is a little disappointed in me and I think he is even thinking of bribing one of the instructors.' She grins. 'You can't buy everything just cos you have money.' She pours two orange looking drinks from a jug on the table into two glasses already filled with ice cubes.

He responds quickly. 'You are right. Money helps a lot but for instance; money can't buy love?'

'Isn't that a Beatles record. Can't Buy Me Love?' She giggles. She is teasing him once more and it is obvious but still he has not really worked it out just yet. He is thinking more in terms that he is not in her league. His confidence is rocked. He is struggling to stay focused on the conversation. He is trembling a little and is struggling to hide it. He has to snap out of it and quickly because he could lose the best chance he has ever had to impress such a beautiful human being as Emily.

A little belatedly, he laughs as he recalls the tune in his head but fortunately for all concerned he did not attempt to sing it to her. 'I Feel bad sitting around and getting paid for it but I must admit I have been looking forward to this day all week. It was so nice of your father to engage me for this extra work and to spend some quality time with you... well I think I should give the money back.' He has overcome all the hurdles swimming around in his head. His lack of confidence has disappeared too by the sounds of things.

'He is nice but in my case he is far too over protective. I suppose most fathers' are like that with their daughters?' She has an immediate solemn look appear upon her face. 'But he is overpowering at times. He fails to realise I am just a teenager and human, after all.' Tears begin to well up in her eyes.

'Not a bad thing these days. Especially with his standing in the community anything could happen... but of course nothing will. You are his pretty little princess and I don't blame him for looking after his prize possession but of course I would want you to be happy. That would be my main objective as a father. Although, I can only imagine what it must be like to be a parent?'

'Possession! That's the problem, Leo. He is too obsessed. Sometimes I feel imprisoned in my own house. Don't do this and don't do that - study, study and more study. That's all he says to me these days. He has been so wrapped up with his business he doesn't even give mother much affection anymore.' She looks genuinely upset now.

Leo moves closer to comfort her a little but is obviously trying to be careful not to be to full on because he has only known her for such a short time. She appreciates it and responds by putting her head onto his shoulder. After a short while she is back to her normal jokey self. As they sit under a grass looking parasol, sipping their juices and enjoying the hot sunny weather, Emily looks him up and down and says, 'you are a little over dressed for the work you are going to do today? I hope that is not just for my benefit.' She smiles knowingly.

'I will be taking my shirt off and I have a pair of shorts in the boot. Just need a quick change and I'm good.' He thinks he's avoided a little embarrassment about being so smart but he does not know what lays ahead.

'I'm hot. Think I'll go for a dip in the pool. Fancy jumping in?' She takes off her shorts and top to reveal a red bikini underneath.

'I don't have any trunks with me,' he says, wishing he had brought some for this golden opportunity. He has secretly been fantasising about a moment like this with her since the first moment he set eyes upon her at his interview. That all seems a million miles away now.

'You're probably the same size as father. I'll get you a pair.' She goes inside and quickly comes out with a pair of red cargo looking swimming shorts with the word "Baywatch" in large black letter down each side. She giggles once more as she sees the look upon his face. 'Baywatch? Things I do for a laugh. Where should I change?' He is looking a little bashful.

'You can get changed out here. No one will see. Only me.' She teases once more. 'I'll look the other way - if you want. Didn't have you down as being a shy one Leo.'

He feels he has to act cool and say nothing but do something. So he takes his top off and gets an immediate look of approval from Emily. She has still not turned around but it is probably part of her teasing. He takes his trainers and socks off, just his jeans and underwear to get off now. He slowly unzips his jeans and looks her directly in the eyes. It has become a game of "chicken". Will she turn around at the last moment or will he turn around at the last second?

'I give in!' she says as she turns around to give him some privacy. What she did not see was Leo almost fall over getting the last leg of his jeans off. Within seconds they are both in the pool splashing each other and giggling like naughty school children.

'Race you to the other end,' she yells out knowing she had at least a metre head start.

'That's not ...' he swallows some water as he tries to speak at the same time as breathing. She is laughing once more. He manages to keep his head above water long enough to say, 'it's not funny. I nearly drowned then.'

As he reaches her in the shallow end of the pool they both stand. They look at each other and there is a sudden moment, a rush of excitement filling their bodies. He leans towards her thinking this is the right time. She looks ready to commit but there is something still holding her back. She really wants to kiss him but knows if her father finds out it will be curtains for Leo. There is an intensity building between them as they have a moment but Emily decides to break it by deliberately splashing him. The moment has been lost for the time being.

Chapter 29

THEY ARE ONCE again standing opposite each other in the pool. There is another opportunity for Leo to show her his real affections. Having been rebuffed on his first attempt it did not appear to be a whole hearted snub but more like the door is still slightly ajar. He splashes her once more and she does the same back. They start with a little wrestle and suddenly the pushing and pulling stops. They are back to staring each other in the eyes. One of them has do something otherwise the moment could be lost forever.

Leo takes the initiative. 'You have such beautiful hazel eyes, Emily.' He then plucks up the courage to put his right arm around her and pulls her closer. He does it in a gentile and slow action in a way to allow her plenty of time to rebuff him once more. She is not hesitating this time.

They kiss passionately but it is short lived as Emily pushes him backwards. He actually falls over into the water but this time she is not laughing. 'Sorry, Leo but we cannot do this. It has no future. My father will go berserk if he finds out. It is best for you not to come here anymore. Stay away, Leo. If you know what's best for you, please leave now. I'll tell father you had heat stroke. He'll understand.' She leaves the pool in a hurry, grabs a towel and dries herself quickly.

He is stunned. At first he has no clue what to say but then thinks about everything for a little while. 'What he doesn't know can't hurt, can it? Besides, I'm a big boy now. I can look after myself.'

'Please go, Leo. Just in case someone comes home early.' She rushes indoors and closes the door shut behind her.

'What about the lawns? Shall I go and ride Big Bertha?' He has not realised just what he has said.

She slides open the patio doors, pokes her head out and says, 'oh you do make me laugh, even at times like this. Yes, do the lawns but please don't look for me afterwards. We cannot see each other again, Leo. It just won't work.'

'Okay, if that's the way you feel, then fine. I'll just be the handyman who only lives around the corner.' He walks off in the direction of the workshop, assuming this is where they keep the famous Big Bertha.

She runs up to her room crying. She feels a little ashamed of herself for having desires and being a little flirtatious. She has a deep hurting feeling inside her stomach area, it is like a frustration burning deep inside. If she was not Terry Banks' daughter she would be free to act upon her sensations and have a mind of her own but then she wouldn't have a pool, a Mercedes Sports Convertible, a lovely home or a privileged education - just to mention a few things.

Somehow Leo and Emily managed to get through the day without any further moments of passion. He did a good job on the lawns and had gotten on really well with Big Bertha. Emily stayed in her room studying but she could not help but look out of her window to see Leo working hard with his top off. There is so much chemistry between them it is going to be hard to see just how they will cope without seeing each other on a regular basis but they are really leagues apart - so much to overcome.

They did not have to wait that long until they saw each other again, just a couple of days went by until Emily turned up in the office at the Sawmills. She was taking every opportunity she could without being noticed, to look out of the office windows and stare at Leo as he worked the sander machine down below the office. He was fully aware she was in the office and he was sneaking some gazes her way at the same time.

'You don't seem with it today, Leo' Stefan says.

'Yeah, sorry my friend. I think I ate something that did not really agree with me. Just like some people.' He says as he once again thinks back to what went wrong at the poolside at Emily's.

'I know how that can be. You not having women troubles are you?'

He is shocked by Stefan's clever observation but is also a bit concerned as he will need to rein it in if he is to keep his feelings for Emily a secret. 'Oh, you've seen that before then? Yeah, some girl I knew from school... we just broke up.'

'If it weren't meant to be... then it weren't meant to be.' He laughs as he realises the obviousness of it.

'I think I know what you mean, Stefan. Is that what they say in Hungary?'

'Szakitas.'

'Do you get fed up talking English all the time? Really we should make more effort to learn other languages. What does that mean anyway?'

'Break up. You will soon be saying szeretlek again, Leo.' He laughs once more.

'I am guessing that means something like; I love you.'

'Do not let Bateman hear you say that to me. He will split us up.' They both laugh out loud. Leo is exaggerating his happy mood and appears to be playing to the gallery so much so Bateman comes over towards the sander machine.

'What's so funny? You know you are not here to enjoy yourselves. Now make sure we make our figures this week or no bonus.' Bateman grins in a sinister looking way as if to let them know he does not like the way they are getting along.

'Yes, we are over the quota already!' Leo shouts back above the sounds of the machinery.

Bateman just turns away pretending as if he did not hear anything above the loud machinery noises.

'I told you. He hears everything. He makes out not to hear anything positive.' Stefan looks a little concerned. He has a wife and two children to support. He has learned not to answer Bateman back or to try and outsmart him as it always backfires.

All of a sudden there is a loud announcement over the internal speaker system; 'Can Leo Parker come to the office?'

'What have you been up to now, Leo, my friend?' He smiles but is a little concerned for his new friend.

'Probably another pay rise.' He looks at Stefan's face and momentarily he had been suckered in but then he laughs.

'Hurry up back or Bateman will put someone else on here. Oh and Leo... good luck with the girl in the office. I think she is too good for the likes of us my friend.' It's Stefan's turn for a little wind up.

Leo checks his hair in a small mirror at the bottom of the stairs and walks up to the office. He knows Emily is in there alone but for how long? 'Hello, you rang.' He tries to keep a stern look upon his face as though this disruption has been inconvenient. He also thinks acting this way will keep him from looking overly keen.

She has a similar problem with him but is more determined to at least remain friends. 'Hello, Leo. How was your weekend?' She laughs and eventually Leo laughs. 'I'm sorry for what happened, Leo. I hadn't planned anything. It just happened.'

'Yes, I know. Feel the same. I don't want you to think just because you've got money and come from a well to do background...'

She interrupts him. 'Stop, Leo! Please don't think it is all about wealth and privileges because it's not. I can't help my position, just like you cannot help yours, so let's not let something like that overshadow what could be a really good and lasting friendship.' She looks close to tears and Leo was going to comfort her but then realised where they were. He looks over his shoulder to see Stefan working away but glimpsing up at the windows every now and then. He can tell Stefan looks genuinely concerned.

'Friends? Is that what you really want Emily?' He looks infuriated by the suggestion.

'No, of course not but I cannot have any ... any close friends otherwise my father will destroy them. Please see it as it is and don't try to fight it. It is in your interests as well as mine.' She has tears rolling down her face and Leo is still unable to be seen comforting her. So he just tries to show a sympathetic look upon his face.

'Okay, what do friends do then?'

'We can hang out.'

'Is daddy going to be okay with us being "friends" do you think?' Leo looks a little dejected and quite solemn. 'Are friends allowed to go to the cinema without a chaperone?'

She sees how his demeanour appears to be deteriorating by the minute and so says, 'it's your 21st birthday on Friday, so have you any plans? Party perhaps?'

He quickly recovers and is looking more himself. 'I haven't planned anything actually. Probably just go over The Crown for a couple of pints on my own. Stefan is away this weekend. Going back home for a quick visit.'

'Have you not got any family living in Becclesfield?' She finds it hard to believe that such a handsome young man would be all alone on such an important birthday.

He hesitates as things are getting a little personal and he is secretive about his family at the best of times and this is nowhere near one of those times. 'No. Got an Aunt somewhere in Tranby though. Not seen or heard from her in over three years not since....' He stops himself as he does not wish to reveal anything further.

She senses some sadness involving his memories of family life and so changes the subject. 'We can't have you being all alone on your 21st birthday can we. Why don't I come along with you - you know, as "friends"?'

A little disgruntled at being demoted to a friend after such a short period of time. He is a somewhat hesitant to go along with this but on the flip side he will get to spend some real quality time with her and you just never know?

'Okay. See you there about 8pm - is that okay?' He suggests.

She smiles and looks far more happier than before Leo walked into the office. 'Great! I'll see you in there. Please don't tell Stefan or anyone will you? Just my father...'

'I know your father will have my legs shot off!' He laughs to show it was just a bit of sarcasm that he could not resist.

She smiles but is frustrated deep inside. She has strong feelings for Leo and hates the way she has to sneak around behind her father's back but it is far better than what the alternative could be if he were to find out.

Leo leaves the office, his heart is beating rapidly and he knows he has to think up something to tell Stefan as to why he was called up to the office. He is bound to ask and he does.

'Sack or redundancy, Leo?' he asks.

'Afraid not, Stefan. You'll have to put up with my silly jokes for a little while longer. It was about my National Insurance Number.'

'You mean you have one?' They both laugh but it was enough to get Stefan off the scent of the real truth.

Leo knows the next three days will drag by as he counts the hours until the next time he will have some precious time with Emily. He has already tasted a little success but now wonders if the setback to being just friends will be a difficult challenge to overcome.

Chapter 30

IT IS FRIDAY night and Leo has found a quiet little alcove along the left hand side of the bar area, away from the flashing fruit machines and the entry/exit doors. He has been seated for around twenty minutes and is anxiously awaiting the appearance of Emily. He is nervous, which he finds a bit strange considering he is only meeting a "friend". He looks all around the pub to ensure no one from work is anywhere near, which was done more for Emily's sake rather than his. There is no familiar faces anywhere in the pub and so he feels a lot more comfortable. It is ten past eight and so she is late but is that not a woman's prerogative?

She was worth waiting for as she saunters into the pub. She is dressed in a red strapless, mini dress and looks immaculate. He does not get up straight away. He is enjoying sneakily looking at her. He suddenly thinks; *not bad for a friend.* Suddenly she turns towards him and they spot each other. He stands and says, 'you look amazing, Emily. Are you meeting someone?' He could not resist a little joke.

'Don't I always look amazing?' She sits right next to him and crosses her legs so he can see just how tanned they are. 'You don't look half bad yourself.' She remarks as she takes a quick glimpse around the bar to ensure there is still no one familiar nearby.

He is hanging onto his composure but only just. He stands and says, 'which half?' he laughs. 'What shall we drink tonight?'

'Rose wine would be nice. Just in case I spill it onto my dress, it won't show up so much. That is how you decide what colour wine you should drink - pair it up with the colours you are wearing. Nothing to do with etiquette.' She tries her best to keep a straight face.

He knows she is just jesting but plays along. 'I've got a white shirt. So better get a bottle of white for me and a bottle of Rose for you. Think we will definitely be spilling it.'

She giggles. 'Rose is my favourite despite what colour I'm wearing and no matter the type of food on the menu. Thank you, Leo. Oh, happy birthday.' She leans over to her red bag and pulls out a gift wrapped box.

'Oh, thank you, Emily. You shouldn't have.' He graciously starts to unwrap the gift.

'Funny how everyone always says that. I wonder what they would say if they *didn't have?*' She laughs once more. She is in good spirits tonight and has not had any alcohol yet.

As he finishes unwrapping the gift, he leans over and kisses her on the cheek, remembering they are just "friends". 'Wow! A gold St. Christopher.'

'I'll clip it on for you. This will keep you safe wherever you go.'

'Even safe from your father?' he laughs but she does not.

'Let's not worry too much about him tonight. Happy birthday, Leo.' She leans over and kisses him quickly on the lips. Then she looks all around the pub to make sure no one saw or more importantly no one she knows is within eye shot.

'I'll cherish this forever. Let me get those drinks. I'll be back in five.' He walks off to the bar area and is quickly back seated with a tray, two glasses and a cold bottle of Rose. 'I'll be mother.' He fills the two glasses and they gently clash them together, both saying, 'cheers.'

'So Leo Parker tell me all about yourself. I know you were in the army and JD's Fencing but what else have you been up to?' She slowly sips her wine, gazing at him in an adorable fashion.

He likes the way she is looking at him. He suddenly feels smug and is thinking how the other pub goers must be envious of him sitting with such a beautiful young lady. 'I left school with the usual certificate... 100 yards breaststroke...' he awaits her response and it is immediate as she nearly chokes on her wine. 'It actually took a while to get a job around here when I first left school. So my only option at the time was to work along the seafront but that was only seasonal. At least at JD's they sent me off to study a few courses and of course I have the famous forklift driving licence.' He grins but really does not like talking about himself and so switches the subject by asking, 'what about you?'

She has a serious look upon her face as if to show she really does not wish to discuss her life much but as she started it all, she has little choice. She says, 'not a lot really. My life is pretty much mapped out. I guess I will follow the same path of my older sister, college, uni and boring husband.'

'How old is your sister? She got married young?'

'Got married about three months ago. She's 22 years of age. Father wanted it and so it was a done deal.' She looks full of remorse. 'I miss her so much. She's coming home soon for a break from university at Oxford.'

'Oxford? She must be brainy? Anyway, getting back to your position. You said your parents want this and that but what is it you want? That's sounds like the most important thing of all.' He smiles as if to comfort her in some way.

'I am not sure yet but I would like to have a say in things. I'm 17 years of age and soon I'll know what I really want to do. All of this studying is making me feel sick. '

'I sympathise with the studying but it is important to learn. Look at me, no qualifications and working as a labourer. Wish I had done more whilst it was all free. I am at night school now just to get some qualifications and I have to pay for the privilege.' Now it is Leo's turn to look a little remorseful.

'Oh, I'm sorry, Leo. I didn't wish to sound ungrateful. I know I have an advantage in life thanks to my parents but I want to make the important decisions about my life - that's all.'

'My favourite teacher at school, Mr. Webb, told me to work on the things I like the most and that may be a way of discovering what you are good at. I haven't done that well with those, Gigolo, Pro footballer...' He pauses to make sure Emily realises he was just jesting and she does. 'So seriously, what sort of interests do you have? Perhaps, you could do something you want to do?'

'I like horse riding but I doubt if my parents would let me be a jockey.' She laughs once more. Her spirits have lifted. 'I actually have two horses; Rocky and Toby. I love riding them and looking after them.'

'That sounds fun. Why don't you have your own stables? You could train little Emily's up and look after the horses.' He smiles as he tries to be compassionate.

'Would you like to come up the stables and ride one of the horses?' She attempts to gauge his immediate reaction.

'No fear! I'm bad enough on two legs but the stables sounds a nice idea. I'd like to see you ride and groom.' He is pleased with himself as he just recalled the word "groom" in time as he was about to say "look after them".

'We'll have to arrange that when you're not too busy working for my father. He's got you cleaning all the windows this weekend. Did you know?' She smiles as she refills their glasses.

'No, I didn't know but that sounds cool to me. I get to splash you with the hose... if you're going to be there?' He has delivered this well. His number one question was always going to be whether she would be there or not.

'Yes, but we'll have to pretend we don't know each other that well. I don't think father will be in but mother may come back from the hairdressers whilst you are there.' They chink glasses once more.

The bottle is now empty and she gets up, wriggles her dress down a little. 'I'll get a bottle of champers. It's your birthday and we need to celebrate in style.'

They debate over which one of them should pay for the champers but Emily wins and is soon seated back at the table with a bucket half full of ice, bottle of champers and two flute glasses. 'Cheers, happy birthday, Leo.'

'I like this. I could get used to this. Cheers, Emily. So where did you live before your father hit the big time and bought that mansion in Front Lane?'

'It's hardly a mansion. When I was little we lived in a two bedroom terraced property in Amstead Drive. I have a lot of happy memories back then. Father was much more easy going back then.'

'I know Amstead Drive, I used to live in Maplin Way. That was just around the corner. Wow! We may have at some point in time bumped into each other without even knowing it?' He leans over for a hug and hopes for a kiss but she is still hesitant. She knows anyone could be in the pub. Even the bar staff may know whose daughter she is?

'We can't. My father will not allow it.'

'He's not here.'

'I thought this was going to happen. I'll have to go now. Call me a cab.' She gets up wriggles her dress down a little and heads for the restroom.

He is once again full of emotional upset. He knows deep down Emily has feelings for him in the same way he has for her but how to get around the issues surrounding her parents strict upbringing is going to be a serious challenge. He calls a cab and waits patiently for her to come back to the table. She is a good ten minutes adjusting her make - up and looking at herself in the mirror. She returns to her seat.

'Did you have any luck with the cab, Leo?' She is not as sharp tongued as before.

He can see she has mellowed. 'Yes, it'll be here soon. Shall we go outside and wait for it to arrive?'

They wait outside. It is still a nice summers night. The cab pulls up next to where they are standing. She turns to him and says, 'I will have to be dropped off last, just in case father is looking when the cab pulls up. He must only see me. I told him I was going out with Charlotte from the stables.'

'Charlotte from the stables? That sounds like a film.'

'She'd like that. She's like you. Funny.'

'I prefer Emily from Amstead Drive though.'

She giggles and they get into the cab. She whispers . 'Leo, I really like you but my father will not let me go out with someone...'

He interrupts. 'You mean with someone like me?'

'I didn't say that. He will not let me go out with anyone until I've finished all my education.' She is looking serious and unhappy.

'Oh, I see. He wants you to be the most educated virgin in Becclesfield?'

She slaps his right cheek so hard even the cab driver shudders. 'That was a terrible thing to say! Very hurtful!'

'I'm so sorry, Emily. I didn't mean it but it's so frustrating for me. You don't know how much I like you and the thoughts of never to have you in my arms is unbearable.'

She is sobbing but yields and cuddles him. 'Oh, Leo, what are we to do?'

'I'm your rock. Remember that. When things ever get tough, I'll be there. I have your back, Emily - always.' They gaze at each other in the eyes and in a loving moment they move closer. Leo puts his right hand around the back of her neck and gently pulls her closer towards him. There is no resistance. They kiss. Their passion for each other is obvious to the cab driver as he is ever so careful as he turns a sharp bend. Even he does not wish to spoil the moment.

They stop kissing and Leo tries to impress her by saying, 'I'm attending night school. I have taken a business management diploma.'

'You are doing well but I like you just the way you are.' She nibbles at his side neck area.

'That is definitely a title to a song. Barry White sang that one. Big hit back in the day. Anyway, I don't suppose I'll be enough for your Dad unless I win the lottery.'

'Don't be silly. You have to get out now. We're here.' She leans forward for another passionate kiss as the cab pulls over outside Leo's home.

'Wow! Where did you learn to kiss like that - at prep school?' He asks.

'Very funny. It was an all girls school.'

'Well, you still could've learned it there?' He says as he laughs and even the cab driver is having a private little chuckle to himself.

Emily is just grinning. She loves Leo's sense of humour and is really appreciating his understanding of her parenting issues. 'We'll have to meet up at the stables. What do you think?'

'Definitely. Is Charlotte from the block going to be there though?'

'No, only Rocky and Toby. I had better go now, my father is expecting me home by midnight... and no, before you say it, I'm not Cinderella.'

'Hadn't crossed my mind. Have you got both of your shoes? Just checking.' He says as he moves towards her and they kiss again. The cab driver is patiently waiting as he has heard most of the conversation and is showing a great deal of empathy.

'Come to the stables on Sunday morning. That's if you've finished cleaning my windows by then.' She giggles and blows him a kiss as he gets out of the car. He walks around to the driver's side and hands him a twenty pound note telling him to keep the change. Leo knows the cab driver will be discreet if he gets a good tip.

He then wanders to the kerb side of the road and watches carefully as the car drives off. He is hoping she will turn around to look at him once more and she does. He feels a rush of adrenalin and huge lift in his ego at the same time. He waves back to her and then walks off towards Waverley Road where he lives. He is soon inside his apartment and the first thing he does is look at himself in the mirror with great pride. He has had the best ever birthday and kissing Emily was the best present he could have wished for. His thoughts are already turning to their next meeting but he still wonders if it is enough to being moved up from "friends" to something more meaningful but he'll have to wait a little longer to find out.

Chapter 31

LEO HAS BEEN waiting with a certain amount of excitement and a little apprehension for Sunday to come around. He dances out of bed and runs into the shower. For some reason he starts singing; "I love you just the way you are!". His mood is extremely positive as he puts on his best designer gear. He is out to impress and wonders just what sort of reception he may get. He knows on Friday night at The Crown they both drank a lot and is worrying whether the kissing was mostly down to that or whether she has genuine feelings for him. It will not be too long for him to discover as he drives the fifteen minutes down a winding country lane in search for the stables. As he negotiates a real sharp bend on the left hand side he sees the sign come up; "Banks Stables". He says to himself, 'I might've known he owns that as well.' He pulls into a muddy area and can see Emily tending to a large chestnut horse in the distance. He gets out of the car and avoids most of the puddles.

'Hey! Good Morning, Emily! I see it bloody rained last night.' He moans as he looks down at his muddy trainers, which were only brand new last week.

'I see you come dressed for it again, Leo.' She says as she giggles and thinks back to what he was wearing when he first turned up at her house to do the gardening. 'I like your trainers - are they new?' She laughs.

'They were new last week but I suppose you're worth it.' He walks over towards where she is standing. She looks stunning in her riding attire. Tight navy blue top and tight cream coloured trousers. 'You haven't got a whip as well?' He laughs to show he was only joking?

'Funny you should say that. If you don't behave you know what will happen?' She grins.

'Promises, promises,' he says, 'what's the name of that one?'

'This is Rocky. Do you want me to saddle him up. He's only thrown me off three times this week.' She is back to teasing him as she bends down to wash a hand brush in a bucket of water knowing full well Leo will be unable to resist taking a secret glance at her perfectly shaped figure and he does.

'You are kidding. I need to be in tip top form for next week.' He says flexing his muscles out.

'Where did you get muscles like those from?' She gives him a long lingering look of admiration.

'Your fathers sawmills!' They both laugh but it is short because Emily has picked up on his little lack of confidence. She throws her arms around him, pulls him close to her and they kiss.

They have somehow made their way into the stables where there are piles of hay strewn all around on the ground. Still hugging and kissing, they find themselves laying on a small hay bale in the darkened corner of the stables. Their passion and excitement towards each other has led to much caressing. Within moments they are undressing each other. 'You are so beautiful, Emily, not just on the outside but on the inside as well. You are whole.' Within moments they are both naked and making passionate love.

After an hour or so they are partially dressed and sitting up on the hay stack. Leo smiles at her and takes some straw out from her hair.

She is first to speak. She says, 'Leo, you are so gentle and loving. I'm so pleased we... we got to know each other more.'

He is feeling on top of the world. 'You are so beautiful. I don't know if I ever told you that?' He laughs aloud because he knows he has several times.

'Thanks, Leo but we had better get ourselves looking fully decent as my father will be here in about five minutes.' She has a serious look upon her face.

'What! Bloody hell.' He stands up and then falls over trying to put a sock on his right foot.

She is giggling uncontrollably by now. 'Got you! Of course he's not coming here. Do you think I'd be laying here like this if he was even five miles from here. He's at the golf course like he always is on a Sunday. Come on lay with me. I've not finished with you yet. I want that massage you promised me on Friday night.'

'Massage? I don't remember ... well I'm ready.' He has a huge smile on his face as Emily removes her top once more and lays on her stomach.

'No funny business, Leo. Just a massage.'

'Yeah, right. Just a massage. No charge of course.'

'Oh, Leo, I wish we could stay overnight in a proper room somewhere.'

'There's plenty of places. Why not?' He rubs his hands between her shoulder blades and she groans with pleasure.

'Ooh, you've hit the spot there, Leo. Let's get a room in Tranby. That should be far enough from preying eyes.'

'Okay, leave it with me. When?'

'I'll have to get Charlotte...'

'Charlotte from the stables? I like her already.' He moves his hands upwards from the lower spine to the shoulders and then she turns over. They are passionately kissing and caressing each other once again. Poor Toby will not get his grooming today as they spend the whole afternoon in each other's arms.

It is Friday and Leo is at the Turkish Hairdressers. He wants to look his best for the Friday night he has planned with Emily. He has booked and paid for a room in the White Hart Hotel in Tranby. Having taken the day off as annual leave, they can leave early and spend some time in the shopping centre but Leo has a big surprise for her. He picks her up in a prearranged secret place near to Front Lane but far enough away from her parents eyes.

'Hi, Emily, sorry the car is old but it still has some life left in it. It should get us to Tranby and back.' He smiles. 'I'm going to swap it one day.'

'What on earth for?' She is grinning and cannot wait to hear the response.

'A black Audi.'

'With all due respect, Leo, who is going to swap an Audi for an old Fiesta?' She is still grinning and intrigued.

'I don't mean a straight swap. I'm getting the money soon and I will buy one. I will have my own personalised plate as well.' He is smiling at the thought of it all.

'Father must be paying you too much,' she giggles and then asks, 'what are you going to have on the plates? My other car is a Fiesta?' She burst into laughter but cuts it short as she can see the seriousness upon his face.

'Ha, very funny not. I'm going to have "LEO 1" on her and it will be famous in Becclesfield, they will all know it's me when I drive past them.'

'Oh, so the car is a "she" then? I thought I was your baby? I'm so disappointed.' She pretends to be upset.

He puts his arm around her and pulls her closer. 'You're my number one. I think I've gone and done it again - another song title. "S. Club 7" remember them?' He has deliberately changed the subject to get back on favourable terms.

She gives up playing around with him; she looks at him and leans over for a reassuring kiss. She has not done anything like this before; ignoring her father's express wishes of not having any kind of relationship with anyone until she finishes her education.

'Leo, I like your hair have you just had it done?' She kisses him on the cheek.

'Yes. Especially for my little princess. You look so amazing. I like your white silky top. Is it real silk?' Feels like it.' He starts up the engine and checks his mirrors not just for traffic but to make sure there is no one following them.

She nods in a positive manner and says, 'of course it's real. Just like me.' She reaches over to the radio/CD player and starts fiddling with some buttons but cannot get anything out of the speakers. 'Does this work?'

He laughs. 'Of course not. Everything about me is false.'

'Please don't tell me we are going to have to sing our way to Tranby. I've not rehearsed since the audition I had on the "X Factor" two years ago.' She smiles and looks out the window awaiting his reaction and she did not have to wait long.

'Did you really? How did you get on?' He is trying to concentrate as they head down Denbar Lane en route to Tranby.

She still looks out of the window acting a little innocently. 'Daddy said I was the best and the show is fixed.'

'He would.' He has said it out loud and has to come back with something quick. 'What I meant he would stick up for his little princess wouldn't he?'

'Well, I'm glad in a way. I didn't much care for all that glamour. Besides, we may never have met.'

'I want to take you somewhere special before we book into the hotel. Are you up for that?' Leo looks content with himself.

'That sounds interesting. Am I dressed for the occasion?'

'It is just around the corner now.'

'Oh, it's close to Tranby town centre. That's good. I like these kind of surprises.' She huddles up to him and puts her head on his left shoulder.

They turn a corner and he parks the car next to a large area of wasteland. 'We're here.'

'What's here? I can only see long grass and a few hills.' She appears a little disappointed.

'That's why it's Tranby's best kept secret. Follow me.' He leads her along a narrow footpath and suddenly it all opens up. 'See that lake over there and the way those willows trail into the water?'

'Oh, Leo, it's so beautiful and very quiet.' She suddenly becomes impressed.

They make their way to the lake and Leo takes a blanket out of a carrier bag he had carried from the car. He lays it neatly on the ground. They sit down together hugging and appreciating the stillness of the surroundings.

He turns to look her in the eyes and says, 'I'm so glad we can spend this special moment here together. It is where I spent so much of my childhood. They were happy times here.'

'No humans anywhere to be seen. That is a rare sight these days. So tranquil.'

He points to left hand corner of the far end of the lake. 'See that corner over there, that's where I fell in when I was about seven. Luckily for me a farmer came along and pulled me out.'

'Is he still around? I'd like to thank him.'

'The farm's long gone now but I shall remember him forever that's for sure.' He looks very serious as he remembers how he had panicked splashing around in the water.

'Soon these types of places will have new builds crammed all together. I wish we could stay here forever, Leo. It's so beautiful and restful.'

'I'm so glad you like it. That means a lot to me.' He leans over and they share a long passionate kiss. 'Emily, I know we haven't known each other long but I think I'm in love with you. You are on my mind day and night.' He feels perhaps he should not have said all of that so early in their relationship as it may frighten her off. Also he has issues with the difference in their living standards and worries if he is ever going to be good enough for her or more to the point - her father.

She pulls him close and kisses him once more then whispers, 'you have made me the happiest person in the world. I feel the same way about you but was scared to tell you because we have only known each other for about a month and my father... well you know the problems I have in that direction.'

'I will look after you. Don't worry about you father. I will tell him he has to accept it. We won't be the first couple to go against a parent's wishes. Of course, you may have to accept a lower standard of living for a while.'

'You are so brave, Leo but you really don't know what you are getting into. If I tell you something will you promise not to tell anyone?' She actually turns her head to see if anyone is close by.

'Yes, okay.' He is looking very intrigued.

'Well, have you heard of the Reynolds gang in London?' She asks looking quite pensive.

'Who hasn't. They are the maniac brothers running protection racketeering.' He looks quite concerned now.

'My father, when he was young, was part of the gang. He only has to make a phone call and it is done. You know what I am saying?' She begins to sob.

He tries to comfort her and says, 'we'll elope. He won't know where we are.'

'Don't you think they have contacts all over the country? They even got someone in Argentina two years ago. We'll just have to be careful. Take these stolen moments while we can. It's safer that way.' She hugs him once more and kisses him on the right side of his neck. Suddenly the tranquillity of the lake and surrounding areas do not look so beautiful as the reality kicks in. To make matters worse, the rain starts to pour down.

He takes off his leather jacket and wraps it around Emily. 'Here take this. My route 66 jacket.' He smiles.

'Route 66? Oh I see it is written on the back.' She smiles and although getting a little wet feels snug.

'Yeah, it's a long road in America - I think? I like it for how comfortable it feels.'

'A long road - you could say that 2400 miles is long, Leo.' She giggles.

'Wow! that's massive. You would have to keep filling up petrol just to get through it.' He chuckles to himself at the amount of stops it would have to take to get from start to finish. 'We had better get back to the car or we will have colds by the time it gets dark.'

'I told them I was staying around my friends house tonight. I just hope he doesn't send anyone around to check. He has hired people to follow me in the past you know? I have left my mobile phone with her, so if he is tracking me, which I suspect he is, he will think I'm around her house all night.' She has her head on his shoulder as he drives towards the hotel.

'He's a control freak! Does he do the same with your sister?'

'Not anymore, she is married now. He approves of him but I don't. He's a creep. I don't like the way he looks at me sometimes. My sister doesn't even notice. I also have my suspicions about his temper. I heard him shouting at someone one day outside The Angel. It didn't look good. He's a wrong one, Leo. Take my word for it. I wouldn't be surprised if somewhere there is a connection with father's past.'

'How did he approve him then?' He sees a ray of hope suddenly appear.

'They met at university and his parents actually have a house in Oxford. His father runs a large haulage company. Money as usual. He loves money.' She sits upright as she sees the entrance to the car park of the hotel.

'Well, I'll just have to rob a bank.' He laughs, 'or Banks?'

'Very witty but even the taxman doesn't know where his money is.' She says with quite a serious look upon her face.

'I've bought you a little present.' He says as he leans over towards her.

She looks pleased and raises her eyebrows. 'You shouldn't have.'

'You see, you said it, just like everyone else. Here you are.' He passes her a medium sized box with gift wrapping paper all around it.

'You've even wrapped it. I'm impressed, Leo. You are such a little sweetie.' She quickly rips the paper away to reveal a handbag. She hugs and kisses him.

'Open it. There's something inside.'

'Oh, stockings, thanks so much.' She kisses him once more. 'I will treasure these for the rest of my life.' She declares.

'Don't worry too much about that. I hope to soon be in a position to buy something much better.' He looks a little inadequate.

'I'm happy just having you, Leo. They are great. I'll have to hide them away from my mother, she is quite nosey when she wants to be.' She smiles and once again they kiss each other.

They get out of the car, book into the hotel and spend a passionate night together but all the while there is this obstacle in their way. They will speak much about how to overcome it, even bordering on illegal ideas but for now everything will have to be kept secret. In the meantime, Emily will have to come to terms with getting ready to go off to university amongst other things whilst Leo will be working away at the sawmills but keeping one eye on the office.

Chapter 32

LOUISE BANKS IS speeding through Denbar country lanes. She is in a hurry to get back home before her husband, Terry arrives. She is particularly well dressed for what was supposed to be a cup of coffee and a chat with her best friend Tara Shaw. She screeches around a particularly sharp bend and as she straightens up sees a police officer with a speed gun mechanism in his hand, and it is pointing straight at her car. She curses her bad luck and as she slows down she is waved over by another officer positioned in a lay by. She stops the vehicle, unwinds the window and then for some reason hitches her Chanel pale blue skirt higher up her legs. She quickly unbuttons two more buttons from her cream coloured silky top to reveal the tops of her breasts. She deliberately leans forward towards the oncoming officer. 'Good afternoon, officer. What is happening?' She is trying to look as vulnerable as she possibly can.

He leans forward. 'Good afternoon, Madam. Do you know what the speed limit is in this part of the lane?'

She deliberately crinkles her face as though she is close to tears but in reality she is a million miles from crying. 'Oh... is it 60mph?' She has driven these lanes a hundred times and never even given it a single thought, until now that is. 'I'm so sorry if I have accidentally broken the law. I promise I won't do it again.' She pretends to be even more tearful than before. She pretends to pick something up from the floor in order to reveal more of her body.

The policeman has a stern look upon his face and it appears as though it has been there since the very day he was born. 'May I take your name and address please?' He says rather abruptly.

'Louise... Louise Banks. I live at Timber Vale, Front Lane.' She suddenly changes her look to one of real worry. For the first time, she actually realises she could get charged with speeding, which will be a fine but more damaging to her, points added to her licence.

All of a sudden, the officer's stern looking face has changed. 'Are you related to Mr. Terry Banks?'

'Yes, I'm his long suffering wife.' There is a glimmer of hope appearing upon her face as she knows just how important her husband really is in these parts.

'Oh, right. I didn't realise who you were. My apologies, Mrs. Banks. Please make sure you drive safely as some of these bends can find you out when you least expect it. Oh, will you give my regards to Terry and tell him Gerry says hello.' He is smiling graciously as if he is trying to be forgiven for an error of sorts.

She smiles appreciatively towards him and says, 'thank you, Gerry. I'll tell him how polite you was with me. May I go now, please?'

He steps back and says, 'of course, sorry for any inconvenience but please do take it a little easy around here.'

She smiles at him but this time it is as though she had suddenly became his superior in some way. 'Thank you, officer. Have a nice day.' With that she starts up the engine and speeds off. She looked as though she was trying to prove a point. Once out of sight she speeds up even more and soon arrives home in Front Lane.

She parks up and rushes indoors. She is soon in her bedroom quickly undressing. For some reason she wishes to get all her top designer clothes off before any one sees her. Suddenly, as she is removing her Chanel suit, the bedroom door opens and she hears a familiar voice. 'Hi, mum. Where have you been all dressed up like that?'

She turns around quickly and says, 'Oh, Millie, didn't know you were coming home this week. Lovely to see you. You look so pretty. Hope Julian appreciates you?' They hug and kiss each other. 'Just went to meet my best friend, Tara Shaw in Tranby. We had a coffee in this new bistro. You should see the owner, he's a right dish. Think he's French or Italian? Either one will do for me.' She laughs to indicate she was only joking.

'Oh, I see you are still up to your flirting tricks. Good job dad doesn't know what you're really like?' Miley smiles as if to show it is all a little piece of harmless fun.

'I'd watch what you are saying about me, Millie. Remember you are at least half of me, maybe more.' They both hug and laugh at the same time.

'So where's your handsome husband, Julian?'

'He's joining us tonight, mum. He had some things he had to attend to before he could leave Oxford.'

'Oxford. It just oozes class don't you think?' She looks so proud of her daughter and how she has done so well marrying into money.

'Stop being a snob, mother. Becclesfield sounds just as good to me. In fact, apart from you and dad, there's not that many pretentious people around here compared with Oxford, I can tell you.'

'Pretentious, moi?' She laughs once more. Miley just shakes her head as if to say - "I don't believe you sometimes".

Louise gets dressed into some black ski pants and white cotton top. She is still chatting with her daughter in the bedroom. They are now both sitting on the bed as Louise turns her mood to something a little more serious. She says, 'have you seen your sister since you got home?'

'No, I've not seen Ems for over three weeks now.'

'Well, Millie, please promise not to tell anyone but she has been so happy around the place lately. I want to find out who he is?'

'What! Little Emily has a boyfriend?' She looks shocked as she still imagines her sister as being that little girl with ponytails, freckles and buck teeth but of course she is no longer that person.

'Don't whatever you do, tell your father. Don't tell Julian. In fact, don't tell anyone but a couple of Sundays ago she came back from the stables a different person. A mother knows. Anyway, on Monday morning I was clearing up...'

'Being nosey, you mean?' Miley interrupts quickly.

She laughs a little but then continues on with the story. 'As I said, I was nosing around in her room and I found a brand new handbag with stockings inside. She wouldn't buy stockings as she never wears them and the bag wasn't even designer.'

'Mother, that is nowhere near enough evidence to hang someone with. If I used this as an example in one of our tuitions everyone would laugh. You need concrete evidence. Leave it with me. I'll give her the talk tonight.'

'Talk?'

'Birds and the bees. Bet you and father haven't even done that yet, have you?'

'I haven't and I don't think for one minute your father has. Oh, I see what you mean. What a bad mother I am.' She pretends to really care. 'Anyhow, don't they do all that at school? That's what we pay for.'

Miley just laughs at her mother's flippancy.

Emily is laying on her bed with her earphones on. She is listening to music and chilling out. She did not hear the knock on the door. The door opens and she sees her sister Miley standing in front of her smiling. 'Hello, sis. Pretending to study are you? That's what I used to say when mother or father walked in on me.'

Emily is so happy to see her, she stands up and they hug each other. She quickly takes off her earphones and closes her music app. 'Millie, when did you get back?' She asks with a big smile upon her face. They are so close.

'Got home this afternoon. Didn't mother tell you?' She sits next to her on the bed. 'How grown up you look today, Ems. You must

be the prettiest girl around here for miles bar me of course.' They
laugh and hug each other again.

Emily knows she has to be careful with her thoughts but has
always taken her elder sister's advice through the years and it has
not failed her yet. She says, 'you look so lovely. How long have you
had the blonde hair?' They continue chatting for over an hour until
the subject of boys crops up and it was not Emily who raised the
issue first.

'You must have a lot of admirers, Emily. Have you got your eyes
on anyone? I remember being your age you know. Remember my
secret romance with Tony from the college?' She thinks back as she
says it and recalls just how badly it ended once her father had found
out.

'Yes, he seemed such a nice guy. Shame... the price we have
to pay for being a Banks - hey?' Emily sympathises and is now
thinking about her romance with Leo. She is secretly praying it will
not end the same way as her sister's.

'So come on, Ems, who is it?' She is doing her best to coax her
along but it is still not enough at this point.

'I don't have anyone, Millie. If I did, I would be knocking on
your door for advice. That's what sisters are for.' She is really
struggling about lying to her sister but she knows the consequences
of her father finding out are far too harsh to contemplate.

Miley puts her arms around her and whispers, 'what about the
handbag and the stockings?'

Emily pulls away and is obviously embarrassed but thinking on
her feet she quickly says, 'well this guy at work keeps sending me
stuff but I don't have feelings for him. He seems a nice boy but he
works for father...'

'Oh, Ems, you are so charitable. You must send them back to
him. Tell him you're not interested and tell father to sack him. Get
him out of your life for good.'

'I can't do that! He needs the job. Besides, I've already told him to back off and he has. I will be returning those gifts .' She looks convincing.

'Okay Ems, so long as you have told him and he does back off. I mean this stuff he bought you... looks like he only spent about £20. You deserve a lot more than that.' She lifts up the bag and gives it a quick once over. She then throws it towards the wastepaper bin in the corner of the room. Wiping her hands with a scented wipe as though she may catch something by handling it. 'Honestly, Emily, you are worth so much more than this. Take Julian and I, you will meet someone like that one day and all of these obsessive guys will still be doing what they do best ... stalking. Now you really don't have anything to say to me about him? He hasn't been pestering you whilst you have been attending the horses at the stables, has he?'

Suddenly things are getting uncomfortable for her. She wonders if anyone had seen those special moments down at the stables. 'No, of course not. I would tell father if he did. Please don't fret sister dear, as I said earlier I would always come to you first. I kept your romance with Tony a secret didn't I?' That was her way of telling Miley to back off and it worked. No more personal questions were raised and they went downstairs for their dinner. Emily had been looking forward to all the family sitting around the table together as it has been quite a rare occasion since her sister went off to university in Oxford. This happy vision was about to be shattered as Miley's husband, Julian turns up with a bottle of champers and a big bunch of flowers for her mother. He knows just how to keep in with the parents but not so with Emily. She loathes him.

Chapter 33

EMILY AND LEO have just visited the wasteland and the lake once more. They are happy and holding hands. She says, 'I really love that place, Leo. You actually feel as time has stopped and given you some precious moments to treasure for the rest of your life.'

'Yes, it's so quiet. I'm so glad you like it, Emily. It will from now on be our special place. Whenever we are apart, one of us can come here and we'll always feel close to the other no matter how many miles away the other one is.'

'I think I get your meaning, Leo. That is so sweet. Yes it is our special place and always will be.' She leans towards him and they kiss. She then says, 'we had better get a move on if we are to have lunch in Tranby, remember I have to be home by 4pm before father gets in from work.'

'Oh, yes. I forgot about him.'

'Wish I could at times like these but there we are. We have to be happy for these stolen moments. I love you with all my heart!' They kiss again.

'I love you Emily Banks with more than my heart.'

'You're so competitive, Leo. You have to try and upstage me all the time.' She giggles because she really appreciates the sentiment. She has not had such a caring, sensitive and loving relationship like this one at any time in the past.

They are soon in the car and looking for a parking spot in the town centre. 'There's one there, Leo.' She points to the side of the road.

He easily manoeuvres the car and parks up. 'See, Emily, that's the beauty of having a small car it is easy to park up. You wouldn't get your Merc in that spot would you?'

'I wouldn't get any car in any space the way I am driving. Come on let's go, I am famished.' She unclips her seatbelt and gets out of the car first.

Leo slowly gets out and ensures the car is fully locked up. They head across the road towards "Daniela's" a trendy wine bar in the heart of the town. Leo stops all of a sudden. 'That's not your mother over there coming out of the White Hart Hotel, is it?'

'Oh my God! What is she doing here? Why is she hugging Ray Shaw? That's Tara's husband.' She grabs Leo and they hide behind a white parked up van.

'They seem to know each other really well. They're kissing now. Perhaps, it's some sort of business meeting?' He tries to turn her thoughts about her mother into positive ones.

'Business! More like dirty business. If father finds out about them they will both regret it. I've a good mind to go over there.' She pokes her head further around the van to get a better look without being seen herself.

'You can't. Remember you are supposed to be at the cinema with Charlotte from the stables.' He tugs her arm to reel her back in a little. He can see sadness amongst the shocking looks upon her face and so gives her a reassuring embrace. 'I'd leave it if I were you. We don't want to spoil what we have. It may jeopardise everything if she finds out.'

She begins to sob. 'How hypocritical is she? I'm not allowed to choose who I want and yet here she is parading around town with some fancy man... What about poor Tara? She needs to know what a scumbag her husband really is.'

'Leave it, Emily, please leave it. You will not even feel any better for getting involved. It'll probably run its course, they usually do.'

'You are so mature, Leo. I wish I had your mannerisms and worldly thoughts. You're right. What good will come of it? They deserve one another. Pair of cheating bastards.' She looks a little embarrassed as she realises that is the first time she has sworn in front of Leo.

'Exactly my love. Come on let's go and get something to eat. Time is running out for us.' He cuddles her gently. He then runs his right hand around the back of her neck and up the back of her hair. 'You are so beautiful.' He whispers.

Emily arrives home and rushes to her bedroom. She is in a confusing emotional state; She is happy for the time she has spent with her lover but at the same time furious about what she saw on the streets of Tranby. She needs to settle her emotions before she sees her mother again otherwise she will not be able to hold back. So she just concentrates on the times spent with Leo and the future arrangement already in place to meet him at the stables on Sunday afternoon. She is laying on the bed listening to her music through her bright red earphones when her bedroom door opens and in walks her mother. 'Hello, Ems. How has your day been?' She asks looking a little coy.

Emily was a little unprepared but was not going to let this go by without some reference being made to cheating. She says, 'not too bad, although I did see someone I know from school's mother in the shopping centre with another guy. They were very close; you know kissing and stuff. He is a married man as well. How disgusting is that?'

Louise goes bright red in the face. It is not just a blush but more of a sudden rise in blood pressure. 'Who was that?' She asks sounding rather nervous.

'Oh, you wouldn't know them, unless you stayed at the White Hart Hotel in Tranby. That's where my friend told me they always go.' She is keeping a solemn look upon her face but is also enjoying getting what she thinks is her own back in some way.

'Well, sometimes we don't know the full story. For example, we don't know if her husband has been up to the same nor do we know their marital arrangements or disagreements.' She feels she has swerved it all quite well but Emily is not done for yet.

'If they are unhappy in their marriages why don't they just get divorced?' She turns away from her mother and lays back onto the bed. She then adds, 'is that why you are so strict with me? Worried I may find a wrong one? I do know my own mind.'

'You're only a teenager, you need looking after. I had it, your sister has and look how well that's turned out for her.' She is not finished with her daughter just yet.

'I want to make my own decisions in life. Especially now I'm all grown up.'

'Grown up? You are not acting like an adult now are you? You need to know where you came from and how many privileges you enjoy.' She turns to leave the room but is stopped short by Emily's response.

'Millie may have got lucky so far but what if not? Will it be okay if she then goes off sleeping around with whoever?' She attempts to finish the conversation whilst still thinking she may be ahead but her mother is having none of it.

'What's his name then?'

'Who?' She suddenly looks as though she is losing the debate now.

'The boy you are obviously getting so emotional about.'

'I haven't got any boys. Where are you getting this stupid idea from?'

'Well, you had better not - otherwise... you know what your father will do?' She attempts to leave the room once more.

'So how can I ever have any relationship with someone? Tell me when that will be allowed or am I supposed to remain the silly little rich kid who comes from Front Lane until daddy says it's okay for me to be with someone?' She has gone all in and has no more comebacks to what her mother may say next.

'You are right about one thing; You are a spoilt little rich kid. You should not turn your nose up so easily. If only you knew what your father has to do to make us all live the way we do - you wouldn't be saying things like that. Put your music on now. Don't think for one minute I'm fooled into believing you were studying with your headphones.' With that she walks out of the bedroom slamming the door shut.

Several hours later Julian and Miley are sitting in the west wing of the house. This is the area where they go to be alone and away from earshot any time there is some issues arising. Today is one of those occasions as Miley needs to speak with him in a hurry.

Julian is first to speak, he says, 'your sister looked upset at dinner tonight. Has she had a row with your mother. They looked like they were giving each other the cold shoulder treatment. I should know, I've seen it enough from you. I can see where you get it from now.' He laughs to ensure she knows it was meant light heartedly.

'Oh, funny. Remember where you are, Spikey.' She has called him by his nickname from university and he likes it. 'I'm glad you picked up on that. I know what it is all about but you must promise never to tell anyone - especially father.' She pauses to see him nod in agreement and he looks really interested. 'Well, mother thinks she is having a relationship of sorts.'

'What little Emil? Never! She's such a goody two shoes.' He grins as he imagines her having a romantic fling.

'It's true. Apparently some guy has been showering her with gifts. I think he could be infatuated with her. Not healthy is it?'

'No, it's not. Do you want me to sort this guy out?' He offers because he is certain of the answer and he is once again right.

'My father will do all that if he ever finds out but Ems is adamant it is all harmless and she doesn't even like the guy. She's told me he has already backed off. So I told her to tell me if it gets serious at any time.' She stands up and walks towards the large double bayed windows looking out onto the pool area. 'I hope she has told him. She says she has.'

'We need to monitor the situation closely. I'm home this weekend and I'll keep an eye on her. She won't even know.' He stands and walks up behind her, puts his arms around her and kisses her.

'Oh, you are such a lovely man, Julian. I really love you.'

'I love you to, angel. Always and forever.'

She responds. 'Yes, always and forever.' They embrace further and passionately kiss for some time. They leave the west wing and head outside to the pool area. The blue cover is stretched right across the whole pool. It is ready for the winter months approaching but it still looks quite inviting. Miley's thoughts are however fully focused on protecting her little sister but will she be able to do this without telling her father? What if her father finds out and discovers she knew about it all? Emily will not be thanking her if she tells her father, she is in an unenviable position whatever way you look at it.

Chapter 34

EMILY AND LEO are back at the stables stealing some precious secret moments together. They are still lying together on top of a hay bale. Emily is first to start the conversation following their hour or so of expressing their love to each other. 'I'm going to be 18, in May next year, I'll be able to make my own choices then.' She smiles tenderly and hugs him tight as if to suggest they'll be together then.

He doesn't look convinced and says, 'yes that's all well and good but if you are still living under his roof then you'll still be under his spell.'

She pulls away from him looking in disbelief. 'I didn't ask for all this designer clothes and stuff. I would rather just have the simple things in life, if it would mean my freedom.'

'That's quite ironic,' he says, 'do you know there are thousands of people who would love to be in your position.'

'Really? Would you like to be in my position then?' She is staring at him in the eyes. She wants his truthful response.

'Well, if that means I wouldn't have to shave everyday...'

She interrupts. 'You know what I mean?'

He drags out his real answer a little longer. 'Does it mean I would have to put up with your father and that creep Julian?'

'You want everything your own way.' She looks upset now.

'I'm happy with what I have, so long as you are by my side, I can take anything they can throw at me.' He smiles and is immediately rewarded with a lingering kiss.

'It took you long enough to get there.' She smiles as they sit up and stare at each other in a way as though it is vital to staying alive.

He then says, 'okay, that's enough of that. Now where were we...'

IT IS SIX o'clock the next morning and Julian knows Terry will rise around this time. So he heads down to the breakfast room and waits for him to show up. Terry walks in fully dressed for work but looking very tired. He has not slept well for weeks now. His worries over the financial state of his business lay heavily upon him. In all of this time he has had to pretend to be his normal jolly self but this is also taking its toll upon him. He sees Julian filling a kettle. 'Blimey, Julian. What are you doing up this early? Has she kicked you out of bed?' He is still pretending to be his cheerful self.

Julian turns around as if being surprised to see him. 'Oh, Terry, I forgot you get up this early to go off to work. Want a cuppa, just filled the kettle?'

'Great thanks. One sugar please.' He seats himself by two large windows overlooking the rear lawns. He is thinking how much more time will he be able to hold onto it all. 'Not too bad today. Looks like snow is on the horizon though.'

'Well, it is winter. It probably will hit us again at some point. How's things at the mill?' He thinks he is being polite but if only he knew.

'It's had better times. Think the epidemic and Brexit caused some damage to us but we have to plan for everything - right?' He is looking for some support to ease some of his self pity.

'Yes, definitely. I'm surprised so many businesses have made it through all of that. It all seemed to happen at once.' He looks closely at Terry's face and feels it is time for the real reason of getting up so early to be revealed. 'Terry, I have to tell you something in strict confidence but I think you should know.'

Terry puts his cup down on the table. He knows with what has been going on lately, it can only be further bad news. 'What is that, young man? I will keep it to myself - I promise.'

'You've been so good to me since I met up with Mills but you should know this. It's about Emily.' He pauses in order to see if there is any signs he already knows this information he is about to share and there is not. 'She has an admirer and I think it could get out of hand. He has been sending her gifts. He has an unhealthy

obsession with her. I thought you should know and I told Mills...'
He appears to have deliberately let the cat out of the bag about
Miley knowing and not telling her father. 'Well, I told her I would
be happy to take care of it.' He tries to keep a serious fixed look
upon his face but deep inside he is purring at the thought of just
how many points this will score in terms of their relationship.

'So Millie knew about this all along?' He looks more
disappointed with this part of the information rather than his
youngest daughter potentially getting involved with someone.

'Yes, but she only found out yesterday. She said it was nothing
to worry about. Apparently she had the same thing happen to her
when she was Emily's age.'

'Really? That's news to me. How many other secrets going on
around here?' He pauses, 'thanks for letting me know. I can see how
awkward it is for you and it is safe with me. I think I know who the
little scallywag is. Leave it to me... and Julian... tell no one I know.
Okay?' He stands up and hugs Julian to show his appreciation.
Julian feels ten feet tall. It has been a hard journey winning him
over during those early weeks with Miley but now he thinks he has
truly arrived.

Just before he walks out of the door he turns to Julian once
more and says, 'I took my eyes of the ball. Let that be a lesson
learned for you when you have kids. Thanks a lot and mum's the
word.'

'No worries, Terry, you can rely on me.' He gets up and makes
his way back to the bedroom. Suddenly all the personal items he
sees around the place, which he always felt belonged to other
people now feel part of his personal possessions.

Terry has arrived at the Mills and is sitting in his office on
the first floor. He is going over so many things in his head; the
financial state of the business, the creditors, Emily and the money
he owes the Reynolds brothers. It is all getting to the point where

something has to give. He has already cut staffing levels, lowered his prices and cut costs on energy by switching back to a five day week but the lost orders to some of his best clients has now taken its toll on the balance books. He stands up to take a lingering look out of the double windows in his office, he appears to be observing the factory floor area. His eyes are fixed on one person. He is the one on the sander. The one he trusted to do handy work around his house. The one he trusted not to make any moves on his youngest daughter. It has not been confirmed but he has a strong gut feeling. He has observed the way they look at each other and the way they deliberately ignore each other at the same time, it has to be him?

His deep thoughts are interrupted by the sound of his landline ringing. He is now deciding whether to answer it or not. It is bound to be a creditor but on the slim chance it could be a fresh order, he has to answer it. 'Hello, Banks.' He has his hands free so he can walk around at the same time as speaking.

'Ah, Terry. I've been trying to get hold of you for several days now. You promised I would have the funds by now but they have not been received. Is there any problem with the payment? I hate to bring it up but I have the monthly wages for the maintenance team to pay next week.'

'Hi, Eric. How's Sharon now? I know just what it's like getting that sickness bug. It lasts for weeks.' He has deliberately changed the tone of the conversation into one of being more friendlier.

'She's fine now thanks, Terry. How's your good lady wife, Louise?'

'Still the same - I'm afraid.' They both laugh. 'Now back to the matter in hand let me see what's gone on. Please hold on while I get the information up.' He just gets up and stretches his arms, gives it a few minutes and thereby gives himself time to think up a good explanation as to why the bill for £11,250 has not been paid for the maintenance contract of his machinery. He times it to perfection. 'Oh, Eric. I can see where it has gone wrong. I'll get it to you straight away. If you want a job done properly don't let anyone else do it. Sorry, mate.' He stops talking to see if his excuse has worked and it has.

'Great thanks, Terry. Knew I could rely upon you to sort it out. Didn't want to bring it up but under a bit of pressure at the moment. You know how it is. Thanks once again. I'll leave you to get on - bye.'

He slams the phone down in a rage. He has hated having to lie to Eric as they go back so many years but he has no money left. Time is now running out everywhere and he needs to come up with a plan to keep everyone off his back, especially the Reynolds brothers from London. He does however have many dark contacts to rely upon if he needs to get out of this jam by illegal means. He unlocks a hidden compartment in his desk and pulls out a small red notebook. He flicks through the pages and suddenly he stops at one page. Gets a small mobile phone from the compartment and turns it on. As he waits for the phone to power up, he looks down at the gun, fully loaded just sitting there. This is his emergency drawer, more than that, it is his desperation drawer and he is more desperate than at any other time. The bills are coming in from everywhere and even his wife, Louise is adding to the pain with the clothing and jewellery she buys each week - all adding up.

He calls one of the numbers in the book. He goes by the name of "Flame King" and there is good reason for the name. 'Hello.' The voice at the other end says.

'It's me, Butch. You have all the plans and details by now. Go ahead as planned on Sunday at noon, not a minute before and not a minute after. That is vital. Okay?'

'Got it Butch. Count it as done. High noon on Sunday.'

'Good. I'll leave the money at the agreed place on Monday evening at 8pm. Whatever happens don't get caught. If you do, you know what not to say - right?'

'Been doing this for years, Butch. It will be done or my name's not "King". Nothing else, I take it?'

'No, bye.' Terry hangs up as he reminisces back to the days when his nickname was "Butch" but he knows he is no longer the "Butcher of Plaistow" that was when he was younger and now appears to him to have been in another life.

He sits back in his chair and tries to relax as the phone rings once more. He is still hesitant to answer it but does. 'Hello, Banks here.' He hears the voice at the other end and quickly switches off the speaker to the phone.

He picks the phone up and says, 'I told you never to ring me here unless it is very urgent. It had better be.'

The caller relays the information he has discovered and it does turn out to be urgent.

'You say Tranby... overnight? Are you sure about that? What's his name? No, leave it to me. I have something special lined up for that little bastard. Thanks. I'll leave your money in the usual place. It goes without saying to keep this quiet from anyone else. Just the two of us. Okay?' He hangs up the phone. Now he has the name and a plan. The only thing he needs to do now is get him in the plan somehow? However, time is running out and he needs money and fast. If only enough to pay the Reynolds brothers their monthly "commission". He clears all the items from his secret drawer and a picture he has of his wedding from his desk. He decides to get home before anyone in his family arrives. The one thing he must not let any of them know is the truth, certainly not the whole truth.

Chapter 35

LEO HAS SPENT the last two days cleaning up his apartment as Emily will be calling today. He has got all his best crockery and glasses gleaming in the midday sun. He has the balcony doors wide open and has a table with two chairs placed out there. He knows it will not be as impressive as her poolside set up that he so enjoyed the first time they kissed. He has taken all the bachelor posters off the wall and replaced them with something more agreeable. It is fair to say his apartment still lacks a woman's touch. He is just taking one last look around the place when the doorbell rings. He tries to look cool by taking his time answering the door but deep inside he is sprinting. 'Good morning. You found it okay then?' He says as he ushers her into the living room.

She kisses him and takes a good look around the place. 'It looks a lot cleaner than I thought it would.' She is teasing him once more.

'I know it's not Buckingham Palace but I've worked hard to clean it all up for your visit... your majesty.' He laughs.

'Glad you know your place. ' She smiles and kisses him once more.

'Make yourself comfortable on the chaise lounge, or whatever you call it.' He sneaks out to the kitchen and runs back into the lounge. 'Anyway, you'll find the oven and everything you need in that room there... it's called a kitchen.'

She looks concerned. 'What? You want me to do something in there?'

He laughs. 'Got you! One - nil.'

'The nights young. I have two nice bottle of champers I stole from fathers wine cellar. He won't even notice. I trust you have more than one glass?' She grins.

'I know I live on my own but I'm not that stupid. I've got two pint glasses, I'll bring them in.' He goes to walk off to the kitchen once more.

'You are pulling my leg again?' She cannot help but grin.

He turns around and confesses to her. 'I've got flutes, a takeaway ordered and some really lovely slow music.' He then turns the dimmer switch down to a darker mode. She looks as though she really appreciates all the hard work and preparations he has carried out. She pulls him closer and they kiss passionately once again. She stays until around eleven o'clock because she has to get back before her father starts questioning her where she had been. She gets indoors and goes straight to her bedroom without seeing any of the family members.

The following day Terry has been at work for just over three hours when he suddenly feels he has had enough of being at the Mills. There is nothing he can do to turn the tide back into his favour. Every attempt he has made to square the books has failed and he is sinking further into debt. So he decides to head home early. He gets home and quickly races up to his bedroom before he sees any of his family members. He is still in a state of high anxiety. He needs to calm down or they will all be asking what is wrong? He quickly gets changed into a pair of blue Calvin Klein jeans and a white Ralph Lauren polo shirt. He carefully removes his Rolex watch and places it into a hidden safe behind an expensive painting of his parents. He places the gun, book and mobile phone inside. As he is looking at himself in the mirror he hears the door swing open. 'Are you there, Hun?' It is his wife Louise.

'Hi, Angel. What have you been up to today?' He asks, just in order to pass the time of day. He is not at all interested really, he has too many other things to worry over.

'Oh, just this and that.' She grabs him and they embrace with a lingering kiss. It looks as though she has missed him today.

'What you after? Not another car I hope?' He sort of laughs but really he is praying it is not something too expensive. Then he takes a good long look at her. She is standing in front of him in a black low cut dress and her blonde hair is perfectly drooping over her shoulders. He then wonders what will happen if he loses her and his business, not to mention the house and cars.

'Nothing, just thought I would let you know how much I love you. Now you need to get changed we have a special dinner tonight. Julian is coming with Millie.'

'Get changed? I've just changed.' He looks a little put out by her comments but knows he must now put on his black Gucci trousers and his old faithful Le Coste white shirt, which he has had for over fifteen years but still looks brand new. He opens up a golden box, which is laying on top of a dressing table and takes out a heavy golden chain. He puts it around his neck and then turns to her and says, 'Julian is one of us now. Why have we got to go to all this fuss every time he comes to dinner?'

'Because... because I want it that way. He comes from a well-to-do family and we have to show our worth.' She kisses him on the cheek and then leaves him to ready himself once more.

Just as he was about to leave the room his mobile rings. He has a sudden look of real fear appear upon his face. He knows who is calling from the unknown number flashing on his mobile screen. He plucks up the courage to answer it as he knows he has to. 'Hello.' He tries to sound upbeat.

'Ah, Butch. How have yer been?' A sinister sounding voice says.

'Hi Frankie. Fine and you?' He knows the niceties are not going to last long and has prepared himself.

'You're still late with the commission, Butch. Is everything alright at the Mills?'

'Just a bit of cash flow. You know how it is Frankie. I'll have it within the month. I am waiting for a big payment to come in from a client. He's a bit slow this month. That's all it is.' He is sweating now and quite profusely.

'D'you want us to send the boys over to see if they can rush it up for yer? Only Lenny's getting a little restless. Yer know how he can be when he gets like this. You remember that night at the Palais, those poor bouncers, three of 'em in hospital and not a mark on Lenny.'

'Lenny knows I'm good for it. Just give me a little more time. I've got a plan in operation as we speak and when it comes off, I'll send you a lovely little bonus on top. Just to say thanks for your patience.' He closes his eyes and prays he has done enough. He remembers just how violent Lenny Reynolds can be.

There is a deliberate pause at the end of the phone as if the caller is discussing their options. After a minute or so, the caller says, 'okay Butch. For old times' sake. Four more weeks but if you let us down, we'll have to forget those happy times we used to spend together. It's not personal, Terry but it's business. By the way how are those two lovely young daughters getting along. One at Oxford, that must cost yer. Let's hope they continue to blossom. Bye.' He hangs up not giving Terry a chance to say anything not even goodbye.

Terry throws his mobile on the bed and cringes at the thoughts of just what may happen to him or even members of his family should his newly formed plan fail. He has to get the money, by hook but most probably by crook. In the meantime he has to act as though it is business as usual both at work and at home.

Miley has taken the time to check in on her younger sister who is laying on her bed listening to music thinking of Leo. Emily is as always pleased to see her sister enter her bedroom. 'Hello, sis,' she says, 'have you come to give me a grownups talk?' She smiles.

'Not really but I would like to know if everything is okay with your stalker. I hope you have sorted him out now. She is standing over her with her arms folded and attempting to look quite sternly.

'I told you. I don't even like the guy. How's married life treating you? You look happy and content.' She attempts to change the conversation.

'Nice try, Emily. You promise he is not stalking you or anything like that? I need to know before I go back off to university.' She joins her on the bed for a brief hug.

'Nothing to worry about, Millie, honestly.' She hates lying to her elder sister but knows everything with Leo has to be kept a secret.

'Have you seen mother around today?' Miley asks.

'She could be anywhere. Probably in Tranby.' Emily says sounding a little fed up with her.

'Tranby? Why would she be there?' Miley looks somewhat surprised her mother would take an 80 mile round trip unless it was important.

Emily quickly realises she has made a mistake to mention Tranby. 'I think I heard her say something about meeting Tara there. She does go there a lot for shopping nowadays and she said there is a new posh restaurant in town.'

'Oh, they're best friends from college. Been friends for all of those years. She probably met her in the new restaurant then? Amazing how they have stayed friends for all of these years. Anyway, I better be going or Julian will be getting fed up watching TV on his own.' She gives her a little hug and leaves Emily to her music.

It is Sunday 14th October approaching midday and Terry Banks is on the 8th green at Becclesfield golf course. He is £200 up and there is another £50 riding on his next putt. Stuart Johnson is staring and cringing at the same time. He is hoping he misses in order to claw back £50 from the £200 he currently owes. Terry bends and sizes up the hole even though it is a relatively easy putt. He is now standing over the ball and picturing just how the ball will travel towards the cup and sink inside when Stuart interrupts him. 'Wow! Look at that fire over there. Isn't that near your factory?'

'Nice try. I'm not falling for that one.' He assumes it is just a piece of gamesmanship and prepares to take the putt.

'No. I'm serious Tel. Look at the flames and smoke. It must be next door or maybe a train has caught on fire?'

They both suddenly stand in silence as they watch the raging flames leaping well above the tree lined fairway to their left. 'I think it's my place! Take care of my clubs, Stu and I will investigate further.'

'Be careful. The smoke is toxic by the looks of the darkness of it all. Looks as though some tyres are being burned.' Stuart grabs both golf carts and starts to wheel them towards the clubhouse whilst Terry rushes through the trees to get a better look.

Terry's whole behavioural features in his face have changed to looking less serious but still a little nervous. He knows exactly where the fire is coming from and secretly he is beaming deep inside. The plan has worked to this point. He is actually hoping the whole place is destroyed, as he can then move onto the next phase - proving who did it.

He gets himself ready for when he walks into the clubhouse knowing much sympathy and best wishes will be forthcoming. There were many of them. Stuart says, 'was anyone working today?'

'No, we had stopped weekend working a couple of weeks ago. Orders were down since Brexit. Good job in a way, I suppose.' He looks saddened. 'Oh well, I shall have to drive around there and see what's going on. Thanks everyone. Don't know when I'll be back here but thanks for your support.' He turns and races out of the clubhouse not just because he needs to show his concerns over the factory but more to the fact he was finding it hard to keep a straight face in front of the members.

He arrives at the entrance to Ferry Lane but it is cordoned off by police. A uniformed officer walks over to his car and says the obvious. 'Good Afternoon, sir. I'm afraid the road is closed off because there is a large fire at one of the warehouses. You will have to take another route.'

'Yes, I know, officer. I can see it but it is my factory by the looks of things. I am Terry Banks and I was playing golf over the back there.' He is pretending to be heartbroken. 'The Mills has been in operation for many years now. What a pity. Is it bad?'

The officer has no diplomacy whatsoever. 'Bad? It's finished, sir. The whole place is gutted and the fire brigade say they will be here for two days. That's how bad it is. Oh, sorry it's not better news, Mr. Banks.'

'There's nothing I can do for her now. I may as well start phoning all the workers and tell them...' he pretends to breakdown a little.

'Okay, Mr. Banks. Think that is probably all you can do given the circumstances.' He looks as though he is also close to tears.

Terry turns the car around and drives back to his house. This is the best he has felt for over three months now. Ever since he started to fiddle the books at the Sawmills. He is certain the insurance cover will be enough to pay off all his creditors and as for the Reynolds brothers, they will not only get their payment but it will be the last time as there will be no business left to take their "commission" from. The real bonus though is he will not have to tell his wife or sell the house and her jewellery. He rushes up to the bedroom. He quickly changes from his golf attire into something more casual. He is expecting some call or appearance from the police but he knows most of them by name and so is not too concerned. He walks downstairs and sees Emily sitting in the front room. He smiles in her direction and she says, 'good game of golf, father?' She is smiling back at him.

His facial expression has changed to look more solemn. 'I have some bad news to tell you... the Mills has been burned to the ground.'

She jumps up from the couch. 'What?'

'There was a big fire. Don't know anything else yet about it.' He then remembers she is set to go to the stables at some point and he knows who she has secretly arranged to meet. 'Yes, it's so bad. I think we all need to be together today. Your mother is going to be devastated by the news.'

Emily looks more than upset. Not just about the fire but missing out on seeing Leo at the stables and she has no way of telling him. 'Oh... but the horses won't get done today.' She attempts to sway her father to her way of thinking.

'Oh, ask that girl... you know, Charlotte. Tell her I'll pay her for her trouble but we all need to be together. The police may call and we will have to give them our movements, I suspect.' He hugs her gently.

'Police? What do you think it could have been done deliberately then?' She is now thinking about all the employees losing their jobs, especially Leo. 'That means everyone is out of work?'

He pulls away from the embrace and says, 'there's nowhere for any of them to work... except for clearing the debris. I'm glad you mentioned that because we need to ring around everyone and tell them.'

'Yes, we do need to ring them all.' Suddenly she has realised she can ring Leo now and it will all look okay to her father.

He then says to her. 'You take all the surnames from A-M and I'll take the others.' He is beaming inside as he knows just which ones she would prefer to ring and she falls for it.

'Why don't I do the ones from N-Z and you do the other ones?'

'I want you to handle the ones I said. You will be far better and more sympathetic to people like Bateman and Cooper for instance. No, we'll do it that way.' He knows it is just a temporary measure and if she is anything like him she will find a way to ring Leo at some point before the day is out.

Leo Parker has been driving around aimlessly as he now knows about the fire and remembers placing the petrol cans in the office. He is really concerned the fire may have started from there. Then he realises the attendant in the garage will most certainly remember him. Also, he has missed his romantic meeting with Emily. He decides to ring the number Terry Banks called him on. He gets a message telling him this mobile phone is out of service. He actually fears going home in case the police are waiting for him. So he drives to the place where he always feels free and a place where he will be able to think things through. He knows he cannot turn up at the Banks' home, as he thinks they will be in no mood for visitors following the news of the fire. He heads to Tranby and within an hour and a half he is seated by the lake on the wasteland. The sacred place where he spent those magic moments with Emily. He was actually trying to see if the theory about one of them being there without the other would work. It does. He feels her presence even though she is forty miles away in Becclesfield. His thoughts turn back to the fire. How is he going to get out of this? For some time he has been giving his full attention to the thoughts of it being proven to be an arson attack. He then thinks back to how his parents died following an arson attack three years earlier and he was not at home. He remembers all of the questioning by the police and the finger pointing by the neighbours every time he walked down the street. Then there was the media coverage and how they implied it had to be Leo and how he was the only one who would benefit from it in a financial way, being the only child. He recalls how his father in his final days was acting; withdrawn, unhappy, nervous and the obvious money concerns both his parents were experiencing. Those strange phone calls in the middle of the night. To this day there has not even been anyone arrested in connection with it. He knows he cannot go through all that again but he has reasoned Mr. Banks will back up his story about the petrol but even so he has made a decision to lay low for the time being.

As he is contemplating his next move his mobile phone rings and it is Emily. He quickly answers the phone. 'Hi, Emily I have been trying to find a ...'

She interrupts him. 'Mr. Cooper, I am afraid I have some bad news.'

'Cooper? What are you going on about?' Is it the fire?'

'Yes, Mr. Cooper. So you already know about it?' She is staring directly at her father as he is on another phone talking to one of his employees. She whispers, 'where are you?'

'You know where? Our place. What's going on? Are the police involved?' He is getting very anxious at this point in time.

'Yes, that is correct. We don't quite know at this point how it started.' She is continuing with the charade as her father looks over adoringly towards her.

'Okay, can you get to the stables this afternoon?' Leo asks anxiously.

'No, but thank you for offering. Perhaps we can speak again next week when we know more?' She is secretly arranging a rendezvous with Leo.

'Stables?' He asks as he tries to decipher the cryptic message.

'Yes, I know. I will tell him. Ever so sorry but we don't know what's happening just yet.'

'Right, next Sunday at the stables. what time?'

She looks over and her father is still looking over at her. 'I'd say morning we could have a better idea of what has gone on and what we can do going forwards. I had better go now as I have to ring up so many people. Thank you for your understanding under what are extremely sad times for all of us.'

'Next Sunday. At the stables. Got it. Look forward to seeing you there and Emily, I didn't do the fire! I have to tell you something when I see you next Sunday. I love you so much.'

'Yes, me too. Thanks and bye.' She disconnects the call and turns to her father. He is just finishing with one of his employees and has hung up the phone. They both have real deep looks of sadness upon their faces but both have completely different reasons for it.

Chapter 36

LEO HAS EVENTUALLY returned home. It is approaching Saturday afternoon and he is trying his best to get some sleep in. He spent the most of the week in Tranby and on the wasteland. He suddenly hears the sounds of muffled vehicle doors closing outside his apartment. He stands and goes over to the window. He can see a number of vehicles parked in the middle of the road but no occupants. He then hears the front door rattle. 'Police! Open up!' He gets to the door and opens.

He is stunned. There are six burly police officers looking menacingly at him. One of them then says, 'Leo Parker you are under arrest for the arson attack on Banks Sawmills in Ferry Lane.' He reads him his rights and cuffs him. He is then led down the stairs to the ground floor. He can feel there are neighbours watching this rare occurrence with some interest. He is quickly bundled into one of the vehicles and driven off to Becclesfield Police Station. The only chance to get out of this situation now lays in the hands of Mr. Banks himself.

He gets questioned and tells them the arrangement he had with Mr. Banks. How he had run out of petrol and been asked to take some petrol to the Mills. Police question him all throughout the evening and then again in the morning. Eventually, he is taken to court charged with arson. He pleads not guilty and an application for bail has been granted. He must turn up at the police station by 1100 each morning, as he will be monitored whilst the investigation continues and more evidence is gathered.

Sunday 21st October, it has been one week to the day since the fire and Leo is scrutinising all the news channels to see if the police have made any breakthroughs but none have been forthcoming so far. He has spotted some suspicious activity outside his flat and figures it is either the police or Terry Banks' henchmen keeping a close eye on him. He has not been able to contact Emily for fear of their relationship being discovered. As he goes into the kitchen there is a knock on the front door. He goes to answer it. He sees a very smartly dressed man standing in front of him and he is extremely well built. 'Hello, can I help you?' He asks quite nervously.

'I can help you,' the man says. 'I had better come in if you don't want the neighbours finding out just what I have to tell you. It's in your interests, Leo.' He tries to look more accommodating.

Leo is reluctant to let him in but wonders what else could possibly go wrong now? 'Come in,' he says as he opens his front door wider.

They walk into the lounge area and sit on a couch. 'I'm from an interested party. You need to hide somewhere whilst we get those responsible for the arson. You are in danger and so are everyone you hold dear. Get your belongings together.'

'What? I don't understand?' He is looking petrified at this moment in time.

'Get your stuff together now and leave while you can still walk. There are some nasty people on their way down from London and they won't be as nice as me. You have to leave now. Here's some cash.' He passes a thick brown envelope over to him.

'But what about my bail conditions?' He stands in protest.

'Live or die and die slowly in much pain. It's your choice. If you don't go now they'll be here soon. You don't have long to escape them.' He tries to reassure him by smiling.

He is in a state of turmoil but thinks he had better do exactly what he is told. 'Okay, thanks. I suppose it gives the police time to find the real culprit.'

'The other thing, Leo, whatever happens from here on in, you don't mention that story about Banks being involved. He is connected you know?' He is back to looking quite menacing.

'But he is my alibi in all of this. He told me to take the petrol and put it in the office... he... he run out of petrol you see?'

'Don't ever say that again if you value your life and anyone you value in your life. Live or die. That's what it amounts to. Who do you think is sending the boys down from London? Now get away while you still can. It's your only chance of freedom... and Leo, give me your mobile phone. I will get rid of it so no one can track you. Also, you must tell no one for if you do it could be a death sentence for them. No one. Really important!' He stands up towering over Leo and says, 'I'll go now and watch you drive off. Remember these guys could be anywhere. They could even be outside now. So quickly get out!' He walks out of the apartment alone and heads back to a parked car.

Leo is frightened. He has to go but what about Emily. Surely one quick call from a public phone box but then it could be traced or she may not answer? It could be her father answering the phone? He quickly grabs a suitcase and piles some clothes into it. He looks inside the envelope and counts one thousand pounds in used notes inside. Someone is desperate to see the back of him and now he knows his fate. The one person who could have got him out of this mess is responsible for him now having to go on the run and not just from the police.

Meanwhile, outside sitting in a parked car is the man who had just visited Leo. He makes a phone call. After a few moments he says, 'it's me. It's done. He should be off shortly and he has been warned not to ring anyone. So your daughter will be safe from him. I told him never to mention the dealings with the petrol cans so you are in the clear. Money in the usual place, Butch?' He hangs up and turns off that particular mobile phone. He then checks his other phone and sees a missed call from his wife. He rings her quickly. 'Hi, Sharon I am ever so sorry I missed your call. I had a little bit of business to attend to. I'm on my way home.' He sounds quite meek and mild now. He waits to see Leo racing to his Fiesta with a case and speeding off. He has a little chuckle to himself and then calmly drives off to his home.

Leo heads for Tranby, buys camping equipment. He then goes into a supermarket and gets supplies to last at least a week. He pays for them with some of the cash from the brown envelope. Now he has everything he needs to get out of the area and see from afar just how the media is going to report this tragic fire at the Sawmills. He drives off to Sunborough knowing it will take a good three hours from Tranby but takes heart in the fact it is no Route 66. He is totally devastated by the discovery that in all probability Terry Banks not only did or arranged the arson attack on the Mills but has framed him for it. Trouble he is also having now is that he knows Emily will never believe her father would do such a thing. He is frustrated as he cannot contact her just to say, "hello" and tell her where he is heading.

Emily is getting ready to leave for the stables. She is hoping Leo will be waiting for her when she arrives. She goes down the stairs in her house. She is greeted by her sister and her husband, Julian. She just says, 'I'm off to the stables, see you later sis.' She completely ignores Julian and walks out of the door with a spring in her step. The cab is waiting for her down by the double gated entrance to the house.

'I wonder if she is going to be pestered by that creep, Parker. He has been released on bail. They only kept him in for a short while. If father gets to him first, his life won't be worth living. Don't know how he got bail but he better watch his back.' Miley says as she slices a carrot with a long sharp knife. 'What are you doing today?'

'Me? Oh, nothing much. Have you got anything planned for me then?' He sort of grins as he knows she is up to something.

'Thought I would go and see father at the Mills. He is seeing if anything is salvageable.' She checks the weather by looking out of the large double rear windows.

'Okay, I'll probably pop into Tranby to get the car serviced as there is a special promotion going on today. It needs a complete overhaul.' He hugs her and leaves the house to take his car to Tranby but decides to make a stop off first somewhere.

It is approaching five o'clock in the afternoon and Terry, Louise and Miley are all seated in the lounge. They are waiting for Julian to return from Tranby. He has been gone longer than had been anticipated but suddenly he walks into the room.

'Where you been? That must've been some promotional offer? Was it busy?' Terry is first to speak and is a little impatient at being made to wait so long for dinner.

Miley looks him up and down and asks 'How did you get all that mud on your shoes? You had better remove them and get dressed for dinner.'

'Had no choice. Had to push this car for an elderly looking lady. She had broken down in the Denbar Lanes. You know how dangerous it is around there?' He shrugs his shoulders in a way as if to portray it was an act of chivalry.

Louise is showing signs of admiration towards him and says,' oh that's so nice of you, Julian. You're so lucky to have him as your husband, Millie.'

Julian intervenes and says, 'that's what I keep telling her.' They all laugh.

Terry suddenly says, 'where's Emily? Shouldn't she be home by now?'

Then within a moment or two they all realise, she has not come home from the stables. Miley rings the cab firm responsible for her transport to and from the stables. They advise their driver dropped her off at the stables but when he went back at 1600 hours she was nowhere to be seen. Apparently the cab driver sounded his horn and waited over ten minutes before departing for another fare. On hearing this news relayed to him, Terry stands up and grabs his car keys. 'I'm going to the stables to see what the hell is going on.'

'I've tried her mobile, dad but it appears switched off.' Miley says as she takes a quick look out of the windows.

'That's unlike her. She's always got that phone stuck to her ear.' Louise says.

'I will come with you.' Julian offers his support and it is gratefully received.

They leave in a hurry and are at the stables within a quarter of an hour. Terry makes an observation. 'The horses are still out. Perhaps, she's fallen off one. Oh no, I hope that is not the case, she could've been on the ground for ages?'

'That could be the reason the cab driver did not see her? Quick let's get out there and look for her!' Julian says as he unclips his seatbelt and jumps out of the car first. He is quickly followed by Terry. It is now dark and so they find a torch in the barn area. They call out her name but there is no answer. They search all the surrounding fields and call her name every few moments or so but still no sign of her. The rain has started to pour down and they are not really dressed for this weather. Terry still has his dining clothes on and is now soaking wet and the bottoms of his trousers are covered in mud. Julian is in a similar state. They have no other option but to return to the barn area. They put the horses away and Terry gets in his car and parks in a way where he can put on his full beam across the large fields in front of them but still no sign of Emily. He checks his phone and sees a number of missed calls received from Louise. He calls her back.

'Has she returned home, Louise?' He asks sounding quite frantic.

She sounds exactly the same as she says, 'no. I was hoping you had found her at the stables. I called Charlotte and she says she has not seen her today as well. What can we do?'

'I'm not giving up just yet. What about any boys?' He is wondering if there are more Leo's in the picture.

'Boys? Oh you mean boyfriends? Don't know but she has been acting a little emotionally recently.' Louise calls over to Millie. 'Do you know of any boys involved with Emily?'

Miley remembers the obsession someone at work has with her. 'There is this boy at work. She said it was just someone being silly. She returned all of the gifts back to him.'

'Gifts? What gifts?' Terry asks but he knows just who the boy they are referring to is and he knows exactly where he lives. He says, 'don't worry about that. Leave it with me, I've got an idea.' He closes down his call on the mobile and turns to Julian. 'We know just who that boy is that has been obsessing over Emily, don't we, Julian?'

Julian nods in total agreement. 'Let's go and get him. I think he lives over the Waverley Road area?'

'I've got his address. Let's go and pay the bugger a visit.' Terry says as they get into the car and speed of in direction of Becclesfield town centre.

'See what happens when you take your eye off the ball? I'll never let that happen again. Open up the glove compartment.'

Julian opens the glove compartment and sees a gun inside. He is momentarily shocked. 'Is that thing loaded, Terry?' He asks.

'It's a toy but it'll frighten the life out of him and he'll tell us where Emily has gone.' Terry grins in a very sinister way. He knows it is not a toy but is a loaded gun and he will use it if he really has to.

They arrive in Waverley Road and have tried to get an answer from Leo Parkers apartment but there appears to be no one in.

They call upon a neighbour next door. A middle aged woman answers the door. 'Hello, what can I do for you?'

'Oh, sorry to trouble you,' Terry says, 'but you haven't seen Leo today please?' He is smiling and trying his best to look friendly but he is burning up inside. Every minute seems like an hour since his daughter has gone missing.

She looks at both of them. 'Are you the police?' She asks.

They both actually laugh and Julian says, 'no, we are his friends from college. This is my father, Jonathon.'

It appears to work. 'He went off in a hurry this afternoon. Haven't seen him since.'

Terry can wait no longer. 'Did he have a young lady with long black hair with him about 17 years of age?'

'No, but I know the one you mean. She has visited him on a couple of occasions. Are you sure you're not the police?' She looks concerned she may have said too much.

'No, you have been very helpful. Thank you. If you could ring me on this number when he gets back or the young lady shows up here, I would be eternally grateful and I will make sure you are given something special... for your trouble.' Terry hands her one of his business cards and they leave.

All the while Terry is now regretting the decision to pay Leo off and get him out of town because he has reckoned they may have eloped off together somewhere. He thinks this could be the reason she has not come home. The one thing he does not know is where Leo Parker has actually fled to. He believes they could even be planning to get married. Time is of the essence and he has no choice but to reach out to the Reynolds brothers once more. If anyone can find him, they will but it will come at a high cost to both Terry Banks and especially, Leo Parker.

Chapter 37

LEO ARRIVES IN Sunborough. He finds the campsite. He has had some happy times here as a child when camping with his late parents. It will go some way to settling his nerves. He has skipped bail and knows the police will be out looking for him but he is more fearful of the Reynolds brothers finding him first. He has pitched his tent up in the far right hand corner of the farmers one and a half acre camping field. He is a little disappointed at the amount of tents there are camping out as it will not give him the cover he had imagined. He has no mobile phone but plenty of cash and groceries. So he will hide up here for at least the next week or so. He is regretting not being able to say his goodbyes to Emily but thinks this will all blow over soon, once the police catch the real arsonist and they will once again be together.

Three days have passed and Leo is feeling safer by the day but the one thing he does not know about is the Reynolds brothers have put a bounty on his head in the underworld of £10,000. They just want the information of where he is hiding out. The other thing he is totally unaware of is Emily has been missing since the day he left town and now people are pointing the finger at him not just for the arson attack but the kidnapping of Emily Banks. Soon someone will no doubt go back in time and try to put two and two together, pairing up the arson attack on the Mills and the one on Leo's parents home as being linked.

It is Thursday, 25th October and Emily has been missing for 4 days. Things are getting desperate inside the home of Terry and Louise Banks. Terry has just come back from the stables and surrounding fields. He has been out day and night. He looks so fatigued, withdrawn and constantly in a state of shock. He walks into the lounge where his wife, Louise is sitting. She has been there for nearly two days just praying the phone will ring bringing her good news of her youngest daughter, Emily. She looks up and sees Terry entering the room she says, 'still there has been no word. She hasn't even been on the news yet. Why are they dragging their heels? Can't you talk to Bobby, surely he'll do something for us?'

He approaches and gives her a hug. 'I've already spoken with Bob and he says he has his best detectives on the case. They want us to appear on tv on Saturday night to give an appeal if there is still no news by then.'

'Terry, where is she? Who would do this? Is it that Leo Parker? Why did you let him into our lives?' She is uncontrollably sobbing. 'Why can't you ask your old friends to make him talk?'

He knows just who she is referring to and feels he has to tell the truth now. 'Already been done.' He pauses to see what her reaction is but there is little room for any other emotion other than deep sadness. 'They'll soon catch up with him. They have contacts all around Europe.'

'We don't want to go back to those days, Terry but we are desperate and if you really think it will bring our Emily back then it is worth a try.' She puts her head on his shoulders.

'It hasn't come cheaply you know. I have to give them a slice of the action when we get the insurance payment but as you say if it brings our little Ems back then it will be worth it. Especially if it leads to whoever did this terrible thing.' He grinds his teeth in anger.

'There's not even been a ransom note or anything like that. It's just done out of spite. We must hurry up and find her.' She is crying once more and he tries to comfort her. 'It must be personal? First the fire and now...'

Terry had not given that idea much thought before and there are plenty of skeletons in his cupboard. He has to disrupt her before she starts to build up some kind of credence to her latest theory. 'It's nothing like that. I have enough people out there looking for her and if it was a personal thing they would know - believe me.'

Their conversation is interrupted as Julian comes walking into the lounge and says, 'I've been everywhere; the woods, the parks and even the beach but there is no sign of her. I've put lots more posters up along the seafront just in case any holidaymakers may remember something.'

Louise is quick to reply. 'Oh, thanks Julian. You have been a rock.'

Terry backs that up by saying, 'yeah, thanks a lot, Julian. I just don't know where to look next? I keep thinking it is my fault.'

Julian responds immediately. 'Of course it's not your fault. I reckon it's that Parker character. If I could get five minutes with him...'

'Five minutes? Give me two and I'd have him wishing he hadn't been born.' Terry stands up and pats Julian on the shoulder in an act of appreciation for all the support he has given them both but it looked a little strange. The type of affection normally shown by somebody who is going to be going away for some time or even forever?

Terry leaves the lounge and goes to his bedroom. He then opens the safe, gets out the loaded gun and places it inside his pocket. It would appear Terry has made a decision and it is not a good one as there is a loaded gun involved. He takes a long look into the mirror and is thinking how hard he has worked to get out of all those old racketeering days but now he feels he has no choice. Who would not do anything to get their daughter back? He is now looking a little brighter now he has a plan of action and has no thoughts for himself regarding how things may play out at the end. His only priority is to get his daughter back home safely and dish out his idea of punishment to whom has been responsible for this abhorrent crime. He gets a call on his mobile, it's DSU Bobby Derby.

'Hello, Terry. We found him. He's holed up in Sunborough. I'll txt you the address. I can sit on it for 6 hours but after that, I'll have to pass the info on. Be discreet and you didn't get it from me.'

'Thanks, Bob. I owe you one.' Terry hangs up the phone. He goes downstairs and into the lounge. 'I've got to pop out and see someone. I'll let you know how I get on.' He gives Louise a tight embrace and whispers. 'You're right. I will see him and get anything he knows out of him. Don't say nothing to the others.' He knows he cannot tell her about the phone call but now there is a glimmer of hope.

She is familiar with these veils of silence from many years ago and knows never to show any emotion when she is whispered any information. She nods in total agreement and they kiss. He turns and says, 'see you later, Julian and thanks again.' Julian nods over towards him and senses a change has occurred but he is not sure if it is positive or negative.

He gets into his car and speeds off. He is going to get to Sunborough within the detective's suggested timeframe of six hours. but in case he doesn't, he texts the address to Frankie Reynolds, as he has an arrangement with them and they probably have contacts nearer. He is desperate to get there first but knows it will be a three hour drive. Time is of the essence, every passing hour seems like a day to him. Of course, the police, the Reynolds gang and most of the general public who know about it already have Leo down as the arsonist who burned down the Sawmills in Becclesfield. He has much time to wrestle with his conscience and his anger will need to be controlled if he is to arrive without bringing any attention to himself with any erratic driving.

The time had come. The time Leo was dreading. He has run out of supplies and so has to chance going to the grocery store in the village. He has let his hair grow longer and tried to grow what resembles a moustache as well. He has been rehearsing the local dialect in order not to stand out on these occasions. He makes it to the till without the need to speak but a friendly lady asks him. 'Are you on 'oliday then?'

He cannot say he is local as they all know each other in the village. 'A little breaks I have been on.' He tries to imitate her voice.

She looks him up and down. Something is not right. 'You not from 'ere then?'

He just wishes to pay for his groceries and leave but he must engage in conversation or that will also look strange. He tries once more to speak like her. 'Not that far you. A few miles yonder.' He quickly pays for his items and rushes out of the shop. He is sweating and nervous. He hopes he managed not raise any suspicions. He need not to have worried for waiting by his car were two 6'6" men with shoulders to match. They are looking straight at him and he knows they are not police.

'Can I help you gentleman,' he says looking as nervous as he sounded.

'Yes you can Leo. You've given us a right run for our money haven't you? Now we can do this the hard way or the really hard way.' One of them says to him as they grab him and frogmarch him off to an awaiting large grey van with its engine running. They throw him in the back and they get into the front. He is laying in the dark but feels the presence of at least one other person in there as the van moves off.

'Hello, Leo.' A voice in the darkness is heard and he is next to him.

'Who are you? What do you want with me?'

'I'm going to ask yer a few questions and so long as yer answer them correctly you have nothing to fear. Get me?' He has an accent from somewhere south but he cannot place it at this moment.

'Okay but I didn't do it.' He pleads.

'Where is she? What have yer done with her?' He has a very creepy tone to his voice.

'Who?' Leo suddenly feels something hard hit him in the lower abdomen. He thinks it looks like the shape of a baseball bat. He is in instant pain.

'Where's, Emily? Come on you can tell me. We just want to know so we don't have to keep looking for her.'

'Emily's missing?' Suddenly a rush of adrenalin makes him try to strike his assailant in the face but he misses in the dark. He gets another pain in his stomach. He has been hit again.

'You're lucky the last one to do that is six feet under. Now for the last time where is Emily?'

'I don't know. I love her. Your guys told me to leave town so I did. Why have you suddenly changed your mind?' He is panicking and in great pain. He can see no way out of this.

'Nice try. Now what have yer done with her?' It is sounding like his assailant is getting extremely inpatient with him.

'Let me search for her with you. I want to find her. I didn't even know she went missing. Have you tried the stables? All of a sudden he feels another pair of hands grab his right hand. There are two of them in the back of this darkened van. Suddenly he screams out in agony as he feels his right for finger snap.

'Stop whingeing you've got lots of others... for now that is. Now where is Emily?'

He is in agony but knows he has to answer immediately or something else nasty will come his way. 'I honestly don't know. I want to find her now I know she is missing.'

Then a lighted flame appears from nowhere. One of them has flicked a cigarette lighter open and now he sees the outline of the two assailants for the first time.

'You see this flask I'm holding? Do yer know what's inside? Now where is she?'

'I don't know.' He sits back and closes his eyes expecting the worse but then the van swerves at speed and comes to a sudden halt. The double back doors swing open. One of the men from outside the store is standing in front of them all.

He says, 'we have to be going. They've got the reg. That old woman called the cops. Get the stuff out of the box. We'll take him down that alleyway there.' He points to a gap in-between two derelict shops.

They drag him down the alleyway. One of them gives him a kick in the stomach as some sort of passing shot. They grab one of his arms and roll up the sleeve. Then a tight tourniquet is tightened around the top of his arm. They get an injection out of the box and pump it into his veins. He groans but almost instantly feels no further pain from his wounds.

One of them slaps him gently around the face. 'Now Leo, tell us where she is. You only have hours left to live so you might as well tell us.'

He utters something incoherently but it sounds like "I love you". He feels another kick but this time it is in the groin area.

'He doesn't know anything, Lenny! Butch is not going to be happy with us.'

Lenny looks him in the eyes quite menacingly and says, 'don't worry about, Butch. This sends a message to him as well. He owes and this'll remind him of what's coming if he don't pay up.' They then get into an awaiting black BMW and speed off leaving Leo in a state of heroin overdose. They know at best he will have many problems with his mental thinking in many ways for years to come but at worse he will not survive the night.

As Terry Banks is driving he receives a call on his mobile. He puts it on hands free as there is no one else in the car with him.

'Hi, Butch, it's me. We caught up with him. He's been taken to Sunborough General. Probably intensive care, I would say.' The caller sounds a little hesitant.

'Intensive care? How did that happen?' He is really annoyed and thinks they went too far in getting the information but before the caller has time to respond, Terry says, 'he didn't say where she was then?'

'He don't know, mate. No one could've held out from Lenny.' Suddenly Terry goes a little quiet and after a short pause. 'I didn't know Lenny was personally supervising things. Can you tell him how grateful I am and I'll be in touch.' He quickly hangs up. The problem he has now; Leo is bound to have a police guard if he survives that is. Either way, Terry is likely never to be able to gauge just what Leo knows now this has happened to him. He has his gun on his person and if he gets pulled over by the police they could discover it. He books into a hotel in Salisbury, overlooking Stonehenge. He needs time to rest and time to think his next move. For sure, if he survives, he will be taken back to Becclesfield for questioning and he may have a better chance of getting to him back there rather than in a place not that familiar to him. So after much thought he has decided to return to Becclesfield in the morning after resting up overnight. He is bitterly disappointed there have been no sightings of Emily and the one person who may be able to tell him where she is may not make it through the night.

Chapter 38

7th November

SOUTHERN GENERAL HOSPITAL, Sunborough, Intensive Care Unit. Leo Parker has been in a coma for 8 days now. Still he has a 24 hour police guard at the side of his bed. There is still no sign of Emily Banks and no other arrests have been made in connection with the arson attack on the Banks Sawmills as the police have the number one suspect laying in a hospital bed.

PC Walker, a 24 year old woman, has been sitting patiently beside his bed for the past five hours. She has been sent down from Becclesfield to take some relief off the local constabulary. She has been doing a crossword puzzle to pass the time when all of sudden she is startled by the sounds of several alarms going off from some of the VDU screens up against the wall above Leo Parkers head. He is moving slowly and making a gurgling sound. She rushes out and is already joined by two nurses. 'He's coming around! Call doctor Stevens!' The other nurse rushes out of the room.

'He's made it then?' Walker asks as she stands and straightens her legs.

'Looks likely now but we need to get these tubes out and sit him up.' She is taking out the tubes and turns off the alarms. 'Come on Leo. Can you hear me?' There is little response coming from him at this moment, it appears he is finding it hard to breathe.

At this point a doctor rushes in. 'Great. Hello, Leo. You're in hospital can you remember?'

Leo is unable to react. He looks incoherent and dazed.

'This is to be expected. Just keep trying to talk to him. Keep him sitting up.' The nurses nod their heads in an adorable fashion. 'He looks to have pulled through. Does he have any family?'

One of the nurses looks up his notes. 'He doesn't have anyone listed to call.'

261

Walker butts in. 'He's on bail for arson in Becclesfield and is a suspect in a missing woman case. He doesn't have anyone as far as I can recall but I'll get in touch with DI Daniels he is heading here and should be here some time tonight.' She puts her book away and is preparing herself for when he awakens properly. She will have a few hours to wait for that to actually happen though. She sits back down and for some reason begins to recall her childhood days spent growing up in Nottingham. A time full of complications; parents divorcing, moving down to Becclesfield with her mother and two brothers. She remembers the reason why she joined the police, her elder brother addicted to drugs and found dead in an alleyway. It is this that spurs her on each and every day. She vowed to her mother that she would make a difference when she puts the uniform on. She looks at the sad figure lying on the bed and see her brother's face for that was exactly where she had seen him last. Her thoughts are interrupted as DI Daniels walks into the room.

'Don't get up,' he jokes with a grin on his face. 'How's it been, Zara? Not easy sitting around these lowlifes is it?'

She does take offence but is pleased her superior has referred to her by her first name and she knows he is unaware of her past, so just says, 'well, someone has to do it.'

'Has he said anything yet?' He asks looking at his notes at the end of the bed as if he really knows what they mean.

'Not yet, sir. He grunted and looked as though he was choking to death when they removed the tubes but he's gone off again. The doctor says he is likely to pull through but probably unable to talk for several hours, if not longer.' She walks over to the window overlooking a busy ring road outside. 'How long did it take you to drive here, sir?'

'Bloody three hours, twenty minutes and then another twenty minutes to get a parking spot but at least I didn't have to do the driving.' He laughs as he recalls the looks upon George's face at all the traffic jams they occurred on the way.

'Who was the driver?' She smiles.

'George Freeman. Do you know him?' He drags another seat over to the side of the bed.

Know him? He is the twinkle in her eye. She met George on her first day at Becclesfield Police station. She remembers how kind he was taking her under his wing for the first six weeks or so. 'Oh, yes, I think I do. Is he the guy with the short brown hair, 6'2" tall and of slender build, sir?' She is trying to impress him with her eye for a detailed description.

'Wow, Walker. You haven't been seeing each other on the quiet have you?' He jokes.

How she wishes that were true but alas the 27 year old is married with a child. She tries her best not to blush but has failed miserably. 'Of course not. He's married isn't he?'

'You could say that. I've told him to rest up for the evening as he's got the nightshift. We're in the Red Lion. Where are you staying?'

'Same. How long will we have to wait for him to come around, sir?' She tries to change the subject and has succeeded but she also wished to hide the fact she is pleased George is staying in the same hotel.

'As long as it takes, Walker. That's the downside to this job. No, I mean that's one of them there are so many and they are increasing by the week.' He looks quite a bit disgruntled and a little disillusioned by the continued changes in detective processes.

'We could be in for a long night then? Shall I go down to the canteen area and get a couple of coffees?' She stands and slowly walks towards the door. She has the need for some fresh air outside and considers this a good way of getting it.

He looks quite pleased by the kind offer and says, 'yes please. That's a good idea. Don't forget to put it all down on expenses.'

It takes over three more hours for Leo Parker to come around and be lucid. 'Where am I? Who are you?' He's utterly confused.

'We're your protection. I am DI Daniels and this is PC Walker. We're from Becclesfield Police station. We need to ask you a few questions.' He is standing now and looking down upon him laying in the bed. 'Do you remember how you ended up in this state?'

It takes a long while for the response. 'I'm in hospital and I can't feel my right hand. What's happened?'

'That's why we are here, amongst other things. Don't worry about your hand it is already on the mend. You had a broken finger or two. How did that happen?' Walker is taking notes and listens intently for his response.

'Where am I?' He still looks panic stricken.

'In a Sunborough hospital recovering from a drugs overdose.'

'Overdose? You must have your facts wrong detective? I've never ever taken a single drug in my life.' He attempts to sit up further but hurts his right hand in the process. 'Are you here to arrest me for drugs or something?'

Daniels looks at Walker and then back at Leo. 'What were you doing in Sunborough?'

'I remember camping for some reason. Then there was a shop. Can't recall anything after that.' He nearly drifts off to sleep.

'Don't go off again. We need to know how you got yourself in this state. If you say you didn't do it then someone must have pumped your veins full of the stuff. You're lucky to be alive.' Daniels says, getting himself a little frustrated.

'Tranby... I went to Tranby. Why?' He is finding it extremely difficult to focus his thoughts and a doctor has been studying him throughout this line of questioning.

'He's had enough for the time being. Please rest now Leo. You will get stronger each day and your memory may return but it is going to be a very long process.' The doctor shows the police outside the room. 'Come back tomorrow morning. I'm sure he'll be feeling a lot better. You have to remember the shock to his system and we don't know for sure just what brain damage has occurred.'

The police officers leave the hospital and head to the Red Lion. Sitting up at the bar is George Freeman and he has had a few drinks already by the looks of things. 'You can't beat expenses, sir? Oh, Zara, hi!'

She is pleased to see him as well. 'Hi, George.'

'You getting them in then George, Pint of Guinness for me and what do you want, Zara?' He says as he takes a look around the bar area.

'I'll have a vodka and coke please, sir.' She says, 'but I'd better get changed first otherwise everyone will think I am drinking whilst on duty.'

'Call me Ray as we are off duty. Good idea, Zara, that's all we need is some reporter to get hold of us. Especially as we have got a constable from Sunborough doing the night shift for us at the hospital.' He grins and sits down at a corner table. They will all spend the night drinking heavily and discussing Leo Parker, the fire at the Mills and the missing Emily Banks investigation but there will be no solutions arrived at except for questioning their number one suspect in the morning at his bedside.

It is eleven o'clock and DI Daniels together with PC Freeman are waiting patiently outside the room for the doctor to come out and see them. The doctor has been speaking with Leo and reassuring him things will be okay as long as he does what the medical teams tell him to do.

The two detectives have been given fifteen minutes to interview him. DI Daniels is first to speak. 'Good morning, Leo. I have to say you look a lot better today.'

Leo just nods to conserve energy for when the questioning commences and he did not have to wait long.

'Leo, who did this to you?' Daniels is standing over him and Freeman is busy scribbling the notes down.

'I didn't do it to myself. I've never taken drugs. All I remember is hitting the concrete floor. Prior to that my mind is a blank.'

'What about the fire at the Banks Sawmills. Do you remember starting that?'

'I never started anything. Has there been a fire?' Leo looks utterly confused.

'What do you remember about Emily Banks? You know... the presents?'

'Emily. Is she coming to visit me?'

'Hardly. What did you do to Emily?' Daniels is now looking a little impatient with the time it is taking Leo to answer these basic questions as the doctor looks on.

'Emily? I love her. Why isn't she coming to visit me - is it her father?'

'Okay, when did you last see her?'

'Yesterday in Tranby.'

'That's impossible, Leo. You've been in here for 8 days. So what have you done with her? If she's still alive somewhere we need to get to her quickly.'

'She's missing 8 days? it feels like hours to me. What's going on?' He looks even more confused than he did before.

The doctor intervenes and calls a halt to proceedings as he can see his patient beginning to hyperventilate and has to deal with that immediately. The two detectives leave the hospital looking rather dejected and return to The Red Lion for the rest of the day to consider their next moves. So long as Leo makes it to another day, they will have another chance to interview him at his bedside in the morning. The one thing all three officers could not fathom is how someone got to him before they did?

Chapter 39

LEO PARKER HAS recovered enough to be taken back to Becclesfield Police Station for further questioning and is being held on remand for the arson attack at Banks Sawmills. He is the number one suspect in the Emily Banks disappearance and it has been two weeks now since she has last been seen. DCI Long is leading the investigation in both cases and is seated in interview room 7b along with DI Daniels. Leo Parker and his solicitor, Mr. Dwight Patterson walk in and take their seats shortly afterwards. The following is a transcript of the interview.

Transcript of interview with Leo Parker. Representative. Dwight Patterson (Chesterston and Co.) 51123999430 case number. 0207 660 1070 DCI Long, DI Daniels. 15th November @ 1115 hours.

P Is there anything you need before we start?

LP No thank you.

P Can you tell us where you were on the 21st October?

LP I was at home relaxing.

P Did you go out anywhere?

LP I went to Tranby.

P What for?

LP Going away.

P Why were you going away when you were not allowed to do so?

LP It doesn't matter. You've all made up your minds.

P This is your chance to tell us your side of the story.

LP You won't believe me anyway but here goes. I had a visitor. I don't know his name but he was a big guy. Anyhow, Terry Banks sent him.

P How do you know that? Where is the proof?

LP See, I told you - what's the point?

P Okay, let's assume this is correct what happens next?

LP He tells me I have to skip town as they are coming for me - he was right.

P Who was coming for you, Leo?

LP Terry's boys, I think? Anyway, I bought my camping gear and got away as far as possible.

P Sunborough?

LP Yes.

P Did you meet up with Emily first?

LP No. I couldn't even ring her. He took my mobile as well.

P What was his name? The guy who gave you the advice to leave town?

LP I told you. He didn't leave his calling card. He gave me the money you found on me. About a grand.

P You sure it's not drug money, Leo?

LP I don't take drugs and I certainly don't deal in them.

P So how did you end up in hospital then?

LP They must've injected me with the stuff. They gave me a bit of a beating.

P Who gave you the beating?

LP Don't know but they were big. About four of them in total. The last thing I remember is my finger being broken and then I felt the cold concrete hit me as they threw me to the ground.

P Who are they, Leo?

LP No idea? Ask Banks.

P Where is Emily?

LP Wish I knew. I want to see her before her father fills her head with a load of nonsense about that fire.

P So when was the last time you saw Emily?

LP Sunday. Can't remember the date but middle of October would be a good guess.

P When did you last talk with Emily?

LP After the fire she called me. She was pretending to call one of the employees to notify them about the fire.

P What did you discuss?

LP We arranged to meet up at the stables on the following Sunday.

P That would be 21st October, agreed?

LP Yes. It was a day I'll never forget. That was the day when that heavy from Banks came and visited me telling me to get out of town and I did.

P It's also the date when Emily Banks was last seen by anyone.

LP She's been missing all of this time? Why haven't you found her?

P We are trying our best but you see how this is beginning to look, Leo? The arson attack at the Banks Sawmills and now his daughter, who you were obsessed with, has disappeared on the same day you went on the run. See how it looks? This is your chance to help us find Emily. Where do you think she has gone?

LP I didn't do the fire and I wouldn't do anything to hurt the girl - we're in love with each other and so if that means I'm obsessed, then you're right I am obsessed. The only place I know of is the stables - have you checked that area?

P Yes it was one the first places we checked. Is there anywhere else?

LP Tranby.

P Tranby? Can you be more specific?

LP We stayed at the White Hart Hotel. You can check with them. See it was a real relationship not an obsession or some silly crush.

P Why did you take two big cans of petrol to the Sawmills on Sunday, 14th October?

LP I've told you before... Banks asked me to bring it there. He had run out of petrol and he didn't want the people over the golf course to know he had done something silly like that.

P He denies having made a phone call to you and denies asking you to take the petrol to the Mills at any time.

LP There you go. If you want to find the real arsonist it is him.

P You can prove he called you that day. Just hand over your mobile phone and we'll confirm your story or not.

LP I told you that heavy guy took it from me. Can't you see I've been framed by Banks. Probably an insurance job?

P He is not going to kidnap his own daughter is he?

LP Has there been a ransom note?

P Can't tell you that information. Now your last chance to get this off your chest and do the right thing by the Banks' family - where is she, Leo?

LP I don't know? Let me out and I'll help in the search.

P Where would you start your search?

LP Stables then Tranby.

P Is there something special about Tranby?

LP Yes there is. We go there a lot together.

P If there is something secretive you are holding back, now would be a good time to tell us.

LP Nothing. She is here with me now. I can feel her.

P What do you mean she is here now?

LP Her spirit is always with me. She's the one who pulled me through after that drug overdose.

P You say spirit? Is she dead, Leo?

LP Don't say that. She must be alive. Perhaps, she's had enough of her controlling father?

P So you don't know where she is?

LP That's what I've been telling you since I woke up. I love her and miss her already. You must find her.

P Okay. We'll leave it at that then.

LP Can I go now?

P You are being held on remand pending further inquiries. Interview ended 1215 hours.

Miley and Julian are undressing in the bedroom getting ready for bed. She glances over as he removes his shirt. 'Where's that golden locket I gave you for your wedding present? Why are you not wearing it?'

He touches his chest and for the first time in weeks he remembers he has not been wearing it. 'I probably put it down when I had a shower?' He struggles with a suitable response.

'Well, go and look for it. You know how much I love the photo of us inside of it?' She looks bitterly disappointed he has not taken greater care of such a cherished item.

Within the time it has taken him to think up an excuse, he comes back into the room. 'I think I know where I dropped it. It must have been when I helped push that lady's car in Denbar Lane?'

'Perhaps someone handed it in to the police?' She says looking very concerned.

'No, we don't need to involve the police. I'll go and look for it tomorrow when it gets light. If I am unable to trace it then I'll have to go and buy another one. I can easily put our picture back inside.' He leans over to hug her but it is rebuffed.

'I'm so disappointed, Julian, that was so special and you have gone and lost it already.'

'I'll make it up to you, I promise.' He says as Miley switches the lamp off and turns her back to him in protest.

Chapter 40

IT HAS BEEN over three months since the fire at the Banks Sawmills and almost three months since Emily Banks had gone missing. Leo Parker has been charged with arson but charges on suspicion of murdering Emily Banks have been dropped due to a lack of evidence. He still remains the person of interest in the ongoing case but no fresh evidence or clues have been discovered in all of this time. Much criticism of the police at Becclesfield Police Station has resulted in an internal investigation and the whole force is under review. Terry Banks' former association with the Reynolds brothers in London is now the subject of much speculation as a direct result of this. The insurance company has not paid out on the policy, they are carrying out their own intense investigation. Terry Banks health has begun to deteriorate and he is showing signs of mental illness. He has the Reynolds brothers on his back demanding their money he owes them as well as a dozen creditors trying to get their money from him. His marriage is now looking to be in a bad place. His daughter Miley is inconsolable and having treatment for nervous exhaustion. She is too ill to attend the trial, so Julian agrees to testify in her place with the knowledge he has about the fire at the Mills.

Terry Banks knows time is running out. He needs money and fast. He has sold off some cars and some jewellery, which is probably the reason his marriage is beginning to fail but there is another big reason, which he knows nothing about; she has been having an affair with her best friend's husband for several months.

Terry rings an old friend, Charlie O'sullivan. 'Hello, Charlie is that you?'

'Hello, Tel, how's things going? I heard about the fire and your daughter - any news?'

'No, she's still missing and the bloody insurance company appear to be taking forever to pay out.' He tries to hold it all together but his emotional thoughts are making things really hard for him.

'They're quick enough to take the money though.' Charlie is quick to support his old friend.

'Charlie, I wouldn't ask, mate but I'm in a bit of a corner at the moment until the insurance comes through.' He tries to cover up the desperation in his voice.

'I bet. Do you need a bit to get you over this bad spell?'

'Thanks, Charlie, I knew I could depend on you.'

'What do you need? A few hundred or more?' Charlie is a little hesitant but sounds willing enough.

'I need a lot more if you can stretch that far... about five grand would do it.' He closes his eyes as if to pray for a positive answer.

'Five grand! I don't have that much, Tel. I can probably commit about a grand but it'll take a couple of days to get to it, if you know what I mean. My money's all tied up. You know how it is?' He is sympathetic but has to be realistic at the same time.

'Okay, that's fine mate, thanks. That helps a great deal. Should keep some of them off my back until the insurance comes through. Shall I come over to you?'

'Yeah, pop over tomorrow. I'll have it for you then.'

'Thanks, Charlie. I'll pay you a bonus on top of what I owe when my money comes through.' He hangs up and then considers just how the Reynolds brothers are going to react to such a small payment off the £15,000 he owes them.

He has arranged to give over £9,000 to one of the Reynolds's couriers but he has been warned once again what will happen to him or any of his family members if the balance is not received in a week and to make matters worse they have added another £3000 as interest on the outstanding amount owed to them. He has no other cash or means to get a further £9000 in a week's time. His house is still under mortgage and it is expensive each month. On top of all this, he will have to attend the Leo Parker trial commencing on Monday as a witness and has been warned what will happen if the names of the Reynolds brothers comes up at the trial at any stage. He knows the defence team will touch on it at some point and there is nothing he can do to stop it now. His world is crumbling apart and he is fully aware of how desperate the future looks.

The trial is coming towards its closure and he receives copies of the counsels' summing up. He reads through them very carefully. He knows one insinuation or hint of the Reynolds brothers involvement will mean further aggravation from them.

Prosecution Summary

MEMBERS OF THE jury. You have heard how Joe Watkins, the attendant at the garage, said without any doubts he served the defendant with two cans of petrol. This was supported by the CCTV footage. The defendant admits he did purchase them from that garage and at the time stated. The defendant also admits to taking it to the Banks Sawmills and taking it inside the premises. Once again this is witnessed by the entry CCTV system. The defendant said he left the premises immediately after dropping off the petrol but the CCTV shows a different story. It was 12 minutes before he left the premises and sped off in his car. Enough time to set the fire. Footage shows smoke bellowing out from the premises within 18 minutes of when he entered the building. Then we heard the ridiculous claims made by the defendant. He says he bought the petrol for his boss, Mr. Terry Banks because he had ran out of petrol. He then said Mr. Banks was embarrassed and so told him to drop it off on the first floor of the building and he would come through a gap on the golf course to collect it later. Yet, Mr. Banks was seen driving his car away from the golf course in the direction of the Sawmills and a police officer testified that when he spoke with Mr. Banks, his car engine was still running and he saw Mr. Banks turn his car around, driving off in the direction of his home. The police officer also testified to say he thought Mr. Banks was mortified to hear about the fire at his factory. We heard from Mr. Banks himself, who emotionally explained just what losing his business has meant to him and his family. He also expressed deep sorrow in having to lay off over 100 employees. That is 100 people out of work.

We then heard an account from the defendant who claimed Mr. Banks had set him up because he had found out about a secret relationship with his youngest daughter, Emily Banks. This claim was rejected by Mr. Banks and Julian Sanderson in their testimonies. Mr Sanderson told the court how Emily had confided in him about how obsessive the defendant had become. How he showered her with gifts; flowers and chocolates not to mention a handbag with stockings inside. Mr. Sanderson also told the court how Emily was going to give the gifts back and that she had no feelings for the defendant whatsoever. Emily was on the verge of telling her father.

Mr. Banks also denied knowing anything about this obsession and actually gave him extra work at his home during weekends. Obviously, this would be the last thing any father would do if they knew their youngest daughter of 17 years of age had an unhealthy obsession, such as the defendant. Then we heard the strangest of stories from the defendant trying to insinuate Mr. Banks had connections with some gang from London - how ridiculous is that? He then goes on to suggest a mysterious giant angel came to ...'

'Sorry your honour. I'll rephrase. The defendant then told the court a giant of a man had attended his flat on the 21st October, a week after the fire, to tell him to get out of town. This kind hearted man, which the defendant said was sent from Mr. Banks, then gives him a thousand pounds to help him on the way. So the defendant skips bail and goes into Tranby buys camping equipment and groceries before driving the three hours or so it takes to get to Sunborough. Once in Sunborough, somehow Mr. Banks has found out and once again sends some men to question him about his missing daughter, Emily Banks, the person the defendant claims he was having a secret relationship with. The facts we do know; he ended up in hospital with a heroin overdose with some other injuries, he was technically on the run having broken his bail conditions for this arson crime.

He bought the petrol, he transported the petrol, he entered the building with the petrol and he came out without the petrol.

Minutes later the Sawmills was ablaze. Police have no other evidence, clues or suspects for this arson attack other than those brought before you here in this court and the only suspect is the defendant. Mr. Banks gave the defendant a job and he trusted him with his family by engaging his services around his home. He showed nothing other than kindness and what did he get in return? He has lost his entire business amongst other things...'

'Sorry your honour. He has lost all of his business and has currently had to sell much of the family's personal effects; cars, jewellery and all of his personal investments. Members of the jury, there is no other person guilty of arson other than the defendant standing before you. I rest my case.'

Defence Summary

MEMBERS OF THE jury, we have heard the prosecution emphasising the word "fact". Here are some facts, just in case they have somehow been missed. FACT; The defendant was beaten in Sunborough. FACT; He did have a heroin overdose. FACT; He did nearly die and spend those 8 days in a coma. What we do not know is just how that all happened but there must have been a really important reason for it to have happened. Another fact is Leo Parker knew no one in Sunborough and was just camping there. He told no one where he was going.

Let's take the prosecution's claim that the defendant had an unhealthy obsession with Emily Banks. They appear to have ignored the evidence given before this court of Charlotte Kemp. She stated on record that her close friend Emily and the defendant were not just friends but lovers. She stated that Emily confided in her and told her just how much she loved the defendant. How Emily had told her father she was staying at Charlotte's home when in fact she was staying overnight with the defendant in a hotel in Tranby. She also stated that Emily was afraid her father may be tracking her mobile phone and so she left it overnight at Charlotte's. They were lovers of that there can be no doubts. No obsessions just honest love for each other.

The defendant's life was beginning to really improve; he had a job, a car, an apartment and a love of his life, Emily. The police confirmed he had no previous related criminal charges. No drugs dealing or taking. No health problems. He was in love. So this drug overdose does not make any logical sense to have been done in some kind of suicide attempt as the prosecution would have you believe. Quite far from it. He was in love.

Here is another fact. We showed you copies of the financial situation Mr. Banks and his Sawmills were in at the time of the fire. The special financial witness brought before the court stated the business was sure to fail and pretty soon. There were too many creditors owed money and not enough orders to even pay half of them. Mr Banks argued that point by telling the court he had pulled the company out of this kind of mess before and he would have done it again. Asked how and he refused to give us his business plan on just how he was going to do it.

The prosecution argued there was no evidence to suggest underworld criminal activity in all of this case. I do not recall ever seeing in a court of law, a calling card from any underworld associations. What happened in Sunborough? How did four men turn up at the grocery store and then frogmarch the defendant into a waiting van? How did they know it was Leo Parker? How did they know where to find him? So many unanswered questions. But they do however, raise arguments supporting the involvement of criminal associates.

The police found over £800 tucked into a money belt. This was still there whilst he laid in his hospital bed. So you can see the attack was not even money orientated. He certainly had not been long enough in Sunborough to make such nasty enemies. So why did they attack and try to kill him?

The defendant told us that a big man called at his home on Sunday, 21st October with a brown envelope with a thousand pounds inside. Why the prosecution do not believe this is...'

'Yes your honour. The defendant's own financial records were shown to the court and we could see there was no way he could have accumulated such an amount in the short time he had gained regular employment. Too many gaps in the evidence. Once again if the man who visited the defendant's home was acting for another party, he is not going to leave any traces of his identity behind. He took the defendants phone and told him to get out of town...'

'Yes your honour. The defendant stated the man took his phone and told him to leave town immediately.

He admits to buying the petrol. He admits to taking it inside the Sawmills but he does not admit to setting fire to Sawmills. If he did it, then he would have to go all around the offices then downstairs to the wood yard and even the canteen had traces of petrol. So the fire was started in at least four perhaps even five places. I seriously doubt if the defendant could do all that in the time it took him to enter and leave the building. Upstairs and downstairs. That would probably take a lot longer than 12 minutes. Up and down the stairs alone probably 6 minutes and out to the yard. Just cannot be done in that time...

'Yes your honour. I doubt if it could all be done in 12 minutes. We contend that there was a second person already within the premises just awaiting the arrival of the petrol. The defendant has been framed, all the evidence proves it and the missing pieces also point in the defendants favour. I trust you the jury will do the right thing and find the defendant, Leo Parker, not guilty. I rest my case.

Chapter 41

TERRY BANKS IS sitting in his lounge watching TV awaiting the verdict on the Leo Parker arson trial and is interrupted by the sound of something being posted through his letterbox. He gets up and goes to see what it is. It is an official looking letter and he has seen plenty of them recently. Though this one has come from the insurance company. He assumes it is the cheque to settle his claim for the Sawmills but he is wrong. As he reads the letter his face turns from happiness to sadness within a few moments for there is no cheque inside the envelope. He reads the letter and it is the worst possible news he could have imagined. The insurers have instigated an immediate and thorough investigation into the arson attack following certain revelations in court. This will mean a further delay at best but worst case scenario could be a refusal to pay the claim. His immediate thoughts turn to the Reynolds and their recent threats. Then he considers just what this bad news may entail for his family members. He assumes if a guilty verdict is returned the insurance company will have no choice other than to pay out.

It takes the jury three days to reach a guilty verdict and Leo Parker is sentenced to seven years in prison. The first piece of good news he had received for some time but then he receives a phone call and he knows just who it is from. He slowly picks up his mobile and answers. 'Hi Frankie. Did you hear the news?' Deep down he knows this is not the reason for the call.

'You've let us down again, Butch. The locals have been sniffing around here since that hearing. Lenny is well unhappy.' There is a very sinister sound to his tone.

'It'll blow over, Frankie. We've had all this before, remember?' He is struggling to keep the conversation upbeat.

'That may be but where's our money? We've got all the heat for this and you're sitting on a small fortune. Lenny says the price has gone up by another £20,000. That's on top of the £9,000, so let's round it up to £30,000. When are yer getting this money from the insurance, Butch? Only it's been a long time coming.'

He tries not to sound hesitant but is really concerned about the extra money being added on and he has seen this a hundred times happening to other poor souls in the past. 'Oh, you know what they are like? They were waiting for the verdict, that's all. I'm sure it'll come very soon.'

'It had better be soon, Butch. Lenny is getting impatient and the only reason he hasn't taken any action so far is because of your missing girl but his patience, as yer know, is very limited.'

'You don't know where she is do you, Frankie?' He sounds extremely desperate at this point.

'What do yer take us for? She's just a kid! Whilst on the subject, Lenny says to tell yer he asked after your trouble and strife. What's her name... Louise isn't it? Has she got life insurance, Terry?' This sounds very threatening and to make matters worse, he ends the call without allowing Terry to make any further comments. He had expected it and had witnessed it before when other unfortunate souls were in this type of predicament.

He is now fearful for his wife's safety as he knows the Reynolds do not make idle threats. His thoughts are now consumed with how to improve upon Louise's safety. He knows he cannot tell her anything but needs to make some alterations and quickly.

He phones the insurance company and speaks with the lead investigator in their case. After much conversation he asks the crunch question. 'So when can I expect to receive my money?' He deliberately emphasised "my money".

'If we find everything to be satisfactory then it could be paid out immediately after that.' The voice sounds somewhat regimental and it is all a question of doing things by the book it would appear.

'So when will the investigation finish?' The obvious next question has been asked.

'It could take weeks, it could take months and I have known certain cases to go on for years.' Not an ounce of sympathy shown towards Terry.

'Years! You will hear from my solicitors!' He slams down the phone and curses aloud. So loud Louise comes running down the stairs.

'What the hell, Tel?' She says.

'Sorry, but that bloody insurance company is not playing ball. They say despite the guilty verdict proving it was an arson attack they are still investigating and it could actually take years in some cases to payout.' He is immediately hugged by her and they then sit down on a couch. 'I don't know what to do? The Reynolds want their money for their... so called work in hunting down Parker. The mortgage needs paying soon or we'll lose the house.'

'What? Lose the house? That's not fair. Get in touch with Reginald Bartram. He'll sort the bastards out!' She has temporarily regained her fighting spirit, which is so adored by Terry.

'I know he is a friend of ours but it still costs more money but perhaps I'll go and see him for some advice. He probably won't even charge for that?' He gets up from the couch and grabs his car keys. 'I'll go see him now. Don't worry yourself, I'll find a way. I always do. Where you off to today?'

She hesitates and then says, 'well, I was going to go to Tranby to have coffee with Tara but as we are in so deep... perhaps, I'd better not.'

'Please go. Don't let any of this affect your daily arrangements. Besides, I think we can still stretch to a couple of cups of coffee?' He laughs as he leaves the room.

Two weeks later and Terry is still in the same predicament as he has been in for some time. He has rang the insurance company on daily basis but has been getting the same answer; "the investigation is still ongoing".

It is three o'clock on a Tuesday afternoon when he receives the call he had been dreading for some time. He knows he is running out of time but far more worrying, he has run out of excuses to give to the Reynolds. His mobile phone rings a number of times and he has ignored it for the past three days now but knows it is time he faced the music. 'Hello, Frankie. I...' He is interrupted.

'Not Frankie, Butch. It's Lenny here. What's going on?'

His face changes to one of extreme fear. 'Oh... Hi Lenny, how's things down there in London?'

'Where's my money? I don't want any of yer fobbing off neither.'

He knows if he hesitates he will pick up on it but this looks like the time to come clean. 'I've been having trouble with the insurance company. They've started an investigation and are dragging their heels. There's nothing else I can do, Lenny. You know me, this is the last thing I would ever dream of doing to my old friends?'

'Don't give me that old flannel. I tell yer now - times up!' Then silence from the other end of the phone as the call is abruptly ended by Lenny. There is a moment of silence too in Terry's lounge as he realises it is going to get much worse from now on.

Knowing his wife is in danger, he calls her mobile but it goes straight through to voicemail. He decides to drive the 40 miles to Tranby in order to make sure she is safe. She will be the Reynolds main target now. Terry has calculated they will get to his wife and get their money afterwards from her life insurance. He is desperate and at his wits end. He goes to his bedroom and opens the safe. He stares inside for a few moments before reaching inside and picking up the loaded gun once more. He tucks it into his pocket and leaves the house in a hurry. He has to act fast. The sweat is running down his forehead and he is becoming more anxious by the minute. He drives off to Tranby.

It takes him forty five minutes to arrive in the town centre. He is looking for a car parking space when he sees Louise coming out of the White Hart Hotel. He wonders what she has been doing visiting the hotel. He decides to sit and observe her for a while longer. Then he sees Ray Shaw coming out shortly afterwards. They kiss and hug in a way lovers do when they leave each other's side. They then go their separate ways. It takes him just seconds to realise just what has been going on. He is frustrated with himself and feels extremely foolish. He curses himself and calls out aloud; 'Stupid! I should've known!' Now he is thinking back to all of those times from the past - how he never even gave those missing moments a thought. Those times when she arrived back late to the house. The times she drove all the way to Tranby and back. The new outfits and lingerie, some of which he has not even seen her wear. All this time and secrecy, all for Ray Shaw and to make matters even harder to bear, he loaned him several thousands of pounds when the Shaw's Investment Company got into financial troubles. He has his gun and his thoughts are consumed by taking his revenge but this will not sort out the bigger picture; the Reynolds, the creditors, the insurance company and his missing daughter, Emily. Enraged by what he has just witnessed, he revs up his car just as Shaw crosses the road, he accelerates and runs him over. He gets an instant rush of satisfaction that he has got some form of revenge and then his thoughts turn to his wife. He considers running over her lover will be more than enough punishment for her especially as he considers how bad the future is going to get for her. He has now to deal with the thoughts of the police catching up with him at some point for the crime he has now just committed. He continues to drive down Denbar Lane on his way back home. He suddenly pulls off onto a farmer's field. He finds a clasp of trees and parks up inside. Now he feels free to consider all of his problems and sees no way out whatsoever. He is pretty certain the Reynolds will have placed a tracker on his car just in case he attempts to flee at some point. So he knows deep down the clock is ticking. He cannot go home and there is no other place to lay low. He decides where he is should be a safer bet but how long can he remain hidden by the trees on a farmer's field?

Chapter 42

LOUISE HAS MADE it home and quickly rushes to the bedroom to get changed into more suitable clothes. Julian and Millie are still out putting posters around the town centre in Becclesfield. She is curious because she has noticed the picture of Terry's parents looking as though it has been moved. She takes a closer look and removes the portrait. She then discovers the secret safe and it is open. She wonders if there has been a burglary and what the safe has been used for. It looks as though it has been there for years. She looks inside and discovers a mobile phone and a little red book. She flicks through the pages and sees the names of the Reynolds brothers, Flame King, Scar and many other former associates of Terry's. She turns the mobile phone on and sees it has been used recently but only unknown numbers are listed. As she is sitting on her bed wondering what Terry has been up to her mobile phone rings. She thinks it is Terry but then sees it is Tara Shaw.

'Hi, Tara, is everything okay?'

'No, Ray has been run over by a hit and run driver!' She pauses in order to gather in her emotions.

'Hit and run? Where was this?' Suddenly her thoughts are turning back to Terry and her secret affair with Ray. She knows Terry is more than capable of this sort of revenge, if he has somehow discovered their affair.

'He was in Tranby. What was he doing there, he told me he was in London?' Tara sounds confused and obviously upset.

'How is he?' This was the question she had been dreading but it had to be asked.

'He's in intensive care but may not make it through the night. I have been told to prepare myself for the worse.' She sobs loudly down the phone.

'I'll come. Where are you? Tranby General?' Louise asks as she stands up and rushes back to her walk-in wardrobe.

'Yes, please come. I need someone I trust to be with me at a moment like this.' She begins to sob once more.

Louise hates herself but says, 'of course. I'll be there within the hour.' Cheating on Terry was bad enough but on a friend she has known for nearly all of her life is unthinkable but she did do it. She quickly gets changed and rushes out to her car, starts up and races down her long winding driveway. As she looks at the double gates, she notices somebody loitering but does not have time to engage him. He is on the public footpath outside in any event but he looks too scruffy to be a detective or a journalist. She drives past him making sure he sees her staring at him as she drives by. Her mind is focused on Ray, Terry, Emily and now Tara. She needs plenty of courage to overcome breaking down when she meets up with Tara at the hospital. En route to Tranby she gets a call from Tara. 'He's gone, Lu!' She is sobbing uncontrollably.

So is Louise but for a number of different reasons. She finds it hard to reply but does manage something. 'Oh, I can't believe it. Do they know who done this?'

'Police are here with me now. They are investigating. I'm being driven home. I have to tell Alex... what do I tell him?'

'I'll divert to your house if you wish?' She offers her friendship for what it is worth.

'No, it's okay. I need to be with Alex. He is driving back from London to see me. I think he was having an affair with someone. He's been acting strange lately. I'll find out who it was and... will you help me, Lu?'

Louise is unable to respond until she controls her continual sobbing but it is in self pity at the realisation of just what the affair may have cost her friend, Tara. She eventually responds. 'Of course, but you need to focus on telling your son for the time being.'

'Thanks, Lu, I am so lucky to have you. I have to go now. Bye.' She closes the call down leaving Louise with her deep thoughts. There are many of them now. She takes a slow drive home. She has figured Terry has found out about her relationship with Ray Shaw and wonders just what else was in the safe before he opened it?

She makes it safely home and there is no sign of the man who had been loitering outside earlier in the day. Still she takes it very cautiously as she knows the temper Terry has and if he has found out he could be waiting for her to come home. She ponders the thought of her husband having carried out this crime and is fearful for her own safety. She sits in her car outside for a little while and phones Millie asking her to come home as soon as possible. She refuses to enter the house until Julian and Millie go in to check first. The area is deemed safe. Now there is more drama in the house as Louise tells Millie the news of Ray Shaw.

Millie responds immediately in shock. 'Dead? I can't believe it... how's Tara and Alex?'

'What do you think? I can't believe it. Who would do such a bad thing? He was in his prime and ...' Louise breaks down in tears as Millie comforts her.

'Where's father? Shouldn't he be here by now?' Millie asks as she looks over to Julian who is now standing in the doorway wondering what on earth has been going on.

'Is it... Emily?' He asks rather nervously.

Millie responds. 'No, it's mother's best friend's husband, Ray Shaw... he's been... hit and run. He's dead!'

'What! ... Where did this happen?' He is not sure why he is asking the questions but feels he needs to.

'Where did it happen?' She asks her mother.

'Tranby.' She replies.

'I was looking for Emily in the town centre area only yesterday.' Julian comments. 'Where's your father? He needs to be here.'

Louise is quick to respond. 'I haven't heard from him for several hours. He is not picking up or answering any messages. I'm a bit worried about him, he has been acting very peculiar these last few days.'

'Yes, I noticed that.' Julian replies. 'I'll go and look for him. He can't be that far away? I'll check in with the guys over the golf club and see if they've heard from him.'

'Oh, thank you so much, Julian. I don't know where we would all be without your help over the past horrible weeks.' Louise sobs once more and Millie says no more but shows her appreciation to Julian by smiling adoringly towards him.

Millie then whispers to her mother. 'Does Tara have any idea who could have done this?'

She just shrugs her shoulders.

'I'll go and make us a nice cup of tea. I know that probably sounds silly but we have to keep up our spirits we still have no news about Ems.' Millie stands up and leaves the bedroom.

It is six thirty in the evening when Julian arrives back to the house after doing a thorough search of the local area including the golf course and the burned down factory. He heads for the kitchen area where he finds Millie washing up. 'What are you doing?' He asks.

She turns and smiles a little. 'Got to keep myself busy. So much going on. Any news from father?'

He nods his head in a negative response. He tells her all the places he's searched and then says, 'what do we do? I mean how long do we wait?'

She looks mystified by the questions. 'What?'

'We have to report him missing. It may be linked to Emily?' He hugs her as he can see she is trembling in fear.

'Mother will need to make that decision. Can you imagine the media frenzy this is going to cause?' She sobs gently.

'I'll go and talk with her. Perhaps she has some other ideas as to his whereabouts or the reason he has gone off somewhere without telling anyone?' He leaves the kitchen area and heads upstairs to where Louise is lying on her bed with an ice pack on her forehead.

'I've been everywhere, do you have any ideas?' He asks.

'No, I have no idea this time. He's under so much stress, he could be anywhere or doing anything?' She removes the ice pack and sits up. 'Thank you, Julian, it's really appreciated. Think it's best to give Terry a few days to get rid of any issues he may be dealing with. I'm sure he'll be back by then?'

Julian just nods and smiles sympathetically towards her. He leaves the room whilst Louise lays back down placing the ice pack once more upon her head. She is now thinking about all of the underworld connections he has and how he had to reach out to them. She ponders the thoughts of just how much that would have cost and what the consequences would be for not being able to pay for such a service as still the insurance company are not paying out. She sits deeply in thought, staring at an empty chair opposite her and considers just what the real reasons are behind her husband's sudden departure?

Chapter 43

IT HAS BEEN three days since Terry Banks went missing and the time has come for Louise to accept the advice of her closest family members and contact the police. She is dreading all the media frenzy, which will happen as soon as the news gets out. The daughter and now the father both missing. She has an ace card to play first and so decides to go this route. She phones a number from Terry's contact list and knows exactly who it is.

He answers his phone politely. 'Detective Superintendant, Derby speaking.'

'Hi, Bobby. It's Louise... Louise Banks here.' She says rather hesitantly but she really needs at the very least his advice.

He pauses momentarily and then says, 'oh, hello Louise. I am sorry we still have no news but I have all the best detectives on the case and I'm sure...'

She interrupts him. 'No, it's about Terry.'

'Terry?'

'I'm afraid he hasn't been home for three days. He has his mobile turned off and he hasn't withdrawn any money from our bank accounts.' She tries not to sob.

'That doesn't sound like Terry. How was he when you last saw him?'

'He's been acting very strange and secretive. He has not been handling the Emily thing very well. None of us have.' She starts to sob.

'I'll send Daniels around to you. He can take a statement from you and get the ball rolling. I'm sure he has just gone off for some alone time. Under the circumstances, I can see why. Don't whatever you do let the press know anything. They'll turn your home into a

circus. Please do not worry, we'll find him... we'll find both of them.'
He sounds sympathetic and reassuring.

'Oh thank you so much, Bobby. He always said good things
about you. Bye.' She closes the call down and feels a little relieved
she has at last got some help but all the time she cannot help but
think whether the Reynolds brothers have a hand not only in this
but now she is thinking about her daughter, Emily too. In view of
all of these recent activities she has considered whether to hand
over the red book from Terry's safe to the police. The book has
a number of contacts from the criminal underworld. She has to
judge whether it will help find her daughter and husband or what
the consequences will be for her should she part with such critical
information.

It has been an hour since her call to DSU Derby and as
promised DI Daniels has visited and taken all the necessary details.
Louise, manages to refrain from giving him any of the information
from the red book at this point but is still taking it into
consideration. She will however not have to wait long to discover
Terry's fate as within another three hours there is a knock on the
door. Two uniformed officers are standing in front of her. She
knows this going to be bad news but which one are they here
about?

'Mrs. Banks?' One of them asks.

She just nods.

'May we come in, please?'

'Of course, have you any news?' She asks looking anxious.

They walk into the lounge area and advise Louise should be
seated. She complies and it is just as well because her legs are
trembling so much it is getting hard to remain standing.

'I'm afraid we have bad news about your husband, Terry. He has
been found dead.'

'What? Where? Who?' Louise is unable to control her thoughts and her emotions.

'We will know more after the tests are carried out but you need to go along the hospital in Tranby at some point. I would strongly suggest you have someone with you for support.'

Louise is now crying and is being comforted by one of the uniformed officers. When Millie having heard the commotion and seeing the police car parked up at the front of the house, rushes into the lounge. 'What's going on?' She knows it can only be bad news.

Louise puts her arms out towards her and they are soon on the couch together hugging each other. 'I'm afraid it's your father, Millie. He is... he is dead!'

'Dead? He can't be? Are you sure it is him?' She looks to the uniformed officers for their confirmation.

'Yes, I am ever so sorry. We have a F.L.O. on her way to pay you a visit.'

'F.L.O. - what is that?' Millie asks.

'Sorry, it is a Family Liaison Officer.'

'What good is that going to do? Will it bring back my father and what about my sister?' Millie is looking more angered than shocked at this point.

'She will be able to deal with any issues you have and be there for you every step of the way whilst the investigation is carried out. I am sure we will know more soon.'

'Okay, thank you. I know it's a hard job you have but I think my mother and I will prefer to be on our own at the moment?' Louise picks her head up off Millie's shoulder and nods in approval. The uniformed officers leave.

'Where's Julian?' Louise asks.

'He's out looking for... I better ring him to tell him.' Millie gets up and takes her mobile phone with her. She goes up to her bedroom so her mother does not have to hear it all again. She rings

Julian and relays the sad news and he promises to come straight home. It will be three weeks until the family discover how Terry had died; a single bullet shot to the head but there will some doubts as to just who pulled the trigger. His car had been set on fire and was totally burnt out. Louise promised herself she will gain revenge upon those responsible; she is pretty sure it had something to do with the Reynolds brothers and so she handed over the red book to DSU Derby with some other information she had managed to find. Within a number of weeks of gaining this and some other evidence, the Reynolds brothers, Flame King, Scar and many others from the gang, were safely locked up awaiting their trials.

Louise has somehow managed to gather up enough strength and will power to attend the funeral of her lover, Ray Shaw. One week later she attended the funeral of her husband, Terry Banks but it has taken a toll upon her. There was still no news of her daughter, Emily and police were not able to gain any further evidence. Leo Parker was still the number one suspect and was still serving his time for an arson attack on the Banks Sawmills. She has become addicted to drugs and nearly all of the life insurance on her husband Terry had all but been spent. There is still no news from the insurance cover on the fire gutted Sawmills. There was another new worry for Louise as she had discovered Julian Sanderson had turned into an aggressive wife beater. This had all happened after the death of Terry Banks and it looked as though he had started to show his true self once Millie's protector had died. Louise's health had deteriorated even before this latest problem but everything was getting too much. There was still no sign of missing, Emily and now her other daughter was being beaten on a regular basis. She could take no more. She had no one strong enough around her to turn to. She had lost her lover and husband in a matter of days, the very two people who could have sorted out the Julian and Millie issues. She had no money to pay someone to take care of Julian and now she had given all the evidence to the police on the Reynolds gang, her life has become pretty precarious. She tried to pay Julian off some time ago but he just took the money and laughed at her.

It was the 1st of May, this would have been Emily's 18th birthday. Millie had at long last managed to escape Julian's controlling and aggression by fleeing to a secret address in Spain with money her mother had given her out of the life insurance on her father before she started fixing up on a regular basis. With Miley gone, she had no choice but to live with all of her memories and regrets alone. She was having to get through what would have under normal circumstances been a day to celebrate. This was about to become the hardest day of her life and ended up to be her last day alive. Her body was found in her bath at home. She had taken a mixture of alcohol and drugs. On the dining table was a note left for Millie;

"Millie, I am so sorry. I can't take it any longer. I feel responsible for your father's death and for allowing Julian into our hearts. I hope you can forgive me. Please don't be sad, you have the rest of your life ahead of you now. You have always been my inspiration in life and I just have to see Emily again. Think she's waiting for me somewhere along with your father. Bless you, Millie and stay safe. Love you forever - mum. xxxx"

Chapter 44

IT HAS BEEN just over two years since the death of Louise Banks and still there has been no news on Emily's whereabouts. It is now safe for Millie to return from Spain as Julian Sanderson has started a new life in the USA and most of the Reynolds gang have been locked away for many years. The family home has been auctioned off due to the outstanding mortgage and debts owed upon it when Louise Banks passed away. The insurance company finally paid out for the fire at the Banks Sawmills and as Millie is the only known living next of kin, she received the money but she has put half of it into a savings account for Emily, just in case she is somehow found safe. The very first place she goes to visit are her parents graves inside the churchyard at Becclesfield. She has purchased an apartment in Minster Way close to the town centre and has decided this to be a good place to start all over again. She has not yet got her divorce papers through and so has not changed her name just yet. She has also figured on the name of Sanderson may act as a shield against any underworld reprisals. So at this point in time she is not reverting back to her single name, Miley Banks.

As she lays a reef on the graves she sees someone approaching her. She does not know who he is. He looks about thirty years of age and has dark short hair. He appears to be friendly as he looks her up and down.

'Well, haven't you grown since I last saw you?' He says with a grin upon his face.

'I'm sorry, I think you look familiar but just can't place you.' She says, as she rises from a kneeling position to stand directly opposite the man.

He laughs and that is when she really discovers who he is. 'Alex! I'd recognise that laugh anywhere. What are you doing over here?' She asks without giving the question too much thought.

They hug a little and he says, 'I came over to put flowers on my father's grave. Looks like we did the same thing?'

She then remembers. 'Oh, of course. I'm so sorry about your father. He was a lovely man. How is your mother coping?'

He looks a little solemn. 'Oh, she's got herself another man. She needs company, so it's good for her. Thanks, he was a lovely father to me but mother hinted on more than one occasion that he was seeing someone else at the time of his death. Never found out who she was? It doesn't matter to me anymore. I still miss him though.'

She hugs him once more but this time out of pity. 'I know. So sorry too. Your mother and mine were friends for so many years. She regularly used to meet up with her for coffee. They liked Tranby.'

'Yes, I remember how well they got on. Look at me wallowing in me self pity when you have it a lot worse. losing... well you know what I mean?' They hug again. 'What about that husband of yours? What happened to him as I see you're not wearing your wedding ring?'

'Very observant of you, Alex. Divorcing him as we speak. He turned out to be a controlling wife beater.'

'No! The swine! Wish he was here now, I know what I would do to him. Give him a piece of his own medicine, mate. Can't stand cowards like that!'

She smiles in agreement. 'Oh, thanks for the support.'

'Where are you living as haven't seen you around these parts since I moved back here?' He changes the subject quite quickly.

She is pleased to answer. She has known Alex since he was a child but lost touch with him when he went off to London to work. 'I've got a little apartment in Minster Way. Had to sell the house, it would've been too big for me on my own, anyway. What about you? No wedding ring neither I see.'

'I have a place just outside Becclesfield. No, not married. Never seemed to have the time.' He pauses for a moment, takes a look at her pretty face and then says, ' I'm going over for a pint in The Crown, would you like to come?' He smiles hoping for a positive reaction.

'Do you know what? I think that will be a great idea. I haven't had much to drink about lately... How's that friend of yours - Paul, wasn't it?'

'Great. Paul is getting married soon. He is marrying Maxine Hughes. Do you remember her from college?' They start to walk off and continue talking as they go along the narrow footpath leading out onto the main highway.

They are soon in The Crown. He says, 'what would you like to drink? Shall I get a bottle of wine or something?'

She looks happy with his choice. 'Rose wine would be great, thank you so much, Alex. It's so nice to be out again. I had to hide away in Spain for a couple of years just to keep safe from that creep and... I can't believe he has someone else out in the States. Poor cow, she must be desperate.'

'Scumbag. One day he'll get his. I'll go and order the drinks. Do you want something to eat? Smells like fish is on the menu.' They both laugh out loudly. She declines the kind offer of fish and chips.

He soon returns with the wine and two glasses. He pours them both a glass each. Millie is first to start off the conversation once more. 'I've got a cat called, Tom. He's such good company. Living on your own can get a little lonesome. How about you?'

He smiles and replies. 'No cats or dogs, just myself and the TV. Still I am quite young and you never know when Miss right will come walking through the doors.'

They both look over to the main entry and she says, 'what those doors over there?'

He laughs as he remembers how Miley likes to tease. 'You know what I mean, mate.'

'Mate? I suppose you got that from living in London? You actually sound a little cockney now. Not that that is a bad thing. I think it sounds a little sexy.' She takes a large gulp of her wine as she realises just what she has said but he does not appear to mind one little bit.

'Oh thanks... mate.' He exaggerates the accent.

She laughs once more and says, 'do you want to know something? Today is the first time I think I have laughed in getting on for over two years.' She suddenly looks sad as she thinks back over those years.

'You deserve a bloody medal, mate. All you have been through. I don't know how you coped and you still look amazing on top of all of that.' Now it is his turn to take a large gulp of wine for courage.

She appreciates his kind words and leans over and gives him a little kiss on the cheek. 'Thank you, Alex. You're such a kind soul. You remind me of Tom. Pets never let you down do they?'

Alex is quick to reply. 'Only when they mess on your new carpet.' They both laugh once more. They continue drinking and discussing their happier times when they played together as children.

Alex returns from the bar with another bottle of Rose wine. 'Here we are, Millie. Let's wet our whistles.'

She looks at him strangely. 'What does that mean? I don't have a whistle.'

He laughs. 'Yes, you do and it's the best whistle in town. It means lips. Let's wet our lips.'

She leans towards him and whispers. 'I've got a better idea.' She approaches him for a kiss and they embrace each other for the first time.

'Wow!' he says. 'That was fantastic. You're so beautiful and I've always...'

She stops him from talking by kissing him again and it is a long passionate kiss. 'I've wanted to do that from the moment I saw you today.' She says, 'and by the way - you have a lovely whistle too!'

'Just today. I've thought about you for years. Not since we were kids but from our teenager days together. Remember Smokesey's party? We nearly had a moment there.' He pauses to see if her memory is as clear as his.

'Oh, yes, Smoksey, wonder what he is doing these days? He was a character but you wouldn't leave your valuables anywhere near him, would you?'

'So you don't remember me that night. We danced and then just as we were about to kiss, Bugsy grabbed you for a dance and the moment was lost. Do you remember?' He appears desperate for her to recall this special moment he has been deliberately retaining deep within his thoughts for many years.

'Was you that spotty, skinny looking youth with a striped tank top on?' She is purposely teasing him now.

He knows. 'Yeah and you was that pony tailed, braces on your teeth, wearing a maxi dress, girl.'

Now she looks a little put out by his remarks but then he grins and bursts into laughter. She knows he is now teasing her back and she laughs along. 'Takes one to know one.' She says.

They finish their wine and head for an Indian restaurant across the road. There they have a lovely meal together and agree to meet again. They exchange their mobile numbers. After around fifteen minutes of kissing and caressing each other they depart but will Miley ever be able to trust a man again after her terrible experience at the hands of her ex husband?

Chapter 45

IT HAS BEEN just one week since Alex and Millie met. Millie decides to phones him. She says, 'Alex, thank you so much for the lovely flowers. I have put them in my favourite vase.'

'I'm glad you like them. I nearly got arrested stealing them from outside the Town Hall.' He laughs.

She giggles. 'Seriously, it was such a lovely thought and it came on the right day as well. Did you hear that scumbag Parker has handed in yet another appeal request?'

Alex is quick to reply. 'Don't worry, Millie. He has only served around three years of his sentence. He'll be in there for several more years yet.'

'Yes, although he still hasn't coughed up about Emily.' She sounds solemn.

'I know. He needs to be sorted out. If you get what I mean?'

'I've got some serious ideas on how to do just that but I will need some help along the way and it could get dangerous.' She is holding onto her thoughts and hoping for a positive response.

There is a little silence on the phone as Alex tries to wonder what that could mean. Then he realises she needs his support. 'I'm definitely in. Let's meet up and discuss further.'

'Oh, great. Thanks, Alex. My cousin, Chloe and her husband, Colin are going to help too.' She is sounding more upbeat about things as she considers her plan inside her head.

'What about I come around yours tomorrow night? I can get a takeaway and bring some wine?'

'Sounds a good idea to me. See you tomorrow stud.' She giggles once more.

Alex is pleased she sounds so happy. 'Ha-ha!'

Alex arrives early at Miley's apartment. They are sitting cosily on the couch hugging and kissing. The door bell rings. 'That must be the Chinese takeaway?' Alex says as he stands up quickly. 'I'll go and sort it out, be back in a mo.'

Miley goes out into the kitchen and returns with a bottle of Rose wine and two glasses. She places them on a beautifully prepared dining table. It has a large glass chandelier in the centre and four candles. She lights the candles as Alex returns with the meal. 'That chandelier looks expensive?' He says.

She smiles in appreciation and replies. 'Thanks. They were a present from my father to my mother on their 25th Wedding Anniversary. One of the few things I managed to get out of their before...'

'It looks even more expensive to me now.' He says as he places the containers onto the table. 'Chicken Chow Mein?'

'Yes, that's for me.' She replies.

They continue unwrapping the rest of the meal. They finish their meals within an hour and Miley is at the sink washing up the empty dishes. Alex walks in behind her and places his arms around her slender waist. She turns around and smiles, they kiss once more. Miley starts laughing as she realises her hands are full of soap suds and most of it is now resting upon Alex's hair. 'Hope you didn't wash your hair today?' She giggles.

He is still unaware but takes a quick look in a small mirror next to the sink. He sees the joke now and says, 'that reminds me of when you was watering your mum's garden and got me straight in the face at full pelt with that jet hose you used to have.'

She laughs as it is still a vivid memory. She pulls him closer and kisses him once more. Moments later they are sitting on the couch together going over Miley's plan to get the police to re-open the investigation into Emily's disappearance, which is now getting on for four years ago. Alex has waited patiently to get involved but has listened with much attention and thought. He says, 'Millie, you are putting yourself in too much danger. Remember what he could be capable of? I don't like the idea of you being alone with him, even if this part works.'

She responds immediately. 'It's the only way to get to the truth. I could slip a drug in his drink or something like that?' She pauses to see if he is not too shaken by this suggestion and he is not. 'We must get the investigation started again and this is the only way to achieve it.'

'What about this therapy bit? You may get a criminal record if it goes wrong? I don't mind playing the victim and I'm sure my mate Paul will go along with it but what happens if they don't put you into therapy?' Alex is now sitting upright and looking straight into her eyes. He needs to know she is fully committed to such a plan if he is to go along with it.

'I will get my solicitor to recommend it. Besides, after all I've been through it will be almost certain to happen.'

'You could get it anyway. I would've thought after everything, you should get it?' He looks saddened as he recalls all the things Miley has gone through; losing her parents, her home, her abusive husband and the disappearance of her younger sister.

'Yes, I know what you mean but it will take too long. I have checked and the waiting lists are over 18 months unless by order of the court and then it is immediate. I need to get into therapy at least a few weeks before Leo Parker gets out of prison. This way I will have a head start on him for the time when we meet up. The way he keeps on appealing, he could get out a lot sooner. So we need to be ready for any sudden changes.' She is beginning to look rather desperate and Alex notices this.

'I'll help you. Of course, I will. Not happy about some parts of the plan, though. What happens if he doesn't even come back to Becclesfield?'

'I'm pretty certain he will but if not, we'll find a way to entice him back. It's great the way you support me, Alex but enough of this, the time is ticking away.' She gets up and puts her hand out towards him as if to gesture "follow me". He stands and holds her hand as she leads him into the bedroom on the left hand side of the small hallway. They will spend the night together for the first time. It has taken someone very special for Miley to overcome the scars of her past relationship and to give herself to another man after what Julian Sanderson had done to her. Alex being fully aware of her past has done everything expected from him and has tried to ensure any fears she may have remain where they belong - in the past. He has treated her with respect, kindness, tenderness and above all, dignity. He has been patient and allowed her to come to terms with this relationship.

'It's half past seven, Alex!' She shakes him and he slowly awakens.

'Half past what?' He is still struggling to open his eyes properly as Millie flings open the curtains to the bedroom allowing a sudden burst of sunshine into the room.

'I thought you had to be in work this morning?' She is quickly getting herself dressed. It is either because she is in a hurry or perhaps she is a little bashful still?

Suddenly Alex returns to the reality of his life. 'Oh. I need to get my skates on.' He jumps out of bed naked and Millie turns away to give him some privacy. 'You don't have to look away, Millie. I'm not shy, mate.'

'I know that but I am... mate.' She leaves the room and heads to the kitchen to quickly make a small breakfast for them both whilst Alex is having a quick shower.

She shouts out to him. 'Coffee or tea!'

He pretends not to hear her as he wants her to come into the bathroom. She moves to the door and shouts it out again but still no response. She slowly opens the door and sees Alex naked in the shower. 'Come on in, Millie. It's great in here.' He slides the shower door wide open and grabs her left hand. She is tempted.

'I've got to get to college. Come back this evening if you are not busy? It was a fantastic night, Alex. Hurry up and stop messing around.' She cannot help but admire his physical presence but finds the will power to leave the room. She is quickly joined by Alex with a towel around his waist.

'Thanks, Millie. Coffee, just what the doctor ordered.'

'Didn't know you was a doctor.' She giggles as she teases him a little. She passes over a plate with two slices of toast already buttered. 'Now stop larking around and get yourself dressed. You're going to be late for work.'

'I don't care. I just love spending time with you but I suppose bills have to be paid?' He half eats a slice of toast and picks up the other one before leaving the kitchen area to go and get himself dressed.

Within half an hour they are both outside the apartment kissing each other goodbye.

Chapter 46

MILEY'S COUSIN CHLOE has invited both Miley and Alex over to the pub she runs with her husband, Colin. They all meet upstairs of The Swan in Tranby. It is a small but private area and they are discussing further aspects of a plan, which they hope will entrap Leo Parker when he gets released from prison.

'Assuming he comes or we get him back to Becclesfield, what do we do then?' Alex has raised a worthy question as all the others in attendance nod in agreement. Chloe is sitting next to Colin and she says out loud. 'We'll get him to Becclesfield don't worry about that but Alex is right, what do we do next?'

Millie replies. 'That's where Alex and I come in. I will somehow encourage him to have a relationship with me whilst Alex will make friends with him. Let's not think too far ahead than that at this moment. We need to put all our efforts into the first two parts of the plan.'

Chloe says, 'where do we come into it?'

'If you don't mind... we could lure him into the pub. Perhaps, I can work behind the bar or something?' Miley looks pleased with how the reception of her suggestion was received by Chloe and Colin in particular as she needs their cooperation for this part of the plan to work. 'The trick will be to get him to come here in Tranby but we'll just have to see how things progress with the early stages... Okay, so Joe the private detective I've hired, will be following him on the day he gets released, so we'll know every step he takes. Then we'll all have to take turns to follow him on a daily basis as we cannot afford to keep paying his fees indefinitely. How does that sound?'

'Sounds good to me, mate. I'm owed a lot of annual leave so I can take some time off when this part happens.' Alex shows his full support for Miley and she looks very pleased as she gazes over to him in admiration.

Colin is next to support her. 'I can get extra staff in as well as being able to put some time in with Chloe.' He nods over for Chloe's agreement and she is smiling back towards him showing her unification.

Millie then turns to Chloe and says, 'you will need to report me missing to the police. Perhaps suggest you are my sister and I think it essential not to mention my maiden name until we really have to. We need to string Parker along for as long as possible. So if pressed say I have only lived in the country and Becclesfield for the past three years. Besides, I did live in Spain for a number of years before coming back to Becclesfield. I'm pretty sure they won't be able to discover the truth in the short time it will take to get this business over with. Australia sounds a nice place to grow up?' She giggles.

Chloe says, 'so use Sanderson. Are you sure you still wish to be associated with that creep?'

'It's only for a short time. Anyway, I have to go now as I have my first therapy session at the Merryfield Medical Centre tomorrow morning.' She giggles a little but is not really looking forwards to it. It is going into the unknown for her and she does not like anything like this but knows it is an essential part of the plan.

Alex grins and says, 'give them hell girl.'

Chloe adds. 'Good luck but be careful you don't say too much about yourself, otherwise they'll send you off in a white jacket.' They all laugh and in minutes they have left the room for some drinks up at the bar downstairs.

It is Wednesday morning and Miley is getting herself ready for her first therapy session. She chooses a short pale blue skirt and a tight white cotton top. She is looking as though she is about to go out for a night out somewhere special. She takes a long look at herself in the mirror, it appears she is rehearsing something, similar to an actress readying herself to go onto a stage of a theatre?

Within half an hour she has passed all the questions thrown at her by the receptionist and is now standing outside a small office on the second floor of the Merryfield Medical Centre. She takes a breath or two and gently knocks upon the door. She hears a welcoming voice call out. 'Please, come on in.'

She pushes the door open and sees a middle aged man rise from a chair to greet her with a warm smile. 'Welcome to our humble dwelling. Did you find us okay? My name is Jacob Lyall?'

She likes the sound of his friendly personality and can tell immediately he is one of the good guys. 'Hello, Jacob. My name is Miley but most prefer to call me Millie.' She walks into the centre of the room. 'Yes, I found it easily. I've walked past it so many times without even given the place much thought.'

'It is not that striking, as far as buildings go.' He smiles once more. 'Please take your choice of seating or laying on the couch and whilst I remember, if you ever need a break at anytime there is some utensils over there... even the kettle works.' He grins a little as he approaches a large leather chair directly placed in the middle of the room.

She deliberately opts for laying on the couch and as she lays down she slowly pulls her short skirt down a little. 'This is nice and cosy.' She remarks.

'You are comfortable to begin?'

'Yes, I need your help. Some of things going on lately are really weird.' She looks satisfied with her opening comments.

'You say you need help, what has been troubling you, Millie.'

She is pleased he has called her Millie. It feels to her they have known each other longer than the five minutes or so. 'Well, I suppose you have the paperwork from the court? It all started when I met Paul in the Angel pub. Do you know it?'

He nods. He would as the pub is near enough opposite where they are sitting but he refrains from talking and encourages her to continue.

'Anyway, I was out having a really good time when these two guys come over to me and started buying me drinks. I liked them both. They are very handsome but I do tend to wear my heart upon my sleeve.' She pauses and takes a quick look around the room as if to buy her some more time to think. 'So at some point Paul's friend has disappeared somewhere leaving just the two of us together. We danced and had a really good time but I drank too much. Luckily or as it now turns out, unluckily for me he took me home in a cab. I asked him in for a coffee, well I had to didn't I?'

'I understand. Please continue.' He shows no emotion or any body language signals to suggest any disapproval.

'Well, one thing led to another. We ended up in bed together and he stayed the night. I thought at last I had met someone really genuine and considerate but how wrong could I have been?' She appears to be tearful so Jacob gets up and walks over to his desk, picks up a box of tissues. He places them next to Miley and she clasps some to wipe her eyes. She recovers her emotions and continues. 'So, after a few weeks I was getting quite serious with him but there were some red flags. He could only see me on a Friday night and then he wouldn't answer my calls or texts. So I tracked him down to where he lived. I watched him come and go a few times but then I saw a pretty young woman come out of his house. I stopped her to ask for directions and saw she was wearing a wedding ring. That was it! I saw red. I spoke with him and he said it was over but still refused to admit he was married.'

'He was married? How did you know the lady you saw coming out of the house was his wife? It could have been sister or anyone?' Jacob has stopped momentarily taking notes to gauge her response.

'He was married!' She has raised her voice in response. 'I watched them for weeks. I saw them together in restaurants, pubs and they were truly in love. All the things I wanted in life - she had. I couldn't help myself. The thoughts of revenge had overwhelmed me and so one day I wrote with white paint on his new black car; "Paul is a dickhead".' She pauses once more. Now it is her time to gauge the looks upon Jacob's face but it shows no emotion. 'Then the strangest thing happened; his mate Alex meets me in the Angel one night. We start drinking and I just don't know how I fall for these types of users. To cut a long story short, he buys me lots of drinks and we end up back at my place. I don't know why I fell for that trick twice from two guys who are besties? I think I have this childish fairytale in my mind that I will meet my Prince Charming one day and every time I think I have, it goes terribly wrong. I cannot take much more of this treatment. I am getting too old for that sort of rubbish now. Can you help me?' She begins to sob and grabs some tissues.

'I am here to help you. So long as you remain truthful like you have today we will soon be making progress. You have done so well for a first session. Try to think more positively about yourself. Think of all the good things this world has to offer. You may feel you are in a bad place today but the future is all yours, it is up to you to embrace it.' He stands and walks back towards his desk, places his notebook down. 'Now Millie the other thing we must discuss is your medication. You are taking it as prescribed as it is really important to your recovery?'

She stands wriggles her skirt down a little. 'Yes, they appear to be working a little.'

'It will take time, Millie but you are showing some positive signs already. Now we need to go through some breathing and relaxation methods, you will find they help too.' He shows her the methods and tells her to keep positive. The session ends and Miley leaves for a rendezvous with Alex in The Crown.

Alex stands as she arrives inside the pub. 'Over here!' He shouts. As she gets close they kiss and he whispers. 'How did it go?' She is tearful. 'He's such a lovely man. He's said so many nice things. I don't know I can go through with it? I mean, he probably has a wife and children. I may ruin his career.'

Alex comforts her and encourages her to sit down. 'I've got the wine and glasses.'

'I could do with a stiff drink.' She picks up one of the glasses full of wine and has a large gulp.

'You have to do it, otherwise it may not work. Besides, Millie, you know worse is yet to come if you wish to discover the truth from that pig, Leo.' He hugs her tightly as if to suggest she can overcome this first hurdle.

'I know. I know... but he's a lovely man and he actually has made me feel more positive. I wonder if we should just carry on with our lives and forget about Parker?'

He takes a sip of wine and ponders her suggestion. Life is good at the moment. 'It's up to you, Millie but I fear you will regret this for the rest of your life and it's the only way we can find... you know - find Emily.'

She suddenly has a more positive reaction to the plan. 'Yes, you're right, Alex, I would regret it for the rest of my life. We must nail him, he has ruined my life and my parents' life's. He must pay. He will pay!'

'That's the spirit, Millie. So let's chill while we can. We have a lot of stress ahead of us but it will all be worthwhile if we can get to the truth.'

Chapter 47

TWO DAYS AFTER Leo Parker is released from prison, Miley receives a call on her mobile phone. 'Hi, Millie here.' She says.

'Hi, Millie, it's Joe here. I'm calling from France. I have tracked him here to a small village, St. Mere Eglise. It's off the Normandy coast. I don't know why he has come here but I thought would call you because of the expenses. You know they will be running over the budget pretty soon. Do you want me to continue following him?'

'Hi, Joe. Thanks for the information. Please keep following him, we need to know where he is at all times. If it goes over budget just let me know with some updates of his movements. Is that okay, Joe?' She is looking pensive and serious at the same time.

'I will continue until you tell me to stop. I'll send you emails on the address you gave me. I'll get back you when I find out what he is up to. Bye.'

'Thanks, Joe.' Millie quickly relays this information to the other three; Alex, Chloe and Colin. The initial stage of the plan has commenced but is not going as expected.

It is two weeks later and Millie receives a phone call from Joe advising Leo Parker has returned to the UK and is actually living in the next block of apartments in Waverley Road, Becclesfield to where he had previously lived. Millie and Alex are walking in a park in Minster Way. Millie relays the information over to him.

'That's unbelievable! It couldn't have worked out any better, mate.' He is excited and gives her a tight hug.

'It's meant to be. I believe things are meant to happen for a reason and we know the reason for this don't we, sweetheart?' They sit on a park bench and share a passionate lingering kiss.

'How long shall we give it until we start the next part of the plan?' He asks as he attempts to guess the answer in his head and show his undying support.

'As soon as we can get him to the pub. I'll get some of Emily's clothes and personal belongings together. I'll ring Chloe and get fixed up behind the bar so the regulars get used to seeing me. We want him to think I've been there for some time when he arrives.' She looks Alex in his eyes and with what appears to be a heavy heart says, 'you know what that means to us? We'll have to be more careful together and cannot afford for him to see us both together at any point in time.'

'Yeah, thought that would be the case. Perhaps, you can come around to mine a bit more?'

She smiles at the thought but still has a much more serious look upon her face. She knows the next part is the most dangerous of all. She has to ensnare him and keep him interested in her for whatever amount of time it will take to completely expose him.

One week later, Colin has visited the apartment block where Leo Parker now lives in Waverley Road. He is observing from across the road and sees him leave in a black car. He seizes this opportunity to knock on a neighbours door to see if he can find more information such as; daily habits, relationships and anything else that may be useful. He discovers Leo Parker is not the identity he is now using. He has told neighbours his name is Harry Sutton. He immediately phones Miley. 'Hi, Millie,' he says, 'Parker has either changed his name or is using a different name?'

'What? He obviously doesn't want anyone to know who he really is. That's a good sign. Bloody good job we found that out otherwise the whole plan could've failed. Thanks, Colin. What name is he now using?' She asks in bewilderment.

'Harry Sutton. An elderly guy living on the ground floor told me.'

' We had all better get used to that new name. That's really important. I think we can stop the surveillance now and move to the next part? Getting him up The Swan.'

'Okay, Millie. I'll let Chloe know. Are you seeing Alex?'

'Yeah, don't worry, I'll let him know. Well done and thank you ever so much for all of your help.'

'No problems. Just hope we can get the bastard locked up for good and find your sister.' Colin closes the call down and heads back to Tranby to let Chloe know the news.

One week later Harry Sutton has to appear at the local magistrates court and Chloe sits in at the back of the court to discover just what it is all about. She had spotted his car in the town centre and so followed him there. Sutton has pleaded guilty to a road rage incident. She cannot believe the sentence he got and so rushes out of the court to phone Millie. 'Millie,' she says, 'Parker... I mean, Sutton has just pleaded guilty to a road rage offence and has been sentenced to undergo a course of therapy. You know what that means?'

'Wow! That could mean he will have to attend the Merryfield Medical Centre in Becclesfield? It must be that one it is the only one for 40 miles.' She is smiling and feels this is a major breakthrough. The piece of luck they have been praying for. 'This could mean, even if we can't get him to go to the pub, I could have a "chance" meeting at the therapy centre?'

'Fantastic! I'll tell Colin. Are you going to let Alex know?'

'Will do. Thanks, Chloe. I can't believe this is really going to happen.' She looks overjoyed and closes down her mobile phone as she takes a long look in the mirror as if to give herself the courage to carry on with the next phase of this dangerous plan.

Two days later, Alex has overnight, posted a note through Harry Sutton's letterbox advising him Leo Parker will be in The Swan at Tranby on Friday night. It is more in hope than in belief he will actually go to Tranby but it had to be attempted as a first resort. It works and Harry Sutton makes his way into The Swan pub in Tranby where Miley is dressed in her sister's clothes and wearing her sister's perfume. She has dyed her blonde hair black. She has coloured contact lenses in that make her eyes give off an appearance of being hazel in colour just like her sister's.

She is behind the bar working but has noticed him the moment he walked into the bar. Her heart is racing and she is becoming extremely anxious. It has come to her turn to play the biggest performance of her life. She actually turns to the breathing techniques Jacob has showed her and finds it has calmed her. She watches as he approaches the bar. She races straight up to him and has served him out of turn. They begin their conversation and she attempts to act like her sister. It works, he is staring uncontrollably towards her every move. She knows this and deliberately bends down to pick a glass off the bottom shelf behind the counter. Still he looks her up and down. She gathers her courage and walks back to him with two lagers. They exchange a little banter. She tries to tease him. It works. Even when he is standing in the corner of the pub he is looking over at her.

Chloe comes into the bar area. 'Is he here yet?' She asks.

Miley can hardly control her mixed emotions. 'Don't look now but he is standing by the front doors. It has worked. He is looking for Leo Parker. I'm pretty sure he has noticed Emily's clothes I've got on.'

Chloe could not help but take a quick look over to the entrance and gets her first glance of him. 'Knew he'd be on his own. People like him don't make friends.'

'Just got to get him to like me now.'

'Like you? Look, he's not taken his eyes off you. He's in, I'm pretty sure. Now the next bit is going to be dangerous but Alex is upstairs waiting for the signal, so don't threat.' Chloe walks away from the bar area to go upstairs to let Colin and Alex know he is in the bar.

It appears to be the longest evening ever for Millie as she is trying to work the bar and keep an eye on Sutton. He comes to the bar again. She races towards him and serves him. She tries to lure him with some sexy innuendoes and it works. She decides to write him a note asking to meet by the burger van around midnight when she finishes her shift. She slips it in his hand with the change from his round of drinks. Still she does not know whether he will show or what will happen directly after that. Alex is keeping an eye on him from a darkened corner in the bar. The pub closes and Millie walks to the burger van. She sees him standing there. Alex is standing behind a large oak tree observing his every move. They buy burgers and move off to the canal area. They sit and after a short while they kiss for the first time. The plan looks as though it has worked but the hard bit for Millie is still to come. Alex has kept a safe distance away from them but still he observes. He knows things could at any moment become extremely dangerous. Still they sit, hugging and kissing. Finally, some movement as they stand. It looks to Alex as though an argument is happening. He gets himself ready for action. He begins to walk towards them and then he notices them hug once more. He walks past ensuring to keep his face covered with his coat collar. He takes up another position and is sheltered by a wall. They eventually walk off with their arms linked together. It is a relief for Alex but the night is young and still he follows.

They eventually enter The Lodge, a large hotel. Alex watches them for the last time. He cannot do anything other than to await Millie's call on his mobile phone, should anything go wrong. He is feeling extremely jealous at this point. He is upset having to watch his girlfriend kiss, hug and now go into a hotel room with another man but he had been forewarned this would need to happen. He just prays Millie's plan to render Sutton unconscious really works for both of their sakes. For Alex it will be a long and anxious wait outside the hotel in the freezing cold night but he will not leave his post unless she calls him. Colin is still sitting up with Chloe in their now closed pub. They are both on edge and are awaiting a call. Any sign, just to say everything is okay. It will be a long night for all the conspirators as both Millie and Harry spend the night inside the hotel.

It is ten minutes after two in the morning. Alex notices Harry leave in a cab. His phone rings and it is Millie. 'Alex, are you there?' She says sounding rather anxious.

'Is it over, Millie? I see he has gone off in a cab.' Alex is even more anxious sounding.

'No, he's just gone to get some...' She pauses as she realises she is speaking to her boyfriend and he will not like the truth. So instead of telling him he has gone to buy some condoms, she tells him he is off to the garage to buy some alcohol. Even though she has no intention of allowing Harry use them. 'I've got everything in place. It's going really well. He likes a drink and so it won't be a problem. I'll slip a couple into his drink and then I'll get out. Don't worry it is going really well. Better than I had thought.'

'Has he tried anything on yet? I don't like the idea of you even kissing but I know you have to and I know you don't want to either...'

'Hush now. It's going well and with a bit of luck we could get this over really quickly. Just make sure you are outside and keep an eye on your phone. I'd better hang up now in case he comes back unexpectedly. I love you, Alex. Just remember that and I promise not to let him get too amorous.'

'Don't take any chances, sweetie. Remember what he is capable of and... I love you too.' Alex closes down his mobile and prepares for what could be a long night.

Chapter 48

MILEY AND HARRY meet several times after their first night together at The Lodge. Miley is pleased with the way in which the relationship is heading. She has visited her therapist on a regular basis and has currently built up a large case file. She has told Jacob how loving her new boyfriend is and how they met. Now she is portraying Harry Sutton as being aggressive, stalking and obsessive. Jacob has been taking all of these notes down so the next part of the plan is now becoming ready to put into motion.

'Alex, it's Millie here.' She says whilst holding her mobile phone in her right hand. 'I have followed him again last night. Why does he keep going to 6 Cherry Walk? It's really weird. Last night he walked right up to the front door but turned away at the last moment. I could see him clearly through the conifers. There must be some connection to Emily there?' She pauses as she lets her cat, Tom out of the front door. 'I've just come back from the therapist. I think all the notes are ready. Just need you to go and do your bit with him now.'

'Looking forward to it, mate. Been polishing up on my drinking skills. I'll soon get him under me wing.' Alex is grinning as he awaits her response.

'Don't forget to wear that leather jacket with the Route 66 on the back. He won't be able to help himself.' She laughs loud enough so Alex can hear at the other end.

'Right, I'm off to the pub then. Wish me luck. Don't know when he'll turn up so may have to go every day.' He laughs loudly this time.

It is two days and Alex has visited The Crown both days. He walks in on the third day and goes up to the bar. He has the leather jacket on, which Leo had given to Emily some time ago. It works as Harry Sutton aka Leo Parker approaches him and taps him on the shoulder. Alex pretends to look puzzled but soon they are laughing and drinking together. It could not have worked any better. Now Alex has him where he wants him and so does Millie.

The final part of the plan is about to commence. Alex is in The Crown pub awaiting Millie's entrance but he will not be talking with her. He is there in case there is a bad reaction to what Millie is about to do to Harry. She enters the pub. She has a loud row with Harry and she tips one of his lagers over his head. There are plenty of witnesses to this chaotic behaviour in the pub. Whilst Harry has his back to her, she picks up his mobile and places it into her handbag. She leaves the pub. Alex wanders over to Harry looking at him in disbelief but supporting him at the same time. Whilst Harry goes to the toilets to clean himself down, Alex leaves the pub and meets Millie outside. She hands him Harry's phone. He carefully places it inside his leather jacket pocket. They have a quick peck on the lips and she leaves whilst Alex goes back into the pub. He is seated in another alcove area with what's left of Harry's drinks. He then goes about getting him drunk with beer and shots, pretending to be drinking them as well but he is not actually drinking any. He takes a drunken Harry home back to his apartment. A neighbour comes out and offers him some help but it is refused. Alex does not want any nosey neighbour getting in his way and so struggles up the stairs to Harry's apartment. He places him down on a couch, takes his car keys and waits until it gets dark. Harry is asleep for a long time. He has been drugged by Alex at the pub. When nightfall begins, Alex leaves the apartment and drives off in Harry's black Audi car. He waits in The Ship and Anchor car park for Millie to drive by in her car. She slows at the entrance and Alex then follows her. He follows Miley into Denbar Lane. The both pull over in a lay by on the left hand side of the road. Miley gets out of her car, leaving all her personal belongings and the key in the ignition. She gets into Harry's car, which is being driven by Alex. They drive off and turn left into Long Lane. They stop half way and meet up with Chloe who is waiting in her car to transport Miley back to the pub in Tranby. Before she gets into Chloe's car, Miley places some droplets of her blood into the boot of Harry's car and then Alex drives back to park it up outside Harry's apartment in the same spot where he took it from. He then goes back up to Harry's apartment, places the keys on a table, takes a look at him sleeping and then quietly leaves. He then goes around the corner to Waverley Road where he had parked his car up earlier and then drives to Tranby to meet all the others in The Swan pub. Miley will stay upstairs at the pub in an attic room for however long the police investigation will take. They have done all they can now it will be up to the police to not just start a missing persons enquiry about Miley but re-open her sister Emily's investigation again and find the truth. They are all fully aware that once the truth is uncovered each and every one of them will need to face up to the consequences of their actions. One by one they will probably get called in to help with the investigation at some point but they will also be using this time to point the finger firmly at Leo Parker, now know as Harry Sutton, and highlight his infatuation with 6 Cherry Walk, Tranby.

Chapter 49

CHLOE AND ALEX have met up at The Swan. They are discussing just what may likely happen to all of them when the police discover just exactly what has really been going on. They are disturbed by one of the bar staff who has come in looking for a coat. Alex had not noticed him as he says to Chloe, 'meet up on 23rd November?' He turns around and sees the bar person rummaging around behind him. The room goes all silent until the bar person leaves the room. 'Sorry, Chloe, I didn't see him there.'

Chloe's replies. 'It's only, Tony. I shouldn't worry too much. I doubt if he heard anything. Besides, we could be talking about anything.'

He nods in agreement and then leaves to go up to the attic room to see how Millie is coping. 'You've made the news my love.' He grins and approaches for a kiss.

'This is the part I am regretting. Just hope it leads us to the truth. How is Jacob taking it?' She sits back down on a sofa.

'He stayed outside your apartment all night on Thursday. He looked really concerned. You must've played the wounded soldier really well.' He sits down next to her and they cuddle each other tenderly.

'I hope he's going to be alright? He's such a lovely guy. Just wish this was all over now.'

'Will be soon. He's been charged with kidnapping you and it won't be long until they put two and two together, will it?' He brushes he blonde hair with his right hand ever so gently.

'I've been watching the progress on TV. It seems to be taking them an age to get to my sister. They are more interested in me but at least he's banged up at the moment. It will be his DNA test that will lead them back to Emily's disappearance as they discover he is really Leo Parker.'

'Yep, it won't be long until they pull me in, I guess? It'll all be worthwhile in the end, mate. You wait and see.' He kisses her once more.

She sits upright and has a serious look upon her face. 'What if they don't find anything new out and then they come for us? We will all have to go to prison and for what?'

'Prison? You never said anything about prison.' He laughs to let her know he was joking. 'We're all adults and knew what we were getting into. Besides, the public will have nothing but sympathy for us bearing in mind our motives.' He pulls her closer to hug and reassure her. 'I have to go now as Chloe is giving me a lift home, a I've had a few pints to calm down. I'll see you on the 23rd, Saturday at the White Hart Hotel. Chloe told me you're moving out on Friday night. So I'll come over after coming here to get an update on how the plan is going.' They kiss once more and Alex goes downstairs to meet Chloe. They leave the pub together and she drives him home.

23rd November

DAVIES AND JENKINS arrive outside The Swan in Tranby. Their driver, Bates has found a safe spot to park up.

Jenkins says, 'good spot. We can see the side elevations and the main entrance. We may even be first to see him before he even gets into the pub?'

Davies replies, 'yes, let's hope so. We have so much riding on this weekend. If nothing materialises here or in Cherry Walk we will have a certain amount of egg on our faces.'

Bates interrupts and says, 'is she inside the pub alone, guv?'

'No, don't worry, she's got our operative working behind the bar. He is fully up to speed with the whole operation. He'll keep an eye on her and probably give her some free drinks.' Davies looks out of the rear window. 'Bloody hell! There's a guy urinating up against a shop doorway and it's only ten o'clock. Shame, you two could have got another easy nick on your CV's.'

Jenkins quickly says, 'I'll pass on that one. Bates can have it. He needs it more than I do.'

'Very funny. It's been a bit quiet lately.' Bates replied.

'A little patience is all you need chaps. We're on the crest of bringing home the real deal tonight. So stay sharp.' Davies is quick to advise.

Jenkins is in deep thought and says, 'you must remember those days, guv? The 1970's when free drinks for us coppers was the norm.'

He smiles and is definitely reminiscing back to how things were back then. 'You better believe it. Many of our officers actually ended up as alcoholics back then because of that very perk.' Then a text tone sounds on his mobile phone. 'It's from Wicks. Damn it! She can see no sign of Colin Richards. That's bad news. He could be meeting Shaw somewhere away from the pub but at least Chloe Richards is present.'

'He may be in the cellar or even up there in his office. The light is on.' Jenkins attempts to lift the spirits in the car.

'There's nothing we can do about that now. Just keep our fingers crossed we haven't just wasted hundreds of pounds of the taxpayers money. Not to mention valuable police time and resources.' Davies is as always pragmatic on these occasions. 'What's the time, Bates?' He asks even though he has his own watch on. Perhaps he is just checking they all have the exact time as each other, which they did have half an hour earlier when they sequenced their watches.

'Ten thirty, guv,' Bates is quick to respond.

'We only have another hour or so before this operation is dead in the water. We'll just have to arrest Chloe and Colin Richards, that is if he is there?' Davies looks extremely dejected but is experienced to know things can change in a moment.

Jenkins is first to console him. 'It will be alright. Where's the Dunkirk spirit gone, guv?'

It does lift his spirits as it makes Davies laugh out loud for the first time this evening. 'Not that bloody desperate yet, Jenkins.' As he finishes speaking another text tone sounds upon his phone. 'I hope this is good news?' He reads it aloud. "Still no sign of Shaw or Colin Richards. Will keep you updated."

'Nothing lost and nothing gained. Something's going to happen soon. I've got that feeling in my water.' Bates tries to be positive.

'We're running out of time. Come on Shaw. Where are you?' Davies is clinging to hope now. 'Do you think he is going to show?'

Both Jenkins and Bates both agree at the exact same time as though there was a prize for the person who answered first.

Davies gets another text. He rushes to read it out. "Colin Richards has just entered the bar, sir. Will keep you updated." 'Bloody great! It could still be on chaps, so get yourselves ready. If it happens it will be very soon or not at all.'

Suddenly the atmosphere becomes tensed. This has to be played correctly as one sudden wrong move could prove fatal. Davies has started his nervy and tensed habits that always occur when he feels he is about to make an arrest. He looks at his watch every ten seconds or so, scratches his head with his right hand and moves his head from side to side. The tension is mounting inside the car.

Jenkins breaks the silence and says, 'what she doing outside the pub brushing her hair? Shouldn't she stay inside the pub and keep...'

Davies jumps up. "That's the signal. It's a go! Come on Jenkins let's get in there! Bates inform the squad car to come around the front and tell them to come straight into the pub.'

Jenkins, for once, says nothing. His adrenalin has just kicked into overdrive. There is excitement and a little fear all mixed up together. He has been on many of these operations before and they can get violent on occasion.

'Over there,' Davies says, 'out in the beer garden in the left hand corner at eleven o'clock.'

'Got them, guv. Let's go get them! The squad car has just arrived by the sounds of it. Good timing.' Jenkins gets out a pair of handcuffs he had been hiding inside his jacket pockets.

Shaw and Richards are in a deep serious conversation and are unaware they are about to be arrested. As the uniformed police enter the pub, the music stops and the regulars look aghast. Whilst this was happening, Wicks took her chance and arrested Chloe Richards at the bar area. They watch as Shaw and her husband Colin Richards are escorted out of the pub by two uniformed officers whilst the premises is emptied. A search of the premises did not reveal any clues as to the whereabouts of Miley Sanderson. Davies and Jenkins are a few steps behind. Jenkins breaks off to join Wicks at the bar and ensure the arrest has gone smoothly. Within the hour all three suspects are locked up in cells at Becclesfield Police station but news has quickly filtered out to the local press offices. They are there just at the time when the pub was being locked up by a caretaker publican. Alisha Nicholson arrives first as per usual.

She reports the following;

'A development in the missing 29 year old Millie Sanderson investigation has just occurred here in Tranby. Three suspects were taken from the pub behind me and arrested. Two males aged in their early thirties and a female of similar age. I have with me an eye witness. Mr. Thomas Stewart, who was inside The Swan when police made the arrests. What did you see?'

The camera focuses on a male in his mid twenties with dark hair and of medium build. He says, 'I was right there when it happened!' he says rather excitedly. 'I was vaping at the time. I saw two guys having a conversation over in the corner of the beer garden. Two plain clothes officers entered and approached them. The two in uniforms raced in with their cuffs at the ready. It all happened pretty quick. I thought it was a drug bust? You know you see the sort of things on tv. Didn't think I'd ever see something like that happen in Tranby. Then I heard the older guy say "conspiracy to kidnap". Pretty sure he said that. Then they were carted away with a female up at the bar area.'

The camera swings back around to Alisha Nicholson. 'There you have it. Three arrests made within the past half an hour or so. Police will no doubt update us all at some point tomorrow but for now we know they have charged 28 year old Harry Sutton with suspicion of kidnap. We hope to have further as the we go through the night. This is Alisha Nicholson outside The Swan in Tranby.'

Chapter 50

JACOB IS LOOKING forward to a chilling, relaxing and quiet Sunday morning at his home in Priory Park. It is too cold for him to go out on the lawn as he usually does on a Sunday, even if it means hat and coat. The snow is beginning to fall. Ayaka looks excited about this as she appears to be trying to watch every single flake fall. She turns to Jacob, who is seated in his leather rocking chair and says, 'it looks as though it is going to settle? The children love the snow. I remember when I was a child. My father used to take us to Naspa Ski Garden. It was kawaii... cute. It used to take father one and a half hours in the car from Tokyo...'

'I used to have a car like that!' He could not resist the temptation.

'Oh you are listening then? Just for that I am going to tell you the whole story.' She smiles, refrains from proceeding with the threat but then says, 'we used to build a snowman though... I wonder what we should call them today? Snow Man, Snow Woman or Snow Person?'

Jacob laughs and actually puts his paper down on the dark oak coffee table next to him. He then says, , 'you are determined today, Ayaka. Although you do have a valid point. Perhaps we had better look it up somewhere?' He changes the subject as the news is going to be on tv soon. 'They arrested three people last night in connection with the kidnap of Millie.'

She looks upset as she suddenly remembers the ongoing searches being made for her and then says, 'we had better put on the news to see if there have been developments.,

He nods and put it on using the remote control. 'Let's hope they find her now they have so many suspects detained.'

The local news channel is breaking the latest news. There is a male reporter standing in a street. He is halfway through his report;

'... the three suspects remain in custody at Becclesfield Police station. Meanwhile, Harry Sutton formerly known as Leo Parker had been charged with suspicion of kidnap but given the latest discovery these charges may change?

If you are just joining us, we can report that police have this morning discovered human remains in Cherry Walk. It is all cordoned off and a tent has been erected. They are asking members of public to avoid the area whilst forensics carry out their work and not to speculate at this stage. The remains have yet to be identified. Stay tuned in for further updates throughout the day. This is Isaac Brontes reporting from Tranby.'

Ayaka hugs Jacob and says, 'it may not be her. They said remains and not body. It could even be male? Remains generally means the body has been there for a long time.'

He replies, 'I can see why they said not to speculate - it's hard not to when you know the person. So much for chilling out today.' He grins but it looks more like a wince. 'Leo Parker... I should have known that by the way he was talking about him all the time.'

'Why don't you go off sick tomorrow? Take a few days off to get some of this out of your system. What would you be saying to one of your patients now? Think of that.' She kisses him on the cheek.

'That is all they need. They are already carrying out a witch hunt on me. This would just add fuel to the fire.' He picks up the paper again but this time he is just staring at it. He is unable to concentrate on even just reading as his mind is full of questions. He knows he will not be able to relax until the remains are at least identified and then they need to be anyone other than those of Millie Sanderson. Although the discovery is a grim affair it has some hope. The detectives now have further clues to work, three suspects arrested and one suspect charged. It all now depends on the forensics and the DNA results of the remains to move the investigation to its final phases. The team brief for the afternoon has been moved forward and all the team are anxiously gathering in the incident room.

As DCI Davies walks in he gets a round of applause and cheers from every single member. His leadership over the past month or so has been so invaluable to the investigation and his insistence on moving resources to Tranby over the weekend paid off handsomely. He looks extremely humbled by the reception he is receiving as he stands in front of the desk and applauds each of the his team individually. 'Great work! First thing I have to tell you is the remains are not those of Millie Sanderson. Early indications are estimating the remains have been there for five years or more. They have however, pinpointed the remains to be female aged around 16 to 18 years of age.'

At first there were gasps of disappointment but then a realisation appeared to fill the room. Detectives were first to start smiling and punch the air with their clenched fist. Then the others caught up and were hugging each other. No speculation the police said but here they were more than speculating, they would have hung Sutton/Parker if they were a lynch mob.

Davies raises his hand in the air to hush the room. He says, 'disappointing in terms of the Millie Sanderson case but if these remains turn out to be... to be who we think they are - we would have solved a six year old cold case. We await on forensics for confirmation and hopefully some firm DNA clues at the scene or on the victim. In the meantime, we will today be questioning the Richards couple and the man we have been waiting a life time to question - Alex Shaw. We still need to find Millie and her ex Julian. So all resources now will be moved to achieve this. Organise yourselves in small teams and let's get this all done. Thank you all for your great efforts so far in this investigation and soon you will all have a little more free time to spend with your families.' He smiles and then leaves the room.

Wilkins has entered DCI Davies office. He has some new evidence from The Crown in Becclesfield. He is invited to sit and does. He wants to make this count as his superior Simpson has done a good job of keeping him in the lower ranks by taking all of his good work as his own.

'Okay lets have it then. I can tell it's good by the looks upon your face.' Davies leans forward to grab his silver Parker pen.

'Well, guv, I've got CCTV footage which blows open this case!'

'Really? Let's have it then.'

Wilkins passes him a memory stick. 'On here, is CCTV footage from the lunchtime of Friday 8th November. It clearly shows Sutton and Shaw when they approach the bar area to buy their rounds. Let me talk you through it.'

Davies inserts the memory stick into a USB port on the side of his laptop. Presses a couple of buttons here and there. It opens just like a video. He uses the fast forward. Wilkins says, 'stop it at 1242. You will see Shaw up at the bar. Here see him there? Freeze it just there. He has actually ordered a shandy for himself and he has a lager for Sutton. Watch what he does next. See, he has a Shot and pretends to drink one at the bar but if you look closely his glass is actually empty and he produces it from his pocket. He doesn't get a shot for himself. All the rounds were purchased by Shaw and at no time does Shaw have a pint of lager or a single shot. In other words, guv he is getting Sutton smashed but staying sober himself.'

'Fantastic Wilkins! This is really good work and comes just at the right time. I can't wait to question him this afternoon. You not doing anything around 3pm today are you?' Davies is looking elated with this piece of evidence even though it probably means Sutton was telling the truth.

'No. I'm only here in the office today chasing up on Julian.'

'Okay you're in with me to question Shaw. Tell Simpson he can stand down.' Davies picks up the phone leaving Wilkins to make his way out of the office.

He makes his way slowly back to the incident room. He is happy about being in on the Shaw questioning but he has to find a way to tell his superior, Simpson that he is actually taking his place in the interview room. That will look as though there has been some back stabbing, whatever way he relays this information back. As he approaches Simpson's desk there is a shout from the other end of the room. One of the junior investigators has discovered that Julian Sanderson has been living in California for the past three years. There is no record of him ever visiting the UK at anytime in the past three years. Simpson grabs the paper off the guy and heads up to DCI Davies office to pass the exciting news. Julian Sanderson can now be eliminated as a suspect but inquiries will need to be made to see if he was involved in any of the planning but it is looking like the police now have all the suspects they need to solve the case or do they?

Chapter 51

DI JENKINS RETURNS to the station and has an urgent meeting with DCI Davies. He walks into the room and can see a disgruntled look upon his boss's face. 'Afternoon, sir.' He says timidly.

'Is it? I suppose you've heard by now that Millie Sanderson was married and had an abusive relationship with her estranged husband? No? Then why not? You should've known this after visiting her home. It makes us all look bloody stupid Jenkins! Not only that, she was raised in Australia. That is according to Chloe Richards anyway. So tell Wilkins to look into that. We're supposed to have everything about her background if we are to crack this case. I don't suppose the Aussies will be very quick, so better get that part going. You know; maiden name, boyfriends - bloody basics!'

'It wasn't me who checked her background, sir. Who told you it was me?' He has a very good idea just who it was but still wants to hear the name aloud.

'Simpson, says you and Wilkins went to look for the clues and get all the background information.' Davies is still looking rather sternly.

He knows whatever he says next will either drop someone else into trouble or show up further errors that were made right at the outset of the investigation. 'Well, I thought that information was made available by the "MPU" (Missing Persons Unit). Aren't they supposed to pass this information over to us?'

He deliberately takes a long time to respond in order to make Jenkins sweat even more than the visible amount on his brow. 'Luckily, it didn't lose us too much time and we've been able to eliminate him now. Please take more care about what appears to be routine inquiries because as you know, a clue missed is an investigation pissed.' When you get one of DCI Davies' made up sayings you know you are in trouble.

He hangs his head in a little shame but quickly rebounds as he still has some exciting news to share. 'I think we know a lot more now, sir. I visited a Fred Watkins from Waverley Road. A neighbour of Harry Sutton. He states categorically he not only saw a man answering the description of one Alex Shaw but spoke with him on Friday the 8th November. He also says he saw the man drive off in Harry Sutton's car. Wicks is bringing him in to do a full statement and he is happy to pick him out in a line up.'

'Bloody hell, Jenkins. Why wasn't this picked up before?' Davies is pleased with the result but displeased with the amount of time it has taken to unravel. 'This is unforgiveable. Someone's head is going to roll for this one. We could have had him locked up by now. I'm going to put that lot into further training. These are the bloody basics!'

'Well, sir, you will need to talk with Simpson as he went there a week or so ago and perhaps for some reason forgot to ask him the right questions? It was early into the investigation, it may just have slipped his mind. I don't want to get anyone into trouble, sir. You know that's not my style. As you always say, sir; results speak louder than action.' Jenkins is very pleased he has managed to get one back on Simpson after being put in the frame for not getting the information about Millie Sanderson's husband and it is a big one.

'Well done, Jenkins. I'm sorry for having a go at you earlier. I guess the stress gets to all of us. I can't believe Simpson didn't get this information when he questioned the witness? Schoolboy errors, Jenkins!'

'Yes, sir. I'm sure he will be gutted when he finds out. Bit out of character though.'

'I think it's time to get Shaw down to room 7b, what do you think?'

'Definitely, sir.'

'Come on then let's go and have a cuppa while we wait for the interview to be arranged. I suppose he'll have a brief in attendance? Oh, can you get hold of Wilky and tell him he's not needed at this interview. Perhaps he can read up on some of the basics in detective work. He surprises me sometimes. One minute he comes up with some really good clues and then he doesn't ask a witness the right questions. Baffling?'

'Will do, sir.'

'Okay let's go get this guy tied up in knots then.'

The transcript of the interview in room 7b;

Alex Shaw - representative Mr. Ben Sharp (Ely and Stewart co)

Transcript d/d 22nd November @ 1505 hrs

5111000380 case number 0207 660 6025 DCI Davies and DI Jenkins

P As we agreed earlier. You are happy for us to call you Alex?

AS Yeah.

P Is there anything you need before we start?

AS No.

P OK thanks. I would like to take you back to the drinking session in The Crown on the 8th November. Were you the person with Harry Sutton?

AS I'm afraid so.

P It looked as though you were good friends. Is that now not the case?

AS I was until I found he got charged.

P Okay we'll come back to that later. He said you both got into a heavy drinking session. Was that the case?

AS Yeah. I won a bit on the horses and treated him. He was saying some strange things not just about Millie but mostly about a girl called Emily - I think?

P What sort of things?

AS I don't wanna get him in trouble.

P He's already in trouble and if he was planning something then someone may be or has already come to harm. So what sort of things?

AS He was talking in the past tense, so it's already happened I reckon.

P So what things?

AS "She deserved everything she got. I wish it didn't happen but it was her own fault". Those were some of the things and then he went on about - Cherry Walk being important to him. Had no idea why though. Is that helpful, mate?

P Anything else?

AS Can't remember too much. I was drunk weren't I?

P Did you both drink the same amount?

AS Well I weren't counting but we roughly had the same amount.

P What sort of drinks did you both have?

AS Pints of lager and shots. He was on a mission. He kept going on about how he had hurt a girl called Emily. That's why I thought it strange he was charged over another girl.

P Did you have shots as well? Only he says you got him home.

AS Yeah. I guess I can hold my drink better than he can.

P Have you ever heard of Millie Sanderson before she was kidnapped?

AS Inaudible.

BS I thought you had the person responsible for her kidnap. So why are you still questioning my client over it?

P We just needed to know if your client knew of Millie Sanderson prior to it all being on the news. So Alex, did you know her before?

AS You know I did. I have a restraining order against her.

P How did you meet Harry Sutton?

AS We met in The Crown by chance and become friends. I was shocked when I saw the papers about Millie but really she had it coming the way she was treating guys.

P Did you know Sutton was involved with her at any point in time?

AS I knew he had a girl. I should've guessed it was her the way he said she was treating him.

P How did you get Sutton back to his home following the drinking session?

AS He didn't live far and so we sorted of leaned on each other. Staggered - would be a fair answer.

P Did you go inside his apartment?

AS No. I just opened his front door for him and he made it in.

P Has Sutton ever let you drive his car or given you his car keys?

AS No to both questions.

P How do you know Colin and Chloe Richards?

AS They run The Swan. I drink in there and met them then.

P Why didn't you come forward when there was media coverage asking you to get in touch?

AS Was there. Blimey, I'm famous, mate.

P So on a scale of 1 - 10 with 10 being the highest. How drunk would you say you was on the 8th November?

AS Definitely at least 9.

P How many shots did you drink - roughly?

AS Probably about six or seven at a guess.

P How many lagers?

AS 8 or 9.

BS Are you going anywhere with this line of questioning only my client has a life to get back to?

P Did either of you change your drinks to say - shandy or something like that? It's a lot to drink in one session?

AS Shandy is for wimps.

P So you never drank any that day?

AS Don't touch the stuff.

P So you know Chloe Richards from the pub?

AS Yes. I've already told you that.

p So you have a restraining order against Millie Sanderson but it is okay to socialise with her sister, Chloe Richards?

AS She is not her sister. You need to check your facts, mate.

P Did you fit Sutton up for this kidnap?

AS How on earth could've I done that?

P Have you ever heard of Leo Parker?

AS No.

P Do you know Millie Sanderson's ex husband Julian?

AS No. Poor sod has my commiserations.

BS Okay that's enough now. Can you produce any evidence to support your untimely arrest in a public place in front of so many people and for what?

P We just have one last question. Have you at any time had access to Harry Sutton's mobile phone?

AS No. He hardly ever used it when I was with him.

P Have you ever driven down Denbar Lane?

BS Don't answer that. You said you only had one last question. Times up. He has fully cooperated with you. I think you either charge him or let him go. I've seen no evidence of any sort just a lot of useless questions about his drinking habits. So what's it to be?

P We have a witness that says he saw you and Harry at Waverley Road on the afternoon of the 8th November.

AS I've already told you, mate. I took him home. He was legless.

P But you weren't?

AS I'm used to it. I'm out all the time.

P We have a witness that saw you get into Harry's car - reg HARR3 - on the afternoon of the 8th November.

AS He must've been drunk as well?

P But you weren't were you? You were drinking shandy and you did not drink any shots did you?

AS I was well drunk.

P You stayed sober and so then you could drive Sutton's car to Denbar lane, whereupon you kidnapped Millie Sanderson. Where is she, Alex? Come on it will save a lot of time.

BS Do not have to answer.

AS Ridiculous claims. Your Jackonary mate!

P So you won't mind attending a line up for us then?

AS I'm not going to let you lot fit me up. It's time I upped and left.

P Where's Millie?

BS I have told my client not say anymore. He has fully cooperated. Release him or charge him.

P Alex Shaw you will be taken down, where the Sergeant will charge you with suspicion of the kidnap of Millie Sanderson.

Interview ended 1546 hrs.

Chapter 52

IT IS SATURDAY morning and Jenkins has arrived early. He is sitting in his usual chair near to the evidence board. He looks up and goes over all of the clues. There are new clues being added each day and today the investigation is about to take a dramatic turn. The identity from the remains found in Cherry Walk are due in around eleven. Everyone on the team are expected to be milling around the incident room around that time. This is the moment they have been awaiting since the remains were dug up. It will end speculation and for some, torment. The detectives are all convinced they have the right suspects detained. Just a little more evidence will no doubt secure a much needed conviction but still no sign or news of Millie Sanderson. She appears to have vanished into thin air and it does not look good for any kind of happy outcome for family and friends. The days have turned into weeks and soon it will be a month since she went missing and they are nowhere nearer finding her but they have charged Alex Shaw with her kidnapping. Jenkins sips a little from a hot mug of tea and ponders everything for a while. There is something troubling him about Harry Sutton/Leo Parker. He has already got him down for the abduction and most probably the murder of Emily Banks but as for Millie Sanderson they need Shaw to either confess or they need to find her either dead or alive to solve the case.

'Morning, sir,' a cheery female voice interrupts his thoughts.

He looks up and sees Constable Wicks back in uniform. She is standing next to him. 'Morning, Wicks. Well done the other night, by the way.'

'Thank you, sir. Good team effort I would say.' She is humble and trying to include everyone in the compliment she has just received.

Jenkins just nods his head and grunts, 'I suppose?'

She is used to his body language being off in the mornings as he is not a good early riser nor known to be a good sleeper. The bags under his eyes verify that very point. He feels older than at any other time. His brown hair is beginning to fade away and there are some grey strands appearing to front. He has not told anyone but it is his birthday. He has stopped celebrating them since he turned 45 three years ago. It is as if he does not wish to be reminded of each passing year but the upside is he will be able to retire on a full pension if all goes well for another ten years. He looks at members of the team and wonders if there is any single one of them he would rather be than himself. There is not. Perhaps, being his birthday has brought on some form of mild depression. He has been on the go now nearly nonstop since this investigation commenced in earnest on 11th November and still no sign of Millie Sanderson. He thinks Davies has already called Simpson in and given him a rollicking over the Fred Watkins evidence he or Wilkins failed to get some time ago. He has been getting the cold shoulder treatment from both of them but he is used to getting these sort of moody blanks over the years, as he remembers back to when he was a DC. He got promoted above Simpson back then.

Simpson and Thompson are now in the interview room 7b awaiting the arrival of Chloe Richards. Simpson says, 'I'll ask the questions. You take some notes - for your experience. If you think of something then write it down on a piece of paper and pass it to me. Okay? I don't want any cock ups on this one. Bloody Wilky has got me in trouble already this week. Think you'd do a better job than he does and you're only young. If you know what I mean?'

He looks a little put out about these instructions but just nods in agreement. He is used to being treated like a junior. He is after all a trainee and one wrong word in sensitive cases like these could blow it permanently. 'So what happened to Wilkins? he was up with the old man for nearly an hour and when he came back he grabbed his coat and left. Rather red faced.'

'Don't worry he'll be back nice and early tomorrow morning. It isn't the first time and it won't be the last... and Thompson, it will happen to you at some time, you wait and see.'

Transcript of interview with Mrs Chloe Richards. Representative. Brian Ingle (Chesterston and co)

5111000387 case number 0207 660 6030 DI Simpson and T/L Thompson.

23rd November 1125 hours interview room 7b.

P Is there anything we can get you before we start?

CR No thank you.

P You reported Millie Sanderson as missing on Sunday, 10th November is that correct?

CR Yes.

P You then reported seeing a black car parked outside her address in Minster Way and you went to challenge the person inside that car. Is that correct?

CR Yes.

P Did you know who the driver of the vehicle was?

CR Not at that time. No.

P When you reported Millie Sanderson as missing you gave your name as Chloe Richards, sister of the missing person. Is that correct?

BI Inaudible.

CR No comment.

P Are you her sister?

CR No comment.

P Our information is that you are not her sister but in fact, her cousin. Is that correct?

CR What does it matter who I am. It is Millie we should be spending our resources upon.

P If you are to help us find her then we need your full cooperation. You understand? What relationship do you have with Millie Sanderson?

CR She's my cousin. We've always called each other sister. So it was just a slip of the tongue - I guess?

P Thank you. That helps us a little. When did you meet Alex Shaw?

CR Don't know any Alex Shaw.

P You was seen talking to him on a couple of occasions. So you must know him?

CR I suspect he's a regular at the pub. I talk to loads of people. It's my job.

P Did you know that Alex Shaw has a restraining order served against your... your cousin?

CR No. That's a shocker. I knew there were two people with these orders but they are the ones that need sorting out not Millie.

P Have you ever met a Harry Sutton?

CR Yes that was Millie's dodgy boyfriend.

P Dodgy? What do you mean by that?

CR He wasn't the person he was trying to portray but Millie couldn't see that. She wears her heart on her sleeve. He used to change personalities at the drop of a hat. Every time he couldn't get his own way, he would turn into this aggressive person. I told Millie about it but she couldn't see it. Have you got him to confess yet?

P We still have him in custody for questioning further. If you know something about her disappearance then now is a really good time to tell us. So do you know what happened that Friday evening on the 8th November in Tenby Lane?

CR Don't you think I would've come forward right at the beginning of this - investigation?

P Don't you think it rather strange that Alex Shaw makes friends with Harry Sutton and they both had relationships with Millie Sanderson?

CR Becclesfield is a small place. It must just be a coincidence?

P Another coincidence is Harry Sutton and Millie Sanderson having the same therapist. Did you know your... cousin was seeing a therapist?

CR Becclesfield is a small place. Yes I did know she was forced to attend to see some sort of shrink or another. It is the only one in the town.

P What do you know of her court cases for stalking and harassment?

CR Probably the same as you - except she is the victim in all of this.

P How many times has Alex Shaw visited your pub?

CR I don't know. He's a customer of probably several hundred each week.

P So you don't know him that well then?

CR No.

P Is he a friend of your husband, Colin Richards?

CR Not that I am aware of.

P What about Julian Sanderson. Do you know him?

CR No comment.

P You never mentioned Millie Sanderson's ex husband at any time when we first spoke with you over her disappearance. Why was that?

CR No comment.

P You appear to have stopped cooperating. I thought you wanted us to find Millie. So please just try and clear up this issue.

It could be important to the safety of Millie. So once again. Why didn't you tell us about Julian?

BI My client has fully cooperated throughout this interview. I would like to hear just what evidence you have to justify remanding her in custody?

P If we could just have the answers to those final questions we may be in a better position to understand exactly what has gone on.

BI Once again. Can you get to the evidence you have or you must release my client without any charges whatsoever.

P Well, firstly, she lied about being Millie's sister. Then she is seen taking Alex Shaw into the back room of the pub for a cosy chat. We have information telling us Julian Sanderson was an aggressive and abusive husband. Something I am sure your client would've known and yet she says nothing about him in all of this time. Her cousin is missing and in who knows what kind of danger. Why are you not cooperating fully. Now is the time to tell us. If Millie is still alive we need to find her now. Where is Millie?

BI Just circumstantial at best.

P We'll be holding her pending her husband's interview later today. I would come clean over some of these areas we will be highlighting.

Interview ended at 1215 hrs.

JACOB AND AYAKA are sitting in their living room watching tv. They have been checking periodically the news channels to see if Millie has yet been found. There has been much speculation over the human remains found in Cherry Walk, Tranby. There are four persons in custody; Harry Sutton, Alex Shaw, Chloe Richards and her husband, Colin Richards. DCI Davies is about to give a news conference and the main newsreader passes over to her journalist.

The camera switches to Alisha Nicholson. She appears a little breathless as if she had been running a marathon but it is the excitement of what may about to be revealed in the Millie Sanderson case.

She says, 'I'm outside Becclesfield Police station where we are awaiting any moment now for Detective Chief Inspector Sean Davies to give an important update. You may recall Harry Sutton, a 28 year old from Becclesfield has been charged with suspicion of the kidnap of Millie Sanderson. Police have already informed us about the discovery of human remains in Cherry Walk, Tranby and recently police arrested three more suspects, which are currently being detained pending further inquiries. So... here he comes let's see what he has to say.'

'My name is DCI Davies. Good afternoon and thank you all for coming. I can confirm the following; Harry Sutton's charges of kidnapping Millie Sanderson have been dropped. We have today charged Alex Shaw with the kidnap of Millie Sanderson. We have charged Chloe Richards and Colin Richards with Conspiracy to Kidnap. We can also confirm the following;

The human remains found at a property in Cherry Walk, Tranby are those of missing 17 year old, Emily Banks. Emily went missing over six years ago. We have today, following extensive police work, charged Harry Sutton aka Leo Parker with the murder of Emily Banks. Questions?'

R Has Sutton confessed to the murder of Emily Banks?

P We have the evidence and are still making inquiries.

R Do you have any idea where Millie Sanderson is now?

P We are still gathering evidence and I can say with confidence it will only be a matter of time.

R Alisha Nicholson - Detective can you explain why given you had Parker in custody six years ago - it has taken you this long to solve the crime?

P Hello Alisha. It has been a complex investigation but we never gave up on Emily and we haven't given up on Millie either. Sometimes, things take a long time to come to the surface but progress in DNA testing and detective advances have helped us a great deal. One last question please, Andy you've been patiently waiting there.

R Thank you. Andy Stones from the Herald. The three new charges; isn't Chloe Richards, Millie Sanderson's sister? and what about Julian Sanderson?

P That's two questions as normal, Andy but yes Chloe Richards is related to Millie Sanderson and thank you for bringing up her ex. He has been eliminated from our inquiries as he was in the USA at the time. We have no evidence of Julian Sanderson being involved. Thank you all. Bye.

Alisha Nicholson turns to her camera and looks down at the lens and says, 'there you have it. Harry Sutton aka Leo Parker charged with murdering Emily Banks. You may recall she is the daughter of the owner of Banks Sawmills, Ferry Lane, which Leo Parker burned down around six years ago. Police had him in custody at that time but due to lack of evidence, they could not charge him in connection with the missing Emily Banks investigation. He served five years for the arson attack on the sawmills. Charges for kidnapping Millie Sanderson dropped but Alex Shaw has now been charged with the kidnap and Chloe Richards, a relative of the victim along with her husband have been charged with Conspiracy to Kidnap. There is a lot going on here in Becclesfield and I am sure we still have a lot more to find out. So just to recap on this extraordinary investigation; Harry Sutton has been charged with murdering Emily Banks. Alex Shaw is charged with kidnapping Millie Sanderson. Chloe and Colin Richards are charged with Conspiracy to Kidnap. Sadly we still await news on the whereabouts of Millie Sanderson. This is Alisha Nicholson reporting.'

'Emily Banks! I cannot believe I missed that.' Jacob leans on his wife's shoulder close to tears. 'He went on about her all the time in our sessions. Oops, sorry please ignore you heard that.'

'I'm your wife, Jacob, you do not need to worry about that. It is not your fault. The police are doing a good job and they have you to thank for a lot of their evidence - I imagine.' She kisses him on the cheek and goes out to the kitchen.

'They still have not found poor Millie yet. I am fearful, Ayaka, she may be...'

'Do not even think that, Jacob. You do not know what her fate is and whilst there is still hope - there is optimism. Please be positive. This is what you probably tell your patients all the time.' She has popped back in from the kitchen to be with him. They sit down on the red leather couch to comfort each other.

Chapter 53

A BLONDE WOMAN aged in her late twenties has walked into Becclesfield Police station. She is claiming to be the missing woman Millie Sanderson. DI Jenkins and Constable Wicks are going to take her statement. They are eagerly gathered and seated in interview room 7d.

Jenkins is looking her up and down. He has a puzzled look upon his face. He says, 'before we start, may I just say, you look nothing like your photographs. You have black hair and hazel eyes. The lady I'm looking at now has blonde hair and blue eyes.'

She smiles and crosses her legs. She looks at ease considering the confessions she is about to make and the consequences they will almost certainly bare. 'All will be revealed, detective. All will be revealed.'

He is quick to respond. 'So you will not mind taking a swab for your DNA so we can match it up with the ones taken from Minister Way?'

'I am pretty certain you are going to do that anyway. Especially after what I am about to tell you - if you'll let me that is?' She says deliberately being sarcastic.

Jenkins nods and then says, 'okay, as my vicar always used to say, "let us begin". You are happy for us to proceed?'

'Yes, please.'

'Just for the record. You are voluntarily giving us your statement?'

'Yes.' She is now looking a little impatient.

'Please go ahead. In your own time and in your own words. I may have to interrupt just for clarification purposes - you understand?' Jenkins adjusts his seating to be more comfortable and is looking really interested to see what she has got to say.

She nods her approval and says, 'the first thing you need to know is I have solved the case of my murdered little sister for you.' She pauses as she knows there must be a question to such a dramatic opening sentence and there is.

Jenkins eyes almost pop out of his head, he is stunned. In all of his years he has never heard such an opening statement from any suspects or victims. 'You say murdered sister? Who is that?'

'Even now, you all don't know do you? Emily Banks was - is my little sister. Whilst on the subject of names you lot and the media have been getting my name wrong all along. My father named us with the same letters in our first names; Emily and Miley, that's M-I-L-E-Y, Miley and not Millie but I have been called Millie for many years now.' Her face is a little flushed as she shuffles around on her seat a little.

'Yes we have just discovered the fact you were married but your sister - I mean cousin, didn't do us any favours by withholding so much information about you. Was this part of the plan?'

She deliberately ignores his remarks and continues with her criticism of the investigation. After a short break, she says, 'anyway, whatever way you want to look at things... it hasn't been the greatest investigation has it?'

This time both Jenkins and Wicks choose to ignore her remarks. They urge her to continue with the facts but Jenkins knows this is going to be far worse a mistake than any of the others made so far. He knows Davies will pull someone over the coals for this negligence and he is praying it was not his fault.

She looks up at the cracks in the old ceiling plaster as if to signal her patience is becoming a little frayed but eventually continues with her statement. 'As I said, Emily Banks is my sister and things changed just prior to the fire at my father's sawmills in Ferry Lane.

My father employed Leo Parker as a general labourer some months before. Poor little Emily used to work in the office to help out and that was where Parker first laid eyes upon her. He kept persisting with her to go out but she had better taste than that. He bought her unwanted gifts, telephoned her and generally became obsessed with her over time. My father liked Parker but was totally unaware of his attentions to Emily and gave him extra personal work. He painted our home, landscaped the back garden and even washed the windows. To think he had the full run of the empty house at times actually makes my skin crawl and gives me the shivers.' She pauses and reaches out for a paper tissue from a box which had been strategically placed on her side of the desk prior to her arrival.

He looks over towards her in a sympathetic manner, which is not usually that forthcoming and especially not in the interview room. She appreciates the gesture and sits up straighter.

'Now you have Parker locked up for the murder and my sister can now be laid to rest with my parents, my job is done - I must face the consequences of my actions.' She pauses for a moment. 'Anyway, a couple of days after the fire and after you guys let Leo Parker go after questioning him for the arson attack, my sister went off for her weekly hairdressing appointment in the town. Except she never made it there. We reported it to you immediately but nothing was taken seriously until three or so days went by. My father had lost his business and now one of his daughters has gone missing. I don't know how anyone can deal with such trauma in such a short space of time? The months went by and the only news we were getting was Parker had been charged with the arson attack but he had to be the one who took Emily as well? You had no other suspects but still you failed to find any evidence on him. You probably know he was found guilty of arson and sentenced to 7 years in prison. Well, that gave us plenty of time to plan our next move. I spent the next five or so years just doing that and planning for when he would get out.

Killing him would be no good, so don't worry that was never in the plan, besides I still needed to know where and what he had done with Emily.' At this point she has broken down in uncontrollable sobbing. A refreshments break was called for and a time for Miley to recover her composure in order to continue with her statement.

The three return to the interview room and are seated. Jenkins has reassured her once more and confirms she can request a break at any point if she feels the need. She takes a deep breath and then recommences her statement.

She says, 'as the time was approaching his release, I dyed my hair black and started to get used to these special contact lenses that can change the look of your eyes. I bought hazel coloured ones to match my sister's eyes colour. I remember how she used to walk, talk and bought the perfume she used to wear. I took a number of her personal jewellery and clothes, held them in a cupboard in my apartment in readiness for the right time. Then I was going to wear some of it on the first occasion when I was to meet up with him. I was ready for when he gets out. I had to find a way of getting into some medical care and being able to have a case file drawn up on me. This would enable me to manipulate everything for when the time came for these files to be made known to you. So a couple of friends of mine pretended I was obsessed with them and had been stalking them. They took out restraining orders against me and I obviously broke them. I was taken to court and managed to talk my solicitor in putting forward a plan for me to undertake much needed obsessive therapy. It worked a treat. Now I was officially in therapy and could say anything I wished. It would all be recorded in my file. We kept an eye on Parker when he got released from prison. We followed him to France and back.' She pauses and takes a sip of water.

After a short break to recall all the events, she says, 'we did not anticipate him to ever set foot in Becclesfield again but shortly after his release he had undergone several changes in his appearance. He had transformed his hair colour to fair, put on a little weight and some Botox had altered his facial appearance quite significantly. I still knew him. I would always be able to recognise the animal anywhere. The one thing we didn't know at this point was the change in name to Harry Sutton. That threw us off to begin with but the neighbour on the ground floor of the apartments in Waverley Road was extremely helpful. He told us his name and basically his movements over the past few weeks. We were able to start monitoring and followed his every move. Then a major piece of luck fell in our laps. He got arrested for a road rage incident - his temper rising to the surface once again. I couldn't understand why he didn't get sent straight back to prison as I thought that would've been the normal procedure but Leo being Leo had most probably charmed the judge with his fake personality. Anyway, this turned out to be real lucky because not only did he get forced to undertake therapy for his anger management - he was seeing the same therapist. Of course, that shouldn't come as a major shock as there is only one therapy centre in Becclesfield. This now meant there would be two sets of case files and all I had to do now was to have a chance meeting with him to lay the trap.' She pauses to take another sip of water from a white plastic cup in front of her on the desk. Picks up a tissue and wipes her eyes dry.

Jenkins has been patiently waiting to butt in with some questions but it has been so remarkable he did not wish to spoil the flow and so he restrains himself. He smiles in a way to encourage her to continue.

'That's better. So my cousin Chloe and her husband run The Swan pub in Tranby. What better place to bump into someone than a pub? A note was posted through his letterbox telling him Leo Parker would be in a pub in Tranby on that Friday evening. We weren't sure if he would actually take the bait or not but deep down

I knew he would. I thought as he had changed his name from Leo Parker to Harry Sutton, he may think of Leo as either not being alive anymore or being somebody completely different to himself. I had been reading so many medical books over the years, I had heard of this distancing some people do when they have had a serious trauma and need to move on in a different kind of life, so I was hoping it would be this. The other reason he would turn up must surely be to see who had discovered his true identity but it was still a gamble.' She pauses again but this time it is in order to get the details correct.

She continues. 'I got a job behind the bar and worked around four Friday night sessions in a row, so the regulars were getting used to me and everything looked as it should for when he turns up. I spotted him immediately when he walked in and went about my routine of trying to walk and talk like my sister Emily. I was also wearing my sisters clothes. I could see the looks upon his face. He was walking into the trap. A little bit of flirting and some laughing was all that was needed. We met at the burger van in the square after I finished work that night. We then walked down to the canal. Here I had to endure his stupid little jokes and then, this was something I could not tell I'd be able to do until I did it, we kissed. I knew there would have to be a lot of this if I were to succeed in hooking him proper. We already knew he had booked a room at The Lodge and the idiot actually booked it in the name of Leo Parker. Thought he was being clever I suspect. The bottom line is we went back there. This is the part of the plan I had been dreading from the very start. Pretending to get all amorous with the creep who had killed my sister - well, it would be the only way to find out the real truth. I led him on and as luck had it, never thought I would say this but he didn't have any condoms. So he left the hotel and bought some at the 24 hour garage in Tranby. I had everything ready for when he came back. The fool fell for it so easily. We had some drinks and when I poured him some I put a drug inside, which in a short amount of time would render him useless and then put him in a deep sleep. Whilst he was asleep, I ripped open a condom packet and left the empty wrapper on the floor for him to see when he wakes up. I then wrote something on the mirror to let him think how wonderful in bed he is, together with my mobile phone number and in order to keep the charade going longer.

When it came to my next therapy session with Jacob; I hated using him in this way but it was the only way to get the truth, I spilled the beans about this wonderful guy I had just met and how lovely he is. I didn't tell him the name of this wonderful man at this point. I wanted to build the relationship up and then weeks later I could start describing his sudden change; his aggression, his anger, fixation and the fear I was now feeling. In order to get to that point I needed a distraction and someone who could watch my back in case it got out of hand in some way. That is where Alex came in again. For having already taking a restraining order against me he was now becoming best buds with Parker. He played his part perfectly. Even getting him drunk on the final day, 8th November.'

Jenkins can bare it no longer he has to disrupt her with a question or two. 'So you drugged him two nights running at The Lodge? What about all those other times? There must have been other times in all of those weeks you were seeing each other?'

She laughs for the first time. It would appear he has said something to amuse her. She says, 'it was the same every single time. It was easy. He likes a drink and he was taking his medication. So every time I drugged him, we both just put it down to the alcohol mixing with his meds. I would leave an empty condom wrapper for him to find and in his head and with his big ego - he believed we had been intimate. Jacob warned me time and time again about not drinking alcohol whilst on meds. So that part was easy as well.'

He looks a little disbelieving. 'So you were never intimate with him in all of that time?'

Once again she gets a kick out of it all and says, 'that's correct. Empty condom wrappers on the floor. He must've woken up feeling well hung-over but taken a little solace in the apparent sex he thought he had the night before.'

Both Jenkins and Wicks look at each other. They both have similar looks upon their faces. It is a look of shock but it has an air of pleasure at the same time. Jenkins is next to speak after this short pause in proceedings. 'Do you wish to have another break, Miley.' He has intentionally called her by her correct name. This may be in an attempt to show a little admiration or it may be more to do with extracting further information. Either way it has been appreciatively received by the reciprocate. She is smiling back towards him and for the first time is actually beginning to trust him.

A half hour break has been taken and all three are back sitting in their chairs in the interview room 7d. Jenkins says, 'okay, Miley please continue where you left off. He was drugged and you never were intimate.'

'That's right. That was the part of the plan I didn't think would come to fruition. I dreaded the thought of him succeeding in... in getting his way with me. It may have happened. There was always the possibility he may not drink on one of the occasions but thankfully I didn't have to cross that bridge. It was bad enough exposing my naked body and having him caress me. Anyway, moving along as I'm sure you want to hear the rest?' She pauses and sees two smiling approving faces opposite her and so continues. She says, 'the one thing I hadn't accounted for was my cat Tom getting involved but as it happened anyway, I decided to use this to my advantage in my sessions. It helped paint the picture of how nasty that Leo or Harry whatever you prefer, really is. I didn't expect

Jacob to actually solve it for me. What a nice guy that man is. He even sat outside my apartment all night to ensure my safety. I hope he is going to be okay after all of this. I wouldn't want him to feel bad or anything like that.' She stops for some reassurance.

Jenkins says, 'quite the opposite actually. He has really helped us in this investigation. He was, like everyone else, really concerned for your welfare.'

'Ah bless him,' she says, 'there are not that many nice ones around these days.' Then after a little thought she recalls further events. 'So having built the case files up in a way that Harry Sutton now looks like the dangerous maniac with anger issues that he really is, it was time for my final day. I went around to his apartment, spoke with Fred from the apartment below. Making sure I was seen being linked to Harry Sutton. Then I went over to The Crown where there would be a number of witnesses plus Alex was hiding in a corner to ensure my safety - should something go wrong. I had the stand up row with him and did what most women would no doubt love to do - tip his precious beer all over his head. This wasn't done just out of spite or in a fit of jealousy but as he moved away from the table putting his back to me, I was able to take his mobile phone and place it in my bag. No one was looking at me they were all looking at him cursing out loud for everyone to hear. That was an unexpected bonus because we now have him shouting aloud abusive life threatening remarks towards me in front of staff and customers alike. I'm sure you found this useful in your investigation, assuming someone did go to The Crown to investigate this matter?'

Jenkins is quick to respond. 'I personally went along and interviewed bar staff and customers. You're right, they all said how Sutton threatened you and it did add to the motives side of things. Please continue.'

'That's good,' she says a little sarcastically. 'Alex came outside of the pub when Parker went to the toilet to clean up and I then handed Alex the mobile phone. I then rushed out of the area back to my apartment to pick up some belongings. We now had everything in place for me to disappear, except for his car of course but that was going to be another job for his new best friend Alex. Having got him very drunk, Alex took him home to his apartment and laid him on his bed. Yes, he was drugged again so would not resurface until many hours later. Alex waited until just before 1730 hours. It was dark then so he easily managed to leave his apartment with the car keys and Parker's phone in his pocket. I left my apartment shortly after. As I drove past the Ship and Anchor, Alex flashed his lights at me from the car park. He then pulled out in the black Audi he had taken from Waverley Road and started following me. We knew there would be a lot of CCTV cameras in that vicinity and both cars would be caught on camera. It would look as if he was following me into Denbar Lane. At the lay-by on the left hand side just before the farm, I pulled over. Leaving all my personal belongings including the key in the ignition in the car, Alex pulled up behind me and I jumped inside. We quickly drove off and turned left. Knowing full well there are no homes in this area and no chance of being caught on CCTV. Alex threw Parker's now switched off phone in the lake on the left hand side. When we got a little further up the road, we opened the boot and I placed my blood droplets, which I had prepared earlier in the day, onto the boot carpet. I closed the boot and jumped into Chloe's car with her and we went the long way to Tranby. I stayed upstairs in the loft room whilst she reported me missing. Alex took the car back and went into his apartment, carefully placing the keys upon a table. He looked in on him and he was fast asleep - out for the count.

Jenkins has to speak. 'That was some plan but how did you think it would lead to finding your sister?'

'It had always been a calculated risk but with me missing and the row in the pub being the last time anyone saw of me, add to that his past and being his so called girlfriend, he would certainly be number one on the list of suspects. His infatuation with my sister was always going to be his downfall. I knew he could not resist some form of bragging to the therapist about her and it was certain at some point, his true identity would be revealed. The two case files from the therapy sessions must've made good reading. It would show me as being vulnerable, frightened and getting more anxious as the weeks went by. The other case file of Harry Sutton would probably be showing some signs of desperation and anger towards the end. He would probably be raging about me by then. So it all fitted in nicely and you lot will certainly be interested in it all once I go missing. Now you were looking for a woman missing in the present, it would surely only be a matter of time until my sister's disappearance, six years ago, would resurface and he would be questioned over that. Besides, we knew he had some sort of infinity with Cherry Walk as we followed him there at least five times over the months leading up to this. I had a gut feeling, I'm sure you do a lot in your job; Emily and Cherry Walk were linked in some way. It turned out to be the case, didn't it?' She looks satisfied with her account of things but is a little fearful deep inside of the consequences of her actions.

Jennings looks at her with a sort of admiration he usually only affords to his two daughters. For quite some time during this statement, he had feelings of pity for her and was staggered by the way in which she carried out the plan. He secretly thought, *what a detective she would make*, but now he had his job to do. He knew she would have to pay for her actions. So many laws had been broken and it appeared he really did not know where to start. 'I think you need some legal assistance. You are certainly going to be detained and charged at some point. You are extremely unlikely to get bail given you have already disappeared once before.'

She looks up at him and says, 'I have a solicitor engaged already. He is actually upstairs right now. He is talking with your bosses as we speak.'

'Really? That's good organising. What's your solicitors name?'

'I think you know him - his name is Reginald Bartram.' She grins and looks him straight in the eyes.

His facial expression changes immediately to one of shock and a little fear. He has had dealings with him in court before and has not been given an easy time of things. 'He is top dog around these parts. How did you get him?'

She is still grinning and looking rather smug. 'Oh, didn't you know? He's a friend of the family but still expensive, I guess?'

'You don't stop surprising me, Miley.'

'Yes and he told me not to sign the statement until he is finished upstairs and comes down to see me. Is that Ok?' She knows it is okay. It is more than okay - she does not have to sign it if she so wishes.

Jenkins looks a little subdued but is happy to go along with events as they are unfolding. He says, 'okay then - we wait for Reginald to come in. Nothing for it but refreshments. I'll go and get them and bring them back for you.'

Chapter 54

WHILST MILEY SANDERSON is being interviewed in room 7d, a meeting is in progress between Reginald Bartram, Davies and Cole. Bartram is representing Miley Sanderson and all the nice introductions have taken place. This meeting is completely off the record. There are no notes being taken. The two detectives had been given a full copy of Miley's proposed statement prior to Bartram's arrival.

Bartram, dressed in an expensive looking navy pinstripe suit, white shirt and navy silk tie, places his brief case on the table. 'The way I see it, you would not have made the arrest of Parker or Sutton, whatever you wish to call him, if it were not for my client's efforts.'

Davies interrupts immediately. 'You are not suggesting we should reward her, are you?'

He smiles as this sort of reaction had been well anticipated. 'I think you need to hear me out. It is definitely in your interests and maybe in your personal interests.'

Cole leans back in his large rocking leather chair as he feels this will not only be very interesting but most probably quite lengthy if past dealings with Bartram are anything to go upon.

Bartram continues. 'The way I see it; there are positives and negatives in this case. The negatives far outweigh the positives from your points of view, that is. Looking in from the outside; you had Parker in custody six years ago, you released him without charge but full credit you did succeed in banging him up for five years on the arson charges.' He stops and gets some paperwork out of his case and places it deliberately on the table so the detectives can read it if they can understand it from being upside down to them on the table. 'So the case goes cold and nothing has been done about it until my client stepped in to save the day.'

Cole says, 'I like the way you are playing her as the heroin and not the villain.'

The sarcasm is completely ignored by Bartram as he says, 'it is a good result for you in the end but look at what may happen to you all in court; you could be torn apart by the media for being incompetent six years ago when the case was bungled and the same for the way you handled the disappearance of Miley - you could not even get her name right could you until today? You failed to discover that Chloe was not her sister but her cousin, you failed to discover Harry Sutton's former identity until Miley put it on your laps - even though you charged him six months earlier. What happened to his DNA? That would surely have told you his former identity, Leo Parker? Had you looked deeper into Miley's background you would have discovered sooner rather than later that she was in fact the sister of Emily Banks. As for Alex - well that took you ages to even find him.

Davies is looking angry and interrupts. 'We were finding these things out as we were investigating. You know how the system works? We were actually investigating a false claim of someone going missing. That sort of thing doesn't happen every day. As for Alex Shaw; well we knew it would only be a matter of time until we got him into custody. Where is he now?'

Bartram just sits there looking smug. He knows Davies is ruffled already and thinks how he would love to get him in the witness box on trial day.

Davies continues undeterred. 'So you are wrong about that part. Also, we had a number of suspects under surveillance. It would only have been a matter of time until we got there. Of course, we had no idea Miley had been planning all of this for so

long but I'm afraid she has to face the consequences and so will we,
I guess?'

Bartram looks pleased with himself. He has them both rattled
already. 'Now the other thing that will happen if you go and charge
her; will cause a major public outcry for her justice. Her sister has
been murdered and she has solved the case for you. How do you
think that will sit with the public and the media? I can foresee
marches on Downing Street, petitions and after a lengthy internal
investigation, there could be demotions or even dismissals. Would
be a shame for those who are nearing their golden pension ages.'
He stares directly at Cole as if to indicate the "golden pension ages"
was aimed directly at him personally as he is nearing that length in
service.

The two detectives both look concerned. It would appear the
personal consequences suddenly hit home to both of them. Cole
is first to respond. 'So what are you offering us? I don't see how
dropping all charges is going to help us in anyway?'

'This piece of paper you have both been trying to read is a
draft legal document that will make all of this go away. I am pretty
confident if we could think of something that benefits my client
in some way, she would be happy to look into the possibility of
signing one. You know the usual? She will not speak to any third
parties about the case etc. You do not need me to fully explain the
benefits of such a document. I am thinking out of the box now but
as Miley has helped you at last to charge Parker or Sutton, whatever
you prefer, her evidence will be vital in securing his conviction. So
having charged her and she will plead not guilty by the way, all that
evidence will come out in her court case before the trial of Parker.
You see what I mean don't you?' He pauses and he is looking at two
confused detectives so he continues. 'You need Miley's evidence
at the Parker trial and you don't want to risk a mistrial or cause
the jury to be biased before the trial starts? As for the therapy

side of things, well they are bound by law not reveal any details of their patients unless - well you know all of that too. If only we could agree to something along those lines it would be so much better for all concerned. Just think of it; you get full credit for the entire investigation, arrest, discovery of body and conviction of a murderer. Your whole police force ratings will go through the roof and your reputations are not just saved but maybe enhanced. Who knows there could be medals and promotions. I know Miley is downstairs and she is making a statement. She has not signed it and so it can easily be ripped up and binned. I think it is a no brainer to be honest. "King's Evidence", best for all concerned.'

Davies is first to react. 'Honest! That is the key word. So you are saying we drop the charges of let's just say; wasting police time and resources, theft of motor vehicle, theft of mobile phone, drugging, conspiracy to do just about anything and much more - just so we can save face and she can go free?'

Bartram nods. 'I would give it serious thought as the conviction of Parker may be at serious risk. Also remember, I will be defending her should a court appearance be necessary and I will expose all of your failings in the Emily Banks case as well as the -Millie or Miley - what do you prefer to call her?'

Cole has been summing things up in his head and says, 'the media and the public will go into a frenzy if we tell them the Millie Sanderson kidnap never really happened. They would never be able to trust us again?'

Davies interrupts. 'The CPS will never go for it. Besides we have a team of detectives downstairs who have been working day and night to find her. How do you convince them?'

'That's your problem. I did not say it will be easy but is achievable. I leave it all up to you. The next time we meet gentlemen will be officially and I will not be able to discuss the issues raised in this meeting, as I am sure you can appreciate. Some wise person once said to me "The ends justify the means", and do you know I use that principle quite a lot in my work. Sometimes I have to go along with things that I truly wish I did not have to but as I said...'

Cole butts in.' The ends justify the means.'

Bartram is looking pleased with himself. He has pitched things just right - in his own opinion. 'Well, I think that concludes our business, gentlemen.' He rises to his feet and shakes hands with the two detectives.

Cole holds onto his hand for a little longer, looks him in the eyes and says, 'you can have our answer now.' Bartram is a little shocked but leans over to listen. Cole whispers, 'definite no if it was up to us but the decision lays with the CPS and I don't think Brad Willis will go for it.'

Chapter 55

MILEY SANDERSON IS still seated in room 7d awaiting the arrival of her legal representative, Reginald Bartram. There is an eerie stillness within the room considering there are three persons in attendance. The door opens and Bartram walks in. He smiles over towards Miley who is still seated. She appreciates the gesture and smiles back.

'We'll leave you two to get on with things. Come on Wicks lets go.' Jenkins says as he rises to his feet.

'Ah, Jenkins isn't it?' Bartram was quick to remember him. 'Weren't you the one involved in the Sherwood case last year?'

He nods but does not engage in a conversation with him. He remembers how badly that ended last time in court when giving his evidence.

'Bye,' Bartram says sarcastically to Jenkins. 'Now, Miley. We don't have long so let's get down to it. I put a deal over to them but basically they refused it but they don't really have much of a say in things. I'll be seeing Brad Willis, he's running the case from CPS.'

'How long do you think I'm going to get?' she asks with a noticeable tremble running down the entire length of her body.

'I think they haven't thought it out yet. You will probably be here for a few days. There's no point in trying to get you bail. You've already disappeared once and they will play on that from their prospective. I am playing golf on Sunday and guess who with? Yes. Brad and I often play golf and chew the fat. He owes me big time after the Harris trial last year and I intend to collect now. So don't worry. The best we can get is King's Evidence against Harry Sutton. You will have to sign a document and cannot reveal any of this case to any third parties. So don't go thinking you can sell your story later on in the Herald.' He smiles and reassures her once more by nodding in a positive way. 'Does that sound like something you'll be interested in?'

She surprisingly hesitates before saying, 'what about the other three? Will their charges be dropped as well?'

'Oh, yes, I forgot about the three wise people. That will all be part of the deal. They won't want any of this getting into the media or the case against Sutton could collapse.' He rises to his feet. 'Just tell the truth and everything will be alright.'

'Worst case scenario?' she asks the million dollar question.

'I never think about that until towards the end of a trial but of course the worse case is obviously a jail sentence of some term but let's not go there just yet. There is a long way to go and we'll know more come Monday morning. Just sit tight and try not to stress. We can discuss further if things are not worked out before then. I have to go now, Miley but get in touch if you need me for anything and leave it all to me.'

'Thank you so much. If my father was still alive he would have been so proud of you and would have thanked you from the bottom of his heart.' She begins to sob at the thoughts of her father and how he would have felt about all of these events unfolding.

'Yes, I know. I miss him. Let's get that bastard convicted now you've done all of the hard work for the police. Bye, Miley.' He rattles the door and it opens. He leaves whilst Miley is escorted down to the cells for another night.

Jenkins has just received a major blow to the investigation and is in Davies office talking with him. 'That woman is refusing to give a testimony in court if she is needed to attend.'

Davies asks, 'what woman?'

'The one that goes by Evita. You know the one Sutton paid to have sex with.'

'We can't have that. We may need her. What was the point of giving her statement is she had no intention of backing it up?'

Jenkins looks up to the ceiling. 'She says now we've caught the man, there's no need for her to get involved - bad for business. She also said now the Miley woman has been found safe - that was the only reason she came forward in the first place. I've had many dealings, sir and they are not usually very cooperative.'

'What about a bit of encouragement - money?'

'Already suggested that to her but I could have a word with Wicks - you know being another woman and all of that. Besides, they seemed to get on quite well when we had her in for her statement.' Jenkins smiles and leans back in his chair.

'Okay, get Wicks to visit her. We really need her testimony so tell her to use her initiative. Keep me informed, we are reaching the crucial stage of the investigation and now we have formed your MIT 1 (Murder Investigation Team), I expect you to deliver Jenkins - at all costs!' Davies picks up his phone. The usual signal to communicate the meeting is over.

Jenkins gets up and leaves the office. He heads down to the incident room looking for Wicks. She is talking to Wilkins about the investigation. 'Wicks!' he shouts, 'I've got a special job for you.'

She is a little happy at being chosen but does not know whether it is going to be another routine assignment. 'Yes, sir?'

'Don't look so worried. You are going to enjoy this one. It is of the utmost importance and only you could succeed. The guv suggested you would be ideal and he will be observing things quite closely. So you will need to be on top...on top of the game.' He sniggers like a school child as he pictures the forthcoming encounter she will soon be having. He explains everything further and Wicks does not look at all fazed by any of it. In fact, she is thinking this is a good chance for her to make a real impact on the investigation and will do no harm in terms of her personal career prospects.

She gets dropped off one street from the address she will be attending. She turns the corner into Albany Road and is looking for number 70. It will be on her right as they are the even numbers. Her heart begins to race and the importance of the task suddenly takes its toll in terms of nerves. As she approaches the dark blue door of number 70 she spots a large sticker by the bell, it reads; "KNOCK, KNOCK, WHO'S THERE? RING THE BELL IF YOU HAVE MONEY TO SPARE". She giggles and it is enough to settle her nerves and bring back her composure. She is ready. She rings the bell. There is a slight delay and then the door opens. Standing in front of her is Evita and she looks dressed for action. Small black leather skirt, stockings and a very low cut red top. Evita looks pleased to see the Constable.

'Hello, sugar. Is this a social call? I see you are wearing your uniform. You had better come in before the neighbours see you.' Evita laughs as she leads Wicks up a number of stairs to the top floor of the maisonette. 'Have they sent you to change my mind?'

She answers in a diplomatic way. 'They're men, you know they only think with their penis?'

Evita laughs. She likes Wicks. 'Do you know what would happen if all the "Johns"' found out I was informing to the cops? At best, I would be out of work and I don't even wish to think the worse thing they could do to me.'

Wicks sits next to her on a large black couch in the middle of a darkened living room. 'We could give you anonymity? That way no one has to know who you are and we could protect you. It's not as though you have witnessed any crime but you have valuable information on Sutton's aggressive behaviour. The guv says he may not even need to call you. Of course, we can arrange some generous expenses - you know - to compensate you for loss of earnings.' She feels pleased with her pitch she has covered all the bases, or so she thinks.

'You're sounding desperate now sugar. I only came forward because of the missing girl. You have the girl and the man locked up. Giving testimony in a packed court is not my idea of fun, Hun.'

Wicks knows she has to do some more convincing. 'We are desperate to a degree but if you just agreed to it now, it may turn out he even pleads guilty. So none of us will have to give evidence besides they do video in some cases, so you may not even have to go into the courtroom.' She knows she has still not sold the idea and so moves closer towards her. She holds her right hand and gently brushes Evita's hair, she whispers, 'I would be ever so grateful if you would agree.'

There is definitely a moment between the two of them as they gaze into each other's eyes. Evita says, 'have you ever been with a woman before?'

She nods in a positive way.

'Have you ever been with a man before?'

Wicks answers immediately. 'Yes, I have.'

'I didn't have you down as being bisexual.'

She looks a little insulted and responds, 'I'm not a label, I am a woman and I am free to choose anyone or anything I like - so long as it's legal of course. I hate it when people put labels over someone's head just because they are individual and proud.'

Evita is impressed but says, 'what label do you put on me? Prostitute? whore? on the game? Hun, there are a thousand labels out there and at some point in your life you will fall under one of them.'

'I don't think of you being labelled as you suggested. You are a beautiful woman trying to make a living for herself. No doubt you have many stories about your past or how you came to be in the business you are in but what has that got to do with anyone else.

You are what you are and be proud of it.' Wicks has said all she can but meant every single word of it.

Evita smiles at her and says, 'I see why they call you PC Wicks now. PC standing for "Politically Correct" that's not a bad thing.' They both laugh out loud.

Evita moves closer and rubs Wick's short blonde hair. 'Are you a natural blond, WPC Wicks?' she says rather flirtatiously.

'Huh, here you go again labelling me. WPC went out with the last millennium. I am Constable Wicks but today you can call me Emma.' She leans closer. 'If you keep on, Evita, I will have to take down your particulars.' She laughs.

'Where did you get that one from, sugar? A Carry On Film?' She laughs, stands and then leads Emma to a bedroom. Where they have a long meaningful kiss. Suddenly there is much erotic excitement in the room as Evita is first to undress. She says, 'keep most of your uniform on, Hun. I've never been with a policewoman before - plenty of male coppers though.' They continue to caress and kiss as they lay on the bed. It will be over two hours before Wicks makes it back to the station.

Wicks is with DCI Davies. They are seated in his room. He says, 'what are you looking so pleased about? I hope you bring good tidings?'

She says, 'I have really good news! Evita has now changed her mind and is going to testify.'

'Brilliant, Wicks! How on earth did you get her to change her mind?'

She smiles ever so sweetly as she recalls just what did actually change her mind and says, 'I made her an offer she couldn't refuse, sir.'

He smiles and says, 'you've done ever so well in such a short time here, Wicks. I think one day you'll be sitting here on the other side of the desk.'

She laughs. 'You'd better not let Simpson or Jenkins hear you say that, sir?'

He joins in with a little laughter. 'Okay then. I expect you have some writing up to do. See you at the next team brief and Wicks. Let's hope she doesn't let you down at the last minute.'

'She won't, sir. I am certain of that.'

She walks down to see the desk sergeant. She says, 'I'm awfully sorry, sir but I have mislaid my handcuffs. They're probably at home somewhere. Could I put in for a new pair?'

The Sergeant gives her the routine spill about looking after equipment and especially handcuffs. He then gives her the form to fill in for lost equipment and says, 'people use them for all sorts of things you know?'

She blushes as she knows full well who has them and also knows how they will be used. She has a big smile upon her face, which has nothing to with any evidence or clues she may have picked up but it is Evita and the stolen passionate moments spent in each other's arms. The fact she was getting paid at the time and Evita was not, is something that really amuses her. She also finds it amusing how Evita has held onto the handcuffs and will have no intention of giving them back. It is not as though she can go and arrest her for the theft - is it?

Chapter 56

BRAD WILLIS HAS called Cole and Davies to his room for an urgent meeting. They arrive together and all three are seated in his office on the third floor. Willis organises tea and biscuits. There is a friendliness about them all considering the issues they are about to discuss. Cole and Davies, in particular, are expecting a favourable response to the charges laid upon Miley Sanderson.

Willis is first to open the discussions by saying, 'we have given this unusual case a lot of careful consideration. The problems we have are one of exposing the evidence before Sutton's court appearance. This will all have to come out and will be known before his case even begins. The other side of this is, we need her full cooperation to make sure we put him away. It has come down to what is the best option. The main objective here is to get the conviction for a murder case and it appears counterproductive to take these four other cases forward. There is too much at stake. So we have decided to offer them all King's Evidence. That way when his trial comes up you will have more evidence and we will be able to prosecute the case with much more confidence. None of the evidence gets exposed pre-trial and no legal arguments over damaging his defence in terms of biasness. We do not wish to get tangled up in legal arguments about the media coverage of a previous case. We need their support in this trial and it has to be done this way. Sorry, gentlemen. I know how hard you have all worked on this investigation but there it is. We have agreed all of this with Reginald Bartram and all parties have signed the legal document. So press on with your investigation on this basis now.'

Cole looks out of the windows in disgust and Davies looks in complete shock.

Willis says, 'any questions?'

They both know it is a done deal. They now have to release all four suspects from detention and then it is they who have to deal with the anticipated backlash from the media.

Davies does decide to launch a passing shot. 'Well, if it's all agreed what can we do? We will have to rethink how we go about arresting people who deliberately waste police time and taxpayers money. All that overtime gone down the drain. All our efforts just taken away from us at a stroke of a pen. Are you going to hold a press conference or is it going to be one of us?'

'I know how disappointed you must be but legal made such a good argument, my hands were tied a little. The sooner you release them and get out a press statement the quicker we can all move on with the murder trial.'

Cole stands up and says, 'you bet we are disappointed. Our team are going to be shattered by this news. Their morale will sink to an all time low.'

'I know you can handle the morale. You have been put in charge to handle these kind of things. Thanks for everything so far but you will have to excuse me as I have another appointment.' Willis stands up and leaves them with their thoughts.

A disgruntled Davies hastily arranges an emergency team brief and within two hours the whole team are gathered inside the incident room. He walks in and the room goes silent. The tension in the room has been building over the past hour or so. Davies says, 'first of all, I would like to thank you all for all your efforts so far in this complex investigation, which has just become somewhat simplified. I have just come back from a meeting with CPS and have to report we have released without any charges; Chloe and Colin Richards, Alex Shaw and Miley Sanderson...'

Jenkins is first to show dissent and says, 'but sir, we have enough evidence on all four to easily secure their convictions.'

'All the hard work, sir - down the drain?' Wilkins had good reason to question this decision as he found himself at the centre of the wrath of DCI Davies for not questioning witnesses thoroughly enough.

Davies intervenes by saying, 'settle down now. I get it. I really do get it but the CPS feels it is too risky not to have these people as prosecution witnesses. The main objective is to put Sutton away for the murder. On the bright side of things, we can now put all of our efforts into doing just that. I don't like it but there it is. We'll all have to live with it. So we start today from afresh. Rework the case from beginning to end. Go over all the evidence and clues making sure we don't miss anything - hey Wilkins?'

He is embarrassed at being singled out but nods his head as if to agree.

Davies continues by saying, 'we will need to take new statements from our new ... new witnesses. Let's show the CPS what a good job we have done with this Sutton guy and nail the bastard for the murder of little Emily!'

By the sounds of the cheering he has done a very good job of lifting the morale back up again but he then says, 'as from today I am afraid overtime will no longer be authorised. So let's spread ourselves over every 24 hour period and try not to inflict any more pain on the poor taxpayers of this great nation. Wilkins, I have a special job for you, can you go right back to Sutton's schooldays and see if there are any skeletons in his closet? You are really good at these type of inquiries. Simpson and Jenkins to my office now.' He leaves the room and heads back to his office so he can be seated when the two detectives arrive there.

They walk in together, looking rather bemused. Perhaps even a little fearful as there have been a number of mistakes in this investigation. Davies says, 'right you two! I've called you up here because you have both acted foolishly in this investigation. I know how competitive things can get at your rank. You can stay stuck on it for what appears a lifetime or ... the only other way is down. I'm sure neither of you want that to happen? I know it is bad timing to have two Detective Inspectors working the same station but in your case it is harder for you to both being equal to work the same investigation. We are stuck with this for at least another eight months or more until this trial is done and dusted. All I ask is you both work together and stop all this stupid points scoring you have been up to.'

Jenkins gets in first and says, 'I didn't mean to come across like that, sir. I only want what is best for the team. Always.'

'Me too,' Simpson says rather hurriedly having to wait for Jenkins to stop speaking so he can get his point over. 'You know how much a team player I am, sir? What will happen after the court case is over?'

'We'll just have to wait and see about that. It will probably come down to them upstairs rather than me. Anyway, I think you need to show you can set an example to people like; Wilkins, Wicks and the likes.' He leans back in his chair and fiddles with his thumbs. 'Now we need to get justice for the Banks' family and friends. Remember what we are all here for - poor Emily, a teenager barely out of school. None of us can tell or know what she went through in her final moments.'

Jenkins stands and offers his hand to Simpson to shake knowing full well Davies will notice he was the one to first offer the much needed Olive Branch.

Chapter 57

TWO HUNDRED AND thirty five days have passed since Harry Sutton was charged with the murder of Emily Banks. His first day at the Old Bailey has now at long last arrived. Outside is a large crowd gathering and they are awaiting his arrival. It is not going to be pleasant judging by the jeering that has already began to fill the immediate atmosphere. There are numerous journalists and a uniformed police presence. This case has now gone from being a local news item to being covered nationally on all news channels. Suddenly the volume of the crowd reaches a crescendo as two police vans and a number of police on motorcycles swing into view. Some objects have been thrown at one of their vehicles and a number of photographers are putting their cameras above their heads and pointing them through small darkened side windows of the vehicle despite not even being able to see inside or if their photographs will capture anything. Some of the police officers have rushed over towards the crowd and warned about the throwing of objects. The heightened hysteria is then followed by what can only be described as an instant eerie silence as the defendant is taken into the court building. Police make no arrests for any public disorders that may have occurred as they know how tensed and fragile these situations become.

Becclesfield journalist, Alisha Nicholson is amongst the many who are standing in front of their cameras awaiting the signal for the live feed. Her camera is a go and she reports;

'I am here outside the Old Bailey where I can report they have just taken in Harry Sutton the 29 year old accused of murdering 17 year old Emily Banks over 7 years ago. You may have seen the pictures of an angry crowd trying to get to him as he was driven into the court entrance and taken down to the cells. There were scenes of extreme anger and frustration as the police attempted to calm the crowds down. There were a number of banners demanding justice for Emily whose remains were finally found nearly a year ago in Cherry Walk, Tranby. I can tell you my sources have informed me the jury has already been sworn in and they consist of seven women and five men. The trial is not expected to get underway until later today as there are a number of legal issues being sorted out as we speak. You may recall Miley Sanderson (Emily's sister), Chloe and Colin Richards together with Alex Shaw were all released without charge for their involvement in falsely claiming Miley was the victim of a kidnap. They are all due to give evidence at some point in time at this trial. Harry Sutton, the defendant in this case was formerly known as Leo Parker who served 5 years in prison for the arson attack on the Banks' sawmills some seven or so years ago now.

As I said earlier, the trial is about to get underway and we will bring you regular updates throughout the stages of this hearing. This is Alisha Nicholson reporting outside the Old Bailey in London.'

The trial having lasted eleven days has now drawn to a close and the jury have been sent out to consider their verdicts. There is much speculation from the journalists covering this case and the many tv viewers who have been following every piece of evidence brought to court and the arguments from both sets of lawyers. With the jury safely locked away for their deliberations, some of the information of the final arguments and summing ups are being shared on social media websites. Jacob has been patiently sitting at home with his wife Ayaka and they have also been following the case closely. Jacob had given his evidence on day four and was fairly pleased with most of it. There were a few uncomfortable moments when the defence team kept asking why he had not informed the police when he first had concerns over Miley Sanderson's safety and he did not escape questions as to why he spent a night parked up outside her home.

Jacob has downloaded copies of the summing up. He reads them both with great interest as he knows one or both may refer back to his testimony at some point and he wishes to gauge how well he actually did do.

Prosecution Summing Up

Members of the jury. You have heard all the evidence and seen many documents. I am sure you will agree there can be no other person guilty of murdering Emily Banks, other than the defendant sitting in the dock today. It is not as complicated as the defence tried to portray. The visits to 6 Cherry Walk are not coincidence. The police did not discover the remains at the rear of this address by chance or some sort of tip off. No, they were led there by the defendant himself. Time and time again he mentions that address. He has been seen there on five occasions that we know off. You have seen the CCTV footage to prove that very fact. Mr. Walsh the owner of 6 Cherry Walk gave evidence to this court that he saw the defendant on his knees, in his back garden at the very spot where Emily Banks' remains were found. Coincidence? Of course not. We heard from the DNA expert who states the match was 100 pct that of Harry Sutton. It was found on the murder weapon, which in this case was a stocking that was still tied around her neck when the discovery was made. His DNA was also found on her handbag, which was buried along with her. Nearly six years her remains lay unfound until the defendant led the police there.

You heard evidence from witness, Miley Sanderson. She admitted to breaking the law and encouraging the defendant into a relationship in order to get to the truth. So it could be argued she lied but why? She lied to get to the truth of what happened to her little sister all of those years ago and she has got the truth. She wanted justice for her sister and today is the day for that to finally happen. Emily Banks has at long last been put to rest in a family plot but the killer still needs to pay for his crime. Today is the day, members of the jury to put all of this hurt the poor family have had to endure for so long - right.

The defence tried to argue the reason for the defendant's visits to Cherry Walk were to do with a form of therapy. Apparently the defendant had some happy memories of the area as a child and yet he has only visited the area at night. When it is dark and I doubt if these would have been the times of day he would have visited as a child? Going back nearly seven years now, there would not have even been a streetlamp within eye shot of this wasteland. I would be horrified to see any child playing over there in the dark. So why visit at night? I am sure we all go back to places from our childhood to reminisce but definitely not at night. When I was a child, I was told by my parents not to talk to strangers and to be indoors before a respectable time. That would certainly be before nightfall.

We heard from the therapist, Jacob Lyall, he said Miley was becoming frightened of the defendant and believed she was in danger. We also heard the times the defendant threatened her both in the sessions and the time at The Crown in front of witnesses. He said and I quote, "I will get you while you are sleeping" among other threats. We know he was attending therapy because of his anger management. Mr. Lyall said on record there had been a deterioration of his mental stability towards the last few sessions they spent together. So it would be fair to say Mr Sutton struggled with his mental health at times? He had the road rage incident, which actually led him to be seeing Mr. Lyall in the first place. We also heard from Mr. Lyall how on hindsight he wished he had informed the police of his concerns over the relationship he had formed with Miley Sanderson, the sister of the deceased Emily Banks.

We have to remember that Harry Sutton had changed his name from Leo Parker and how Miley Sanderson told this court her sister, Emily had no feelings for him. She also told the court about Parker's obsessive behaviour towards Emily. How he gifted her flowers, jewellery and chocolates, all of which were returned to

Parker. Emily Banks never at any stage encouraged a relationship with Parker - quite the opposite. So having his DNA upon her person anywhere would be a bit mystifying to say the least.

We heard from "Evita" a woman the defendant hired for the evening. She told us of how aggressive Sutton was towards her. How he told her to play the role of Emily and to call him Leo. She told us the words he used. He was apologising to Emily for something. He was full of remorse. He was forceful and unrelenting.

We heard from the receptionist on duty the night the defendant booked in to The Lodge in Tranby. She told us he used the name of Leo Parker and he paid in cash. He had parked his car a mile away. We do not know what his intentions were that night but we do know he did not want anyone to know Harry Sutton had visited Tranby that Friday night.

The chilling notes from his session files where he basically says Emily and Leo went off together and that was the last he saw of her, outside number 6 Cherry Walk, the exact place where her remains were found. No coincidence, he kept visiting the area and it was he who led the police there. Why would the police go to the trouble of digging up someone's garden? The expense of it all and the embarrassment if they were wrong? They wouldn't unless there was good evidence to do so and Sutton led them straight to it. Members of the jury, it is the defendant who robbed that young lady of her future. We have no idea what Emily would have become; teacher, nurse, politician or any other profession? She may have been married now with children? He robbed us of all knowing. He took her life, the 17 year old, just out of school. He throttled her and strangled her with one of her own stockings. We have no way of knowing what other things happened to her as she lay fighting for her life. Then he buried her naked body along with her belongings on wasteland, which we all now know to be Cherry

Walk. The DNA proves it. His session notes with the therapist prove it, his own actions of visiting the crime scene on numerous occasions prove it and now having proved it here over the past weeks, it is just up to you all now to return the correct verdict and get justice for poor little Emily. I rest my case.

Defence Summing Up

Members of the jury thank you for your attendance for the duration of the trial. We heard from the prosecution's expert in DNA. You will recall there is not a 100% match but a 100% probable match. Straight away that allows for a small doubt to enter my mind. The other part of this evidence presented by the prosecution stated it was a match to the defendant. The defendant had a relationship of sorts with the victim, so you would expect it to be somewhere upon her belongings or person. He bought her presents; flowers, jewellery and stockings - amongst other things. The fact there were no DNA other than the victims and the defendants found does not rule out the possibility of a third party being involved. There just was no DNA found on her person or belongings of a third party. Do police always find DNA at a crime scene? The answer is no. Because there was no other DNA does not mean someone else could not have killed her, it just means no other valid clues were found at the scene. You have to remember it was nearly seven years ago. A lot can happen to evidence in that amount of time. There was a new building construction of homes in the area, a new road, and much changes in the landscaping of the whole area. Any vital evidence could so easily have been disturbed, moved or buried further in the ground.

I would like to turn to the therapist files of the defendant in his sessions with Mr. Jacob Lyall. You have to consider how much of this information is sheer fantasy. I am sure many patients may even believe some of the fantastic thoughts running through their minds as being realistically true. The defendant actually distances himself from Leo Parker even though he was Leo Parker, just changing his name to Harry Sutton. He wished to make a new start in life, like so many people do these days. He talks of Leo Parker as being someone he knew from school and sees himself as a person who has changed his life. You can see from the case files the prosecution have of course only highlighted the areas that suit their arguments. They quoted the defendant and I quote "That is where I last saw Emily." This was in answer to Mr. Lyall's questions about who lives at 6 Cherry Walk. The defendant was referring to Leo Parker as being the person who saw her there. This could have been at any time. He may be thinking about times they spent together somewhere? Remember, his mental capacity is affected by those cruel events that took place back at the time. The hospitalisation and coma. Our behavioural expert stated that some patients blame everything on a pretence character inside their head. Leo Parker is no longer part of Harry Sutton as we see time and time again in the case files. He blames everything bad on him. He may or may not have seen Emily in that area but he may have seen someone with her and blamed it on Leo Parker. He may even not have been there at all. The tricks our minds play! We see him blaming Leo Parker for everything and we know that some of these events are not real. Take the journey through the country lanes when he speaks with a cyclist and the cyclist tells Harry Sutton that Leo Parker is in a relationship with Miley Sanderson. That in all probability never happened but in Harry's head it looked real. So you see, he may have imagined Leo Parker with Emily just as easy as he believes he met a cyclist in the country lanes. How many cyclists have you seen stop a motorist and ask for directions?

Now I would like to turn our attention to the witnesses brought forward by the prosecution. Let us take Millie Sanderson. Sorry I meant to say Miley Sanderson. Anyway, the person who was supposedly kidnapped by the defendant in Denbar Lane. We heard testimony from her where she admitted all of the details about her kidnap were false and yet we are to believe her every word now. She lied about the kidnap, lied about her stalking convictions, lied in therapy and created a story about how vulnerable she was. She built up a character assassination of Harry Sutton. She pretended to be his lover, She drugged him and strung him along. She set up the row inside The Crown where she made sure everyone in the pub heard an angered reaction to having a pint of beer thrown over the defendant's head. Who would not be able to react in at least an angry loud voice? I know I would.

She lied about her relationship with Chloe Richards, pretending to be sisters. She told her therapist, the defendant and regulars at The Swan. The police failed to discover that Miley Sanderson was indeed Emily Banks older sister until she walked into a police station and confessed. They were still referring to her as Millie. Are we really expected to believe this evidence?

Let's turn to Alex Shaw, one of Miley Sanderson's accomplices. Lied to the defendant time and time again. Befriended him and got real close. Just so he could steal his car, mobile phone and then plant the evidence in Denbar Lane. Got him drunk and took him home to his flat. Then as I said, went about to frame him for the kidnap that never was. He lied to a court pretending that Millie Sanderson was stalking him, so he has already lied once to a court - can we take his evidence as read? No we cannot.

Chloe Richards and her husband Colin. More lies and deceit. They hid Miley Sanderson in their loft room at The Swan in Tranby. So whilst we all went searching for Millie; posters, police interviews, dogs, news releases and not forgetting the door to door inquiries - they had her tucked away nice and snug in their attic.

We know the witnesses have told so many lies. They've even admitted to it. Lying about the kidnap, the session notes are false with the therapist and then the prosecution call a lady named as "Evita". Very interesting evidence but is it not her job to play a role of sorts? Is that not what she gets paid for? So she is even pretending to be someone else - more lies. She stated the defendant became remorseful, well that could be how some clients and I say some, so please do not take offence, feel after they have concluded their... business. I would imagine some may feel a little ashamed of themselves afterwards. I do not feel any credence should be given to this piece of so called evidence.

The defendant stated on more than one occasion that the reason for visiting Cherry Walk in Tranby was because of those happy times spent there as a child. Remember Harry Sutton was the genuine person attending the therapy sessions. I asked Jacob Lyall if going back to places in the past was a good thing in terms of mental health issues. He answered positively but did state so long as they were happy memories it could be therapeutic. The defendant has stated they were happy times. I have gone back to my roots to see the changes and reminisce over childhood days, I think many people do but for some it is more helpful in terms of their wellbeing. Much was given to the fact he only returned when it was dark. Now there are dwellings and people living in that particular part of land. So he could hardly go walking around their properties during the daytime. The best chance he would have is to visit when no one will see him at night. The defendant was honest with the therapist, the police, the court, Miley Sanderson, Chloe and Colin Richards and Alex Shaw, which is more than I can say for those witnesses who have been afforded Kings Evidence Protection. Also immunity from prosecution so long as they give their evidence. A contract of law drawn up and signed by all concerned parties. So they get to stand in the witness box instead of the dock.

You may recall the prosecution put much emphasis on the amount of times the defendant mentioned Emily Banks during his therapy sessions? This is not unusual for when a person has strong feelings for another and haven't seen them for so long, they find comfort in speaking of them even though they are not around. It is certainly not a crime for anyone to hold someone's memory in their heads for a long time, especially as Emily Banks had gone missing for so long. In his head, all he has left are the happy memories he spent with Emily.

Then we come to the evidence of Fred Watkins a friendly neighbour. You heard him tell us how good the defendant has been to him. How the defendant goes and gets some shopping for him. He always pops in to see him and make sure he does not go without. He basically relies upon the defendant not just as a neighbour but as a "friend". They were his words not mine.

Now let us turn to the evidence about Tom the cat. Is there really anything meaningful to be learned from this. The defendant admitted taking the cat but only in order to upset her. It was always his intention to give him back to her. I remember years ago I had a girlfriend, who shall remain anonymous; when we broke up she kept my LPS' - old music albums for those of you too young to know what they were. I loved those records but this is just an example of what couples can sometimes do to each other when they are hurt. Don't forget the defendant was hurting and in deep pain at this time with the relationship having failed. Don't forget also the drugging and deceit Miley Sanderson had enacted in a deliberate and ruthless manner would have added to the pain the defendant was already in. Obviously, I am not saying this should have happened for any kind of revenge or hatred but it is not really enough to say a person is a cold callous murderer either - is it?

Finally, members of the jury, I wish to thank you for your diligence and deliberations in this case but leave you with these final thoughts;

Miley Sanderson pretended to have been kidnapped. She led the defendant into a relationship. She then drugged him. She lied to her therapist. Lied to a court about stalking Alex Shaw. He then assisted her by befriending the defendant, stealing his car and his mobile phone. They together tried to frame him for a kidnap that never happened. As for the DNA, it would be on the victims person and her belongings if they were friendly at that time. As I said earlier, just because the police could not find anyone else's DNA at the crime scene does not mean that somebody else could not have committed the murder. I know this has been a confusing case, it has had me confused at times; Millie, Miley, sister, cousin and all the drugging what went on. I leave it to you now to arrive at the just verdict and return a unanimous not guilty verdict. Remember, the murderer may still be out there. I rest my case. Thank You.

Chapter 58

JACOB HAS FINISHED reading the closing statements from both the prosecution and defence teams. He has a look of anguish bordering on embarrassment upon his face as he turns to his wife, Ayaka and says, 'made me look pretty stupid by the way they go on about me at the end. They are actually insinuating I cannot tell the difference between reality and fantasy.'

'Surely not? You helped them a great deal. You told the truth and you kept your notes meticulously as you always have. Let me read through them. I will give you my honest opinion. I will do my best to be unbiased.' She sits next to him and commences reading the statements.

After a short while, Jacob rises and walks out into the garden. This is where he goes when he needs to clear his thoughts or in this case analyse the situation more comprehensively. He is joined by Ayaka. She puts her arms around him and kisses him. 'It's okay. Honestly. I can only see what a great job you have done and how caring you have been with both patients. No one can calculate for how things have ended up. You did your best. You know that, right?

He embraces her more tightly. 'You really think so? I thought I did okay. It was like attending an intense interview and all those questions. I am glad it is nearly all over. I will be happy when things return back to normality - here and at work.'

'Come. Let us go back indoors and we can see if the verdict has been reached yet. They have been out for a while now. It must be a close run decision?' She takes his hand and leads him back into the living room area where the tv is still tuned into the news channel. It has been on this channel mostly now for over three weeks but they will have to wait a lot longer for the verdict to be reached.

Six days has now passed since the jury were sent out to reach their verdict but the decision is now imminent as Alisha Nicholson along with numerous reporters lining the pavement area outside the Old Bailey are rehearsing their opening salvos in front of their respective cameras. It would appear most of the nation have been gripped by this trial but the people of Becclesfield more than most. Alisha Nicholson's camera is the first to light up for action. She reports;

'Good afternoon. I am live outside the Old Bailey Criminal Courts here in London where the jury are expected to return their verdict at any moment, in the case of Harry Sutton. The 29 year old has been tried for the murder of 17 year old Emily Banks. Inside the court are the friends and family of Emily. They have waited over 7 years to receive this moment of truth. You may recall the police had arrested Leo Parker for the kidnap of Emily Banks back then but he was released due to a lack of evidence. He was then charged with the arson attack on her father's sawmills in Ferry Lane. He spent 5 years in prison but upon release he changed his name to Harry Sutton.

Miley Sanderson, sister to Emily Banks, along with three others have been given Kings Evidence protection for their testimonies. They all took the witness stand and gave their evidence along with local therapist, Jacob Lyall. Police have commended Mr. Lyall for all the detailed information they were able to extract from the case files he had kept on both Harry Sutton and Miley Sanderson.

We await the news now and my sources have just informed me the court is fully operational and the jury are just being led back into their places. We won't have to wait much longer. The family of Emily Banks are soon to discover the verdict and whether this long journey will finally lead to justice for Emily.

Over the street is where they will all come out from the court and we will be there to get their reactions to the verdict... I am just being told the jury have returned a verdict of guilty! Guilty as charged - unanimously. Probably why the decision has taken so long to reach but there you have it; Harry Sutton guilty of murdering 17 year old Emily Banks. My sources have just advised me, there were shouts and cheers from the public gallery. The judge had to call the court to order and has stated he will be passing the sentence in a matter of moments.

Guilty verdict here at the Old Bailey. We await the legal teams response but we have managed to get Detective Superintendent, Cole to have a quick word to us. So what is your reaction to the verdict?'

Cole stands erect and looking a little solemn he says, 'knew we would get the result. Our team have been working around the clock to obtain this conviction. May I just add, it is a time for reflection now, remember the poor child Emily Banks so cruelly taken away from us. I can say with some satisfaction that I put the best officers on the case from day one.'

'Yes. Thank you for your thoughts for the family, I'm sure all of us here are sharing them right at this moment but I have to ask; You had Parker in custody over 7 years ago when this murder took place, why did he get off with it back then?'

Cole looks mortified as he is okay with taking all the credit but not so good at criticism. 'We have made positive moves in both DNA and detective techniques over the last 7 years. It was before the major reforms here at Becclesfield and the whole department has changed since then. I came along 6 years ago along with DCI Davies. So you see, it's not like the movies when the cops always catch the bad guys. Some cases are harder to crack than others. Thank you for your useful coverage - I have to go now. Goodbye.'

Nicholson tries to grab another answer but he has walked off towards a chauffeur driven police car close by. She turns back to the screen; 'There you have it, direct from the Detective

Superintendent himself... I am hearing "life imprisonment". Sutton has been handed down a life sentence for the murder. We still await confirmation of what details that sentence actually carries. Will it come with a minimum sentence to serve or will there be any other provisos? Oh... the prosecution team are behind me and about to make a statement. Let's hear what they have to say.'

'Emily Banks was just 17 years of age when Leo Parker's personal obsession with her led him to take her life and then callously bury her body on wasteland in Tranby almost 7 years to the day. The police and the witnesses for our case proved beyond any reasonable doubts that Leo Parker now known as Harry Sutton was guilty of this act. The parents of Emily died not even knowing whether their daughter was alive or dead but for the other members of the family here today, justice has been served. Hopefully some small amount of comfort can be gained in the knowledge that Harry Sutton will now serve a minimum of 25 years in prison with no chance of early release until after he has served the minimum term. I hand you over to Miley Sanderson, sister of Emily.'

Miley has reverted back to her blonde hair and is trying hard to stand. She has a prepared note of paper in front of her. This is the first time anyone has heard her speak publicly on any of the issues surrounding the case. She approaches the microphones. 'My first thoughts are for my parents. I know they will be looking down on us today full of pride and admiration about the way in which this conviction was reached. I apologise for the distress and any anxiety caused by my sudden disappearance but as someone once said to me "perhaps the ends justify the means" and it certainly does in our case. You have to remember, this man broke my father's heart by destroying his business and then getting Emily...' she is finding it hard but is encouraged to continue by Alex Shaw, standing next to her with his arm around her. She continues. 'Thank you to the legal team, the police... thank you Jacob, I'm sorry but I want the world to know you are a fantastic, caring and professional therapist.' She is quickly ushered away.

Nicholson is once again standing in front of the camera. 'Brave Miley there telling us how upset they were and how her parents would've approved of her efforts to get justice. A special mention for therapist Jacob Lyall there as well. So does "the ends really justify the means"? Well, it solved a cold case, it took a murderer off our streets and poor Emily is now laid to rest with her parents. So I would have to agree with Miley Sanderson. Sutton locked away for a minimum period of 25 years with no chance of parole during the minimum period. This has been a remarkable case to follow and if they do make a film about it all, I for one will be at the front of the queue to see it. This is Alisha Nicholson reporting from the Old Bailey.'

Final Chapter

BECCLESFIELD HAD BEEN enjoying a quiet spell over the past five years since the trial of Harry Sutton and his subsequent conviction of the murder of Emily Banks but following the discovery of new evidence, things are about to return to those chaotic scenes. A golden locket with a photo of a married couple was found in the rear garden of 6 Cherry Walk. The owner, Mr. Walsh had been digging a pond out when he discovered it. He recognised the two persons in the photograph as he had seen their faces on the news around five years earlier. He would remember everything about the mayhem that took place at his property when police brought in the diggers and tore up his back garden. The locket firmly places one or both of them at the scene of the crime. As a direct result of this discovery police will fly out to the USA to interview their main person of interest, Julian Sanderson in this new investigation, who is currently serving a jail term for attempted murder of his estranged wife, Lucie. Harry Sutton's legal team are readying themselves for a legal battle in court as a result of this evidence alone but more recriminating evidence from a former associate of the Reynolds gang has been forthcoming too. The witness who has turned King's Evidence with a promise of immunity from prosecution and a place on a witness protection programme, will give this new evidence in a court of law when the appropriate time arrives. This new evidence is related to an insurance fraudulent claim made by Terry Banks and his involvement in the arson attack on the Sawmills. The informant also has evidence of an arson attack on Leo Parker's parents home three years earlier than that of the Banks Sawmills fire. He claims, it was carried out over gambling debts Hugh Parker owed but it was only meant to frighten him into paying but it went horribly wrong on the night.

Miley Shaw, now married to Alex Shaw has refused to comment on the fresh allegations. She had thought all of this was in her past but it has come straight back to haunt her. If the evidence is correct and the court finds her ex husband guilty of the murder of Emily Banks and her father, Terry Banks, guilty of the arson attack on his own Sawmills, this would have devastating effects upon her not just emotionally but financially. She would not only have aided and abetted in getting an innocent man sent to prison but would most likely have to repay every single penny back to the insurance company as it will then be a case of fraud. Can Harry Sutton get his life back on track but more crucially can he now get the justice he deserves?

To be continued.....

Footnote;

Fred Watkins no longer lives alone. Miley has given him her cat, Tom but he still calls him "Check".